IRONBRAND

The air grew suddenly bright, and in the midst of the white glow appeared a flickering ribbon of darkness. It grew and took on substance, until it was a hooded figure.

"Behold the three brothers of my prophecy," it said, gesturing toward the sons of Vannen.

"The first will have a white blade at his side. First will he be to see his realm, first to fall, and first to rise.

"The second shall have a black blade and be a man of fire. He will guard the plain where the dead and the living will clash in battle.

"The third will be the least and become the greatest, the youngest and become the eldest. He has an iron angel at his back. His life will be short, but he will die at a great age."

The Dark Prophet faced the three brothers. In the shadow of its hood there were no features, only a pale glow.

"You face forces beyond imagining, an enemy more than mortal. Many will suffer and die. I came not to present you with a kingdom but to bring you to your destinies."

"A damn good book, *Ironbrand* is a great big epic that deserves to be read."
                                    —Andrew J. Offutt
                            Former President of the Science
                            Fiction Writers of America

JOHN MORRESSY

BOOK ONE OF THE IRON ANGEL TRILOGY

IRONBRAND

ACE FANTASY BOOKS
NEW YORK

FOR CLIFF SIMAK

IRONBRAND

An Ace Fantasy Book / published by arrangement with
the author

PRINTING HISTORY
Playboy edition / July 1980
Ace edition / September 1984

ISBN: 0-441-37276-7

Ace Fantasy Books are published by The Berkley Publishing Group,
200 Madison Avenue, New York, New York 10016.
PRINTED IN THE UNITED STATES OF AMERICA.

And a Shape that moveth murkily
In mirrors of ice and night,
Hath blanched with fear all beasts and birds,
As death and a shock of evil words
Blast a man's hair with white.

G. K. Chesterton

1

The Legacy of the Sons of Vannen

*First was the sword of Colberane, as straight as a
   beam of light,
With jewel-eyed dragons wreathed around its house
   of gold and white;
   The second he curved like a gentle wave, a
   diamond-dizened sword,
To flash in a web of silver at the side of Scarlet Ord;
   The third, the Iron Angel, he wrought for Staver's
   hand,
With wings spread wide on either side of a simple
   iron brand. . . .*

—From The Last Deed of Ambescand

The candle burned without a flutter in the still and windless night. The little room was silent, save for Vannen's
feeble groans and the dry rale of his breath. He lay
clenched like a wrung rag with the pain that bored
through his body. Two days before, he had been a healthy,
vigorous man, standing half a head taller than his tallest
son, and as strong as any man on the Headland. Then the
fever struck, felling him like the blow of a giant's fist.
Now he was dying.

In the little room were two of Vannen's sons. Though
they were different in stature, their features were so
much alike that one might have thought them the same
man seen simultaneously at two ages, perhaps seven years
apart. Both had thick brown hair, cut short in the manner
of the Headland, and both had pale green eyes and their
father's sturdy frame. Each had the same firm square-cut
jaw, believed by the folk of the Headland to be a sign of
obstinacy, but whether this was a trait passed on by Vannen, no one could tell, since the old man had a thick, gray-

streaked, red-gold beard and his unmarried sons were
beardless, according to Headland custom.

Colberane, the oldest son, went once again to the open
window. He looked out, up the path to the lights of the
settlement, but could see nothing else on this moonless
night. With a grunt of disgust, he turned and leaned
against the wall, arms folded, staring gloomily ahead.

The youngest son, Staver, looked up from his seat by
the bedside. "He'll be here, Col. Jus knows where to find
him."

"At Brower's Inn, no doubt, losing what little he has
left."

"Ord isn't like us, Col. He likes noise and gaming and
lots of people around him."

"I don't begrudge him his pleasures, foolish as they
are. But right now Father is dying, and Ord's place is
here, with us."

"He'll be here," the younger brother repeated.

"You're mighty sure of yourself, sprig. And you're
giving out advice as though you were head of the family."
Colberane settled into the carved oak sidechair, stretching
out his long legs before him and tilting his seat back to
rest against the wainscoting. "What's come over you?"

"I don't like to see you and Ord angry with each other.
We have to stay together now."

A sound of hurried footsteps on the path brought the
brothers to their feet. They heard the front door open and
shut, and two people enter the hearthroom. Staver opened
the bedroom door and a third young man stepped inside,
throwing off his black cloak as he moved toward the bed.
He bore a marked resemblance to the others, but his
clothing was finer and his features seemed pared down
when compared to their more rugged mold. His chin was
narrower; his nose, thin and high-bridged; his eyes, deeper
set. All of his movements were quick. Even when he
stood still, at the foot of the oaken bed, the rapid darting
of his eyes from face to face lent him an air of nervous-
ness and tension. His hair was a bright, blazing red.
Among the folk of the Headland, red hair was the sure
sign of a hot-tempered and volatile man. Ordred, middle
son of Vannen, was certainly such a man, as well as a

devoted gambler, a fine swordsman, and something of a dandy.

"How is he?" Ordred asked.

"Nearly gone. You cut it close, brother," Colberane replied.

"But I'm here, so you can save your disapproval. You're not head of the family yet, Col."

Before Colberane could respond, a fourth man, older than all the rest, entered the room. He walked straight to the bed and leaned over to study Vannen's drawn face closely and to lay a big hand lightly on his chest.

"We're barely in time," the newcomer murmured. Turning to the sons, he gave crisp orders. "Col, Ord, lift him up. Staver, close the shutters and bar them; then go to your mother's picture. Go on, boy, hurry! Now, turn it from top to bottom."

As his brothers lifted their limp father to a sitting position, Staver manipulated the small portrait fastened to the wall opposite the bed. To his surprise, it swung forward, revealing a cache about the size of a man's fist. In it stood a single small bottle.

"Don't gape at it, boy! Bring it here quickly!"

"What are you doing, Jus?" Colberane asked.

"What I swore to do long ago," the old man replied, reaching out to snatch the bottle, breaking the seal with a twist of his hands, keeping his eyes fixed on Vannen's face. "This will bring him back to us."

"Do you mean he'll recover?"

"There's no recovering from what touched Vannen. But he'll get back strength enough to say the things he must say before he dies. Prop up his head, Col."

Jus poured a little of the black liquid into Vannen's mouth. He coughed, gave a great sigh, and then took a deep, regular breath. Quickly, Jus administered the remaining liquid. Vannen swallowed loudly. His eyes opened and he stared vaguely ahead for a moment; then he focused on the old man's intent gaze.

"You've done your duty, Justen," Vannen said, reaching out to clasp the old man's hand.

"I waited until I was certain."

"You were right to wait. You did well, Justen," Vannen said and smiled. "Leave us now, but stay near the door. And be wary."

Jus nodded and left the room. The three brothers, who had been watching in silent bewilderment, turned their attention to their father. The change in Vannen amazed them. His cheeks were red, his eyes bright, and his voice as strong and steady as ever. His big chest heaved with deep, hungry breaths. As they stood watching, their father flung back the bedclothes, swung his feet to the floor, and rose.

"You're well!" Staver cried.

"When this wears off, I'll be dead. I have little time to live and much to do. Quick, help push the bed aside," Vannen said, gripping the headboard.

Together, they pushed the massive bed to the wall. Dropping to his knees, Vannen pried and prodded the floorboards. In a moment he lifted an irregular section of two boards. They were cut exactly to fit the grain at each end, and the joint was undetectable.

Staver looked to his brothers, but their whole attention was on the opening in the floor. For an instant Staver felt weak and unsure of himself. Everything was changing so quickly that his life seemed suddenly to have lost its bearings. It was frightening, too, for such things never happened on the Headland. Life was always predictable here, with little danger and no mystery at all.

The fear touched Staver for a moment, then vanished in a rush of excitement. His father had laid a long bundle on the bed. It was wrapped in soft leather and tightly bound. Beside it, he tossed a pouch that clinked with the sound of coins. Ordred, at that signal, glanced at his brothers and grinned.

Muttering under his breath, Vannen struggled to undo the cords. When they were loosened, he flung back the leather wrappings and revealed three swords, each encased in a scabbard. Laying them side by side on the leather, he stepped away from the bed and extended his hand toward the weapons.

"Swords from the Old Kingdom. Yours by right of blood. But each of you must choose his own blade," he said.

The three brothers stepped to the footboard and looked

down at the weapons. On the right lay a long, slender sword, its gleaming blade drawn a hand's breadth from the scabbard, mirror-bright in the candle flame. The hilt and scabbard were ivory; gold wire closely bound the hilt and crosspiece, and the scabbard was decorated with a twining procession of golden dragons. Twelve had ruby eyes, and the thirteenth, the sea dragon, crowned and wingless, bore a tiny emerald in its brow.

Beside this splendid weapon, in the center of the three, lay a curving falchion, its hilt and scabbard made of ebony and trimmed in a web of silver. Tiny points of light flashed from the diamond chips inlaid in the pommel and in the scabbard. On the left lay a plain iron-hilted sword in an iron scabbard. It was longer than the others and had only one noteworthy feature: the crosspiece swept upwards and was finely chased to resemble a pair of wings.

For a moment no one moved. Then one of Colberane's hands and Ordred's two closed on the gold-and-ivory sword at once. They turned to face each other.

"As oldest son, I claim this sword for myself," said Colberane.

"Oldest by less than a year, Col, and certainly not wisest. I claim it, as the better swordsman."

Neither hand moved. Their eyes remained locked as tightly as their hands gripped the golden sword.

"You must choose for yourselves!" Vannen repeated, his voice loud with desperation. "Hurry, while I yet live!"

Col tightened his grip. Ordred grinned and moved his hand to the curved blade. Lifting it, still smiling at Colberane, he slid it halfway from the scabbard, then slammed it home. "I'll take this one, brother. The ebony goes well with my cloak." Turning to Staver, he said, "That leaves this iron beauty for you. Wear it proudly, little brother."

"It's a bit large for me," Staver said unhappily, taking up the iron sword.

"You'll grow up to it," Ord said.

"Have you made your choice freely?" Vannen asked.

"We have," Colberane responded.

"I'll hear it from you all. Have you chosen freely?"

"We have," said the three together.

"Then take your patrimony," the father said. Reaching into the pouch, he drew out, one after another, three smaller leather pouches, tossing one to each son in turn. "Three hundred golden oaks for each of you."

"Three hundred?" Ord repeated, obviously pleased.

"Enough to keep you comfortably for a long life, if you were free to choose. But you have another destiny." They turned and looked at their father in surprise, and he went on. "You must go to the south, to reclaim the kingdom that's rightly yours."

The room was still for a long moment. Vannen looked at each of them in turn and said, "Yes, a kingdom. Stolen from its rightful rulers generations ago, and all of royal blood slain—so the enemy thinks. But one family escaped to the Headland, to wait, and now you are the only heirs. And though you're not—" Vannen suddenly clutched at his chest and groaned. Staggering to the bed, he collapsed full length on it. He twisted in a spasm of pain, then shuddered and breathed deeply. Staver ran to his side.

"Is there any more of the black liquid hidden here, Father?"

"None. None in the world. Lift me up, quickly." When the three had helped him to a sitting position and propped him up with pillows, Vannen said, "Your mother made that black potion as the last defense against the touch of Hane. It is she who protected us all this time, concealing us, guarding us, against his wasting spells."

Colberane laid a hand on his father's shoulder and said, "Is it a wasting spell that's done this to you?"

Vannen grunted at a sudden stab of pain, gasped, and said weakly, "It is. Hane of the Withering Touch was summoned against me. I sensed him in the field as I fell. I tried to fight, but he was too powerful. Even the amulet could not repulse him. Ciantha's potion . . . my only chance. . . . If it hadn't been for your mother's watchfulness, not one of us would be alive today. She saw the shadow of the Hand and gave her own substance to preserve us. She gave everything . . . everything. On the very day of Staver's birth, she—" He broke off, arched his back, and gave a terrible cry of anguish. His color grew paler and when he spoke next, his voice was hur-

ried and weak. "It's running out. Listen to me and do as
I say. When I'm dead, go with Justen. He has documents
you must see. Read them together and when you seek
your kingdom, seek it together. Remember that. . . . Always work together . . . and there's hope." He closed his
eyes, and his breath became labored.

"We'll stay together," Colberane assured his father.

"Good. You must, for strength. The Stone Hand grows
ever stronger, and so must you. Listen . . . two things
more. . . ."

"What is the Stone Hand?" Staver blurted.

"No time. . . . You'll learn from Justen. Now you must
. . . do two things," Vannen said. He was struggling for
breath now, and his face was as pale as the tallow candle
that burned low beside him. With great effort he shook off
their hands and rolled over on his side. For a brief time
he was so still, they feared he had died, but then he
spoke in a faint whisper.

"Left shoulder . . . the scar. Cut into it. Now, quickly,
Col!"

Colberane hesitated. He gripped the hilt of the golden
sword but seemed unable to draw the bright blade from
the scabbard. Vannen cried out in an agonized voice,
"Cut, quickly, while I live! Take the amulet from beneath
the skin. *Do it!*"

Col felt Vannen's shoulder until his fingers came upon
a faint scar. Beneath it, against the shoulder blade, lay a
flat object. With a quick cut Col opened the scar. He drew
the object out. It was a thin piece of white metal bearing
three symbols. He stared at it wonderingly. Vannen
struggled to a sitting position once again.

"Give it to me. And the blade," the father said, holding
out trembling hands.

Colberane gave him the wafer and the gold-hilted
sword. Laboriously, Vannen scored the metal to separate the three symbols, then bent it until they broke
apart. He held them up.

"Take off your shirts. Hurry! I must insert these before . . . I die. They'll protect you."

"Against what, Father?" Colberane asked.

"The evil . . . that comes closer. Come. Staver first."

Staver stripped off his shirt and presented his back.

He felt a sharp pain when Vannen made the incision, but almost at once the pain was gone and a mild warmth spread over his shoulder and seemed to suffuse his whole body. For the first time since his father had been stricken, he had a feeling that all was not over but only beginning; he felt hope and confidence in the future. From the expressions that lit his brothers' faces, he could tell that they experienced a similar surge of reassurance.

"It began working for you . . ." Vannen said. He returned the sword to Colberane and fell back on the pillows. "I was in time. Now . . . one more thing."

"Tell us, Father," said Colberane.

"My pyre. You must burn my body. Promise me."

"If that's your will, Father."

"It must be done! Now go with Justen. Hear him out. Read . . . study all he gives you. Work together. Go now. Go! Don't stay to watch me die!" Vannen said.

They left him straining for breath. When they entered the hearthroom, Justen turned from his vigil at the outer door. At sight of the swords that hung by their sides, he fell to one knee before them. As they glanced astonished at each other, he took the right hand of each in turn and pressed it to his lips. With head still bowed, he said in a solemn voice, "I hail the sons of Ciantha and Vannen and pledge my life to their cause. Hail, Keeper of the Fastness and the Plain, Master of the Southern Forest, Mage of the Crystal Hills." Then, standing, he said brusquely, "Follow me. We have much traveling to do this night."

"What of our father?" Staver asked.

"Vannen is dead. Come."

Taking their cloaks, they followed Justen and did not look back.

2

Visit of a Gray Man

The night was clear and moonless. Under starlight, Justen led the three brothers along the northern boundary of Vannen's holding, then cut to his left, forded the stream, and crossed the rocky south down. Guided by the light from the nearest croft, they made their way to the sunken footpath that wound across the down to skirt a grove of birches.

Staver could contain his curiosity no longer. Trotting forward from his position between his brothers, he fell in beside Justen.

"Jus, why did you call us by those titles?" he asked.

"You'll soon know."

That was an answer typical of Justen and not at all satisfying. A few paces farther on, Staver tried another question.

"What's the Stone Hand, Jus? Vannen said you'd tell us."

"Vannen knew the Stone Hand better than I. And your mother, the blessed Ciantha, she knew them best of all. But what links the Stone Hand with those who shattered the Old Kingdom and hunted down the fugitives on the cape of the Crystal Hills beyond Northmark—this is unknown to me. I only know that some connection exists," Jus said, his voice bitter.

"I never heard of these places. Where are they?"

"Far from the Headland, Staver. But I'll do all I can to help you find them. I promise you that."

"Far from the Headland? But there's nothing beyond the Fissure, Jus, only forests full of beasts. And to the north and west there's rocks and wild water. Even if there were other places, how could we reach them? No one can leave the Headland."

Justen made a low, rumbling noise deep in his chest. It might have been laughter, if Jus were given to laughter.

"So they tell you. But there's more beyond the Headland than these fat frightened diggers and swillers dare to speak of, and there are ways to leave. And to enter." He cast a quick keen glance at his young companion and asked, "Why do you think the nine towers stand overlooking the Fissure?"

Staver thought for a moment, then admitted, "I never gave it any thought. They've always been there, standing empty."

"They were manned once, to watch for attack from the south. But no attack came, so the towers were abandoned. It was a great mistake. The men of the Headland think in terms of plantings and harvests, Staver. They can't conceive of minds that look upon lifetimes as we look upon a single day. And now I fear an attack is close at hand. And the enemy is no mortal enemy. Not the gray men."

Staver was silent for a time, turning Justen's words over in his mind. He was more curious than ever but he knew the old man's ways. Jus was a closemouthed man and when he spoke, he was as like to give a grunt as a word. He had already said more than Staver had ever heard him say in a single speech before.

But his every answer led to new mysteries.

Justen's hand firm against Staver's chest brought him to a halt. He gathered his scattered thoughts and asked in a low voice, "What's the matter, Jus?"

"Wait. Be still," the old man replied.

Staver felt his brothers close beside him. Colberane pressed forward, shouldering past the others, and whispered, "Is something wrong, Jus?"

"It may be. Stay here until I come back," Jus said firmly. "And remember this, all of you, in case we're separated. You are to go to the fourth tower. Sight in on the triple peak and reach out your left hand. There, under the stone, you'll find it all."

"All what?"

"All you need to know, Ord. Remember that. Do it, whatever happens." Turning and crouching low, Justen scuttled forward around the bend in the path where it entered the birches.

The brothers hunkered down against the bank to await

Justen's return. Unmoving and unspeaking, they became fully aware, for the first time, of a total silence that surrounded them. The wind had not risen all night, and the trees were still as painted pickets. Not a leaf stirred, nor a blade of grass. The night birds were not flying, and their scurrying prey were not abroad. Even the stream ran in silence. In all the world there seemed to be no sound but the breath and heartbeat of Colberane, Ordred, and Staver Vannenson, sitting side by side against the grassy bank of the footpath.

Staver leaned close to Col and whispered, "I've never known it to be so quiet before."

"It's unnatural," Col replied.

"That shouldn't surprise you," Ord put in. "Since Vannen was stricken with that fever, everything that's happened to us has been strange."

"It was no fever. You heard him say it was a wasting spell."

"So he believed."

"But you think otherwise, I suppose."

"I suspend judgment. Just as Vannen taught us to do," Ord whispered.

"You believe nothing."

"Don't exaggerate. I believe very little, Col, but you wrong me when you say I believe nothing."

Staver inched away. He disliked hearing his brothers quarrel, and they seemed to be doing as much quarreling now, when they most needed one another's support, as they had in their younger days. But at least there was no anger in it now, not the kind of frightening rivalry in that moment when both had laid hands on the ivory scabbard.

From around the bend there came a soft thudding sound, a low groan, and the scrape of something falling on the gravel. Staver jumped to his feet; even as he rose, his brothers raced past him with their swords drawn. Around the bend they found Justen. He lay back against the bank, staring up at them with wide, amazed eyes and with both hands he clutched at the shaft of an arrow buried deep in his chest. At first sight they thought him dead, but Col caught a faint sound and leaned close to the old man's lips.

Justen reached out a hand, groping sightlessly, and

in a broken voice said, "Put me . . . at Vannen's feet . . .
when you light . . . pyre."

"We will, Jus. Who did this? Why?"

Justen shuddered. His hand fell limply back, and then
he moved no more. All around them, the night was still
once again.

"Pick him up, quickly," Ord said, looking around uncomfortably. "Where there's one arrow, there might be
two. Or four."

"Why would anyone want to kill us?"

"Why would anyone kill Jus? Many strange things have
happened tonight."

"All right. We'll take him back to the house. He asked
to lie at Vannen's feet when we light the pyre. We can do
that for him."

"We can do anything you like, brother, if only we do
it quickly."

"Give me a hand, then. Wrap him in his cloak, and
we'll carry him between us," Col said. "Staver, you lead
the way."

They retraced their steps, moving as fast as the terrain
and the weight of their burden permitted. The stream was
a slippery crossing, and they paused for a bit once across,
then hurried on, with Staver leading far ahead.

The boundary path was even and wide, and the brothers moved quickly on, meeting no one along the way.
When their house came into view, Col and Ord breathed
a great sigh of relief. Justen was a big man, and their
burden was no easy one. But Staver signaled a halt.

"What now, sprig?" Col said impatiently. "I see no
one."

"The house is dark, Col. We left a candle burning by
Vannen's bed and another in the hearthroom window.
They're both out."

"The candle by Vannen's bed was low. It's burned
down. And the other has blown out, that's all."

"There's not been a breeze all night, brother," Ord
whispered.

Col gave a little grunt of acknowledgment. Thievery
was all but unknown on the Headland, but this had been a
night of surprises. And Vannen had been a solitary man,
little given to dealings with others, close about his own

affairs. Rumors bred quickly about such a man. It would be wisest, Col realized, to take precautions.

They laid the burden down gently, unsheathed their swords, and crept silently toward the house, keeping to the shadows. Ord and Col waited outside the door, Staver by the window, listening. Not a sound came from within.

Col pushed the door open slowly and peered in. The fire had sunk to a red glow that gave occasional little licks of yellow flame. The light was faint but sufficient for Col to see that the room was empty.

They entered, still cautious. Staver fed the fire and lit three candles.

Setting two to illuminate the hearthroom, he pushed open the door of Vannen's bedroom with the point of his sword and, holding the third candle high, looked around the room. Vannen lay dead on the bed, back arched and eyes wide, mouth open in a last silent shriek. Staver glanced away, and that quick sidelong look saved his life: at the sight of the gray-robed figure that lunged at him from the corner of the room, he leaped back and let out a cry of alarm.

Instinctively he flung up his sword to block the downward slash of the gray man's weapon, and the shock of the blow nearly tore the blade from his hand. He flung the candle aside and gripped his sword with both hands. The candle rolled to the wall as Staver retreated, step by step, before a relentless attack.

From over his shoulder came Ord's voice, to say, "Leave him to me, brother."

"I can handle him," Staver said.

The gray man was no skilled swordsman. He was strong and unyielding in his attack but he left himself unprotected. Staver studied his opponent's motion and saw an unvarying pattern: his downward slash left him vulnerable for an instant before he could recover and sweep a backhand cut that brought him into position again. Staver feinted in, dodged the next slash, and lunged with all his strength. His blade sank halfway to the hilt in the gray man's chest, just under the breastbone.

Staver jerked the blade free and nearly had his skull split by the gray man's backhanded swipe. Astonished, he jumped back, tangled his feet in a low table, and fell

heavily to the floor. He remembered to keep his grip on
the sword and roll aside. As he scrambled to his feet, he
saw the gray man turn to strike at Col, using the same
methodical slash and backhand recovery, crude and
predictable, a tactic relying on sheer power. Col waited
for a backhand swipe, then thrust. His blade went into
the gray man's vitals, but the downward slash followed all
the same, and Col had to dive for his life. The gray man,
with Col's sword sticking a hand's breadth out of his back,
turned and started at a shambling gait across the room.

Staver felt a chill of fear. His thrust or Col's would
have stopped any ordinary man, but this creature had
taken both as if they were fly bites. The thing could not be
killed or even injured. A deathblow did no more than
make it hesitate for a moment before returning to the attack. Justen's cryptic words came back to Staver, filled
now with terrifying meaning. He pictured an army of
such beings, a gray army, and his heart sank. No force
on Earth could stand against an army that would not die.

He snatched up the little oaken table as a shield and
circled to his left to draw the gray man away from Col.
The eyes in that gray, wasted face were like sun-baked
pebbles. They turned and rested on Staver and remained
fixed, without blinking or wavering, as the gray man
closed in on him. Then Ord moved swiftly in from behind
and with a single stroke sent the creature's head toppling
to the floor.

It stood motionless for a moment. Col scrambled to his
feet and pulled his sword free, and Staver, blade extended
well in front of him, moved closer. The gray man did not
fall. As if it had caught its second wind, it raised its
weapon, stepped forward, and slashed out blindly. Ord
struck again, cutting the legs from under it, and the
creature crashed backward to the floor. Headless, crippled, it lay unbleeding, and the hooked weapon swung
jerkily backward and forward in a deadly arc.

"What kind of thing is this? What is it doing here?"
a horrified Ord asked as he looked down on the ghastly
sight.

"It came to kill us," Col said. "Look what it dropped."
He held out a bow and three gray-feathered arrows.

"We'll probably find that the arrow in Justen's chest is the match of these. Let's bring him in and see."

"What about this creature?" Ord said, gesturing with his sword. "Where could such a monstrosity have come from?"

"From beyond the Fissure," Staver said.

Both of his brothers turned to him at once, and Ord demanded, "Why do you say that?"

"Justen told me."

"What else did he tell you?"

"He said that something had threatened the Headland once, and that's why the towers were built. That threat came to nothing, but Jus seemed to think that an attack is on the way now."

"Who's going to attack the Headland?"

"People from across the Fissure, I suppose. Maybe these creatures."

"But nobody lives beyond the Fissure. And even if they did, how could they reach the Headland?" Col shook his head. "No, Jus was wrong. Or you misunderstood him."

Ord pointed to the headless gray figure still slashing at the empty air above it. "Did that thing come from the Headland, brother?" he asked sarcastically. When Col made no reply, Ord went on. "Vannen spoke of an Old Kingdom, and there's no kingdom, new or old, on the Headland. And Jus called us by titles that didn't refer to anything we know."

"Jus told me that the Old Kingdom is far away, but he'd help us find it," Staver added.

"Maybe. We'll see when we get to the tower."

Ord turned to his younger brother. "Did Jus say who was going to attack?"

"No. He mentioned a gray army but he didn't say who'd lead them, or why."

"I have little wish to face an army of those things," Ord said, and his voice was uncharacteristically subdued. "Each of us struck it a killing blow, and still it's not dead. How can you fight such creatures?"

"You work together. We did, and we won."

Ord nodded, then he laughed and threw an arm around Staver's shoulder. "So we did, brother. And you handled yourself well, I must say. Though you're a bit slow on recovery. And you, my wise elder brother," he added, turning to Col, "are less than graceful at avoiding an overhand stroke."

"I thought he was finished. My sword went right through him."

"A lesson for you both: never underestimate your opponent. He may be unkillable. Now, shall we bring poor Justen's body in?"

They laid the body on the floor of Vannen's death chamber; they could not bring themselves to put it in the same room as the maimed creature that lay supine in the hearthroom, slashing at nothingness, nor did they wish to look upon the thing themselves.

The arrow that had slain Justen was identical to the three that Col had found. The bow, of a wood unknown to the brothers, was too strong for any of them, even Col, to draw. The thought of the enormous strength of that deathless gray thing struck them anew with fear.

"But who would want to kill us?" Staver wondered.

"And by the hand of such an assassin. Whoever sent that gray monstrosity against us has powers we can't imagine. There's much we don't know," Ord said, half to himself.

"Those titles Jus used—maybe they have something to do with it. Vannen said we have a kingdom, and Jus addressed each of us by a title."

"People have been known to act unkindly toward unexpected heirs, sprig," Ord said dryly. "Perhaps there are some who know more than we do."

"Jus must have hidden the documents Vannen mentioned. We'll seek them out in the morning. They should tell us what we want to know," Col said.

"It's getting close to morning now. And I, for one, do not care to sleep in this house with two corpses and a . . . a headless, deathless assassin. I think I'll take my new cloak and a fresh pair of boots and leave this place for good," Ord said, turning toward the ladder to their loft.

"There might be another of those gray things hiding up there," Staver pointed out.

Ord stopped in his tracks. He was silent for a moment, thoughtful, stroking his chin. At length he said discreetly,

"This was always my favorite cloak . . . and these are my most comfortable boots."

"And with three hundred golden oaks, you can buy all the fine cloaks you want and wear new boots whenever you feel like it."

"True, sprig. You've convinced . . . wait a bit," Ord said, suddenly taut and alert. He sniffed the air. "Don't you smell burning?"

"The candle!" Staver cried. "I was carrying a candle when the thing came to me. I dropped it in the hearth-room."

They rushed to the hearthroom, where the gray crea-ture still lay thrashing in fruitless assault. The air was hot and acrid with smoke, but they saw no flame. Then, as they watched, a plume of smoke rolled up from the floor, and another, and then a tongue of flame that grew and spread, cutting them off from the gray attacker. The wall bellied and split, and flames flung out into the room.

Col drew back from the hot blast. "It's too late. We'll never be able to put it out now."

"Then this will be Vannen's pyre. Agreed, brothers?"

"Agreed," Staver said.

"One thing more. Jus wanted to lie at Vannen's feet. Help me move him one last time, Ord."

They placed Justen's body at the foot of Vannen's bed, shutting the door firmly behind them. Working as quickly as they could, they smashed chairs and tables and win-dow shutters, piling the wood under and around the bed. The door was hot to the touch by now, and smoke curled up from the bottom. Their eyes stung, and breath came hard. Col threw a final bit of smashed paneling on the bed and then thrust his brothers toward the window. Staver tumbled out first, then Ord, and right behind them came Col. They sprawled on the cool grass, gulping in the sweet air.

Ord jumped abruptly to his feet, groaned, and looked helplessly at the flames that now poured from every window of the house. "That gray thing is still in there. It's a monstrous creature, but still . . . to burn alive like that . . ."

They watched the flames rise. The roof went up in

a sheet of flame and began to fall inward, crumbling and cracking.

Staver joined his brothers. The three were silent, watching their only home, the pyre of their father and a faithful friend, sink to red embers, and then Staver spoke. "I think we did a kindness to that poor creature. It could feel no pain and couldn't be killed. Maybe fire is the only thing that can free it from whatever power drives it."

"I hope you're right, brother," Ord said.

The ridgepole cracked and collapsed, bringing down the fragments of roof and wall that still stood. The brothers moved back from the wave of heat. Suddenly a sensation came over them as of a heartfelt benediction of gratitude, and the flames seemd to leap upward and then sink, and all was still and peaceful. In the aftermath of that moment, they knew that Staver's instinct had been true.

"Let us get away from here and find a place to sleep," Col said. "We have work to do in the morning."

They turned their backs on the embers of their past and headed south to the Fissure, where the towers stood.

3

The Tower

Staver awoke first, with the sun in his face and an emptiness in his belly as deep as the Fissure. He unwound himself from his dirty gray cloak, yawned, and stretched the stiffness from his aching bones. The ruined shell of an old gristmill makes a hard and chilly bed, and his few hours' sleep had done little to refresh him.

He heard a stirring at his side, turned, and saw Ordred gazing at him sleepily with one half-opened eye. Ord blinked, scratched his tangled red hair, and yawned long and luxuriously.

"I could use a few fat knucklebacks and a handful of stingberries for breakfast," Ord said. "And a drink of cold water."

"Where are they? I'll have some, too," Col mumbled sleepily from deep in the folds of his brown cloak.

"Our little brother is going to fetch them. Aren't you, sprig?"

"All right. I could use some help, though."

Sighing and groaning like an aged, put-upon man, Ord stiffly arose and said, "I suppose we'll have to wait until sundown for breakfast if we don't all go at it. Come on, Col, let's go fishing. The sprig will gather a capful of stingberries."

They worked quickly and were soon breakfasting on a half-dozen plump knucklebacks from the old millrace, spiced with stingberries sun-warmed and fresh off the bush. Staver had come upon a low-growing zickary and plucked the last sweet fruits remaining on the bottom branches spared by the birds. They made a feast of the meal. All was washed down by clear, cold water from the millrace.

Breakfast complete, they started off at a brisk pace for and fourth tower, southernmost of the nine that stood silent and empty overlooking the Fissure and the lands below. With a long trail ahead, much of it over unfamiliar ground—few ventured near the Fissure anymore—and no wish to spend another day in ignorance of the message Vannen and Justen had hinted at so tantalizingly, they pressed on to the limit of their endurance. They were young men, strong, and accustomed to far journeying on foot, for on the Headland there was no other way to travel; beasts of burden were unknown. Nevertheless, they found themselves less talkative than was their custom. They kept their breath for walking.

Early in the afternoon, they came to a swift-running brook that cut directly across their path. Traces of a footbridge remained, but there was no easy crossing. They looked upstream and down and could see no sign of a bridge or ford. Staver and Ord took the opportunity to splash their faces and drink deeply of the cold water, then sprawled on the bank in the shade of the willows. Col remained at the water's edge, looking into the stream with a preoccupied expression on his face, as if listening to far, faint music.

After a time, Staver sat up. "There's a grove of wild

chula nearby. I'll go pick some. We can take along what we don't eat," he said, starting into the woods.

Col turned and called to him. "Watch out for the witch-finger. There's a thick stand of it beyond the willows. It'll tear you to bits if you're not careful."

"I'll go around it."

Ord looked from one to the other, frowning in puzzlement, but said nothing. Only when they had eaten their fill of the meaty chula cones did he ask how they had come to know this part of the Headland so well.

"I just knew the chula was there. I'm not sure how," Staver said.

"Vannen may have brought us here when we were young," Col suggested.

Ord shook his head. "Vannen never took us this far south, brother. You must have been here on business of your own."

"No. I've never been here before."

"Never? Not even with that girl from the High Ridge settlement?"

"No," Col said, wincing as if at a painful memory.

"Then how did you know about the witchfinger? And how did Staver know about the chula?"

Very tentative and apologetic, Staver said, "To be honest with you . . . it was as if someone told me."

"Who?"

"I don't know, Ord. Someone. A voice," Staver said, rubbing his left shoulder.

"This is curious, but let's talk about it on the way," Col said, rising and brushing the grass from his cloak.

"And where's the way?"

"Right along here." Col pointed to his right, where the brook curved out of sight. "There's a ford around the bend where we can cross without getting our feet wet. Then we follow the stream. We have to make two more crossings, and—"

"How do you know?" Ord cried in exasperation.

"I . . . just know."

Ord's voice was low, controlled, and scathing. "You just know. You just happen to know that there's a ford around the bend, and that we have to cross the river twice more, and where the witchfinger is. And Staver just happens to know about the chula."

"I knew about the zickary this morning, too. I didn't say anything because I thought you'd laugh."

"Tell us, sprig," said Col, and his voice was solemn.

"I had dreams last night . . . someone talking to me . . . and when I woke up, there was an instant when it seemed to me that I could understand what the birds were saying. I couldn't see them and I didn't know what kind of birds they were, but they were complaining about the zickary. They said it was too low and all tangled in the branches so they couldn't reach it. And it was just as they said. I could sense what some of the other creatures were saying, too, but the birds were clearest."

Ord placed his hands on Staver's shoulders and looked hard into the youth's eyes. "Are you telling the truth, sprig?"

"I am, Ord."

"He is," Col seconded. "It's been happening to me, too, only it was the river and the wood that spoke to me. Remember this morning, Ord, when we were fishing and I caught those knucklebacks so easily? I knew exactly where they were. I don't know how I knew but I knew . . . as if the stream had said to me, 'Here, in this place—the fish are right here,' and they were. When I told you about the ford, I was only repeating what I heard."

"Well, this is fine. One brother talks to the animals and birds, and the other holds conversations with brooks. Why don't I hear any voices? Why doesn't a zickary call to me and say, 'Ord, here I am, nice and ripe for your breakfast,' or a brook invite me to take a swim? Trees all around me, and birds and bushes and mice and rabbits . . . and not one of them has a word for me!"

"It will come, Ord," Staver said confidently.

"How? When? Will I find an enchanted ring or swallow a magic chula pit? Or will I wake up one morning and find myself in the middle of a conversation with the world and everything on it?"

"I don't know when it will come, but it must be soon. I think it's from the amulets Vannen put in our shoulders," Staver said. "I've seen Vannen stand in a field alone, rubbing his shoulder, looking as if he were speak-

ing with someone. And don't you remember last summer,
that day we were all out in the middle of Bounty Bay,
with the sun shining and no wind at all, and suddenly
Vannen had us rowing for shore with all our might, and
we just reached land when that terrible storm broke?
Seven people drowned, but Vannen knew we had to get
to shore. Something warned him."

"He always did know where to find trails and crossings.
I never knew him to be lost, and he could find food anywhere," Col added.

"True, he could," Ord said. Then he blurted, "But it's
a wicked thing for you two to have the gift and me to be
without it!"

"It will come, Ord. You have a piece of the amulet in
your shoulder, just like us."

"Little good it's done me so far, sprig. Still, it may
come." Ord looked at them and gave a sudden laugh.
"And if I'm given the power to talk to the throwing-sticks
and learn which way they plan to fall, all your birds and
brooks and trees won't help you if you get into a game
with me."

Their way was as Col had said. They crossed the brook
three times, dry-shod each time, and walking south on
the rolling pasture land, caught sight of the fourth tower
glowing in the last rays of the setting sun. Hurrying on
over rock-strewn fields, they reached it just as the sun
went down over the cliffs of Bounty Bay.

The tower was broad at the base, tapering as it rose.
The height at the battlements was nearly eight marks—
eight times the reach of a tall man. Narrow slits in the walls
admitted air and feeble light through the great rough-cut
blocks of stone. The tower was built to withstand heavy
assault, and yet now it stood abandoned. The great iron-
bound oaken door, thick as a hand's span, was open just
a crack. Col pressed it, and it did not move. He laid his
shoulder against it and heaved, and it gave slightly, with
a deep groan of rusted iron. It took the combined efforts
of the three brothers, their heels dug in and their backs to
the heavy door, to force it open wide enough for entrance.

Inside, the tower had the dank, sour smell of long neglect. Little creatures scampered to their holes, startled,
and Staver smiled at the faint brush of their annoyance.

"What are you grinning at, sprig?" Ord asked irritably.

"We've startled a few of the residents. They're annoyed."

"Residents? Oh, I see. You're having a chat with the wildlife again."

Col, meanwhile, was surveying the lower room of the tower in silence. The simple furniture it had once held—a table, a few stools, and two narrow bunks—had long since been removed. The iron staples that led to the upper platforms had been worked from the wall long ago, to be beaten into household tools or utensils. The lowest remaining staple was well beyond even Col's long reach.

"You're the lightest, Staver," Col said. "I'll give you a boost, and you can see what's up there."

Staver looked up into the dark square opening. "Aren't you coming?"

"Of course we are. Not afraid of the dark, are you?"

Staver tossed his gray cloak to Ord and climbed up at once, stepping on Col's shoulder a bit more heavily than was absolutely necessary. The first staple yielded slightly under his weight, and a white trickle of dried mortar fell from the sockets, but it held. He flung up a hand, clasped the next staple, and hauled himself to the second level.

"Can you see anything?" Col shouted up to him.

"There's hardly any light."

"Here, catch."

Col tossed up his tinder box and a stub of candle. Staver soon had the candle lit. Its flame revealed a bare floor of heavy planks, dry, solid, and sound to the touch. Time and weather had loosened them and they rumbled hollowly under his tread, showering dust on his brothers below, but they held his weight easily. A stone hearth stood opposite the opening through which he had climbed. Above the opening, the staples continued to the topmost platform.

"Anything up there?" came Col's voice from below.

"Nothing at all. I'm going on up to the top."

"Wait. I'll come with you."

"We'll both come," Ord added.

Hauling in stones from the slope beyond the tower, Col and Ord built a ramp that put them within reach of the lowest staple. Once on their way, they climbed past the second level without pause and proceeded directly to the top, with Staver trailing after them.

Before Staver had both feet on the top platform, Col was studiously making the rounds of the parapet, peering through the embrasures to the west and south, searching in the dusk that lowered on the mountains for the sign Justen had given him. He leaned far out, straining his eyes, muttering under his breath in his growing frustration at the fading of the light.

"What are you looking for?" Ord asked.

"The triple peak. Jus said to sight on the triple peak," Col replied without turning.

"How can you sight on anything in this light?"

Staver's shout silenced them. "There it is, over there! Three peaks, close together! You have to lean tight against the side, here, and look straight out."

"I see them!" Col cried. "Now . . . I'm to reach my hand out . . . and under the stone . . . "

Col groped, but his fingers found no crevice, only the solid surface of a broad block of stone. He straightened and peered closely at the massive block while scraping at the mortar on all sides. It was old and dry, untouched for lifetimes. At a sudden thought, he felt under the ledge formed by the top row of blocks, and his fingers touched a loose stone. He pulled it free, scraped loose others to make a hole big enough for his hand, and reached in to draw forth a cylinder of soft, thin material, bound in heavy cloth and fixed with massive seals.

"Don't stare at it, brother—open it!" Ord said.

"Yes. Yes, of course," Col said, plucking at the seals with his fingers, then snatching his dagger and slashing at the covering.

Unrolled and unfolded, the cylinder turned out to be six sheets of thin vellum covered with writing in a small, clear hand. Col peered at it closely, then shook his head. "It's too dark. I can't make it out."

"The candle, Col—I still have the candle!" Staver cried, fumbling in his shirt. He dug out the stub and handed it, with the tinder box, to his brother. Col held up the stub and laughed.

"It's no longer than my thumbnail. I couldn't read more than a few lines before it burns out."

"Then light it and read what you can," Ord said impatiently.

"Yes, do," Staver agreed.

"If you like. But let's go below. And before we light a light, let's make ourselves secure for the night."

Ord's hand went to his hilt. "Did you see something? Are we being followed?"

"I saw nothing, but I want no surprises in the night. If another gray man turns up—"

"Why would there be another?"

"Why was there one? We may learn from this," Col said, tapping the vellum manuscript with his fingers, "but in any case, I want to be ready for anything."

They descended to the first level. Staver went for water, while Col and Ord pulled loose a heavy beam to use as a bar for the door. On Staver's return, they dined hastily on chula cones, gulped down handfuls of water, and then settled in the dark, while Col unfurled the vellum sheets and lit the candle stub.

He scanned the top sheet quickly, frowned, and glanced at the others. "It seems to start in the middle of something. These sheets are in sequence, and the last one is the final one, but the beginning is missing."

"What is it about?"

"War . . . a battle of some kind, I think," Col said.

"By all that lives and breathes, brother, will you read it while the light lasts?" Ord exclaimed.

Col nodded. He moved the vellum closer to the guttering candle stub. The writing was small and sometimes faded, and the light was poor and wavery. Col read slowly and paused often. " ' . . . was broken. Izmann was slain by a single blow from the great axe Jembre, and his men, seeing this, were struck with amaze, and some lay down their weapons, and many, even of the hardiest, cried out and fled. For they had believed Tapran to be be slain and knew that no other hand but his could wield Jembre, which weapon they greatly feared for the virtue of the signs graven thereon. But the sun was now low, and the end of day and the coming of darkness near, and full well the armies of Ambescand knew that night was a time of renewed strength for the enemy. Tapran therefore raised Jembre overhead and rallied his axemen, of whom but two score remained alive and many of those sorely injured, and he led them in an assault against the Balukki guardsmen and with his one good hand he struck the chief of the guardsmen, a certain Shirzuul, and cleft him through the helmet from crown to chin. Then the archers of Lindare . . . ' " Col paused, then looked up and said, "I'm going to skip ahead. This battle has nothing to do with us."

"Go on," Ord said.

Col ran his broad forefinger carefully across the lines of small script. He squinted in the flickering light, brought the vellum closer to his eyes, and stopped. He raised his eyes, stared in bewilderment at his brothers, then licked his dry lips and went on, slowly, as though he could not believe what he saw before him. He looked up once more, dazed, shaking his head.

"What is it, Col? What does it say?"

"Read it, brother! The candle's going out!"

Col's voice was low. " 'In this year, nineteenth of the victory over the usurper, 311th of the tower at Northmark and 643rd of the calendar of the High City, the beloved Ambescand made peaceful voyage to the Land of Light and was much mourned, for he was a good king and a valiant one, and the rule passed to his sons. The three brothers ruled in harmony, and all was prosperous and well with the people, and for long, no enemy dared strike. Then was Colberane Whitblade Master of the Southern Forest, and the Scarlet Ord Keeper of the Fastness and the Plain, and Staver Ironbrand Mage of the Crystal Hills.' "

The candle sank, flared once, and went out. The three brothers sat silent in the darkness, wondering at the words they had heard.

"What does it mean?" Staver asked after a time.

"I don't know. How could I know? I can't even guess. This is an old record, but . . . "

"But those are our names and the titles Justen used," Ord said.

Col sighed, and in the pale beams from the wall slits they could see him rise. "It's too dark to read further, and we can't work out the answer by ourselves. We might as well sleep."

"I suggest the second level," Ord said, moving toward the wall where the staples were set. "The boards are hard, but they're dry. Better to sleep on a hard board than in this muck."

They climbed up, wrapped themselves in their cloaks, and were soon asleep. For all the excitement the words of the document had roused in them, they were so weary from long travel and the shocks of the past few days that they could not keep themselves awake. They gave no thought to setting a watch, for they had barred the heavy door and the tower was unscalable.

Some hours later, Staver awoke from sound sleep with a start. He lay still, holding his breath, listening for he knew not what, but he heard nothing. Col snorted and muttered, then rolled over and was silent. Ord breathed deeply and regularly. Nothing had disturbed those two. Staver yawned, pulled his cloak closely about him, and tried to find a comfortable position on the boards. He was close to sleep when he heard the far faint *tink* of metal on stone.

He raised his head, listening intently, and then he rose, moving as quietly as he could, and went to the opening in the floor. All was silent and pitch black below. He tried to remember where the sound had come from. It seemed distant, perhaps above him. Shifting his sword so that it hung behind him, where it could not strike against stone or iron staple, he began cautiously to climb to the topmost level. He realized as he climbed that the sound he was trying to avoid was the very sound he had heard: the noise made by someone trying to scale the tower.

The parapet was cold and silent, and he could see no sign of life or motion in any direction. Faint light rimmed the peaks of the high range to the east, and he could see the open ground all around the tower; but the Fissure, and the forest beyond it, and the wood of the Headland, were softly dark.

Staver shivered and rubbed his arms for warmth in the chill air. His breath went out in a thin white plume, and he regretted the haste that had made him leave his cloak below. He resolved, on one more slow tour of inspection, to put his mind at ease, and then back to sleep. As he leaned into the embrasure, he heard a faint sound from directly below, a noise as if something were scraping against the stone. He leaned farther—then jerked back quickly, with a cry of fear, at the sight of a gray hand that reached up to grasp the edge of the stone just below his chin.

As Staver fumbled for his sword, the gray man's other hand gripped the parapet, and the creature drew itself up. Staver confronted the pitiless gray eyes and the rutted, wasted features, and for a moment he stood frozen. Then he dashed forward and brought the blade down hard on the clutching fingers of one hand, severing them, and smashed the pommel into the blighted gray face. The gray man toppled back and, turning slowly, fell to the base of the tower, where it landed with the thump of a stone dropped on soft earth.

Staver pulled back, panting and shaking. The severed fingers lay twitching on the stone, and he swept them off with one wild stroke. Running from embrasure to embrasure, sword at the ready, he searched for another gray attacker, but there were no more.

"Staver, are you up there? What's wrong?" came Col's voice.

"I'm all right," Staver called down. "There was a gray man. I stopped it."

Col's head appeared in the opening. As he climbed onto the platform, he said, "Another gray man? How did it get here?"

"Climbed up the side. I heard a noise and came up to look, and it popped up right in front of me."

"Good work, sprig. If it had gotten to us while we were sleeping . . . I'm glad you heard it," Col said, clapping Staver on the shoulder. "Where did it fall?"

"Over here."

Col and Staver leaned far out and looked down to where the gray man lay unmoving. It had fallen on its left side and lay hunched on the ground, looking small.

"Maybe they can be killed after all," Col said.

"Maybe. That one certainly looks . . ."

Staver fell silent as the gray man stirred. It climbed jerkily to its feet and began to move at a lurching gait around the base of the tower toward the door. Its figure disappeared under the archway, and a moment later they heard a great booming as it smashed at the door with its hooked weapon.

"It's still alive, Col. Its side is all smashed in, but it's still alive," Staver said.

"It can't break down that door."

Ord's voice was cool. "It doesn't have to, brother. We have no more food and no water, and there's no way out of the tower but through the door where it's waiting." He perched on the edge of the platform and said, "What now?"

"We fight it."

"Easy, brother. We were lucky once. We might not be lucky a second time."

"What else can we do? We can't climb down the outside without ropes."

The hollow boom of the gray man's weapon on the door echoed up through the tower. No one spoke for a time. Finally Ord said, "You're right, brother. We can't run. We have to fight. So let's plan it carefully."

Some time later, as first light was breaking, the three brothers took their positions on the lowest level of the tower. The heavy flooring of the second level, wrenched loose and splintered, lay heaped in the center. Col and Staver stood before the door, which was already cracked in three places under the gray man's remorseless battering, and grasped the beam that held it shut. Ord, his sword at the ready, stood beside the door.

Col nodded, and he and Staver hefted the beam from its place and retreated behind the pile of dry wood. The door crashed open at the gray man's next blow, snapping the hinges and clattering to the ground. The gray man towered in the arched entry.

Staver felt his gorge rise at the sight of the creature. Its left shoulder was crushed into the rib cage. The arm dangled, twisted out of shape. Half the skull was caved in, and the gray man glared at them out of one pale eye. Its walk was halting, shambling, as if it moved on bones smashed out of normal articulation. And yet it moved and fought, swinging that hooked weapon relentlessly.

It took one unsteady step forward and halted. Staver made a feint toward it and quickly retreated. The gray man lurched a step closer and lashed out, spinning one of the heaped beams across the room with its blow.

Ord struck then. With a smooth slash he took the gray man's head from its shoulders. Stepping to one side, he cut at the creature's legs and kicked it forward, crippled, onto the pile of wood.

Col and Staver toppled a heavy beam to pin the gray man down. Together, the brothers lifted the broken door and added it to the pile. When Col lit the dry wood, the fire caught at once, rising quickly in the chimneylike tower.

Outside, leaning on his sword, Col said, "It seems a barbaric thing to do, burning anything alive like that."

"But when we burned the first one, at the house . . . you had the same feeling . . . as if somehow we'd freed it . . . ," Staver said, his eyes fixed on the flames.

"Enough about that thing. It's light now, and we can have a good look at that document. I want to know why our names . . . What's the matter, Col? Col, don't tell me . . . !"

At Ord's mention of the document, Col had given a start. After a rapid search of his garments, he turned his helpless gaze upon the inferno roaring within the tower.

"It's in there," he said.

4

The Fissure

They took their morning meal at the foot of a bluff overlooking the Fissure. The booming of the early tidal surge came faintly to their ears from the depths; all else was still, save for the wind.

Ord's mood was black and bitter. He ate without saying a word, and when he was done, he sat against a rock, apart from his brothers.

Col made several unsuccessful attempts at conversation. They were greeted by dispirited monosyllables from Staver and stony silence from Ord. At last, in frustration,

Col said, "The sheets must have fallen from my shirt while we were tearing up the flooring. I didn't burn them on purpose. But they're gone. What's happened has happened, and there's no use sulking over it. Anyway, the thing that concerns us now is not some ancient battle or a few nobles with names like ours. We have to make a choice. It's simple enough: do we cross the Fissure and head south to seek the kingdom Vannen spoke of, or do we stay here on the Headland? Isn't that the choice, Staver?"

"I suppose so."

"Of course it is!" Col said, with forced enthusiasm. "Now, as I see it, crossing the Fissure is a difficult task. It may be impossible. No one's ever done it, as far as we know, and if—"

"What about the gray men? Do you think they're from the Headland?" Ord broke in.

"They must be from some unexplored part."

"What part of the Headland is unexplored?"

"Well . . . there are said to be deep caves up by Long Bay. Or the gray men might have come from one of the northern islands. We can't navigate those waters, but perhaps they can."

Ord gave a disgusted groan, pulled his black cloak about him, and turned away. Col addressed himself once again to his younger brother.

"If we assume—just assume, for the sake of argument —that no one has ever crossed the Fissure, then we have to face the fact that we might very well get ourselves trapped down there, possibly killed, before we've even started out. And if we should get across somehow, what do we do then—just the three of us in a strange land, with no followers, no guide, not even a map to tell us where to look—"

"Thanks to you, brother," Ord said, without turning.

"And maybe nothing to look for?" Col continued, doing his best to ignore the comment. "That kingdom may not exist anymore. And if it does, whoever is ruling it now is surely not going to welcome us."

"That's true, Col," Staver conceded.

"On the other hand, if we stay here, with Vannen's land and the three hundred oaks he gave each of us, we can live comfortably on the Headland for the rest of our lives."

"The rest of our lives may be a very short time if those gray monstrosities keep paying us daily visits," Ord broke in.

"We've beaten two of them," Staver said.

"Staver's right. We can handle the gray men. From now on, we'll be ready for them," Col added.

Ord gave them a scathing glance. He rose slowly and walked to where they sat. Standing over them, arms folded, he said, "You talk like little boys after your first fight. One victory and you're ready to conquer the world. Let me remind you, brothers, that the gray man in Vannen's house killed Justen and came very close to killing both of you. And if the one at the tower had turned to his left when he entered, he might have cut me in half before either of you could help me."

"But he didn't. We beat them both."

"And what if we have to face two of them next time? Or ten? Or an army? Will we beat them again? And the time after that, will we beat them?" They did not reply to that, and Ord went angrily on, "Do you want to spend the rest of your lives with a sword in your hand, listening for footsteps? Do you want to post guard every time we sleep and wonder what's waiting for you behind every door? Someone is sending those gray men after us. Maybe it's the same someone who put the wasting spell on Vannen and the one who rules the kingdom that should be ours. If we just sit still here on the Headland, sooner or later they'll get us. If I'm going to be cut down by one of those gray things, at least let me die seeking a kingdom—not snoring in a farmhouse, clutching my little bag of gold."

"The other night you said you didn't believe Vannen died of a wasting spell."

"I've changed my mind, brother," Ord said.

"Yes. . . . Well, those are brave words and a sensible warning, but we must think this over carefully," Col said, rising. "The Headland is our home, Ord. We were born and raised here. All our friends are here."

"Our parents are dead, and our home is a heap of ashes. The folk of the Headland are not my friends, Col, and I never thought them to be yours," Ord said. "I have no wish to be one of them. They work like animals and they think like children, and as the years go by, they get older and fatter and richer, and one day they die. That's all they do—all their lives. But not Vannen. He died like a man. He fought to the end and he asked no tears. He wasn't one of their pitiful lot and he didn't raise us to be. Think, Col—he taught us to read and write, he taught us swordsmanship, he made us think about people and their ways, and about right and wrong. And with his dying breath, he sent us to seek a kingdom."

"Yes. Yes, that's all true, Ord," Col said thoughtfully. "But all the same, we must think . . . Vannen left us his land, and we can't . . ."

"By all that lives and breathes on this earth!" Ord cried. "If a miserable farm and a burnt-out building mean more to you than a kingdom, then take my share and enjoy it as much as you can. I'll cross the Fissure alone."

"No, Ord!" Staver said, taking a firm grip on his brother's arm. "Vannen said we must seek the kingdom together."

"Tell that to the head of the family," Ord said, pulling free.

"I agree with Ord," Staver said. "The Headland is all we've ever known, but I never felt as though we really belonged here. And all of these things happening so quickly must mean something—the gray men, the swords, and the amulet. . . ."

"And the document I stupidly lost," Col said. All resistance gone, he turned to them in a silent appeal for their forgiveness.

Ord's mood brightened. He stepped to Col's side and firmly clasped his forearm. "As you wisely said, brother, what's happened has happened, and there's no use sulking. The way may be a bit harder now, but we'll find it. Let's forget the writings."

"There was no map, Ord, and nothing that looked like directions. I skimmed over it quickly, and it seemed to be a history. Nothing more."

"Then we've lost nothing. I'm sorry for my temper, brother."

"I'm sorry I was so clumsy."

"Forget it. Are you with us?"

Col hesitated, then let out a sigh and nodded his head. "I suppose it's what Vannen wanted us to do. I just want to be sure we follow his wishes. He wouldn't have told us we had a kingdom waiting if he'd wanted us to stay on the Headland, would he?"

"Of course not," Ord said, as warmly reassuring as he could be.

"No. And Vannen really was different from everyone else on the Headland," Col said, clearly trying his best to convince himself that he was making the right decision. "So are we, I guess. I felt it sometimes myself. And Ciantha was even less like the others."

"Do you remember her well?" Staver asked, his curiosity roused.

"Not very clearly. She had long red hair, bright red, even brighter than Ord's, and big bright green eyes. I remember her as being very young and very beautiful. Much younger and more beautiful than the picture in Vannen's room."

"Did she really know magic?"

"I think she did, although at the time I didn't understand. I was only a little boy. She could talk to animals, trees, even the earth itself. She could heal people who were terribly injured. There was a man . . . a woodcutter . . . named Freeland. . . . "

"I remember that time," Ord said. "His legs were hurt."

"They were crushed. His sons were ready to cut them off to save his life when Ciantha came. Freeland was walking before spring."

"What happened to her? If she could heal others, why did she have to die?"

"After you were born, suddenly everyone seemed to need her help. She never refused. Then she fell ill herself. She didn't leave her bed for days. One day an old man came to the house—a very old man—and Ciantha went with him, to be cured. And a few days later Vannen told us she'd never be back."

"I wish I'd known her," Staver said. "All I ever had was the picture on Vannen's wall, and now that's gone."

"You have something more. We all do. That amulet I took from Vannen's shoulder was Ciantha's. She wore it around her neck. But when she left with the old man, she wasn't wearing it. I noticed that when I said goodbye to her, and I always remembered. That was what made me sure she wouldn't be coming back. And it was after she left that Vannen began to act as she sometimes had—as if he could see and hear things that others couldn't."

"That's all very well for you two," Ord said, rubbing his shoulder, "but it would appear that Ciantha's magic can't be divided three ways. Neither bird, nor brook, nor bush has said a single word to me so far."

"It will come, Ord. I'm certain of it."

"I'll try to be patient. But now, since we're agreed, let's be on our way. We have some exploring to do," Ord said, stepping off toward the Fissure. A few steps on he halted and turned back to where his brothers still stood looking back on the Headland. "Haven't changed your minds, have you?" he called to them above the rising roar of the tidal waters.

They turned and started toward him. Col said, "Just one last look. We'll be away for a long time."

"We must cross, brother. There's a kingdom waiting."

"Yes. And someone else is sitting on the throne." Col sighed, gestured to his brother, and said, "Go ahead, lead on."

The Fissure was a broad irregular canyon, the scar of some ancient upheaval, that now served as border between the Headland and the continent to the south, a boundary as absolute as the rim of the world. No man had ever been known to cross it, and few even spoke of such a wild project. There were tales of an ancient bridge linking the Headland and the south, but no one believed them. No trace of a bridge existed, and such a feat of building was beyond imagining.

Yet, as the three sons of Vannen and Ciantha stood at the lip of the Fissure, observing, questioning, and debating, with the thunder of its waters far below rising up to drown out their voices if they sank below a shout, things long forgotten came back to their minds. The gray men,

of course, had to have come from elsewhere. But there
were other things—strange beasts and men, and odd
ways and customs hinted at in childhood tales—none of
them to be found on the Headland. The old man who had
come for Ciantha had come from elsewhere, and the
swords given them by Vannen—swords from the Old
Kingdom, he called them—were the work of no Headland
smithy.

Their deliberations were brief, since there were only
three ways of crossing to be considered. They could
strike for the coast, sail far out to sea on the tidal current
disgorging from the Fissure, and land anywhere to the
south. That was ruled out at once, unanimously, because
it amounted to suicide. The brothers were fair inland
sailors; they could handle a boat on any of the sheltered
bays of the Headland, but negotiating the ocean waters off
the Headland was so close to impossible that it had never
been attempted by any but the most desperate fugitives,
all of whom had come to grief minutes from shore.

The second way was to construct a bridge linking the
two banks of the Fissure. This, too, was ruled out as
flatly impossible. The distance was too great, the angle
of descent too sharp for any simple 'bridge. No tree on
the Headland could reach that distance, and if such a
tree could be found, no three men could drag it to the
edge and place it properly into position. Three hundred
men could not. A rope bridge was equally impossible.
There was no way of getting it to the other side and no
visible anchorage for it on the treeless, rock-strewn
slopes that led back to the fringes of the dark wood.

So they found themselves with no choice but to descend into the Fissure, where tides roared through twice
each day under an eternal blanket of spray, and to seek
a crossing there.

"But how can we ever cross the tiderace?" Staver
asked. "It moves with tremendous force, and the banks
are sheer, and there are huge rocks—"

"Have you seen all that, sprig?" Ord interrupted.

"No, but I've heard of it."

"We've all heard of it. But did the people who told
you go and see it themselves?"

"Well, I suppose . . ."

"Of course they didn't. They'd heard it from someone who'd heard it from someone else, all the way back to the time the Fissure was new. We can see for ourselves that it's impossible to take a boat out or to get any kind of bridge built. I want to see for myself that it's impossible to cross the current," Ord said.

"And what if it is?" Col asked.

"Then we'll just have to find another way. The Fissure can be crossed, brother. Those gray men didn't fly over. If they could fly, we'd be dead now."

"I hope you're right. But it seems to me that if the Fissure could be crossed, it would be. We wouldn't have grown up hearing all the stories of how it was impossible ever to leave the Headland."

Ord laughed and shook his head. "You're thinking like a man now, Col, and not like our Headland neighbors. They're too comfortable here ever to want to leave, so they've had to convince themselves that it's impossible. That way, they never have to face the truth."

Having decided on their course, they set about preparing. Staver went foraging for chula cones, which could be kept indefinitely, and then all three brothers made the long trip back to the nearest settlement to buy ropes, packs, and water bags.

As the sun set, they made camp for the night in an open grassy field. After a feast of grilled knuckleback and cutfin, zickary, and sweet roasted tubers, they rolled up in their cloaks around the fire and went to sleep. This night, though, they took turns standing guard.

By the next morning they were ready. Each had a pack filled to bursting with chula cones and dried meat, two water bags, and a coil of rope. Ord had brought a heavy iron-tipped staff.

They headed east, to where the Fissure widened, reasoning that the current here might be slower, the water perhaps shallower. All the way along, they inspected the rim closely, but nowhere was there a trace of a downward path. For most of the way, the edge was sharp, the cliff sheer, smooth, free of outcroppings, ledges or shelves. Far down, all disappeared in a swirling cloud of mist heaved up by the current that surged below. When they lay at the edge and peered down, the booming of the tidal bore seemed doubled and redoubled in volume, overwhelming all other sound.

They continued farther east, past the wide point in the Fissure. Here they came to another abandoned tower, this one in ruins, standing at the very edge of the chasm.

"Why did they build it so close?" Staver asked.

"They didn't build it at the edge, sprig. The edge moved up to meet it," Col said.

Staver stared at the broken tower. Its top was gone, but no stones lay on the ground. He imagined those great blocks teetering, groaning, and slowly toppling over to plunge one by one into the whiteness so far below. He shuddered and took a few steps back from the edge.

"Don't be nervous. There's usually a warning before the cliff breaks off," Ord assured him cheerfully.

"But . . . so much of it! The other tower was about five marks from the edge. Did that much fall?"

"That much and more. I've heard that the towers were all built to stand nine marks from the edge of the Fissure."

"What did it, Ord?"

"The tide. It eats away, bit by bit, and when it eats enough out down there, the wall collapses all the way up."

"How can a tide do that? It's only water," Staver said suspiciously.

"I don't know, but I've never heard any other explanation. They say the tide will wash the whole Headland away some day."

They shouldered their burdens and set off, Ord still in the lead. A little way on, the Fissure began to widen once again, and their hopes rose a bit. Ord stopped often to inspect likely descents, but he always walked back from the edge frowning, shaking his head.

The morning was gone, and they still had found no way to descend. Ord had twice spoken—only half in jest—of tossing their ropes over at random and trusting to luck, when they came upon an offshoot of the Fissure. It extended at a right angle some distance into the Headland, narrowing to a chimney as it went. At the outermost

point, the faces were less than a mark apart. It appeared
to narrow a very short way down.

Ord dropped to his stomach and peered into the crevice. He rose, grinning, and shouted over the roar that
rose from below, "We've found our way."

5

The Stone Bridge

Ord, the best climber among them, laid out the plan.
They would work their way down this chimney, making
their way out toward the Fissure as the descent narrowed.
Their first objective was to find a place where they might
safely observe the tidal current from a better vantage.
Their greatest need was for clear and accurate information. They had no firsthand knowledge of what awaited
them below. No one on the Headland did.

Ord led the way. The instant they entered the narrow
opening, the roar of the Fissure filled their ears, drowning
all other sound. The descent was slow, for they moved
with great care. The chimney narrowed, and they moved
outward toward the Fissure. Below, Ord beckoned, encouraging Staver on. Since they had entered the cleft,
there had been no verbal communication · between the
brothers. The noise of the Fissure made it impossible.

Staver worked his slow and careful way down, moving
his feet cautiously, one at a time, setting them firm and
flat, and then lowering his back while he pressed his
hands hard against the rock face. His legs and upper
arms were beginning to tire, and his back was sore from
the pressure of the stone. The pack hung against his
chest like an anchor, and the pack strap pulled at his
neck. He felt that he had been in this cold, dark chimney,
with the roar and rumble of the Fissure enclosing him,
for hours and hours.

He became so absorbed in his movements that he was
almost on top of Ord before he saw that his brother had
stopped. Ord was perched on a narrow ledge, and he

flashed a broad grin at his brother, welcoming him to share this refuge. The ledge was no more than a hand's length from front to back, but to Staver it seemed like a broad bench, though unfortunately much harder. He sat stiffly, his back firm against the rock behind him, and flexed his ankles. Following Ord's example, he kneaded his upper arms and his neck to ward off cramps.

Col soon joined them. Nearly touching, but isolated by the surrounding din, they sat side by side on the narrow ledge for a time. No one wished to be the first to urge the others on. Finally, Staver put his mouth close to Ord's ear, cupped his hands, and asked, "How much farther?"

Ord did not reply in words. He tapped the ledge with one hand, and with the other he pointed in the direction of the Fissure. Staver gingerly inclined his head forward and saw that the ledge continued all the way to the Fissure. In some places it narrowed to no more than a toehold, and in others it widened enough to admit both feet side by side; but it went on unbroken.

They carefully drew themselves upright and, in the same order as before, began to work their way to the opening. The opposite face was within reach of their outstretched fingertips now, and their progress along the ledge was faster and less wearisome than the back-and-foot descent of the chimney. Nevertheless, it was late afternoon before they stepped out onto the ledge overlooking the Fissure.

The first thing they noticed was the comparative quiet. The din that had pounded at their senses during the descent had dwindled imperceptibly as they moved outward, and only now, at rest with the climb temporarily behind them, were they able to appreciate its diminution. From the water below there still rose a muffled, rolling roar, but it was fading even as they listened.

From this unaccustomed vantage, the Fissure was a breathtaking sight. The opposite face was in shadow now, but the sky above was cloudless and still bright, and slanting light reflected from the rock high above their heads. Through the misty air, the tide that coursed along the floor of the Fissure was distinguishable far below. At their level and above them, the walls were scarred with long perpendicular seams. Ribs of stone extended fifty marks from top to bottom, where they were sheared off abruptly. As they stretched out on the ledge, which here was nearly a mark wide for a short space, the brothers gazed on the walls—and on the water far beneath them —and marveled at the force into whose presence they had intruded.

Even at its ebb, the water churned beneath a tattered veil of mist and spray that made it impossible for them to estimate its true depth. Above the water level the rock was burnished to a uniform slatey gray surface as smooth as a plastered wall. It widened as it rose, then slowly narrowed again until it reached a point about six marks below their ledge. From there to the top, the walls rose perpendicular in irregular fluted columns.

"How can we ever cross that?" Col said.

"We'll find a way," Ord said confidently.

"How? Magic?" Col's voice rose angrily, louder now than the diminished roar of the waters. "There's no way down. If we could get down, there's no chance of crossing those waters. And if we ever manage to get across alive —by a miracle—there's no way we could climb up again before the tide turned and swept us away."

"There may be handholds on the lower wall. We're too far away to see."

"It wouldn't matter if there were a staircase four marks wide, Ord! We could never get down, and across, and back up the other side above the water level in time!"

"Let's at least get an estimate of the time between tides. Then we'll know how much time we have."

Col went to the rear of the ledge and started digging in his pack. "Do what you like. I'm not ready to begin that chimney climb again until I've eaten and rested."

Ord rolled over on his back and propped himself up on his elbows. Looking coldly at Col, he said, "You give up easily, brother."

"If you find a way for us to get across alive, I'll cross. But I won't throw my life away."

"Oh, don't throw your life away," Ord said scornfully. "Take it back to the Headland and let it trickle away, year by precious year, until you forget you have it."

Col bit savagely into a chula cone and began munching loudly on it. Ord rolled over on his stomach and

stared downward. Sitting apart, Staver looked at them
and wished that the roar of the waters would return to
drown out their quarreling. Bad as that noise was, the
sound of his brothers' bickering was more painful to his
ears.

Staver had eaten a chula cone and a small bit of dried
meat, and now sipped a bit of water, but he ate with
scant appetite. He knew he could not resolve the dispute
between his brothers, and he had no desire to join it.
Using his pack for a pillow, he rolled up in his cloak and
quickly went to sleep.

He awoke in the night to a distant rumble. He buried
his head in the folds of his cloak, but the sound grew
louder. It was not one sound but a medley of many.
Cracking and clattering there was; and sudden booming
bursts; and rattling and crashing as if mountains were
coming together headlong in battle; and long groaning,
as if a tree taller and broader than all the trees of the
Headland were toppling slowly and crushing all before
it; and a steady thrumming, like a long, monotonous
chord on some instrument as immense as all the rock
around them. Over everything was the thunder of water
racing on toward them, bursting through every barrier
and scattering everything in its path, unstoppable by any
force known to mortal man.

Staver glanced up and saw in the faint light the outline
of his brothers sitting upright, grimacing, hands clamped
over their ears. The sound became a dimension that
swallowed all other reality. It was as palpable as the rock
at their backs, as profound as the depth of the Fissure. It
forced its way into their bodies, squeezed the breath
from their lungs, tightened their throats, and set their
blood to racing. It penetrated their minds, driving out
memory and hope and purpose, crushing all thought under its invisible, intangible omnipresence.

The sound of the waters reached the point where they
knew they could endure no more, and still it increased.
There came a terrific crash that shook the rock and the
very air around them, and the din dropped slightly for a
time while the water milled aimlessly, churning and re-
bounding upon itself. Then the tide reversed its direction

and began to surge—with a deeper voice—back up the channel to the sea.

When silence had returned, the three brothers collapsed on the shelf, exhausted by their ordeal. They did not exchange a word. They slept a troubled sleep until dawn.

In the morning, when they had eaten, Col said, "I heard the voice of the water last night—the inner voice, the spirit. It was awful. Sheer brutal power, exulting in destruction. It is merciless. We can never conquer it."

"Then we'll outsmart it," Ord said.

"You haven't seen it, only heard its outer voice. When you've seen it, you'll feel less confident."

Before long they had their first sight of what they had only heard in the darkness. At the first note of warning thunder in the distance, they plugged their ears with bits of cloth torn from their cloaks, but this gave small relief. Sprawled side by side on the ledge, they watched the tide advance.

A great boiling spuming wall of water swept through the Fissure, tumbling before it a vanguard of boulders, some of them the size of barns. Rolling and swirling through its accustomed channel, it gathered force and speed with every second. Spray burst up and filled the air, and the level of the water rose with terrible speed, climbing until it filled the rounded channel and raced by just below the ends of the cliff-high columns. The air grew thick with moisture and dense with sound.

The water rose to cover the bases of the rock ribs. At once it began to eddy and churn along the canyon walls as it was caught by the projecting columns. Wilder, more furious than ever, it ascended to a point no more than five marks below their ledge, and still it rose. Once again the great crash echoed down the Fissure as the westbound water met the tide hurrying from the opposite end. The water reached four marks below their ledge, and then stopped rising.

Staver gaped down on the churning foam-laced surface and let out a breath he had not been aware of holding. He had never seen such power before.

The tide was like a great rasp, thrust in and drawn out of the Fissure slowly but remorselessly twice each

day, year after year, century upon century. It had worn
a smooth channel into the solid rock, and each day it
scoured away a bit more.

When the lull had passed and the thunderous ebbing
of the tide had subsided to a dwindling mumble, like a
bully hurling threats over his shoulder as he stalks away,
Col stood up and began to fold his cloak. He stuffed it
in his pack and swung the pack into place.

"No one can cross that. I'm starting back up," he said.

Ord did not turn. He sat facing out, gazing at the far
wall.

Col paused, then, in a conciliatory tone, said, "Maybe
there's another spot. We can try farther east, and if we
find nothing, we can work our way back to the western
point."

"No. It's here," Ord said. His voice grew distant. "I
feel it. Here, right here, in this spot."

"How can you be so sure?"

"I know it is, Col. I just . . . I know it is."

Staver looked at Ord curiously. His brother was leaning back against the cliff, his legs straight out before him,
his palms flat on the ledge. He stared dreamily ahead,
as if his mind were faring far away, while his body
stayed behind. Staver glanced at Col, and as their eyes
met, there was a thrill of recognition. A voice was coming
to Ord, as other voices had come to them.

"Breaking . . . ," Ord said faintly. "It pulls . . . hurts
me." His face contorted with pain, and sweat beaded his
brow. "It must . . . It's tearing . . . breaking away. . . ."

Whatever more he said was lost beneath a slow rumble that came from the wall behind them. The ledge
shook, and a shower of small stones rattled down the face
of the cliff, bounced off the flat rock, and fell to the water below.

The rumble became a grating shriek that shrilled in
their ears like the creaking of an entire world of rusty
hinges. Col reached out to pull Staver back and pin him
to the wall just as a second shower of dust and stones
hailed down all around them. With a titanic groan, the
cliff to their left spilled forward, halted, lurched and
halted again, slipped, and then began to slide downward

with gathering speed while stones and chips were flung from its sides.

With a crash and a shock that jarred their bones, the giant column of stone slammed against an outcropping below; once more it stopped; then it toppled slowly forward. Its top struck the opposite face, sending a burst of stones spinning through the air. The column split near the middle, and while the upper portion tumbled end over end to the water, the lower half, with a hollow, grinding, rasping squeal of stone against stone, lodged nearly horizontal between the two faces of the canyon.

"By all the winds and waters," Staver whispered reverently. "It was the Earth herself that spoke to him."

"You've found our way across, brother," Col said.

They stared at the miraculous bridge. It hung between the walls, joining them for a time, until the next tide came to sweep it away or to jar it free by the vibrating power of its passage. Barely a mark above the base of the stone columns it had caught. In the wall at its far end, no more than a man's height above its upper surface, was a ledge.

"Let's go," Ord said.

He led the way, and they followed without a word. The approach was not steep, but the loose, fresh-fallen scree made it a slow and difficult descent. Reaching the fallen column, they inspected its anchorage closely. It lay upon a broad ledge, its base jammed flush against the face of the cliff, rising at a slight angle.

"It looks secure on this side," Ord said.

"Secure enough to hold us, I'm sure. But it won't withstand another tide."

"Nothing could," Ord said. Tying a line securely around his waist, he gave the end to Col. Col, in turn, looped his own line around a point of rock. Thus belayed, he ran Ord's rope over one shoulder. When his brother had taken a firm grip and braced himself solidly, Ord stretched out flat on the upper surface of the fallen column and began to pull himself slowly across.

Ord's progress was even but painfully slow. All three of the brothers were aware that this bridge would last only as long as the first onslaught of the incoming tide. There was some time to spare—but there was none to

waste. When Ord at last stood erect on the opposite ledge
and waved the next man across, Col and Staver shared
a sigh and a broad smile of relief.

"You're next, sprig," Col said.

"Me? Can't you go?"

"It has to be you, sprig. If I slip going across, it will
take you and Ord to haul me in."

That was so obviously true that Staver could only nod.
He attached the end of Ord's line to the rope already
fastened around his own waist and gave Col his line. He
felt—and looked—like a condemned man handing the
noose to his own hangman.

"Look straight ahead of you, sprig. Look for your next
grip, and don't think of anything else," Col advised.
"Whatever happens, don't look down."

"I won't," Staver said, and his voice was dry and weak.

"Take a sip of water before you go," Col said, holding
out his own water bag. "Don't feel bad, sprig. I'm afraid,
too, but we can't turn back now."

Staver stretched himself out on the column, trying to
make his body as flat and narrow as the ribbon of smooth
rock that unrolled before his eyes. He set his hands
firmly, drew up his legs, and pushed and hauled himself
forward. As he progressed, he worked into a smooth motion. Though he was still somewhat fearful, the worst of
his fear seemed to be behind him.

He reached the halfway point and passed on without
a pause. He could soon make out Ord's encouraging grin
and hear his brother's exhortations. Soon he had only a
few marks to go. He looked up at Ord, gave a desperate
smile, and then felt an awful moment of panic as the
column shifted—only a slight jar, not enough to shake
him loose, but more than enough to freeze him to the
spot in terror.

Desperately he clung to the surface, digging for non-
existent handholds, his cheek pressed to the cold rock,
his heart racing, his eyes tightly shut. He forgot the ropes
that linked him to his brothers. He forgot everything but
his fear. In his mind was an awful picture of the great
column of stone twisting and turning in its long descent
while he clung to it, screaming, on his way to death be-

low. For a time he was immobilized. Then he felt a tug on the rope.

"It's all right now, sprig. Come ahead," Ord said in a low, gentle voice.

"I can't."

"You must. We can't delay. Col has to cross before the tide."

"Ord, I can't! I'm so scared I can't move!" Staver cried.

"Be as scared as you like—but get moving. If you don't I'll haul you in like a fish." Ord tugged on the rope again.

Staver moved forward a bit, then froze again. Ord's coaxing voice was gentle and reassuring, but the pull on the rope increased. Staver moved again, and once again, and before he realized it he was safe on the ledge with Ord's arms around him and it was all over.

He and Ord anchored themselves fast for Col's crossing. Twice in his progress the column gave a slight jolt, but Col came on without hesitation. Watching him made Staver feel ashamed at first; then he felt his courage slowly seeping back.

They did not pause to rest but climbed at once to a ledge some twelve marks higher up. Here they stopped when they heard the first note of the incoming tide. They had little wish to endure that assault of noise once more, but they had none at all to hear it beneath them while they climbed.

The wall of foaming water boomed into the rounded channel below them, an onrushing palisade of brown and green and dirty white. Swiftly it climbed the smooth walls, and the air was filled with its flung spray and the hissing and seething of its power. It rose to within two marks of their bridge, and the stone all around them quivered and groaned as the great mass shifted in its socket. Still it held.

The water rose, and soon it was rushing past no more than an arm's length beneath the lower end of the bridge, then a hand's breadth, then it touched. A plume of spray shot up, splattering the opposite face of the Fissure, reaching higher than the ledge where they had spent the previous day and night before it fell back, spent. The plume widened into a glassy sheet as the water rose and came into full contact with the bridge. Again the stone shifted, and the walls groaned at its ponderous motion. And then it was gone, swept away by the incoming tide with a force so great that it was carried along some marks before it sank from sight. The crash of its fall was lost under the roaring of the water.

In the stillness between the tides, Ord said, "Someone wants us on this side of the Fissure. We can't doubt it now."

"Someone also wants us dead," Col reminded him.

"True. But we're alive. And we're across."

Staver said nothing. He lay on the ledge thinking of the Headland, the only home he had ever known. Of one thing he was sure—they would never see the Headland again. And he wondered if seeking a kingdom was really such a good thing after all.

It was too late to worry about that though. They had crossed the Fissure, and there was no way to go but southward and nothing to hope for but that the words of two dead men and the writing on a mysterious document were true.

6

The Voice in the Green Glow

They reached the top next day and camped near the edge of the forest. It looked much like the forests of the Headland. The few animals and birds they saw were similar to the ones they knew, and the brothers were reassured. This was not such a strange land, after all.

They saw no people. This did not trouble them, since no one on the Headland lived within five hundred marks of the Fissure, and few were the homes that near. The brother would have liked a covert glimpse of the inhabitants and a chance to hear their speech, but that would come. The important thing was that they were here. They had made the impossible crossing safely. All that could lay before them now was ordinary traveling.

Next morning, they finished the last of the chula cones and the dried meat in their packs, washed it down with the last of their water, and set out with the sun at their backs, skirting the woods in search of a trail leading south.

Before the morning was over they had found a trail. It ran straight and clearly marked into the woods for as far as they could see, a wide track on which two men could easily walk abreast. The grass stood halfway to their knees, and there was no sign of recent passage. But it was clearly a man-made trail, one that had, until recently, seen frequent use.

Even now it was carefully maintained by someone. Before their first rest they thrice passed places where fallen trees had been dragged to one side so they would not block the way. One tall beech had fallen so recently that its leaves were still green and had barely begun to wither. After seeing this, the brothers walked more cautiously.

At a stream bridged by three thick logs, they stopped to refill their water bags and to catch their midday meal. The stream was filled with fish differing from any they had ever seen before: slightly smaller than the knucklebacks of the Headland, plumper, with a firm pink flesh that the brothers found delicious. They ate their fill, and a bit farther down the trail, still within sight of the stream, they found a patch of stingberries and a stand of chula. They filled their packs and went on, a bit more confident now that they had sampled the bounty of the land on this side of the Fissure. They did not relax their vigilance, but they each felt a growing confidence that this promised kingdom of theirs was a friendly land.

That night they slept in a tree near the pathway, in hammocks fashioned from their traveling cloaks. They started off again early in the morning and progressed at good speed, without incident, until past midday, when they came to a crossing.

The intersecting road was wider than the one on which they had been traveling and was obviously in more frequent use. In a marking stone set by the way, the words "Malter's Inn, 9" and "The Woodward, 2" were incised in neat, square-cut letters the height of a man's out-stretched hand, and pointed in opposite directions.

"Encouraging," Ord observed. "Their language appears to be much like ours."

"Now, which road shall we take? The road to Malter's Inn looks like a busy one. More chance of meeting people," Col said.

"But The Woodward is closer," Staver pointed out. "I don't know if they measure distances in marks here, but two is less than nine, whatever they use."

"True enough . . . , but since they seem to speak our tongue . . ."

"We're all thirsty. Let's visit Malter's Inn, brothers," Ord suggested, and the others agreed.

Col insisted on keeping up their caution. With him in the lead, they spread out as far as they could without losing sight of each other. At the first sign of anyone on the path, Col was to shout a loud greeting. At this signal Ord and Staver were to conceal themselves by the path until Col returned for them—or called for their help.

Thus they set out for Malter's Inn and had been walking only a short time when Col gave the signal. Ord and Staver at once plunged into the woods and took cover. After a tense wait they heard heavy steps coming up the trail at an even pace. First Staver, then Ord, had a glimpse of two big and bearded men dressed in green, with axes over their shoulders. The men marched by without speaking or glancing to either side, and not long after they had passed from sight, Col appeared on the road, calling his brothers forth.

"A pair of woodwards—that's what foresters are called here. Their language is close to ours," he told them. "If we avoid involved conversations, and just ask for food and directions, we should have no trouble."

"How did those two act? Did they seem suspicious?" Ord asked.

"Not a bit. There must be a lot of strangers on this road."

"Are you sure? We've been traveling for two days, and those were the first people we saw," Staver said.

"We were on an abandoned trail most of the time."

"What about the inn?" Ord asked.

"It's close by."

"Big or small? Busy?"

"They said it was a small place but sufficient. I didn't want to press them. We'll see for ourselves soon enough."

In a short time they saw the light of a clearing ahead, and soon after that, from concealment, they were looking on Malter's Inn. It was a single, large, two-story building set in the middle of the clearing. A cluster of low sheds stood to one side of the main building, and two small outbuildings on the other. These were all in poor repair, but the main building, in contrast, was neat and appeared well cared for. The roof was not thatched but covered with slates. Every window glinted with glass. A bed of bright flowers lay on each side of the entry, and a tiny garden, carefully fenced, stood beyond.

For a time they saw no one enter or leave. They could not picture this calm setting as the abode of gray men, but they were cautious nonetheless and waited for a sight of the inhabitants.

Their doubts were soon resolved. A girl emerged from the rear of the main building to empty a pail, and no sooner had she reentered than a woodsman left by the front door. A fat man, partly bald, stood in the doorway and called after the woodsman, who stopped and replied. The man in the doorway spoke again, and the woodsman waved his hand in farewell and started toward the trail. The three brothers lay in concealment until he had passed out of sight, then withdrew and conferred briefly.

There was little to debate. The people at the inn were people like themselves and spoke a language much like theirs. Darkness was drawing on, and this was a better place to spend the night than a hammock or an abandoned building. They rose, brushed themselves off, and drew their cloaks about them; with Col in the lead, they strode across the clearing toward Malter's Inn.

Col stooped to pass under the lintel, and Ord ducked his head. Staver walked in without any such precautions, and the three of them took seats at a round table in the corner of the big room. The fat man appeared and came to their table.

"Good day, travelers," he greeted them.

"Good day," Col said. "Are we at Malter's Inn?"

"You are. And I am Malter."

"Bring a pot of beer for each of us, then, Malter, and one for yourself as well."

The innkeeper nodded but said not a word in reply. He disappeared through a doorway, and the brothers heard his heavy tread creak on a long flight of steps. He soon reappeared, heralded by the same creaking of old risers, bearing a big foaming pitcher. Slowly and with elaborate care he filled four mugs with the golden contents of the pitcher. Pushing a mug to each of the brothers in turn, he took up the fourth himself.

"Thanks, travelers. To your health," he said.

"To yours, Malter. And health and safety come to all beneath this roof."

They drank deeply, and after a brief appreciative silence, Malter said, "It is an old blessing you say."

"Learned from our father, who learned it from his," Col said. "Tell me, Malter, can you give us a good meal and a room for the night, and a meal in the morning before we're on our way again?"

The fat man paused for a moment before replying, "I can do that, if you wish it."

"We do, heartily. We've come a long way, and we're heading south."

"Ah. That is some ways hard traveling."

"We're in no great hurry," Col said.

Ord, by his quick frown, appeared to disagree, but he kept his silence and sipped his beer.

"Now that is the good way to travel. Never hurry."

"Even that way of travel gets a man tired and dusty. Have we time to rest a bit before supper?"

"You have," the innkeeper said. "The woodwards and huntsmen come after dark, to eat and drink, and there is time for good rest before then. I will have Meech put a pail of clean water in your room. She will show you the way when you wish it. Shout for her is all you need do."

The brothers finished their beer slowly, then called for Meech. She turned out to be the little girl they had seen emptying slops out the rear door of the inn. She was about twelve years old, small and thin, very dirty, with the narrow lips and pinched brow of the nag already marked on her features. She led them up the narrow, creaking stairs, lit a candle in the darkening chamber under the sloped roof, and though she inspected them furtively at every chance she had, she said not a word.

When she was gone, Ord collapsed on the lumpy bed and said, "Staver, I think little Meech is interested in you. Did you notice how she kept sneaking looks at him, Col?"

"Well, I'm not interested in her," Staver said.

"If you're going to be a king, sprig, you'll have to think about choosing a queen sooner or later."

"I'm not ready yet. And when I am, I'll choose a lot better than that."

Ord generally enjoyed teasing his younger brother once he had him roused, but on this occasion he was too weary to be long interested in such a pastime. The bed was not very good, and the mattress rustled like leaves in a high wind at every move he made. But it was a bed, and for too many nights he had not slept in one. He pulled off his boots, removed his sword and laid it beside him, and drawing his cloak close about him, went directly off to sleep. Col sprawled out beside him, taking up all the room that remained.

In a drowsy voice Col said, "Be sure we don't sleep through supper, sprig."

"What about me, Col? I'm tired, too."

"Not as tired as we are. You can have the bed to yourself tonight. We'll be up late, finding out what we can. Right now, we need sleep and you'll have to watch."

Staver never had much luck arguing with his brothers, and on this occasion it was useless even to try. Col's voice trailed off at his last words, and he was asleep, breathing deeply and regularly, his brown cloak spread over his big frame, before Staver could voice a word of objection.

With a sigh, Staver unfastened his dusty gray cloak, pulled off his boots, and unbuckled his great iron sword, standing it in the corner near the foot of the bed. Making a cushion of his rolled-up cloak, Staver settled into the little window seat and looked out and up at the early stars. The forest was darkening around the inn, and the glow of twilight was deepening into night. The moon had not yet risen, and he could see, just over the horizon, the seven stars of the Lesser Crown, small and faint but distinct as diamonds. High overhead, at the limit of his vision, was the great spiral of light called the Callicrast, with its chain of red stars glowing like a twisted rope of rubies down its center. And below the Callicrast, midway up the sky, was a single star that Staver could not recall seeing ever before. A green star, it shone with a pale and steady light that caught and held his eye.

Diamonds, and rubies, and now a star that shone like an emerald. Staver found himself thinking of those fine swords that lay by his brothers' sides. That gleaming curve of silver, cloaked in black and spangled with diamonds, would have suited him perfectly . . . , and yet Ord had seized it. And that blade of gold and ivory, bright as a sunbeam when it sprang from its magnificent scabbard, was even more splendid. With a sword like that at his side, a man would surely feel like a king, and act like one, and all who saw him would know and acknowledge his supremacy. But the white blade was Col's.

What was a man to do when all he had was a great clumsy iron blade, too big for him, too big for anyone but a giant? Even Col, he thought, would find it hard to lift that sword with ease.

As he thought of Col, Staver grew ever more resentful. Col got the best sword of the lot just because he's the oldest. Ord's the better swordsman.

Staver yawned and leaned his temple sleepily against the cool windowpane. Looking up, he saw more stars in the thickening darkness. The green one, that new and unknown star, seemed brighter and closer than before, and he stared at it until he almost drifted off to sleep and had to rub his eyes hard. He thought again of the swords . . . of his brothers. . . . They quarreled often enough, but they never fought.

Yet, if it ever came to a match between them, Ord would win. And then he would wear the golden sword; and the blade of black and silver, with its crown of diamonds, would then hang at Staver's side.

It was only fair, Staver thought. He was always given the last piece of everything, the smallest portion, the worn-out, nobody-wants-it, hand-me-down rubbish, while his brothers took all the good things for themselves. It was time he was treated as their equal. Just because he was the youngest and smallest of the three, that did not mean that he was the least. He was old enough and big enough to wear a sword at his side, and face gray men, and cross the Fissure. He deserved more.

Staver glanced at Ord, who was lying flat on his stomach, his face half buried in the pillow, one hand lightly on the ebony hilt of his sword. The diamonds danced in little points of light under the candle's glow.

It wouldn't matter which of them won, Staver realized. I'd have the silver blade all for myself, because there'd only be two of us to share. And I'd work, and I'd practice, and become a finer swordsman than Ord, finer than either of them could dream of being. And then one day, when I was ready . . . one day . . .

There was a voice, deep within him, and it was whispering to him, softly, sweetly, of the good things that could be. He was a prophesied king. What need had he of two great blustering selfish brothers? And when they found their kingdom—if, indeed, they ever did, for the way was unknown and there was danger on all sides— if they found it, then what would Staver's portion be? Would they treat him as an equal, or would they laugh, and put a fool's crown on his head, and send him off to rule over bumpkins in a land of weeds and rubble? They had always treated him so, and with a kingdom at stake, they were sure to take the best for themselves. They would see to it that Staver got the smallest portion of any prize that fell to them. They might work it among themselves and their new followers so that Staver received nothing.

Staver's mind recoiled at the thought. No! Not his brothers.

Yes, said the smooth, sweet voice that nestled in his mind. Yes, brothers, too. And friends. Everyone is the same. No one is to be trusted. There's only one way to be safe. Only one sure way . . .

Suddenly Staver's shoulder burned as if a hot iron had been thrust against it, and a current of cold fire ran through his body, shocking him into awareness. He sprang from the window seat, and the dagger that he had drawn

unaware fell from his sweating hand and clattered to
the floor.

The voice in his mind gave a wordless hiss of hatred.
Staver looked dazedly outside, and there beyond the
thick distorting knot of the windowpane hung the green
star. A star no longer, it was a ball of pale green light
the size of a man's head. And before it drew away,
Staver saw, for an instant, the twisted features of a face
beneath the brightness.

He felt Ord's hand on his shoulder and heard Ord's
voice say, "What is it, sprig? What happened? You're as
white as your shirt!"

"The window . . ."

Ord was at the window in a bound, and Col was at
his side. With drawn swords, they watched as the green
glow grew smaller and smaller, rising and turning eastward, and at last vanished over the mountains.

7

Pursuit in Long Wood

The morning came cool and bright. A clear sky and a
mild southern breeze gave promise of a fine day.

Malter offered a breakfast fit to launch a man on a long
march: fresh brown bread with a crust as crisp and delicate as an eggshell, the warmth of the oven hiding in its
middle to melt the firm butter beaded with moisture from
its own chill; new-laid eggs the size of a man's fist; and
milk, cold and foamy and rich as cream. Two fat pots
stood on the table, one of honey, dark as rust; the other
of thick tart stingberry jam. But the three brothers ate
in gloomy silence, alone in the dim main room of the inn.

Their spirits were sagging, and not sunshine nor good
food could raise them. Staver's tale had shaken them all,
with its hint of a new and unsuspected enemy that could
enter their minds and infect their wills, turning them
against themselves. Staver had resisted, it was true, but
only by virtue of Ciantha's amulet in his shoulder. Even

under the protection of the amulet, he had come close to a terrible deed. Would the amulet be able to save him again? Would it help Col and Ord, who were older and stronger willed? There was cause enough for fear.

Added to the fear was frustration. Col and Ord, each in his own way, had tried to draw out the other visitors to the inn, but despite an evening's efforts, they knew no more about this land than they had when they first stepped through Malter's doorway.

"You did your best," Staver said in an attempt to cheer them up. "Pass the honey, Col."

Without a word Col sent the honey pot rumbling down the table to his brother. Staver spilled out a generous dollop of honey onto a chunk of bread. He took a big bite of the bread, munched for a moment, and with his mouth full, added, "You tried."

"And learned nothing. Absolutely nothing," Ord said in a low, disgusted voice. "Nothing at all. I've never seen such closemouthed people. They're unnatural."

"People on the Headland aren't all that talkative."

"Compared to this lot, they're as noisy as sparrows. I lost forty-one consecutive throws of the sticks—believe me, it was not easy—and they kept pulling in their winnings and filling their purses and saying not one word. Then I won it all back, and still they said nothing."

"Maybe they just don't talk to strangers."

Ord gave his younger brother an irritated look. "They don't even talk to each other. Some people grow talkative when they're winning, others when they're losing. But these people never open their mouths." He shook his head, then allowed himself a thin and bitter smile. "At least they'll be a quiet lot to govern. No complaining."

"I think they'll be an accursed nuisance to govern," Col said. "They're surly—a sullen lot. Not like Head-landers."

"You sound as though you're ready to give up and turn back, just because everyone doesn't welcome you with cheers."

"No one's talking about turning back, Ord," Col snapped.

"Well, you certainly sound as though you're ready to quit."

It was almost a relief for Staver to hear his brothers arguing again. Things began to seem almost normal. Col and Ord kept up a crossfire of charge and countercharge, accusation and denial, until Malter entered the room. At once they fell silent. Ord began to push a crust of bread about on his empty plate, while Col saluted the innkeeper.

"A fine meal, Malter. And a fine room, too. We slept well," Col said.

"It is good to hear."

"A pity people aren't a bit more friendly, though." When the innkeeper made no reply, Col went on. "We had hoped to learn directions from people familiar with the way to the south, but no one seemed willing to speak with us."

"We are not much given to the talking. We are solitary people, and it is uneasy we feel with strangers among us."

"Perhaps you can help us, Malter. We're going south —far to the south—and we'd like to know the best way."

Malter stood for a time silent, weighing Col's words. Then he nodded. "Go down road to second bridge. After bridge it is another crossing you will find. You go to left and keep on until you come to river road. Then you follow river south is all."

"That sounds easy enough. Is there any danger?"

"It is always a danger, the traveling."

"We know that, Malter. Is there any special danger we should watch for?"

"Thieves. But they will not attack armed men. It is strange beasts that live in forest, so I have heard, but I have never seen one."

Ord turned and asked, "What about green lights? Have you ever seen one of them or heard of them?"

"No. Never," Malter replied quickly. But for just a moment, his eyes widened and a look of fear passed over his features.

"Are you sure? Never heard of a green light that can come from nowhere and turn a man's thoughts to poison?"

"No," said Malter, and his expression was once again composed and unrevealing.

"Thanks, Malter," Col said. "Tell us what we owe, and we'll settle up and be on our way."

Malter began his tally, and the brothers rose. At that moment Staver recalled that he had left his water bag in the room above and dashed up to get it, taking the high narrow steps two at a bound. At the top of the staircase, he ran full tilt into Meech and sent her sprawling. Her mop clattered to the floor, and her bucket rolled across the landing, spilling its dingy contents down the stair.

"You clumsy! You great clumsy!" Meech said in a low voice, honed to an edge with hatred.

"I'm sorry, Meech. Here, let me help you."

She struck away his hand. "Don't want your help." She climbed to her feet, brushing at her dirty dress with grimy hands, glaring all the while at Staver as if he were some loathsome vermin.

"I didn't knock you down on purpose. I was in a hurry, that's all."

"In a hurry to be about your dirty business, the three of you, with your butcher's blades. And you, like a fool, with the biggest blade of all. A sword for a man twice your size it is, not for a boy who can't even see where he's running."

Staver's pride was stung, and he replied coldly, "I can wield my sword as well as any man when the need arises."

"Aye, you serve your evil master well, the three of you."

"I have no evil master. My brothers and I are our own masters."

Meech laughed at his words and, turning contemptuously, picked up her mop. When Staver took a step forward, she raised the mop defensively before her.

"Don't try to touch me!"

"I don't want to touch you."

Staver stepped past the tense, defiant little figure into the room where he had slept. He soon found his water bag. Fixing it to his belt, he started for the stairs.

Meech was swabbing the spilled water from the landing. At the sight of him, she raised the dripping mop as if it were a quarterstaff.

"I only want to go downstairs, Meech."

"Go, then."

The sight of her pinched, bitter little face, so full of fear and hatred, moved Staver to a sudden feeling of pity. Nasty she was, and soured early in her life with resentment, and though she had no cause to dislike him or his brothers, dislike them she clearly did, and with an intensity beyond all comprehending; but she was a sad creature, and he had knocked her down and added one more bit of drudging labor to her dreary day, and he was sorry for that and wanted to make amends.

"I was clumsy, and I made extra work for you. I want to give you something, Meech."

"It's nothing I'd take from you."

"Please. I want to," Staver said, drawing the little leather pouch from inside his shirt.

Meech lashed out with the handle of the mop and struck the pouch from his fingers. It landed with a heavy ring of metal, and a few coins spilled out.

"It's gold he gives you for your dirty deeds, is it?" Meech said hatefully.

"I did no evil deed for that gold."

"My hands are dirty, but it's clean of blood they are, and I'll touch none of your filthy gold. Take it and go away, so I can scrub the inn clean after you!" Meech cried, almost in tears from the sheer ferocity of her hatred.

Staver scooped up the pouch and the fallen coins and started down the staircase, angry and perplexed. He had done nothing to merit such a reaction, only knocked her down by sheer accident, and she treated every effort on his part to make amends as if it were a vicious attack. These people, he reflected, are certainly not like us of the Headland. Surly, suspicious, full of unreasoning hatred and senseless accusations, that's what they were, to judge from Meech and from what his brothers had said of the woodwards and huntsmen of last evening. If these were to be their subjects, then he and his brothers had a hard job of ruling before them.

Col and Ord greeted Staver with amused glances but made no reference to what they had heard. They left at once, and as soon as they were out of sight of the inn, they spread out along the trail so there was no oppor-

tunity for talk until midmorning, when they paused for a
brief rest in the shade of an old evergreen.

Ord drank deeply, stoppered his water bag, and lay
back on the soft bed of fallen needles. Without looking at
Staver, he said, "It appears to me that the sweet little
girl from Malter's Inn has no wish to be your queen."

"What?" Staver said.

"Meech—that was her name. What a lovely, queenly
name it is, too. Can't you picture our brother in his kingdom, Col, decked out in all his royal finery, with Queen
Meech at his side? Ah, there's—"

"Oh, shut up, Ord," Staver said testily.

"He's sensitive. Meech has injured his feelings."

"If anyone's been injured, it's Meech. I knocked her
down when I turned at the top of the stair. She acted as
if I were some kind of monster."

"You have a lot to learn, sprig."

"I know what I have to know about women, Ord. I'm
no baby. I tell you, Meech acted as if all three of us were
devils, not just me. She kept talking about our evil master, and the dirty business we're here to do, and the gold
we get for our wicked deeds."

"Sweet-tempered little thing, isn't she?" Ord said, grinning at Staver.

"I think she's crazy."

"Ah, you'll see. When you're ruling in your great kingdom to the south, lonely and heartsick, you'll send a
troop of your fleetest messengers to lay gifts at the dirty
feet of little Meech and beg her forgiveness."

"All I'll ever send her is a bucket of dirty water and
a wet mop," Staver replied, rubbing his knuckles and
remembering the sting of the mop handle. "She accused
me—all of us—of doing terrible things."

"What things?"

"She didn't come out and say. But she mentioned
our swords—using our butcher's blades in our dirty business, she said—and our evil master. I told her we had no
master, and she just laughed."

"Did you tell her any more? Did you say why we're
here?"

"No."

"Good," Col said. He rose and brushed the brown

needles from his cloak. "It sounds to me as though there's a ruler here already, and he's not much loved by his people."

Ord propped himself on an elbow. "That would explain the way everyone at the inn behaved last night."

"It would. They hate this tyrant, and they think we're his servants."

"Fortunate for us that they hate him, isn't it? Ought to make things easier for us."

"Maybe, if we're careful. I think we'd do well to cover a lot of ground today. And if we meet anyone, let's be as tight-lipped as these yokels."

They moved faster after that, rested briefly again at midday, then pressed on, passing well beyond the first bridge before they stopped to take a light meal. Ord and Col got into a discussion of the possible distance still to be covered. It soon became a heated debate. The fact that neither of them knew anything of the country they were traveling in did not diminish one bit the vigor of their argument.

Staver, knowing only that it was sure to be a long way to their destination and that every step southward took them farther from the friendly, reasonable people of the Headland, went apart, preferring not to hear talk of distances. He sat on a fallen log at the edge of a little clearing just off the trail, took out the bread and cheese they had purchased at the inn, and began to eat. He looked out at the sunlit grass and at the small birds darting swift and low over the ground, and his mind wandered.

A finch perched on the log, just out of reach. Staver took a few bread crumbs and, moving very slowly, laid them on the log midway between himself and the bird. The finch studied him out of one jet eye, then hopped forward, snatched up a crumb, and quickly retreated. Staver repeated the gesture, this time with a generous helping of crumbs, and the finch again took a crumb. A second finch landed, then a third, and all partook.

Staver could sense their confidence. There was no gratitude in them, simply a feeling—rather smug—of well-being and luck at this find. Staver smiled and found that he was listening to their chatter. The chipping and twittering was beginning to make sense to him, as the birds of the Headland woods once had. He spread out more crumbs and remained very still, listening, and slowly understanding.

Not one of the flock. No, not flock. Groundwalker, but not of the groundwalker flock. Fine food. We lucky. Groundwalker all alone, driven from his flock. Others under nesting-tree, but not true flock. All outcasts. Belly feels good.

Staver cautiously laid out another scattering of crumbs and remained motionless on the log.

We find good food. Groundwalker brings good food. We lucky. Other groundwalkers coming. Good food there maybe. Big flock of groundwalkers coming. Close now. Nice food. Bellies all be full. Groundwalkers here soon, bring nice food. We lucky.

Staver jumped up, scattering the startled finches into the air like darts. Racing back to his brothers, he said, "Quick, let's go. We're being followed, and they're close."

Col and Ord sprang to their feet, and the three of them set off at a steady trot down the trail. They ran on for as long as they could; then Col signaled a rest by a turn in the trail. When they had regained breath, he asked Staver how he knew.

"Birds. I understood them."

This time they did not doubt him.

"Did they say how many?" Col asked.

"They said 'a big flock.' "

"The thieves Malter warned us about," Ord said.

"Probably. Do you think we can outrun them?"

"We can try. We may have to fight."

"If we have to fight, we'll fight," Col said. "But I hope we find a place to make our stand before dark."

They went on at a steady jogging pace that covered distance without exhausting their strength. Before they had expected to, they broke into a meadow, and ahead of them they saw the second bridge. Once across it, they stopped to rest. As Col and Staver sprawled in the shade, Ord, still panting, studied the bridge and the crossing.

The bridge spanned the narrowest part of a ravine that extended as far as he could see in either direction. On both sides the banks fell back to a distance Ord estimated as seven to twelve marks. The bridge itself, a sturdy structure of rough-cut stone, measured about six marks end to end. It was less than a mark wide.

The banks were rounded at the top and grassy. But they fell away sharply to become perpendicular and looked to be a hard climb. The water, about eight marks below, was swift-flowing, even in this low-water season, and the stream bed was full of jagged rocks. Ord took a quick glance back down the trail, saw nothing, and returned to his brothers.

"If we have to make a stand, this is a good place," he said.

"Why not keep running? We seem to have outdistanced them. Maybe they won't cross the ravine after us," Col said.

"I dropped my pouch, and Meech saw the gold. If she sent the robbers after us, they won't give up easily," Staver said.

"Everyone at the inn saw my pouch, too, and they know I won. I think our pursuers will stay with us, Col."

"Maybe. And you think this is a good place to confront them, do you?"

"Look at the other bank," Ord said, pointing. "The forest ends about twenty marks from the bridge. No robber can sneak out of the trees unseen. The sky is clear, and there'll be enough of a moon to see them if they try it tonight."

Staver nodded approval, but Col said, "All the same, if we keep up our pace we might reach the river before nightfall. We'd surely be safe then."

"What if we don't? What if we're on the trail, in the middle of the forest, when night falls? We'd be helpless," Ord said.

"Look!" Staver broke in.

Across the bridge, beyond the meadow, two men in green had emerged from the forest. Soon a third appeared, then two more, then others, in twos and threes, until more than a score of men were assembled on the opposite bank. They paused for a time. Then, at a signal from their leader, they started for the bridge.

8

The Coming of the Dark Prophet

"I guess we stay," Col said.

Ord grinned at him. "I knew I'd convince you, brother," he said.

Winding their cloaks around their free hands and forearms, Col and Ord drew their swords and took up position at the head of the bridge, side by side, a sword's length apart. Staver, his cloak flung back, was behind them, the point of a tight little triangle.

The men in green were almost at the bridge before they saw the three armed figures in the shadows at the far end, awaiting their rush. They halted then, and conferred for a time. At last archers broke from the little cluster of men, trotted off to either side, and took up their stance, leaving ten men at the bridge.

Archers could mean trouble, but they would not make the crossing any easier for the men in green. Col and Ord could take refuge behind the curving stone walls of the bridge and still be able to strike down any man who tried to pass. Staver had only to take a step forward and kneel, and he, too, would enjoy the protection of the walls.

High, arching shots, that would come straight down on them were another thing altogether. The brothers had no protection from arrows that might fall from overhead. Staver hoped the bowmen would not think of that tactic. His heart sank when, at a hand signal from their leader, the archers raised their bows, aiming almost straight upward.

Before they released, Ord stepped forward onto the bridge and called to the ten facing him, "Are you so afraid of three men that you must riddle them with arrows before you stand up to them?"

"It is no fear we feel for you. It is hatred only," said their leader, a sturdily built man with a grizzled beard.

"Then show it like men, blade against blade."

"Filthy butcher—your master allows none but his servants to carry a sword, and well you know it."

"We have no master but ourselves."

"You lie, butcher," the leader of the green-clad men said flatly. "You serve the Cairnlord. You wear those blades with his permission and wield them in his service. Now you will die for him."

"We wear these blades by right—and by no man's permission."

"Another lie. We have you now, devils, and we—"

"Stop jabbering, you windy coward. If you're men, show it."

A big man stepped before the leader and said, "I will." There was a moment of hurried talk, then the leader signaled for the archers to lower their bows.

"You have one who wishes to face you alone, his weapon against yours," he called to Ord.

"Let him come," Ord replied.

The big man stripped off his shirt to reveal a chest like a hearthstone, matted with thick dark hair. He stood a head taller than Ord and was considerably broader. His corded arms rippled as he raised a broad-bladed double-bit axe and whirled it over his head like a child waving a willow switch. Ord lounged coolly against the bridge rail, observing him, looking for a weak spot.

Staver, watching the big man move, could see no weakness in him at all. He began to think that a rain of arrows was preferable to having his brother face that wicked whirling blade. It would take off limbs like a scythe cutting wheat. He was ready to call out to Ord, urging him to withdraw, to run, to do anything that would keep him out of reach of that axe, when two things happened in quick succession.

Raising the axe high, the big man cried, "Kinnaury! For his lost children and his murdered friends, Kinnaury! For his wife and his brothers, Kinnaury!" Gripping the axe with both hands, he started forward at a run to where Ord stood, now braced for his attack.

Before Kinnaury had taken two strides, the air between the adversaries grew suddenly bright, and a great gust of wind blew out of the brightness. Ord fell back, his hand before his eyes, and even his giant opponent halted, withdrew a step, and turned his face away.

Staver blinked and shielded his eyes from the sudden brilliance. When he looked again, he let out a gasp of amazement. In the midst of the white glow appeared a flickering ribbon of darkness. It grew taller and broader, and took on substance, until it was a hooded figure in human shape, hovering in the air above the bridge. It settled slowly to the surface, arms extended, half-bent, and turned to the men in green. At the sight of the figure, they all fell back and lowered their weapons. The glow faded and vanished, and only the dark, hooded figure remained, standing on the bridge between the two forces.

Raising one hand, the apparition spoke. "Drive hatred from your hearts, woodwards, and come forward in greeting," it said. Turning to the brothers, it extended the other hand and said, "Sheathe your swords, travelers."

They all obeyed. Something in the clear thin voice coming from within that dark hood made defiance unthinkable. Even as he returned the iron sword to its scabbard, Staver wondered at that voice.

Beckoning the brothers forward, the hooded figure said, "Come, join hands and meet in peace. These men are good men, friends, and will be faithful to you and to the cause you share." To the leader of the foresters, it said sternly, "You are rash, Goodbowe. You let your hatred overcome your judgment, and that is not the way of a leader."

"They carried gold . . . and swords at their sides. Only servants of the Cairnlord are permitted . . . We thought . . ." The leader of the green-clad men faltered and was silent, his head bowed in shame.

"Will no others come bearing a sword?"

"In all my years . . . in all the time since the fall of the Kingdom, only the minions of that evil wizard have wielded a blade in this land."

"Are my prophecies, then, so trivial that you ignore them? Are the words I spoke to your fathers to be forgotten and the sacrifices of generations swept aside for a moment's bloody vengeance?" the hooded figure demanded in a voice that rose in anger as it spoke on.

"Now is the time, Goodbowe, and these are the men. Their coming has been foretold, and now it is upon you. The struggle has begun."

The voice was still, but it echoed in Staver's mind. He had heard it before and had heard it more than once—but he could not remember where or when, and he strained for the memory.

At the hooded figure's words Goodbowe stepped back, his eyes wide. His jaw dropped, and he pointed to the brothers and stammered, "Are these . . . the three brothers of the prophecy?"

"Have you no longer eyes to see the signs, Goodbowe? Have you grown blind with waiting and dismissed my words from your memory?"

"No!"

"Then speak. Speak the words your father spoke, passed on from his father, sent down from the generation of the days of the Kingdom."

Goodbowe nodded nervously. Licking his lips, he glanced quickly around at his men and at the three brothers, then spoke. "The first shall wear a brown cloak, with a white blade at his side. First will he be to see his realm, first to fall, and first to rise—master of the citadel on the isle, Master of the Southern Forest. White blade shall be his name and his sign. With him will come a second, a brother, cloaked in black with a black blade at his side, a man of fire to keep the Fastness that rises in the living rock and guard the Plain where the dead and the living will clash in battle. The third . . . The third . . ."

"Speak on," the hooded figure urged.

"The third will be the least and become the greatest, the youngest and become the eldest. He will be wrapped in a gray cloak, with an Iron Angel at his back, and he will stand guard over the others. His life will be short, but he will die at a great age, and he will be Mage of the Crystal Hills."

"So, you remember. Now look upon the three—Colberane Whitblade, Master of the Southern Forest; the Scarlet Ord, Keeper of the Fastness and the Plain; Staver Ironbrand, Mage of the Crystal Hills. These are their titles and their destinies. Serve them, Goodbowe, for your

sake and for all who would be free from the grip of the
Cairnlord. All of you—serve these men loyally," the
hooded figure commanded.

Goodbowe fell to one knee and bowed his head. One
by one, the rest of his band bent their knees and lowered
their heads. Ord looked on the sight and then glanced at
his brothers, an expression of great satisfaction on his
face. Col was studying the scene, frowning slightly, unwilling to accept this turn of events unquestioned but
unable to move himself to address the mysterious figure
that stood before him.

Staver looked without really seeing. His attention was
not on the foresters or the prophecy, but on the hooded
prophet. Now he remembered. The voice had come to
him in dreams and in waking dreams. He had heard it
on the Headland, on the morning when he was first able
to comprehend the speech of the birds and beasts. And
in the deep darkness of that awful night at the inn, when
the memory of the whispered enticements of the green
glow burned like raw wounds in his mind, that voice had
spoken healing words and brought him peace and rest,
and courage to face such an enemy again, if need be. He
wondered at this but said nothing.

"Rise, woodwards," the hooded figure said in a gentler
tone. "The day is fading, and this is a good campsite.
Prepare food and resting places for your leaders."

"Will this place be safe?" Goodbowe asked.

"For this one night it will be safe. You must start for
the Southern Forest at first light."

"We will."

"The river is watched. Avoid it. Keep to the forests
and cross the Fool's Head by night. Stay near the western shore and far from the Eye—the enemy has a creature there. You must cross the mistlands. The mountain
trail is too dangerous."

Goodbowe's face clouded. "The mistlands are said to
be worse."

"For a small band, unequipped, they are deadly. But
you will have proper craft awaiting you and men who
know the things of mistlands and how to evade them. I
will see to it. Now go, prepare camp. I must speak with
these three."

Goodbowe bowed respectfully to the hooded figure, turned to go, and then checked himself. He bowed to the three brothers, then was off.

Ord accepted the gesture graciously. With one hand on the hilt of his sword, the other hooked in his belt, he gave a faint nod to the stocky bearded man to send him on his way. Turning to the hooded figure, he said in the tone of voice one might use to address a helpful stranger, "Thanks for your assistance. We were on our way to seek the kingdom ourselves, but these fellows will make it much easier."

"Yes, we thank you, whoever you are," Col added, rather more respectfully. "I thought we were in for a hard fight."

"You are," the hooded figure said. "You thank me too soon. This is only the beginning. The struggle is ahead, and nothing will be easy until it is over. A time will come when you curse the sight and the voice of the Dark Prophet."

"We expect a struggle. We're willing to fight, and we won't forget those who help us," Ord said.

The Dark Prophet's voice became sharp. "You go into battle like boys to their games. Many will suffer and die —some of these good men will be lost—before you take your appointed places. I came not to present you with a kingdom but to bring you to your destinies. I will help you when I can, but the fight will be yours. Much will be asked of you."

"We're not afraid," Col said.

The Dark Prophet was silent for a time. Staver peered into the shadow of the hood but could distinguish no features, only a pale glow. At last the prophet said, in a sad voice, "You understand nothing. You face forces beyond imagining, an enemy more than mortal. Already you have felt the power of the Cairnlord three times."

"He sent the gray men," Col said.

"And the green glow," Staver added.

"Yes. Those were but the slightest brush of his hand compared to what lies ahead."

"My brother spoke for all of us. We're not afraid," Ord said.

"You've spoken to me. I've heard your voice," Staver said.

"I have spoken to you, Staver, and will speak to you again. But now I must go. There is much to be done, much still to be learned before all is ready. The time of hiding and waiting is nearly over. Your followers must be roused and told that the leaders have come."

"But what is to be done? And who is the Cairnlord?" Col asked.

"Goodbowe can tell you some things. I will tell you more when we meet next. Trust the woodwards and lead them well. Rely on Goodbowe," said the Dark Prophet.

A light began to surround the hooded figure. The dark form shrank to a shimmering band of black, like a shadow at the heart of a flame. Then all was gone in a great rush of wind that swept into the aftermath of the vanished brilliance.

Col rubbed his eyes and shook his head. Solemnly, he said, "It came from nowhere and returns to nowhere. It saved our lives, most likely, and gave us guides and followers. And we spoke to it as we would speak to any stranger."

"The Dark Prophet is our friend," Staver said.

"Your friend, certainly," Ord said, looking curiously at his younger brother. "It called you by name."

"Your friend as well, Ord. A few more steps and Kinnaury would have cut you in two."

"I doubt that, sprig," Ord said. He gave a little laugh then and, laying his hand on Staver's shoulder, admitted, "I'm just as glad he came no closer, though."

Col said heartily, "We all are. Come, let's join our men and see what we can learn."

Side by side, the three brothers strode across the meadow to the edge of the woods, where the foresters were busy clearing a camp for the night. The men stopped their work, looked up, and saluted them shyly as they passed, but when the brothers showed a friendly response, the greetings became warmer and less forced.

One little group was straining to move a heavy log to a spot where it could more easily be cut. Col lent them his aid, and the log moved smoothly into place. The men cheered him.

Not to be outdone, Ord called for volunteers to descend the gorge for fresh water and fish for dinner. Six
ran to his side before he was finished speaking. He chose
two young brothers, the Harrismiths, and set off across
the meadow with them.

Staver understood what they were about and chose not
to join in their competition. He had too much to think
about, and he was tired as well. He found a shady spot
beneath a tree and settled back to think and rest.

The Dark Prophet's appearance had certainly been
timely, but it had not solved any of the mysteries that
had been accumulating so rapidly since Vannen's death.
If anything, it had added more.

Staver tried to recall the words of the hooded figure.
Some kind of struggle had begun . . . and the time of
waiting and hiding was past. That much he remembered
clearly . . . and the prophecy repeated by Goodbowe, so
like the words of poor Justen and the narrative on that
lost piece of vellum. Names, and titles, and descriptions
that fit them closely, even though the words were obscure.
And the prophet's fearsome last warning: worse things
ahead. Worse things than the gray men. Staver looked
around warily, and his hand closed on the hilt of his
sword.

The feel of the hilt reassured him, and he thought of
the Dark Prophet's voice, coming to him in sleep, calm-
ing and strengthening, preparing him for whatever might
come. That voice had spoken his name, and the Dark
Prophet had promised to speak to him again. He hoped
it would be soon—this very night, if at all possible—and
that this time the mysteries would be made clear. They
were in a struggle against someone called the Cairnlord,
an enemy of great power, and a hard and bitter struggle it
would be, bringing death and suffering to many before it
was over. That was all he really knew, and even that
little was obscure, and couched in cryptic phrases. Staver
had a suspicion that a sizeable share of the suffering was
going to fall to him and his brothers, though the Dark
Prophet had said nothing about that.

Unresolved questions swam in Staver's head. He
rubbed his eyes and leaned back. The shouts of the
foresters at their work came to him from far away. A soft

breeze blew from the forest, and he breathed deep of the clean, sweet air.

The next thing he was aware of was a hand on his shoulder, shaking him gently, and Col's voice saying, "Time for supper, sprig. You've had a good rest."

Staver grunted, then started up, groping for his sword. "I shouldn't . . . We have to be careful," he said.

"You've been guarded, sprig. Jem Underhill volunteered to keep an eye on you."

"Who?"

"One of the foresters. He said he'd watch so you could sleep." Col pointed to a trio of birches, where a boy stood.

"I ought to thank him."

"Thank him after you've eaten. He was glad to do it. These people have been waiting a long time for us, sprig. Come, eat your supper, and then Goodbowe will tell us what he knows."

Staver turned and waved to the lone figure standing by the birches. The boy waved back, and Staver and Col went off to join the others, with the boy trailing behind them.

9

The History Lost, The Legends Dying

> In ancient days, at a holy forge, the great King
>   Ambescand
> Wrought the blades of liberation by the force of his
>   mortal hand.
>   From steel as pure as innocence, with a hammer
>   strong as youth,
> At a fire fueled by wizards' bones and blazing bright
>   as truth,
>   He dropped his blood on the glowing steel as he
>   murmured magic rites,
> And he shaped the blades three several ways
>   through three unsleeping nights. . . .
>
> —From The Last Deed of Ambescand

"No one knows who founded the Old Kingdom or when. The histories are all lost now, and even the legends are dying," Goodbowe said.

Supper was done. Goodbowe and the three brothers sat by the fire, in the center of an irregular ring of shelters. Kinnaury, Hunter, and Kempe were with them, and young Underhill crouched quietly outside the circle of men, near where Staver sat between Col and Ord, listening attentively. The rest were asleep or on watch.

"We found a fragment of a chronicle. It mentioned a battle and a king named Ambescand," Col said.

"Ambescand is the beginning. He was the last and greatest ruler of the Old Kingdom. A gentle king, a great warrior, and a seeker after justice. It was at his death that the Old Kingdom was divided into the three realms, and one of his sons placed on the throne of each realm." Goodbowe looked at the brothers in turn. "These are the thrones that you must reclaim and then the Old Kingdom will be restored. So says the Dark Prophet. No man now alive will see that day, but in time, from your descendants, a greater than Ambescand will arise and unite the three realms once again."

"Who overthrew the sons of Ambescand? I don't mind fighting for what's mine, but I'd like to know why I must. Who rules the three realms now?" Ord asked.

Goodbowe leaned forward, big hands clasping his knees, and looked squarely at Ord. "It is a long tale to tell. Much is unknown to me, and of what I know, much is obscure and its meaning uncertain. But it is right that you hear it. The Dark Prophet will tell you more when she returns to us."

"She?"

"The Dark Prophet is a woman of great age. She has seen the early days of the Old Kingdom. She spoke to the father of my father when he was a young man and to the father of his father before him. And she has seen the future, too, as clearly as we see the present. She can tell you much more than I, when the time is right."

"Until then, we'll hear you, Goodbowe," Ord said.

The leader of the foresters nodded. Gazing into the fire, he said, "Long ago, in the Old Kingdom, there was much knowledge of sorcery. Some achieved great power and used it for the good of all. But there were evil sorcerers in those days, as in ours. Much harm was done before their magic was overcome. But the evil knowledge was never fully rooted out of the kingdom. Even in the time of Ambescand, a handful of men and women still devoted themselves to the black knowledge.

"When Ambescand went far to the south to turn back the invaders from the dry lands, his brother, supported by a score of nobles, seized the throne. Their army was small, but they had leagued themselves with a company of sorcerers. They hoped, by force of arms and wizardry combined, to scatter the remnants of Ambescand's weary army upon his return, slay the king, and make his kingdom their own.

"Many nobles and commoners remained loyal to the absent king, and upon these the usurpers inflicted great suffering. As time passed and no word came from the south, the usurpers grew ever bolder and more extreme in their cruelties. They feared no retribution. Through their magic certain of the sorcerers had glimpsed Ambescand's army in battle against the invaders. They saw him outnumbered and hard pressed, bereft of all his magic, and they were sure he would never return—or would return so weakened that he would be an easy victim.

"But they were misguided. Ambescand returned to his kingdom in triumph. The usurpers' army was scattered like ashes before the wind, and their leaders fled for their lives. The sorcerers took refuge in their stronghold at the center of the High City and tried to make a stand, but the white magic of Ambescand was too powerful for them. Seven were slain by the people they had so long abused, torn to bloody fragments in the streets as they tried to flee. Four were taken alive and put to fitting torment. Their limbs were broken on the wheel, and they were sealed, still living, in leaden caskets and borne to the Stone Hand."

At these words the brothers exchanged a quick glance of recognition. They looked expectantly to Goodbowe, who still gazed fixedly on the sinking fire.

"What is the Stone Hand?" Col asked.

"An island in the eastern ocean. It was ever a dreary

place, set amid treacherous waters, avoided by mariners and fisherfolk. But when the broken sorcerers were brought there and buried under a great cairn, the island was cursed in the name of all the gods known in the Old Kingdom. Since that day, nothing has grown on the Stone Hand. Nothing lives on it or in the waters near it, and no bird flies over it," Goodbowe said, raising his eyes and looking at Col.

Ord shook his head in confusion. "I don't understand, Goodbowe. If those sorcerers were defeated and killed, what have they to do with the sons of Ambescand and the three realms?"

"The sorcerers did not die."

"How . . . ?"

"No one knows how. It was the Dark Prophet who discovered the truth at last, but even she does not yet know all. Somehow the four mangled bodies were kept alive— perhaps they were brought back to life, no one knows— and their powers restored by a wizard more powerful than they had ever been. His name and his origins are unknown. We speak of him as the Cairnlord.

"Understand that this was not known, or even suspected, until long after, when the worst had already befallen. The four sorcerers vowed to avenge themselves on the line of Ambescand. They had willing tools in the descendants of the exiled usurpers—but now the sorcerers were the masters and the ambitious nobles their servants.

"In the years that followed one misfortune after another befell the three realms. The son of Ambescand, and their children after them, faced the trials bravely and for a time withstood them. But later generations lacked their strength and their magic. The realms began to crumble. A plague ravaged the High City, leaving not enough living to bury the dead. A great army suddenly appeared in the mountain to lay siege to the Fastness. After nine years that stronghold fell, and the defenders were never heard of more. The people of the Plain were victims of a blight that destroyed their crops three years in succession and of sicknesses that killed the fish and animals they turned to for food. They left the land in small groups and never returned. My own ancestors were

among them. Those who dwelt on the lake isle seemed
fortunate for a time. No invader struck at them, and no
plagues assailed them. Food was abundant. But a strange
darkening of the spirit came over them, and they began
to question their reason for living. All seemed futile and
pointless to them. Their music and poetry grew sad, and
they ceased to travel, to work, even to speak to each
other. Within a generation they had died out.

"In all this time survivors had been making their way
to the Crystal Hills, the northernmost of the three realms,
where they found sanctuary. But when all else was in
waste and ruin, an army gathered by the Cairnlord, a
mob of the cruelest, most savage plundering villains to
be found in all the lands, marched on the Crystal Hills.

"They took the tower at Northmark by stealth so that
no warning was given. By night they swarmed across
the causeway and the bridges and fell upon the defenders.
The battle raged for three days without stopping, but
finally the invaders were beaten back. The losses on both
sides were crippling. As they retreated, the invaders
destroyed the bridges, cutting the Crystal Hills off from
the mainland, and the region has been apart and unknown since that day. Strange are the tales told of that
land—a place of spirits and memories, men say, and of
beasts that are more than beasts. The old lore and wisdom survives there, some say. But no one goes there now,
so what we hear may be no more than old men's stories."

Goodbowe sighed and was silent for a time. No one
broke the silence, though the brothers were impatient to
hear him speak on.

"Since the fall of Northmark," he then said abruptly,
"the followers of the Cairnlord have ruled the three
realms. And heavy their rule has been. Some of us have
dwelt long in these forests, but others are newly come,
fled from the cruelty of their rulers. For no cause the
Cairnlord's men descend upon a settlement and slaughter
all within. Travelers are slain upon the roads; even a
large band is not safe. I have heard of human sacrifice
and worse abominations.

"Ah, but that will change now," Goodbowe said, and
the gloom lifted from his face and left his voice as he
looked full upon the three brothers. "The fall of the

Cairnlord is foretold, and now the leaders who were to come are with us."

"I hope we don't fail you," Staver said.

"You cannot. All is ordained. The Dark Prophet has seen what will be."

"I don't understand the role of the Cairnlord. He came from nowhere with terrific power at his command, and no one knows who he is. Why is he such a bitter enemy to us?" Col asked.

"Not even the Dark Prophet knows that."

Ord asked, "Does she know where his gray men come from?"

The mention of the creatures brought a stir and an exchange of fearful glances to the group. Staver heard a sound behind him, turned, and saw Jem Underhill moving closer to the fire. He made room beside him and gestured for the boy to take his place there.

"All we know of the gray men is that they come from somewhere beyond the three realms," said Goodbowe.

"And that they can't be killed. No weapon can harm them," Kinnuary added bitterly. "If my axe could have stopped them, my wife and son would be alive. I'd have been able to save them, at least."

"We have weapons that can stop them," Ord said.

"That's impossible! No one can withstand the gray men!" cried Kempe.

"We've done it twice," Ord said coolly. His statement brought a noisy outburst of amazement mixed with incredulity from the foresters, as he had expected it would. When everyone had calmed down, and there was quiet once more, he told the company of the clashes with the gray men at the farmhouse and the tower.

"Then you bear powerful weapons indeed," Goodbowe said, and others murmured their agreement. "How did you capture them?"

"They were handed down to us. They're swords from the Old Kingdom," Col said.

"Then it may be . . . It may be . . ." Goodbowe looked up, wonder on his seamed and weathered face as he turned to Col and asked, "Is the white blade you

bear bound in gold, with thirteen dragons on the scabbard?"

"It is."

He then asked of Ord, "And the black blade—is it
trimmed with silver and set with diamonds?"

"Yes, it is."

The forester paused, and there was awe in his voice
when he turned to Staver to ask, "Does your great iron
sword bear a winged crosspiece, finely graven, and no
other adornment?"

"It does, Goodbowe."

"Then it is true . . . true. . . . A prophecy I never
thought to see fulfilled . . ." The forester's voice trailed
off, and he stared into the fire. He covered his face with
his hands and drew the palms down slowly, raising his
eyes to the sky. After a time in which all sat silent, ex-
pectant, he spoke again. His voice was soft and distant.
"There is a legend . . . very ancient . . . and until this
night I thought it only an idle tale. Now I think it must
be true. Hear me, and judge.

"It is said that after his victory over the sorcerers,
Ambescand resolved that three swords should be made:
one of gold, one of silver, and one of iron. He mixed his
own blood with the glowing metal and spoke words of
great power over the blades as he forged them with his
own hand. All the white art he possessed he infused into
those three blades. They were to be raised—against an
enemy who feared no weapon of man—by three who
bore names beloved of Ambescand but whose faces he
would never see." Turning to the brothers, he said,
"When you came to us, I did not think of that legend.
We had three leaders, as foretold in the prophecy. That
was enough for us. But now . . ."

"Now we can stand up to the gray men. No more running," Kinnuary said.

"Do you really mean that no other weapon has an effect on them?" Ord asked.

"I've seen arrows shatter against their bodies," said
Kempe.

Kinnuary added, "I brought my axe down full on the
neck of one, just where it joins the shoulder. The blade
bounced off as if I'd struck an iron pillar."

"Our blades don't shatter, and they don't bounce off. They don't kill those gray things, but they stop them," Col said.

"You spoke of fire—of burning them," Goodbowe said.

Col nodded. "The first time was an accident. Next time we knew. When the blaze was highest, we felt . . . I can't explain it, Goodbowe, but it was like a sudden wind blowing over us, bearing gratitude . . . blessing us."

"As if we had set a soul free," Staver said.

"Exactly. As if the creatures didn't want to be what they are and thanked us for freeing them."

"Something else puzzles me, Goodbowe," Ord said. "If the gray men can't be hurt by any weapon you possess, and no one can withstand them, then I should think that all human resistance would have been driven from this land long ago. And yet you're here, and the Dark Prophet spoke of rallying our forces. Can we raise an army?"

"Your army is waiting. It needed only its leaders."

"Where is this army? How can it hide?"

"There are bands of free men in the Southern Forest, and in the fen, and in the mountains near the Fastness. Many still live in the City of the Game. Given leaders who can stand against the gray men, these free people will fight, even against the sorcery of the Stone Hand."

"But how have you escaped the gray men all this time?"

"The gray men are few in number and widely scattered. They strike alone; rarely do they attack in pairs. Only once have I seen as many as five together." Goodbowe glanced up at the others, smiled ruefully at the memory, and rubbed his side. "The leaders of the free men were meeting deep in the forest. We were betrayed. A company of the Cairnlord's human butchers and five gray men burst upon us. Only I and two others escaped, badly wounded."

"And yet you stay on."

"This is our home. We knew that three brothers would come to lead us against our enemy, and now you've come, bearing weapons of great virtue."

"As my brother said, Goodbowe, I hope we don't fail you. We're only human, whatever the Dark Prophet tells

you, and if five gray men come against us at once, we'll
be hard pressed," Col said.

Goodbowe frowned and shook his head. Clearly, he
did not want to hear such things spoken. "You cannot
fail. You are invincible." When Col made no reply,
Goodbowe went on earnestly. "For years we've fled
from the gray men. Now we can fight them. Most of the
Cairnlord's work is done by humans. We have fought
them. Now we can defeat them, and the three realms
can be freed, the Cairnlord overthrown." He rose and
stood before the three brothers. "Others will join you,
but we were the first to acclaim you. We ask now to be
your men and fight by your sides to the end." So saying,
he fell to one knee and bowed his head, and the other
foresters followed his example.

"Of course you can stay with us. We need you to
guide us," Col said.

"We would be more than guides through the forest. We
wish to be your followers to the end of this struggle."

"You have your wish, Goodbowe. Now get up, please.
And no more kneeling."

"But you bear the blades of liberation!"

"Wait until we're properly enthroned. Then we'll see
about kneeling," Col said. "Until then, no more of it."

"As my lords wish," Goodbowe said, rising and gesturing for the others to do so.

Col glanced quickly at his brothers but said nothing.
Ord appeared pleasantly surprised, Staver uncomfortable. The words "my lords" fell strangely on the ears of
one raised on the Headland, where a man's dearest title
was his good name, free of appendages. Col decided to
speak to Goodbowe about titles in the morning.

The brothers retired to their rude shelter. At Col's
insistence they were assigned a turn at watch, but
Goodbowe was equally adamant that it must be the last
watch so that the lords of the three realms might rest un-
interrupted.

Wrapping themselves in their cloaks, the brothers
stretched out on the soft grass. A low roof of cut boughs
lay close overhead, and through the interstices of the
leaves shone single stars.

Col was asleep almost at once, but Staver lay staring

upward, thinking. Hearing Ord stir beside him, he said softly, "Ord, do you believe we're really invincible?"

For a moment there was no reply, then Ord said, "Goodbowe does. So does the Dark Prophet. She said we'd take our appointed places. We can't do that if we're defeated."

"But do *you* believe it?"

"I think I do. We've beaten gray men twice, and no one else has ever done such a thing. And I must say, sprig, that you looked mighty formidable today, brandishing that great sword of yours. A regular warrior."

"I don't feel formidable."

"Well, you look it. That can be even better. I told you you'd grow up to that sword, and I believe you're doing it."

Staver grunted. Words like *formidable* and *invincible* were not words he would have applied to himself. However he may have looked on the bridge, he had not felt like a warrior, certainly not an invincible one. How could he and his brothers be invincible when they faced the power of a sorcerer?

"Ord?"

"What now, sprig?"

"Why is it all happening here—and now? And why us, Ord?"

"Why not?" Ord said, yawning.

Col's voice was muffled with sleep and unmistakably cross. "Go to sleep, you two."

The Mage of the Crystal Hills pulled his cloak about his shoulders and turned over on his side. The Master of the Southern Forest drifted back into sleep, and the Keeper of the Fastness and Plain closed his eyes and began to snore.

The Dark Prophet had promised a safe night. After this night, safety was to be rare and sleep dearly purchased.

10

The Grip of the Cairnlord

They started south before the coming of light. All traces of their night's encampment were effaced, and they moved swiftly, almost noiselessly, along a narrow forest path, not stopping for rest until the sun was high.

Twenty-six set out. Col made careful note of their number and tried to fix the men's names and faces in his mind. By this time he had met and exchanged a few words with all of them. He felt it his duty. Chance had given him this brave band as followers, but he meant to win their loyalty by his own actions. That was the way of the Headland, and he thought it a good way.

After a time he noticed an unfamiliar face. Soon he saw another and then two more. Dropping back down the line of march, he took a count and discovered that their band now numbered thirty-three. Even as he hurried forward to speak with Goodbowe, two green-clad men slipped from the shadowed woods beside the trail, exchanged a salute with those in the file, and took their place among the marchers.

When Col caught up to Goodbowe, the leader of the foresters was talking to an unfamiliar man. Col hung back, and soon the stranger clasped Goodbowe's hand, turned, and disappeared into the forest. Col trotted to Goodbowe's side.

"Who are these strangers?" he asked.

"Not strangers, my lord Colberane. Loyal followers. The Dark Prophet has been among them. They come to see their leaders and go to pass the word to others."

"And what do they tell the others?"

Goodbowe glanced up, and a fierce satisfaction was in his eyes. "They say to sharpen the axe and string the bow. The promised three have come, and we shall strike back at last."

"You said last night that you were once betrayed and led into an ambush. Can all these men be trusted?"

Without hesitation Goodbowe said, "I entrust them with my life."

Col went a few steps in silence, trying to decide how to respond to this statement. Betrayal and ambush would be easy in this thick wood; a small band like theirs could be encircled and killed to the last man by a trained force. And yet a good leader had to trust his men and show that trust, and Col's one wish at this point was to prove himself a worthy leader. Laying a hand on Goodbowe's shoulder, he said, "Then I know they must be loyal. If any wish to speak to me or my brothers, we'd be proud to meet them."

"Thank you, my lord Colberane."

"About titles, Goodbowe . . . I think it's time we dispense with 'my lord.' "

A look of dismay crossed the forester's lined features. "You are our leaders. Our deliverers. Respect must be shown."

"So far, we've led you nowhere and delivered you from nothing."

"No matter, my lord. You will. The Dark Prophet has foretold it."

"I prefer to be called Col until I take my rightful place. My brothers are to be Ord and Staver."

Goodbowe paused before saying in a low, reluctant voice, "As you wish . . . Col."

They were again silent for a time. Col glanced at Goodbowe and saw him crestfallen. It occurred to him then, for the first time, that perhaps a title meant something to these people that a man from the Headland could not easily understand. They had waited, in hiding, for generations. They had suffered and endured the suffering bravely, sustained by a promise that three brothers would come to lead them against an enemy no army of mere men could withstand alone. Now their spirit was reborn, their hope realized, as their promised leaders marched among them. It was only natural for them to want to show their feelings by hailing the brothers.

And yet Col felt awkward and false when addressed as "my lord Colberane." He had looked forward to titles and honors when he first heard the prophecy, but he felt that way no longer. Enthroned in splendor, surrounded by pomp, dispensing bounty and justice to a grateful people, he might feel that the title fit. But now, hurrying furtively along a forest trail, dusty and unwashed, heading for an unknown destination to confront an unknown enemy, he did not feel grand or glorious. He felt untried and unproven, and the words of respect rang hollow in his ear. He tried to think of a way to mollify Goodbowe, and at last said, "You must know, I do this as a precaution against the Cairnlord."

"How so, my—Col?"

"Surely such a powerful sorcerer as he can watch our movements, and perhaps even hear our words—as the lesser wizards were once able to see Ambescand in battle far away."

Goodbowe scratched in his beard thoughtfully. "Perhaps . . ."

"And the longer he remains unaware of us—of who we are and why we come—the better for us and our cause. Far better he thinks us three harmless travelers than the leaders come to overthrow him."

"True. Very wise. A sensible precaution." Goodbowe chuckled with satisfaction and nodded his head. "This is the way a true leader thinks. I should have understood at once and not questioned."

"I'm glad you agree. Spread the word among the men."

"I will, Col."

Col dropped back along the line, pausing now and then to speak with one of the men, to greet a newcomer, or simply to walk a few paces by the side of his newfound followers, listening to their talk, sharing the way in silence. He passed by Staver, deep in conversation with Jem Underhill, and smiled at the sight of the two boys in the midst of this band of men. Jem was the younger by a few years, and from his expression as he listened to Staver's account of the second clash with a gray man, he looked upon Staver as something close to a demigod.

Col was satisfied with his younger brother's conduct and bearing so far, though he had some misgivings about Staver's part in this mysterious business. The boy was husky even now, with a few years' growing before him;

he would most likely end as big as Vannen, if not bigger. He could handle that massive iron blade with fair skill. Most lads his age would have had trouble lifting it. He had courage, too. Twice he had faced a gray man without shrinking, and that was something no forester could boast. He had kept his head crossing the Fissure and had been ready enough to take on his share of foresters at the bridge.

Nonetheless, Col wondered about him. However strong and brave Staver might be, he was still scarcely more than a boy, and this was a man's business. Against an army—or some hideous sorcery of the Cairnlord—Staver's virtues might fail him—fail all of them.

And yet Staver was part of the prophecy. As was the way of all such utterances, the words were obscure and difficult to understand, but Staver was clearly named. And the Dark Prophet had promised to speak to him again—a promise she had not made to his brothers. There had to be a significance in that.

Col recalled the prophecy recited by Goodbowe, weighing the words, but he could make no sense of them. He himself was to be the first to fall, the first to rise . . . and what could that mean? And Staver . . . clearly he was to outlive his brothers. He will be youngest and become the oldest, the prophecy went, and die an old man. But there was something else, something about a short life, that seemed to contradict the prophecy of great age.

Col shook his head, puzzled and annoyed. He was liking this less and less. It was good to seek a kingdom, good to lead a band of loyal men, but all the mystery was worrisome. Prophets who appeared and disappeared in a bright light and a rush of wind . . . puzzling words . . . uncertainty. Even now, they did not know where they were heading or why, only that danger lay ahead.

"Cheer up, brother!" a voice broke in on his reverie.

"What? Oh, hello, Ord. I've just been thinking."

"So I could see. But why the gloom?"

"Everything is so muddy, Ord. We don't know where we're going or why. The prophecy is full of contradictions."

"We're going south to claim our kingdoms. That's clear enough. We have good men to back us and more joining us every hour. Have you noticed them coming out of the woods—just to get a look at their new leaders?"

"Yes, I have."

"Why worry, then? We'll have a good-sized army by the time we get where we're going."

"But where is that, Ord? And what will we face?"

"Who cares, brother? We're invincible."

"So Goodbowe says."

"Don't you trust him?"

"The Dark Prophet wasn't so cheerful."

Ord made a gesture of dismissal. "Wizards are always gloomy. They like to keep people worried."

"I hope you're right."

"You don't want to go back to the Headland, do you?" Ord said, a faint trace of mockery in his voice and glance.

"We couldn't if we wanted to. And I don't want to. I want to claim my rightful kingdom, just as you do."

"That's fine, brother. Just fine. We'll be all right."

Ord trotted ahead and fell into step with Josling and Shields, and at once struck up a lively conversation. Kinnuary, who had stayed close behind the brothers during their exchange, took his place behind Ord, like a faithful dog at its master's heels.

Col let a half-dozen men pass him by, then rejoined the line and walked alone for a time. Talking with Ord always left him troubled. Ord never seemed to understand. He always acted as though a few clever words, the cut of a sword, and boundless self-confidence would solve any problem. And that, Col told himself, could not be right. Perhaps it had been so on the Headland; perhaps in other places he did not know, it was so, still, and ever would be—but not here, not now. Here, all was different.

The band traveled on at a steady pace all that day and the two that followed. At least twice each day they passed a small faring-house of stone. Once open to all travelers as night shelters, the faring-houses were now fallen into rubble. The few who still passed this way avoided them.

Each midday the band stopped to cook fresh-killed meat

over low, smokeless fires, keeping half the meat for evening. There were no fires after dark. They camped in clearings prepared for them by unseen hands and left again before the first trace of light.

Early in their third day of march, as Col was walking near the head of the line, Ord took his place beside him. Col glanced about, but Ord was alone this time.

"Do you feel anything, brother?" Ord asked.

"What do you mean?"

"Do you sense something wrong—anything at all?"

Col thought for a moment, then shook his head. "No. Why?"

"Staver feels something in his shoulder. The amulet. He thinks it's a warning."

"Where's Staver now?"

"He's at the tail end of the line of march, with Jem. I set Kinnuary to watch over them. He's safe enough."

Col rubbed his own shoulder. "I don't understand. I don't feel a thing."

"Neither did I. Staver asked me to walk up the line and see if anything happened. When I passed Goodbowe, I felt a twinge in my shoulder. Like the pricking of a dagger."

"Goodbowe? I can't believe . . ."

"There's a stranger with him. Ordinary-looking fellow, but he gave me a curious look when I passed."

Col weighed this for a time. The amulet in Staver's shoulder had saved them once before. It deserved trust.

"I'll go back and talk to Goodbowe and this new fellow," he said.

"I'll stay here for a time, then I'll start to drift back. If you feel anything, give me a wink as I pass. We'll have a talk with that stranger," Ord said.

Col nodded and stepped to one side to await Goodbowe and the newcomer. As they drew parallel to him, he felt it, just as Ord had said: like the pricking of a dagger in his shoulder.

"Come, walk with us, Col," Goodbowe hailed him. "We have a friend who would speak with you."

Col took his place beside the stranger, extended his hand, and said, "We welcome you."

"I'm called Goss, my lord Colberane." At the touch of

Goss's hand, the imagined point dug a bit deeper into Col's shoulder.

"No titles here, Goss. I'm Col."

"As you command. You are one of the promised leaders, then?"

"So Goodbowe tells me. I believe him."

"Oh, yes. Yes, we all trust Goodbowe," Goss said solemnly. "Three of you, is it not?"

"It is, Goss."

"Yes. Colberane, and the Scarlet Ord, and Staver of the Iron Angel. I have seen the red-haired brother, but where is the youngest?"

"Staver is in the line of march."

"Good, good. May I look upon him?"

The amulet burned in Col's shoulder, and a chill ran through his body. Ahead, he saw Ord making his way back slowly with apparent aimlessness, stopping to chat with every group he passed.

"Perhaps later, Goss."

"I must rejoin my men. I bring a great force, Col— two hundred skilled archers, ready to fight at your bidding. But until I see the third brother, I cannot command my men to follow."

"Think of it, Col—two hundred archers!" Goodbowe said.

"We're grateful, Goss."

"It honors us to serve you. But my men must know that I have seen the promised leaders with my own eyes."

Ord was just ahead of them. He parted, with a low laugh, from the Harrismith brothers who walked some ten paces before Col, Goodbowe, and Goss, and stepped to the roadside to let them pass. His hand went to his shoulder, and he frowned. Col gave the signal.

"Where is Staver, Col?" Goodbowe asked.

"I'd like to hear more about these archers before we call Staver."

"What would you know?" Goss asked.

"How have you maintained such a force all this time? How have you kept them concealed?"

"We have a stronghold . . . far to the west."

"A sizeable stronghold it must be."

"Yes. No . . . not so large as you might think, I

mean. It is concealed. Well concealed. No one suspects its existence," Goss said uncomfortably.

"Did you know of this stronghold before today, Goodbowe?"

At the question, Goss broke for the forest. Col was after him at once. Goss was wiry and agile, but Col's long legs gave him the advantage. When he was close enough, he hurled himself on the fugitive, bringing him to the ground. Goss drew his dagger. Col's big hand closed on the man's wrist, and he hooked his other forearm under Goss's chin.

"Drop it or I'll break your neck," he said.

Goss hesitated. Col jerked his forearm up. Goss gave a grunt of pain and released the dagger.

As Col hauled him to his feet, Ord, Goodbowe, and a third man appeared, their weapons at the ready. Col stood Goss against a tree and drew his sword. He placed the point against the spy's chest, just below the breastbone.

"Who sent you, Goss?"

"My master is the Cairnlord."

"He's not much of a wizard if he needs servants like you."

"He needs no servants. He needs no one. He knows all that you do. The Cairnlord knows everything."

"Then he must also know his days are numbered," Ord said pleasantly.

Goss laughed. "Do you think the Cairnlord fears you? He can destroy you with a word. With a breath! Fools—you throw away your lives on a prophecy."

"If the Cairnlord could dispose of us so easily, he'd have done it. Instead, he sent gray men, and then he sent you to spy on us. Why, Goss?"

The spy said nothing. He glared hatefully at Col. Col gave the sword a very slight thrust and repeated, "Why?"

Goss let out a gasp of pain. He swallowed, shut his eyes, and shook his head. The other man in the group, a slim, middle-aged forester named Warriner, stepped to Col's side and laid a hand on Col's forearm.

"Don't soil yourself with the likes of this. Let me question him," Warriner said. He handed his axe to Goodbowe and drew a short knife from his belt.

Col put up his sword and stepped aside. Warriner walked up to the spy, fixing him with his eyes. He took Goss's chin in his left hand. He turned it slowly from one side to the other while Goss shrank back against the tree; then his right hand flew up with a flash of steel, cleanly severing an ear.

Goss shrieked and clapped his hands to his injured head. Blood streamed between his fingers. He looked about with wild, terrified eyes, and began to moan. Col looked on, stunned, and felt his stomach grow queasy. Warriner stepped back.

"Why, Goss?" he said.

"If I tell . . . he'll punish me. He'll destroy me!"

"As you wish," Warriner said, taking a pace forward.

Col was about to stop him, when Goss cried, "No! Wait! No more, please. But you must protect me. I'll tell you why I came, but you must—"

Goss's voice was choked off as if a giant hand had closed on his throat. His face reddened, and his eyes bulged. He clawed at his throat with gory hands while blood poured unheeded down his neck and chest. His tongue protruded; his face grew ever darker. Staggering, he slumped to his knees, then pitched forward, writhing on the ground. Then he was still.

Goodbowe knelt at his side and tugged the blood-covered hands free. Around the dead man's throat was a thick band, deep red, as if an invisible collar had been tightened from afar to choke him to death.

"Thus the Cairnlord treats his servants," Goodbowe said.

Warriner rubbed his throat uneasily. "What of us?"

No one spoke for a time. Gazing down soberly on the blackened face of the dead man, they all felt the inadequacy of words. Then Ord said, "I think Col was right. If the Cairnlord could kill us off, he would. There must be limits to his power, or he wouldn't need servants at all—not gray men, not Goss—no one."

"But what was Goss supposed to find out?" Col turned to Goodbowe. "Did he ask you about our numbers? Our destination?"

"Yes. And he wanted to know which road we'd take at the fork. I told him nothing."

"Did you suspect him?"

"No. But your words the other day made me cautious."

"A good thing they did. What else did he ask?"

"Only to see both of you, and Staver."

"But why?" Col asked. Puzzled, he turned to Ord. "Can you think why?"

"No. Unless . . . unless it was sheer curiosity."

Col shook his head, dissatisfied with that explanation. Goss did not seem the sort of cool-headed adventurer who would risk his life and his mission merely to satisfy his own curiosity. That could not be. Col frowned, thought on it, and suddenly his face brightened. "Not his own curiosity, Ord—his master's! The Cairnlord wants to know what we look like!"

"But he's a wizard. Can't he . . . look into a magic glass, or . . . or work some kind of spell?"

"Maybe he can't—or chooses not to for some reason. It makes sense, Ord."

"At least we're even. We don't know what he looks like, either."

Col touched his neck thoughtfully. "I hope we never do."

"We'd best get back to the trail," Goodbowe said. "Goss may have men in the woods."

"Go ahead. I'll bury this," Warriner said.

As they hurried to rejoin the others, Col asked Goodbowe, "Why does Warriner hate the Cairnlord's men so much? If I had known what he meant to do to Goss, I'd never have let him near the man."

"You may see worse. None of us has any love for the Cairnlord's creatures."

"Goss wasn't some gray monster. He was a man, like us, Goodbowe."

"When Warriner came to join us, he was alone. For a long time he said nothing of the past. One night, when we were trapped and it looked as though we might not escape, he told me what the Cairnlord's men—humans, like Goss—had done to his family. What he did to Goss was gentle in comparison."

Col said no more. He began to think that he and his brothers were becoming part of something more impor-

tant than reclaiming a kingdom. They had much to
learn, both about themselves and about the enemy they
marched to meet. In this world there was evil that they
had never imagined. And they would have to face it—
and conquer it.

11

The Fool's Head

At midmorning on the fourth day, they came to a place
where the road branched into three. Here they rested for
a time.

To their left was the way to the mountain road. This
was the widest of the three and the shortest route to the
Southern Forest, but it was patrolled by the Cairnlord's
men. No one could travel it unnoticed. To the right was
the way to the coast road. An old road it was—and still
the safest way around the mistlands—but a long and
winding path that required many days of travel. The
middle way led to the Fool's Head. After their rest, they
set out on this road.

Shortly before sundown, they came to the shore of the
inland sea. In outline it resembled a misshapen human
head. A single small island near the center, not visible
from this position, was rumored to hold strange forms of
life, servants to the Cairnlord. Men called the island the
Eye of the Fool and avoided it.

Once a main route to the south, the Fool's Head was
now little traveled. Alone on its vast expanse, men
felt exposed and vulnerable. In the time of the Cairnlord,
these were sensations no one wished to experience, hence
the waterway was shunned.

The Dark Prophet had ordered them to cross the Fool's
Head by night, and this they prepared to do. Waiting
boats were taken from shelters in the forest and carried to the shore. Col was surprised at the lightness of
these craft. They were between three and four marks
long and a half-mark wide, yet four men could carry one

with little effort. He took a turn himself and found that he was scarcely aware of the gunwale resting on his shoulder, so light was the construction.

Their original number had more than doubled by this time, but the marchers fit easily into four boats. Twelve men rowed each boat; one took the steering oar; the rest arranged themselves in the bow and stern.

They pushed off from the shore before moonrise, at the fullness of dark. Col and Goodbowe traveled in the first boat, Ord and Kinnaury in the second, while Staver and Jem Underhill took the third. Buckman was placed in charge of the fourth boat, which served as their rear guard.

The surface of the Fool's Head was smooth. The night was silent, save for the rhythmic slap and plunge of the oars and the regular creak of rowlocks. A mild offshore breeze was at their backs as they moved quickly out into the open water. At a signal from Goodbowe, they pulled to the right and took up a course about thirty marks off the western shore.

Hour after hour they moved steadily south, following the shoreline. The men rowed, rested for a time, changed oars, and rowed on again as strong as ever. After a full day's march, with little rest and no sleep, they seemed willing and able to go on through the night.

Shortly after moonrise, Goodbowe tapped Col on the arm and pointed off to the left ahead. At first Col saw nothing, then he noticed a faint flicker of blue light.

"The Eye. Something evil dwells there," Goodbowe said.

"Are we near it?"

"No. And best it is that we remain far off."

The breeze had died. Col found the air still and oppressively clammy and warm. He flung back his cloak and looked out ahead, toward the Eye. The blue light was no longer visible. The Fool's Head was calm and smooth, with a surface that shone in the moonlight like greased leather.

A breeze came but brought no relief. The sea ahead seemed to be awakening under its sultry touch, with long rolling swells driven offshore by the western wind. The boats rocked as they crossed the swells, but the men rowed on unperturbed.

"Are we passing the outlet of a river?" Col asked.

"We're well past the river mouth by now. It feels like a storm coming," Goodbowe replied.

"There were no signs of a storm all day."

"I sense them now."

Col had to agree, for the signs were unmistakable. The wind was rising, and the swells became steadily higher. He looked up and saw the stars on the western horizon wink and then vanish one by one. A great canopy of sooty darkness was drawing toward them, obscuring all before it as it unfurled across the sky.

"How much weather can these boats take, Goodbowe?"

"The lakemen who built them know these waters. The boats will stand up to any storm on the Fool's Head."

Col nodded and said nothing. Goodbowe may have convinced himself, but Col remembered the feeling of the boat as it lay on his shoulder. So light a craft could not but be fragile. He tried to open his thoughts, in hope that these strange waters might speak to him as the waters of the Headland and the Fissure had once reached deep into his mind, but nothing came. He wondered if his gift had somehow been lost. A pang of fear struck him at the thought that the Cairnlord might somehow have overmastered it and made these waters dumb to him.

The wind pulled at his cloak. He drew it closer around him. Ahead, the blue light flickered once again. As he watched, it began to travel toward the west, across their bow, and then it vanished. Goodbowe seemed not to notice it, and Col said nothing to him or the others.

Now all was impenetrable darkness. Moon and stars were hidden. The boat gave a sudden roll, so sharp that Col was almost thrown overboard. He came up heavily against the rail and clutched it tightly. Goodbowe fell against him, and they both were soaked when the boat pitched deep into a trough and rose half-filled with water.

The wind had come to life. It fluttered and howled and groaned like an agonized monster circling over their heads. Col strained his eyes but could see only black shapes looming against a greater surrounding blackness.

The first drops of rain were indistinguishable from the spray. Soon the rain began to fall heavily, then increased to sheets of unbroken water that streamed from the skies and curled and broke from all sides, turning their garments within moments into a sodden prison that pulled them down and drew all the warmth from their bones. Col, and Kempe at the stern by the steersman, set to bailing desperately.

"Pull for shore!" Goodbowe shouted, pointing to the western bank.

The steersman leaned into the steering oar. The men hurled themselves forward, straining back, driving the little craft directly into the swell that rose at the bow. Up and into a curtain of water, then down again, and they missed not a stroke. The water was high in the boat, and Col could scarcely stay even with it.

Goodbowe's name came faintly to Col's ears. He turned and saw the steersman gesturing wildly, pointing back in the direction they had come. He slapped Goodbowe on the back to gain his attention and pointed to the steersman, whose words came to him in fragments, torn and scattered by the wind.

Col put his mouth close to Goodbowe's ear and said, "What is the steersman saying?"

"Says we're heading wrong—away from shore—wind must have shifted."

"He's wrong, Goodbowe."

The steersman continued to shout. When he suddenly pointed dead ahead, Col turned to follow the direction and saw a faint point of blue light in the blackness.

"He's right—the Eye is ahead—we've got turned around," Goodbowe shouted.

"No! The light moved. I saw it move."

"Moved?"

"To mislead us—lure us out—to drown!"

Goodbowe stared at him for a moment, as if stupefied by his words and by the pounding of wind and water. Then he roared, "Pull, men! This way! Pull for shore!"

The oarsmen bent to their work, and Col bailed at a furious pace. Each wave poured more water into their craft than the one before. When a flash of lightning burst

brilliantly over them, and he saw how low in the water
the boat was riding, Col felt the sudden pluck of fear—
they were sure to swamp.

Water was everywhere. The very air he breathed was
filled with rain and spray. Water streamed down his
face, ran from his clothing, blew into his eyes and ears,
choked him when he tried to speak. It seemed as though
the world had turned to furious water.

The waves grew fiercer. Each time their boat climbed
into an oncoming wave the ascent was sharper—and
when they plunged into the trough, they seemed to be
diving straight for the bottom of the Fool's Head. Hammered by the waves that crashed over their backs, as-
saulted by the howling wind that flung water at them like
pellets from every direction, soaked and chilled and
weary from long labor, the oarsmen still bent to their
work, rowing for their lives.

Their boat rose, and a long streamer of lightning
blazed above them. In that instant of eerie light, poised
at the crest of a mighty wave, Col saw the shore, perhaps
twenty marks dead ahead, and another boat just behind
his. All around, the waves were topped with blowing
foam.

The lightning died. They shot down, plunging deep into
the water, and slowly leveled. The next wave seemed
less ferocious. The ascent was shorter, the plunge less
harrowing, the recovery faster. The bettering of their lot
was purely relative: they were still beseiged by wind and
water, deafened by the crashes and howls and strange
wailing that filled the darkness all around them; the roll
and pitch of the boat made it necessary for Col to bail
with one hand and hold fast to the rail with the other;
but the worst seemed to be behind them.

Then, as another flash of lightning tore open the black
sky, Col looked up, and the bucket fell from his hand at
the sight of a black wall of water racing down on them.
He had not even time to shout a warning.

It fell on them like an avalanche. He felt the boat dis-
integrate beneath him. Still clutching the rail, he was
swept down, deep into the water, then flung up into the
wild mix of rain and sea and wind. Gasping and choking,
he went under again. He tore off his cloak, kicked his

boots free, and fought to the surface. This time he
stayed afloat. Clutching the fragment of rail in a death
grip, he started kicking in the direction of the shore.

That last great wave seemed to have exhausted the
fury of the storm. The swells were high, but no longer
were they the menacing mountains of darkness that had
enclosed them and crashed down upon them. Col was
able to make it to shore, where he collapsed on the sodden ground, staring up into the blackness, gulping air.

The rain soon stopped, and the wind fell. Overhead,
a star appeared, then another, and still others, as the
ragged edge of the storm cloud raced eastward. Col
climbed to his feet. Under the emerging moon, he could
see bits of wreckage on the surface of the Fool's Head
and men clinging to them. Far out on the water the blue
light moved back and forth, then hovered, and then shot
off at great speed toward the Eye.

Col knew then that this storm that came from nowhere, raged and destroyed and abruptly passed, was no
natural event. That blue light was something sent by the
enemy, a magic akin to the green glow that had tried to
turn Staver's hand against his brothers. And at the
thought of Staver and Ord, all else was driven from Col's
mind.

He stumbled into the water, helping survivors to shore.
As soon as they had regained their breath, he dispatched
them along the banks to look for others. When the first
light of morning glinted on the water, Col had assembled
seventeen men. His brothers were not among them.

Col felt the hunger and weariness closing in on him,
overwhelming him and bringing despair in their wake.
He slumped under a tree, drew up his knees, laid his
folded arms on them and let his head droop. It was all
over now. His attempt at leadership had led men to their
deaths. There would be no kingdom for Staver, none for
Ord, and surely none for Col. Lives had been thrown
away on a dream of glory, on an old man's words and
a magician's vague and meaningless utterances—and
that was enough. The three of them had rushed like fools
into the unknown—like boys to their games, The Dark
Prophet had said, and in that, at least, she had spoken
truth. A bit of metal in their shoulders, fine blades at

their sides, and they had thought themselves the match of an ages-old sorcerer powerful enough to destroy a kingdom. It was folly that bordered on madness, and it must end. At least Col could see to it that no more lives were thrown away.

And then, in the depths of his sorrow and self-hatred and despair, reassurance came to him. A comforting hand seemed to rest on his shoulder—within his shoulder, radiating from the amulet—and he knew then that he had been thinking rashly. He faced an awesome enemy, there was no doubt of that, but even the most awesome power could be defeated by the right stroke at the right moment. And the Cairnlord had to be defeated, not for the sake of a lost throne, not for revenge or ambition or adventure—but for some greater cause.

The struggle would be long and hard. There would be other trials, other dark moments, and he would have to endure them. If he despaired, if he surrendered to his weakness and ran seeking safety, all would be lost for him and for the people who looked to him for deliverance. There was no safety, no refuge from the Cairnlord, least of all for those born to overthrow him. They had no sanctuary. They could only move forward, to the confrontation.

He rose, shivering in his wet clothing, and stepped into a little patch of sun. Dark thoughts banished, he saw his situation with new eyes. His brothers might yet be alive, searching for him and his men. The storm was over. Many had survived, and there was hope.

A shout made him turn. He saw Ord, barefoot and ragged, soaking wet, his cloak gone, bounding over the ground toward him. Col seized his brother in a bear hug, lifting him off the ground, laughing aloud in joy and relief.

Set on his feet, Ord took a step back, studied Col, and joined in his laughter. "A fine pair of beggars we are to be seeking a throne. Lucky we haven't lost our swords as well!"

"Did your boat break up, too?"

"They all did. It was the last great wave that did for ours."

"Ours, too. Have you seen Staver?"

Ord's face grew solemn. "No. We have eight men from his boat, but Staver's still missing. So is Jem, and Haggart, and three new men I never met."

For the first time, Col noticed the others who had joined them, apparently arriving in Ord's wake. Goodbowe, Kinnaury, and other familiar faces were there. Goodbowe hurried to join the brothers.

"You're safe, both of you!" he said fervently.

"We're fine. What of Staver? Any word at all?" Ord asked.

Goodbowe beckoned to one of the men who had arrived with him, then turned to explain, "Forben was the steersman in Staver's boat."

"Tell us all you can, Forben," Col greeted the man.

"It was all strange—all mixed up," Forben began, looking from one to another of his listeners as if appealing for their belief. "Never knew such a thing to happen before. Got all turned around, we did. We saw the signal from the boat ahead and turned to head west for the shore. Then, all of a sudden, we were heading for the Eye! We saw that blue light clear as a candle, right ahead of us where it should have been west. I started to bring her around, and the oarsmen pulled to help me, and a wave caught us broadside and smashed her to bits."

"Did you see what happened to Staver?"

"He was in the bow, him and young Underhill. They went over together."

"Thanks, Forben."

"I did the best I could, my lords. I tried to steer for shore, but when I saw that light, I just didn't know . . ."

Ord laid a hand on Forben's trembling shoulder. "We know you did your best. Staver's going to be back with us."

"And we're not your lords, Forben. Not yet. We're all comrades in arms now, all of us."

When Forben had hurried off, Goodbowe said, "I left Warriner with two men to patrol the bank for Staver and the others. They'll join us later."

"How many missing altogether?"

"Seven."

"Considering the suddenness of the storm and its power, we were lucky," Col said.

"Yes, very lucky. But Staver . . ."

"Our little brother is a better swimmer than either of us," Ord said. "And besides, Goodbowe, we're invincible. You told us so yourself."

"Yes. Yes, the prophecy is clear. Staver Ironbrand will rule as Mage of the Crystal Hills."

"Well then, why should we worry if he gets his feet wet? He's old enough to look after himself for a while," Ord said cheerfully.

Goodbowe rejoined his men much encouraged. When he was out of earshot, Ord said, "That's right, isn't it, brother?"

"It has to be," Col said.

12

The Mistlands

The nature of the forest changed as they marched south. The ground became spongy underfoot and the air around them dank. The morning mist grew ever denser and more chill, and it lingered in the air to a later hour each day. Standing pools of dark water were seen with increasing frequency. At last, having skirted the west bank of the Fool's Head and come south along an old trail, they came abruptly to the edge of the Long Wood.

Beyond them the land fell away and vanished behind a curtain of white. Except for the sounds of water, all was silent. Water dripped from branches and ran in rivulets, and from time to time splashed loudly, deep in the milky obscurity. No other sound emerged.

The air was a thick moist cloth saturated with a rainbow of odors. Sweet it was, with the overripe richness of growing things on the point of decay; yet it was pungent, too, with a spicy, musky savor and a suggestion of some heady incense smoldering far away. Under all the other scents, there hung a hint of something rotting and foul.

The Foresters had apparently breathed this air before; they showed no surprise, no distaste, or any other reaction. To Col and Ord it was like the atmosphere of another world. They could not decide if it was wholesome or threatening. It was too new and unknown.

Goodbowe came and stood near Col. For a time he was silent; then, when Col gave him a curious glance, he said, "These are the mistlands. There should be men to meet us with flatboats."

"When will they come?"

"We were expected three days ago. Perhaps they learned of the storm and thought it unsafe to wait. They'll return."

"Can't we wait for them in a drier place?" Ord asked, shivering.

"I fear there'll be no dry places for a few days yet."

Ord, Col, and most of the others had cast off their cloaks and outer garments in the storm. Many of the men had lost their boots. They had managed to make serviceable footcloths out of material salvaged from the wrecked boats, but ever since they reached shore that night, all the men had been wet and chilled without relief. Days were endurable, as they warmed themselves by brisk walking; the cool nights were sleepless, and each night's fatigue added to their sufferings. One roaring fire to dry their clothes and drive the embedded cold from their bones would have restored health and spirits, but a fire was out of the question. Not one man even mentioned the word.

They were fortunate to have only a short wait at their rendezvous. A boat appeared in the mist unheralded by any sound, and Goodbowe stepped forward and signaled to the men in it, using the salute he had exchanged with their visitors on the forest trail. The boat pulled to shore, and a man joined them. The two who had come with him remained in the boat. He drew Goodbowe aside and spoke some time with him, asking many questions that the forester answered to his apparent satisfaction. At length they joined the brothers.

"This is Colberane, Master of the Southern Forest, and the Scarlet Ord, Keeper of the Fastness and the Plain. And this is Meares, a chief of the mistlanders," Goodbowe said.

"Are you the ones come to lead us?" Meares asked.

"So the Dark Prophet has said," Col replied.

"The Dark Prophet has visited us. She spoke of three."

"Our brother was separated from us in the storm on the Fool's Head."

Meares studied them, and his perplexity was obvious from his expression; the brothers marked it but said nothing. He wanted to believe that his deliverers had come, but this pair before him looked to be no more than vagabonds. He was eager to place his forces in the hands of his destined leader but determined not to put his men at the service of adventurers. He looked at their ragged, clinging shirts; their breeches, rent at the knee and split at the seam; their feet, bound in muddy rags, and he plainly doubted all he had heard from Goodbowe and the two men before him. Yet he longed to believe and accept them. Then he saw the blade at Col's side. He looked quickly to the sword upon whose hilt Ord's hand lightly rested, and his eyes grew wide.

"The blades of Ambescand. The third brother carries the Iron Angel," Goodbowe said.

Meares fell to his knees. Then he raised his head to say, "You come. It's true. The deliverers . . . the leaders!" his voice broke with emotion.

Col extended a hand to pull him to his feet. "Our time hasn't come yet. Right now, you're the leader, Meares. We need you to take us through the mistlands."

"I will, my lords."

"We'd like to go someplace warm and dry," Ord said.

"This night you'll have shelter and a fire, my lords."

"And please refer to us as Ord and Col," Col said. When he saw the bewilderment on Meare's face, he added, "A precaution. Goodbowe will explain."

Meares left them, still looking awed and slightly confused at this behavior on the part of figures from a prophecy. His manner became brisk and sure as he conferred with Goodbowe. At his direction the foresters were assembled, and Meares stepped forward, signaling to the men in his boat. They slipped noiselessly into the mist. In a very short time they returned, accompanied by a small flotilla of narrow, flat-bottomed craft. Two men stood in each, one at the bow and one astern, poling the boats silently into position. The foresters were carried three to a boat. Col and Goodbowe rode in the second boat with Meares, discussing plans for the crossing.

They were to head directly, on a safe course, for a stronghold on a rise about a half-day's travel to the southwest, there to rest for the night and for a full day and night after. On the second morning they would start out to complete the crossing in strength.

Col was grateful for the respite. He was chilled to the bone, hungry, and tired, and he knew that some of the men were in worse condition than he. Nevertheless, this sudden slackening of the urgency that had pressed upon them since the Dark Prophet's appearance surprised him, and he asked Meares for the reason.

"We need that time to assemble. It takes a great force to cross some parts of the mistlands in safety," Meares told him.

"Won't the Cairnlord's spies notice a large force?"

"The Cairnlord has no watchers here. His servants never enter mistlands."

"Have you found a way to fight them off? No one else seems able to withstand them."

Meares shook his head ruefully. "They fear the same creatures we fear. Ancient things still live in this place. Things that live in the water but can walk on land as well as a man and even fly through the air. They carry off lone travelers and have been known to attack small bands. We've learned to travel cautiously and only in strength and to avoid certain parts of the bog, so we remain safe from them and beyond reach of the Cairnlord."

"It doesn't sound like a pleasant life."

"It is not. We plan to leave with you. All of us."

"I don't even know my destination."

"You go to strike against the Cairnlord and his minions. We follow gladly."

Col did not share Meares's faith in the sanctuary of mistlands. It seemed to him that a being with the power to raise a storm could easily gather whatever information he desired without human aid and that distance would prove no obstacle to his powers. Yet the Cairnlord did seem curiously dependent on others—on his gray men, his troops, and spies like Goss. It was a puzzle. And Col, seeing no solution, held his tongue.

Just at sunset they came to the mistlanders' stronghold. A dark mass loomed suddenly before them, like a black wall in the mist. The boatmen headed straight for it. Col could see steep banks rising from the water, covered with a furry green growth that shone with moisture. The boatmen poled to an inlet, and there a heavy, barred gate drew back to admit them, one by one, to a narrow channel that wound between high banks. Looking up, Col saw figures in the mist, men bearing long spears, standing silent, on guard.

The channel widened to a natural amphitheater whose banks rose sharply on all sides to the height of about four marks. In the harbor thus formed, boats were tied side by side, creating a wooden floor that covered nearly a third of the water's surface. Col tried to estimate the number of boats—it was surely more than fifty.

The boatmen poled to a long pier, where Col, Goodbowe, and Meares disembarked. Meares led the way to a ramp, and they followed him to the top.

When they reached the edge of the bank, Col was surprised to find the mist almost gone, and the early stars visible above. The ground was springy underfoot but not as moist as the ground at the forest edge.

"There are nine rises like this in the mistlands," Meares explained. "We have settlements on three. The rest we use for fuel and growing what food we can."

Col looked at the few stunted trees and scattered bushes that grew on the rise. "You have little enough wood growing here. Are the trees bigger elsewhere?"

"We cut our fuel from the earth itself."

Col did not understand, but he was soon to find out. Meares led the foresters to a low, rounded building about two marks in diameter and a mark high at its center. There, in a round depression ringed by charred stones, a low and smoky fire burned. The fuel was not wood but dried slabs of some material that looked very much like the surface of the rise. Col squatted before it, extending his hands to the welcome warmth. The smoke was pungent but not unpleasant; he recognized it as one of the unfamiliar odors that had greeted him at the edge of the mistlands. He was there only a short time when Ord joined him at the hearthside.

"Shelter and a fire, as I promised. Two others have been made ready for your men, and food is being prepared. I will find warm garments to replace those you lost in the storm," Meares said.

"Thanks, Meares," Ord said.

"You honor us. Now you must rest. Tomorrow you meet the people."

Warm and dry for the first time in what now seemed like ages, the brothers slowly ate their fill of the unfamiliar but tasty food brought to them by mistland children, who looked upon them with silent reverence. Sprawled by the fire, wrapped in heavy cloaks, they sipped a sweet warming drink made of heated water spiced with an infusion of dried leaves and berries. The storm and its aftermath seemed far away, and all the events of the days since Vannen's death were like the memory of a tale heard long ago. It seemed impossible that so much had happened in so short a time and that they were here, in a hut in the middle of a land unknown to them a score of days before.

"I wonder where Staver is now," Col said.

"I can't imagine. But he's safe. He must be."

"If he's not, then the Dark Prophet is a fraud."

"Exactly so, Col. And I can't believe that. You know how skeptical I am, and yet I believe in the Dark Prophet. There's something about all this. . . . Mind you, I don't understand much of what's happened to us, but I feel that it's all going to turn out right. We may have hardship ahead and danger, but there's a kingdom waiting at the end."

After a thoughtful pause Col said, "I feel the same way."

Ord laughed. Raising his cup, he drained it, as if in a toast, and said, "That proves there's magic in this—we're agreeing on something, brother!"

The next day and night were busy. Groups of flatboats arrived throughout the day, adding to the number already there until it became possible to walk dry-shod from one end of the harbor to the other by stepping from boat to boat. Men, women, and children came bearing all their belongings. And every one of these uprooted people, who had just run a fearful gantlet, was cheerful as a picnic-goer. As soon as the newcomers reached the rise, they were taken in hand by Meares's people, who had everything carefully organized.

Col and Ord spent the day meeting with the leaders and talking to all the mistlanders they encountered. Word of their own arrival had spread quickly. When they emerged from their shelter at first light, their clothing mended, boots on their feet, and mistland cloaks about their shoulders, they were greeted with respect. As the day proceeded, and more and more of the people saw them and spoke with them, the respect turned to warmth. Figures from an ancient prophecy had become real men of flesh and blood, whose very presence was a promise of early deliverance.

They departed, as planned, on the second morning after arrival, with Col in the first boat, Ord in the last, and the mistlanders strung out between, in a hundred and forty boats joined by lines. Every boat was in sight of at least two others and was firmly attached to one or more. In the center of the convoy, the flatboats were three across, almost touching. Toward the ends they poled two across. Only the first three boats were alone.

The original plan had been for the two brothers to travel at the center of the convoy, protected on all sides. This they flatly refused to do, Col declaring angrily that he had come to protect, not to be protected, and Ord sardonically inquiring whether the assembled mistland chiefs believed that he wore his sword merely as an ornament.

Goodbowe watched the debate with mixed emotions. He was proud to see his leaders asserting themselves and assuming command of this undertaking, but he feared for their safety as they did so. He had heard before this of the mist-dwelling creatures, and the tales told were fearsome. Sleek swift bog-dwellers with bodies like barrels and long, strong tentacles dangling behind and below them, these creatures could burst from beneath the dark water to seize their prey and drag it down before an alarm could be given. They could plummet from above on silent wings to carry a victim off to death. Their strength was greater than any man's; they could overturn a boat with ease and subdue a party of armed warriors. Fighting them was rash; they were best avoided—for only a great force could drive them off, and no man could hope to defeat them. Much as he trusted the Dark Prophet's words, Goodbowe was uneasy at the thought of the promised deliverers facing such monstrosities, but the brothers were implacable. Goodbowe resigned himself to riding in the first boat, axe at the ready. He alerted Kinnaury to ride with Ord and guard him at all costs.

The first day's travel was as peaceful as an excursion. At sunset the flatboats were drawn together into a tight wooden island, with a heavy guard posted around the perimeter. The night passed without disturbance.

Spirits were higher as they formed the convoy for the second day. They had reached the deepest and most dangerous part of the mistlands without sight of the creatures they all feared and hated so. If they came through this day and night safely, the worst would be behind them.

All through the morning they saw nothing to alarm them and heard no sound to indicate pursuit or espial. The general mood was still wary but relaxing a bit from the nervous circumspection of the outset. Even Meares, though he admitted his surprise at the ease of their passage when Col spoke with him, could not conceal his relief.

"If they don't attack today, they've lost their best chance. By nightfall we'll be in the shallows. They like the deep water," he said.

"Why haven't they attacked?"

"I don't know," Meares confessed. "I expected at least one attempt—to test our strength, if nothing else."

They poled on at a steady speed. Col sat in the midsection, scanning the smooth surface. He could see nothing threatening. The water was the color of a puddle of dead and rotting leaves. He felt revulsion at the thought of a creature who would choose to live in such a lair.

The first warning came to him faintly. The voice of these waters was slow and sluggish, unlike the thundering defiance of the tidal bore or the childlike singing of the Headland brook. It came faintly, from far away and below, like the muttering of a sleeper, and it spoke of dark forms gathering, coming from the far places, gliding deep, converging silently on their prey.

Col focused all his attention on the blurred voice that whispered within his mind. *Moving low . . . to the dark place . . . the feasting place . . . All come . . . join . . . All gather . . . Feast. . . .*

He unsheathed his sword and said to Meares, "The attack is coming soon. Pass the word, quickly."

Meares warned those in the second and third boats. They cast off to spread the warning. As these two boats —the only visible link with his followers—fell back and vanished into the enfolding mist, Col found his mouth dry and his palms moist at the anticipation of battle with the things of the mistlands. He was relieved when their boat was made fast to the convoy once again.

"Are we near deep water, Meares?"

The mistlander pointed to his left. "The deepest part of the bog lies out there."

"Be ready, then. This is where they'll attack."

Still they moved on, skirting the deep, with no sound but the smooth rush of water by the boards. Col felt the tension in his chest. He was aware of his heart beating loudly. Goodbowe sat behind him, his axe resting ready on his shoulder. Meares leaned on a long pike. They glided on in deepening silence.

The thing exploded from the water at Col's right hand, and the attack began. With a fling of spray and a *croomp* of shaken skin, it unfolded its wings, balancing in the air just above the surface, its fringe of tentacles trailing in the churning water. The spread of its wings was as long as the boat, and its thick body, the size of a big man's trunk. The head was flat and seemed all mouth, save for two round yellow eyes near the corners. The huge mouth gaped as the thing lunged forward.

Col's first stroke went deep into the flat skull. The thing beat frantically at the air, sending twin sheets of spray over the men as it sank into the bog. Col slashed again, shearing off one wing, and the apparition disappeared into the dark water.

He turned and thrust deep into another of the things as it broke water on the opposite rail, and it spurted inky blood and sank like a stone. Goodbowe was hacking at

one that had a grip on the rail, while Meares thrust with
his pike at others in the water. From the shouts behind
them, Col could tell that other boats were under attack,
but he could see nothing of them. Those immediately behind him stood with weapons at the ready, looking on in
horror at the struggle that they had thus far been spared.

Looking over the side, Col saw a hideous flattened face
gliding swiftly by beneath them. He thrust, plunging
shoulder deep into the water, and felt the blade sink
home. The water turned black and the face was seen no
more.

The attack ceased. Meares, Goodbowe, and Col stood
side by side in the rocking boat, looking down into the
bog for signs of the enemy.

"We've beaten them off," Goodbowe said.

"How much more deep water ahead, Meares?"

"We're nearly past it."

"Then we may be safe."

They stared down into the blackened water, intent for
a sign of the enemy. Only the cry from the second boat
alerted them to the creatures that struck from above,
dropping as silently as shadows.

Col felt the tentacles whip around his sword arm, pin-
ning it to his chest, and around his neck. Black wings beat
the air all around. Bracing his feet against the sides of the
boat and tensing his neck muscles, he seized his sword in
his other hand and struck blindly back, over his shoulder,
until the grip slackened. He pulled free and turned. Goodbowe's axe bit deep into the fallen attacker, which lay
in the bottom of the boat, injured but still fighting. Its
wings beat wildly, smacking loudly at the water and slashing forward to enfold Col. He drove his sword into the
thing's midsection until he felt it strike the wood of the
boat. The thrashing wings wavered and stilled. Col thrust
again. They sagged and trailed limply in the water.

Col leaned on his sword, gasping, then tugged it free
from the glistening black body. Goodbowe, axe in hand,
gazed at him glassily. Col looked up, then around, and
only then did he realize that Meares was missing. He
called the polers to a halt, and the convoy stopped behind
him, boat by boat, as word of the leader's fate passed
back.

They probed, and they let down lines, and they waited; but they knew from the start that Meares was gone and nothing could save him. When his fate was clear to all, Col gave the word to press on to the shallows.

13

The Green Court

With Meares gone, Col was the unquestioned leader of their band. He brought them safely to the shallows and had them go on, without stopping to rest, until the mistlands were behind them and they stood on solid ground at the margin of the grasslands. They sank the boats and set out at sunrise for the great Southern Forest.

Col consulted frequently with the mistland chiefs and with Goodbowe, but the final decisions were his alone, and he was obeyed without question. Under a single leader, the travelers quickly fused into a single force. Their old bond had been one of hatred for the same enemy, dread of the same fate; now forester and mistlander walked side by side to their mutual deliverance, sharing work and danger in a spirit of fellowship unknown in former days. Their peril was as real as ever and now more imminent with each southward step they took, but they no longer faced it alone, small and helpless in their isolation. They were becoming an army.

Responsibility seemed to change Col. When his presence was not required, he remained apart, alone, and his mien was solemn. He spoke only when speech could not be avoided. It appeared almost as though the spirit that grew among the followers was being drawn from a reservoir within their leader, leaving him daily more careworn.

Ord watched his brother change and said nothing until they reached the edge of the Southern Forest, where they made camp under the trees. That night he sought Col out and found him alone in a little clearing, looking at the stars.

"I haven't seen much of you since mistlands, brother," Ord said.

"I've had much to do."

"You've been busy before, and it didn't make you gloomy. Is it Staver's disappearance that has you so depressed?"

"Staver's alive. I have no doubt of that. Do you?"

"No doubt at all. I think as you do. Then is it Meares's death that's made you gloomy?" When no reply came, Ord went on. "He knew the danger of the crossing better than any of us. You can't blame yourself for his death."

"I don't. I'm thinking of the others."

"What about them?"

"We lost men crossing the Fool's Head, and we lost nine people in the mistlands. They followed me, and they died. Now I have eight hundred people who look on me as their leader, and I don't know where I'm leading them, Ord!"

"We're going south—to our kingdom."

"How far south? Where's the trail in the forest? We could wander forever. Staver's lost somewhere, and we've taken people into danger, and we don't have anything to guide us but a lot of words we don't even understand." Col sat on a log, hunched forward, and rubbed his eyes wearily with the heels of his hands.

"You're the only one with doubts, brother." Ord said, placing a reassuring hand on Col's broad shoulder. "Everyone here trusts you."

"That makes it worse. I don't know how to lead a band like this. I'll take them all to their deaths."

"They don't think so. They're eating well, they have shelter for the night, and they feel strong."

"I have nothing to do with that, Ord. It's their own leaders who are caring for their needs, not me."

Ord lost all patience with his brother. "What do you think it means to be a king, Col? Do you think these people expect you to hunt their food and build their shelters for them?" he said angrily. "You've got Goodbowe and Kinnaury, and that mistlander, the little yellow-haired fellow—"

"Mullerin. A good man."

"Yes. Mullerin. You've got them to do the daily business, Col, and they do it well. That's not king's work."

"What is king's work? Leading men in battle?"

"For us, yes," Ord said.

"And how do I do that? I'm a good swordsman. I can handle a bow. But I've never assembled an army or led an attack. I don't know tactics. I might lead them all to their death."

"Remember the prophecy. We'll all be kings."

"I remember the prophecy. But it doesn't say how many men will die to make us kings. And it doesn't teach me how to lead my followers into battle against a trained army."

"Stay out in front and never show fear."

Col rose and smiled faintly. "You speak like the Dark Prophet now. It sounds very simple, but it's not that simple to do."

He walked from the clearing into the darkness under the trees, and Ord watched until he could no longer see his brother. Ord remained alone in the clearing for a time. He was troubled by the change in Col. He was aware of no difference in himself, but he could not help but wonder if he might be changing as much as his brother.

The next morning, as they broke camp, two strangers appeared at the site and were brought at once to Col. They were dressed in close-fitting outfits parti-colored in brown, black, and green, and carried longbows. Once in Col's presence, they each fell to one knee until he bade them rise.

"Do you wish to join us?" Col asked.

"We've been sent to guide you, my lord Colberane," said the elder of the two men. "The people of the Southern Forest have been told of your coming, and the forces are gathering. Their chiefs await you in the Green Court."

"What's your strength?"

"Over a thousand bowmen, my lord, and more arriving every hour."

"And how far is it to the Green Court?"

"At a steady pace we'll be there before sundown tomorrow."

"I have eight hundred with me, and children among them. How are they to keep the pace you set?"

"We will assist them," the elder forester assured him.

Col dismissed the two and gave orders that they be fed. He summoned Goodbowe and had him question the guides closely, to make certain that they were trustworthy, and then had Kinnaury and Mullerin organize the people for the march. Goodbowe returned to him with assurances, and they were soon on their way.

The trail was narrow and ran straight as a staff through dense forest, like a corridor roofed in pale green glass. Other men clad in the same tricolored garments joined them along the way, slipping unobtrusively from the forest to take a place in the line of march. Col noticed that the mixed colors of their clothing made them almost invisible against the forest background; these men were more than foresters, he surmised—they were hunters and warriors.

The mistlanders, long unaccustomed to walking, were hard put to maintain the pace. The newcomers offered welcome assistance. They took mistland infants in their arms, lifted weary children to their shoulders, or slung bundles on their backs. Even under these extra burdens, they moved with swift, sure strides along their familiar path. The mistlanders took heart from their example.

The trail widened as they moved southward. Side branches were seen more frequently. Late on the second day of travel, their guides called a halt at one of these forkings.

"The Green Court is a short way down this path, my lord," said the elder guide. "I'll take you there."

"What of the others?"

"A campground has been prepared for them near the next fork. My son will lead the way."

Placing Goodbowe, Kinnaury, and Mullerin in charge of the band, Col took his place at the guide's left hand, while Ord stepped to his right. They proceeded up the grassy path, which rose slightly, then dipped, and at last opened on a clearing, a rough circle about six marks in diameter, overshadowed by the high interlacing branches of a ring of ancient oaks. A dozen men awaited them. All carried longbows, and all were dressed in garments of the same pied stuff as the guide, but of a different cut.

The brothers came part way into the clearing and stopped. Their guide stepped to one side, and the men in the clearing made no move nor any sound. Suddenly wary of betrayal, Col and Ord drew their swords.

The brothers were covered with the dust of the trail. Their boots were filthy, their clothing worn and patched. Fatigue was drawn on their faces, but their naked swords shone forth like the sun and the moon to proclaim them. At sight of the blades, all the foresters fell to their knees.

Col bade them rise, and at his word they climbed to their feet and gathered around the brothers. The silence was ended. Now they chattered like children, and the clearing was filled with their excited voices.

"It is Colberane Whitblade! The Master of the Southern Forest is come at last!" one forester exclaimed.

"And the Scarlet Ord!" said another.

"They come on the day foretold."

"And at the very hour!"

There were bright smiles on the weather-beaten faces of these forest men, and in their voices were hope and joy and wonder. Out of the legends of their childhood had stepped two men, bringing liberation from the generations of fear. One prophecy had come true; surely this was only the beginning. The new age was here.

In the exuberance of the welcome, neither the foresters nor the brothers noticed the first shimmering in the air at the center of the clearing. Then the air grew bright, and they turned and were silent. The brightness increased and became dazzling, and they were forced to turn away or to cover their eyes. A great wind poured from the light, driving the leaves before it, tossing the branches overhead, whipping their cloaks around them. Then the wind died, and all was still. The Dark Prophet stood before them.

This time, to Col and Ord, she appeared smaller and less forbidding, but she was all the more welcome. While the foresters stood transfixed, the brothers ran to her.

"Tell us of Staver! Do you know anything about him?" Col cried, and Ord, at the same time, asked, "What of Staver? Where is he?"

"Staver is where he must be. He has his work, as you have yours," the hooded figure replied.

"Surely you can tell us more than that," Col said.

"Of Staver I can say no more."

"Then speak of us and of our mission. We've done as you told us—come south and gathered nearly two thousand fighting men. But whom do we fight, and where, and when? You promised to tell us more when we next met."

"I shall, this very night." The obscuring hood turned toward Col, and a pale hand rose to point at his chest. "You will learn your role in this undertaking before you rest."

"And what of me?" Ord asked.

"Your trial lies ahead. And last of all, the boy's. You will learn what you must when you must."

Ord was dissatisfied with the response but said nothing. There seemed little to be achieved by making demands of a prophet. Even if one forced out answers, they were sure to be so cryptic and evasive as to be no better than silence.

The Dark Prophet seemed to sense Ord's feelings. Turning to him, she said in a gentler voice, "For your own sakes, I tell you as little as I dare. The greater your knowledge, the greater the danger."

"From whom?"

"From the Cairnlord and his minions."

The foresters had gathered around the prophet. When she spoke that name, they glanced at one another nervously and drew together near their newfound leaders. She turned full upon them. The face deep within that dark hood was a pale blur, but each man felt her eyes burn on him as if he stood alone before her.

"You are wise to fear the name of the thing that has held this land in terror for generations," said the Dark Prophet to the foresters. "But a promise was made long ago, and now that promise is fulfilled. The time has come to strike back against the Cairnlord, and your leader is among you." She beckoned Col closer. "Give this man your trust. Counsel him well, obey his commands, and follow wherever he leads. With him begins the downfall of the Cairnlord. Go now and bid your men prepare for battle. Have the guide remain. I must speak with these two at length."

The foresters left, fading into the deepening twilight and leaving only the solitary guide at the entry to the Green Court. The Dark Prophet sat on a stone, and the brothers took their places on the soft grass at her feet.

"Two nights from now there will be no moon and a cloudy sky. Then you must lead your forces against the citadel on the lake isle," she said to Col.

"I know nothing of war and battle. How can I attack a citadel?"

"Trust the forest chieftains. Let them organize your woodwards and the mistlanders as they have organized their own men, and have them train your followers. They know this forest and they know the citadel. Listen to all that they can tell you and then make your plans."

Col sighed. "Is this what it means to be a great leader, then? Simply to listen to others?"

"Yes. It is a wisdom the Cairnlord has forgotten, and it will be his downfall."

"Why are we the ones chosen to fight him? A month ago we had no idea that he existed, and now we're preparing to attack one of his strongholds. Why?"

The Dark Prophet was silent for a time, as if pondering that question. At last, in a voice softer than they had ever heard her use before, almost like a mother speaking to her children, she said, "A month ago, the Cairnlord was unaware of you. You were still safe on the Headland, and there seemed to be time to lay careful plans before calling you forth. Ciantha had gone away years before to mislead and confuse the Cairnlord, and she succeeded. Only last summer did he begin to suspect Vannen's importance. At once he sent Aoea, the windwraith, to drown Vannen in a storm on Bounty Bay. But the amulet warned Vannen, and he escaped. Then the Cairnlord sent a greater power, Hane of the Withering Touch, and Vannen was overcome."

"Who was Vannen that the Cairnlord should wish him dead?" Ord asked.

"Your mother and father were descendants of the line of Ambescand. His blood is in your veins, just as it is in the steel of your blades, along with his power."

"But his power has done nothing for us, prophet! We're still ordinary men, whatever these southern people think

of us. We have no power to match against a sorcerer's,"
Col protested.

"Are you so ordinary? You have heard the voice of the
waters and used their warning to bring your people safely
out of mistlands. And you, Ord, have listened to the
voice of Earth and found the way across the Fissure. Are
these the deeds of ordinary men?"

"No . . . but I never thought . . . I believed it was
the power of the amulet that Vannen gave us," Col said.

"It was the amulet, and your ancestry, and the swords
of Ambescand, and other forces all working together that
changed you from what you were to what you are. And
the change will go on and make you ever more dangerous
to the Cairnlord. Now he thinks of you as adventurers
who might prove annoying but no real threat to him. Once
he learns who you truly are—and what you represent—
he will turn all his power against you. This is why you
must move quickly and seize the citadel to be both your
refuge and a rallying place for all who oppose him."

"If he doesn't know who we are, why did he send the
gray men against us?" Ord asked.

"He knows only of your father's ancestry. He believes
that your mother was a Headland peasant. He felt it
prudent to rid himself of your family but not a great
necessity. When the gray men failed, he sent Darra Jhan,
the Rouser of Envy, to incite Staver to fratricide. And
when that failed, he again called forth Aoea to raise the
storm on the Fool's Head. Now, because you have followed my instructions and moved south undetected, he
believes you dead. His attention is elsewhere, and you
have the chance to attack the citadel against the opposi-
tion of mere mortals unaided by his sorcery."

Col looked at her with worry in his expression. "What
if he learns of the attack and sends things against us? Not
gray men but other things that we can't fight with a sword
. . . things to turn our minds, or strike us down with fever,
or raise a great storm?"

"I think it unlikely. The citadel is well garrisoned and
strong, and the Cairnlord does not employ his power un-
necessarily. Sorcery is not a gift, Col. It is earned hard
and purchased dearly. Sorcery always exacts a price from
those who use it, and the Cairnlord is already profligate

with his magic. It cost him much to raise Aoea and Darra Jhan from among the lost spirits, where they have wandered since the people of the High City tore them to bits upon Ambescand's return, and he will avoid depleting his powers further unless he perceives a personal threat."

Her words stirred Ord's memory. He thought for a moment, then asked, "Those things—the wizards who roused envy and caused storm and death—are they the ones who rose against Ambescand?"

"They are what remains of them. Out of the company of the twelve sorcerers, eleven joined the conspiracy against Ambescand. Seven of these were slain by the people, and four were broken by Ambescand but later revived by the Cairnlord. In time of need, he can summon the spirits of the lost seven to do his bidding, but it draws upon his power, and for this we must be grateful. If he were to call up Taerhael the Beclouder, or Jashoone of the Frost and Flame, or the Twister of Bones, or the Earthshaker, our cause would be in great peril. You are not yet ready to withstand such forces," said the Dark Prophet.

There in the fading light, Col and Ord exchanged a glance. Ord gripped the black hilt of his sword, as if to reassure himself.

Col asked, "Will we ever be able to withstand such things?"

"One day you must, or the Cairnlord will reign forever," the Dark Prophet replied.

"Tell me, then—after the citadel, what awaits us?"

"When the citadel falls, you, Colberane, will have come into your kingdom. Only one more deed will be asked of you in these times."

"And what of me?" Ord asked.

"Your time is fast approaching. Your weakness will be your strength, and your vice will become virtue to bring you to your kingdom."

"I don't understand that at all."

"When you must understand, you will. Meanwhile, support your brother, and help him with all your heart. There is a task and a time for each of you, and in his appointed moment, each will need the others."

"Staver, too?" Col asked.

"Staver most of all."

"How is he? Where is he? When will we—"

"No more," the Dark Prophet said, rising. "I must leave you. Rejoin your men, and remember what I said. Trust your loyal followers and listen to their advice when you decide—but always act on your own judgment." She walked to the center of the clearing, to the place where she had appeared. "I will be with you after the battle," she said.

All around her the air was filled with light. She seemed to shrink and waver, and the light grew brighter and brighter until their eyes could not bear it. Then a great wind rushed past them into the light, and then there was nothing but darkness and silence and night in the Green Court.

14

The Storming of the Citadel

Deep in the forest the woodsmen assemble—
Raise high the axe! Bare the blade and the spear!
Now let the ancestral enemy tremble—
The leader has come, and the battle draws near!

—War chant of the foresters

Later that night, in a shelter near the encampment, Col met with the twelve chiefs of the southern foresters. The shelter was small and crude, and the dim light of the fire did little more than cause his tired eyes to burn. But he listened carefully, and questioned closely, and learned much.

For years these men had lived as hunted fugitives in their own homeland, victims of random raids by the Cairnlord's followers and in constant danger from the gray men. They had learned to organize and train others; to survive in the forest; to move great distances quickly and quietly on an instant's notice; to spy on their enemy and learn his movements and his strength while remaining themselves unseen; to protect and provide for their families in a time and place where there was no safe refuge and no hope of sanctuary. Now they placed themselves and their forces under Col's banner, trusting him to restore their lost freedom as he won back the lost throne of his forebears.

The foresters were organized into groups of twelve, which served as the basic units of foraging, hunting, and fighting. Each group selected one from among them to be their leader, and these leaders, in full assembly, chose twelve from their number to be chiefs. Col saw the wisdom and efficiency of such organization at once; it was what he had been groping toward when he allowed Goodbowe, Kinnaury, and Mullerin to attend to the daily needs of their band. Ord had perceived that. But neither of them had grasped the underlying principle. The Dark Prophet had advised well: Col resolved to group the woodwards and mistlanders along these lines in the morning.

It soon became clear to him that there was a larger and more important task: their combined force, nearly two thousand at that point and increasing every hour, had to be organized in such a way as to turn their differences to advantage. The men of the Southern Forest were skilled with the longbow; the mistlanders used the pike and the dagger; the woodwards of Long Wood fought with the axe and the shortbow. The mistlanders could fight best on water, while the men of the forests excelled as land skirmishers in small parties. Woodwards and mistlanders were armed for close combat; the foresters' weapons were most effective from a distance. All these skills had to be balanced and properly combined to form the most effective fighting force and to compensate for their lack of swordsmen and siege machinery, and their ignorance of battle tactics. No man in all that mass had ever partaken in an assault on a fortified castle or even dreamed of such an undertaking. And yet in another day and a night, they would be moving against the citadel on the lake isle.

Fortunately they were not attacking in total ignorance of their enemy. The foresters kept the citadel under close observation and maintained communication with comrades forced to labor within the walls. One of the chiefs, Bolter, a stout, bald man with a coppery beard, produced a carefully drawn map of the citadel and spread it out where Col could study it in the dim light. With a broad blunt finger, he pointed out the details for Col to follow.

The citadel stood on a rise at the southeast corner of the isle, of which it occupied about one-twentieth of the total land area. It had two main entrances and three smaller sally ports. The entrance most frequently used was that which opened on the long ramp leading up from the fields on the island where most of the food was grown. The second main entrance was on the lake and was used primarily to bring in supplies that had been carried through the forest. Any visitors to the citadel debarked on a stone pier and entered by the ramp gate.

Col looked over the map carefully and then asked Bolter, "How are the ports defended?"

"Drawbridge over the ramp and a portcullis beyond. Towers for archers on both sides. The lake port is blocked by a portcullis, too, and the passage is so narrow a few men can defend it," Bolter replied.

"What about the sally ports?"

"A guard behind a bolted gate at each one. Any man trying to reach one of those sally ports is in full view of the towers. No cover at all."

"So all five entrances are impregnable. Are there any other ways in and out? Drains? Sewers?"

"They're so heavily barred, we couldn't cut through them in a month, even if we could work unseen and undisturbed."

Col nodded and looked once again at the map. "Can the walls be scaled?"

Bolter's eyes grew bright, and he said, "We believe they can, my lord. This wall, here, on the lake."

The broad finger rested on a wall adjoining a corner tower. It rose sheer from the lake to the battlements, ten marks and more of blank stone.

"It's the only blind spot in the defenses," Bolter said. "The original builders made the walls so smooth, a spider couldn't have climbed to the top, and the present masters have so little fear of an attack from any quarter that they guard it lightly and neglect to inspect it. But there's been settling, and weathering, and now there are handholds and footholds. It's a dangerous climb, but we have men who can make it."

"If one man can get to the top and fix lines, we can bring enough inside to take the towers and open the sally ports. What's the strength of the garrison?"

A small, wiry man named Hawkitts said, "Two hundred men-at-arms and about four hundred archers at present, my lord. The men-at-arms carry longswords or axes and wear body armor. They'd cut us to pieces in close combat."

"Then we must avoid close combat. Is their armor proof against the longbow?"

"If we get within ten marks, my lord, we can put an arrow through them and out the other side," said a third chief.

"Good. But we can't let you get too close. Archers would be helpless confronting swordsmen hand to hand. You need a guard," Col said. A strategy was beginning to form in his mind as he visualized the assault, and the outlines of a battle plan grew clearer. "The mistlanders are skilled pikemen. If they were to form a line ahead of the archers, to hold off the men-at-arms, then the longbows could be used in safety."

"They have archers, too, my lord Colberane, who could attack our pikemen while our own archers are attacking their men-at-arms," Hawkitts pointed out.

"But our archers outnumber theirs three to one. Theirs would be forced to fight from cover. And if we can get my woodwards into their midst, to use their axes, we'd end the threat of those archers."

"What of gray men?" Hawkitts asked.

"How many are there?"

"That we do not know. Gray men come and go, and their arrivals and departures are mysterious. There may be none at the citadel, or there may be a score of them."

"My brother and I have overcome gray men before. We'll see to any in the citadel," Col said. He looked to Ord, who patted the dark sword at his side and nodded placidly.

"Sensible tactics, my lord," said Bolter. "Let's study

the diagram more closely and see how we might work such a plan."

They remained in the shelter late into the night, discussing and deliberating. Goodbowe and Mullerin were roused from sleep and summoned to the council, and Kinnaury was called to join them soon after. Other men were brought to the leaders, questioned, and their information weighed and either added to the stock of ideas or discarded. Gradually a plan of action developed. It was challenged at every step, and either justified or amended, and it grew firmer with each testing. When the group separated, past the midpoint of the night, to get what sleep they could against the next day's demands, each one of those weary men knew his duties and his responsibilities in the assault, and all were certain that they had hammered out the best possible plan for taking the citadel.

Col, who had wrought the plan piece by piece and now held it in his mind like a complex tapestry with many threads but a single design, was sure that they would succeed. But words of the Dark Prophet came to his mind as he drifted off to sleep, and for a moment, he was troubled. Men would die. There was no escaping the fact. Men he had spoken with on this very evening; men he had marched and crossed the mistlands with; men who would scale the walls of the citadel with him and fight at his side; such, and many more, were sure to die. Others would be injured and maimed. Nothing he could do would prevent this.

But when Col remembered why these men were willing to risk their lives, the burden on his heart lifted. They were not dying at his bidding, to regain his throne. They faced death gladly, willingly, for their own dignity and for the good of their homeland and their loved ones. Col was their leader, acknowledged and acclaimed as such, but he led them not in a personal cause—not now, though he had once seen these people of the lands beyond the Fissure as no more than pawns in a game played for his own benefit. That kind of thinking was behind him. Now he was part of a greater cause, and he was as honored by his role as he had once felt himself to be honored by the promise of a kingdom.

* * *

They rose early the next morning, and Col at once set about organizing his followers into their fighting units. When this was done, he passed among the units, spoke with the men and women and their chosen leaders, and explained to them, simply and clearly, their role in the assault, its dangers, and its significance in the overall plan. Everywhere he was received with enthusiasm, and in all his followers he saw a courage that strengthened him.

In the mistland units women bore pikes beside the men. Among the foresters a few women were in the ranks of the archers, but none wielded an axe. The women who were not able to fight were given the task of rescuing and tending the wounded, and the oldest men were assigned to assist them. Children too young to bear arms were attached to each unit to serve as messengers. Everyone had a part to play in the assault, and each accepted the role willingly, for they knew that the battle had to be won. If they were defeated here, the hope of freedom from the Cairnlord's yoke was forever gone.

The rest of the day was given over to training, under the hard direction of seasoned foresters. The mistlanders and woodwards were clumsy at first, but their eagerness was unfailing. By nightfall they had mastered the rudiments of organized combat. They were still a long way from being a well-drilled and disciplined fighting force, but they were no longer a crowd of individuals or a cluster of disorganized groups. They were united, and they had come to respect and trust the strangers who fought at their side—and the man who led them.

The next day they trained again in the morning, then spent the rest of the afternoon on the march to their final encampment, which awaited them near the lake. They arrived at dusk.

After a final conference with the chieftains, Col ate and rested for a time. He was awakened late at night by his guard.

"A man named Warriner is just arrived, my lord, with another. He would speak with you," the guard said.

"Let him pass," Col said, rising and pulling on his boots. He stood, stretched, and rubbed his neck to drive away the fatigue. When he heard footsteps near, he straightened to receive the visitor.

"Welcome back, Warriner. We had feared you were lost," he said, extending his hand.

The woodward was covered with dust, and his face was clenched with the fight against his own weariness. Panting, breathless, he took his leader's hand in a grip that faltered, and Col quickly helped him to a seat against an oak tree.

"No sign. No trace of him, my lord. We searched the banks . . . all up and down. Found three bodies . . . but not the boys'," Warriner said.

"Thanks, Warriner. Staver and Jem will turn up. I'm sure of it."

"I'm sorry, my lord."

"You've had a hard trip."

Warriner shuddered. He shut his eyes and shook his head, as if to drive away a bad dream. "Western road around mistlands . . . safe no longer. Lost poor Netter to a thing . . . with great black wings. It came up from the water as we crossed a bridge . . . pulled him down."

"They attacked us, too."

"We taught them what an axe can do. Killed two of them," Warriner said, looking up with a hard light in his eyes.

"Goodbowe and I taught them a few things, too."

"Good work. Cairnlord's beasts, all of them."

"I don't think so. Not all the evil in this world is caused by the Cairnlord, though we might easily be persuaded that it is. No, I think the mistland things acted on their own." Col sighed and looked out at the dark encampment. "We'll make the world a better place when we overthrow the Cairnlord, but we won't make it perfect. Even Ambescand, with all his magic, couldn't do that. No man can."

Col glanced at Warriner and saw the man slumped forward in the deep sleep of exhaustion. He drew a cloak around the faithful woodward and told the guard to let him and his companion sleep until the last possible moment; then he pulled his own cloak close about his shoulders and walked into the encampment where his forces lay sleeping.

The night was moonless, as the Dark Prophet had promised, but the sky was still clear and bright with starlight. Col walked cautiously down the dim rows of sleepers. He passed unchallenged. The guards recognized him by his stature—in all the camp, only Kinnaury stood taller—and by the sword that shimmered at his side. He stopped to exchange a word or two with each guard and to clasp the man's hand in a gesture of reassurance and camaraderie.

Overhead, the stars were fainter now. Dumelian's Horn began to disappear from view as he watched, and one by one, the stars of the Callicrast winked out. This was no enchantment of the Cairnlord, he knew—not this time. There was good in this.

He felt his mouth suddenly dry and was aware of the quickening at his heart. The waiting was nearly over, and the battle was close at hand. He looked around, at shapes all but obscured in the deepening dark, and thought of his followers. Some who had watched the sun go down this day would see it rise no more. But those who lived would have taken the first step to freedom from the Cairnlord.

Col heard footsteps, turned, and saw the familiar stocky frame of Goodbowe, with Kinnaury towering close behind. Bolter soon joined them, and other chiefs, until the leadership was assembled. All around them, people were stirring, speaking in hushed and sleepy voices, weary still but full of expectancy. The night came to life. The sky was fully dark. It was time to set out on the last march.

They moved in silence along a smooth, well-marked trail. The foresters, who could follow the trail with ease even in the blackest night, led the way and caught up the stragglers. At the edge of the forest they separated, and the great mass of foresters moved westward to prepare for the crossing to the tip of the island, where the underwater barricade had been weakened earlier that night by an advance unit and where no guards stood on watch. Col and Ord led a small force eastward, to the mouth of a stream that fed into the lake nearly opposite the wall they were to scale. The current could be trusted to carry them noiselessly to their destination.

Three volunteers stripped off their cloaks and boots and laid long coils of rope atop a thick tangle of branches floating in the stream. They carried no weapons but a dagger and a sling.

"It's up to you now," Col said. "Good luck to you all."

"We'll do our best, my lord," their leader said.

"We know you will. We'll leave when we get your signal."

They slipped into the water and worked their way into the branches. Casting off, they floated out into the lake, and then followed the current to the rocks at the base of the wall.

The others, while they waited, assembled similar crude rafts to hold their weapons and provide concealment during the crossing. Col paced about impatiently, ever returning to the water's edge to peer into the darkness where the wall loomed like a shadow some fifty marks away.

Then he heard the plunk of a stone in the water nearby; and again, and still again, a stone plummeted from the air and sank into the lake. That was the signal they had been awaiting. All three had made the climb successfully. The ropes were affixed, and the way was open. Col threw off his cloak and undid his sword belt. Goodbowe seized his arm.

"No, Col! You must not risk it now—let others go ahead," the woodward said.

Col shook his hand off. "There'll be no argument about who leads this assault. The men say I was sent to lead them. Very well, then—I shall."

"But the danger!"

Col laid his hand on Goodbowe's shoulder and looked the older man in the eye. "You told me I was invincible. Well, I've come to believe that. And you must believe it yourself, now."

"I do. But if anything should happen . . ."

"If those men reach the top and come upon one of the men-at-arms, they'll be cut down without a chance. They need a swordsman to protect them."

"Protect yourself, Col. We need you."

"Life is sweeter and more precious to me at this moment than it is to any follower of the Cairnlord. I'll not have it taken from me, Goodbowe. Believe that."

Goodbowe said nothing more. He embraced Col, then stepped aside to let him pass. Ord followed his brother.

They fixed their swords in the thick green tangle of their makeshift raft and pushed off into the lake, drifting with the current. They soon reached the base of the wall, where they found three ropes dangling within easy reach. As they climbed, two more ropes were lowered, and by the time they reached the top, others had started up below them.

The brothers slipped through the crenels and onto the platform. To their great satisfaction they found that this platform was unusually broad: it ran a half-mark from the battlements to the edge, with a knee-high stone ledge at the rear that offered concealment as well as protection, and turned the situation much in the attackers' favor. Clearly no one in the castle's history had ever considered the possibility of an attack from this direction.

Slowly, silently, with great care, the assault force gathered on the platform. Pikes and axes, carefully wrapped in cloaks to muffle them against a chance blow in climbing, were lifted over the battlements and unbound. Bows were strung, and arrows laid out close to hand. Men took their weapons and moved into position as smoothly as if they were performing long accustomed actions.

They were on the highest and broadest platform in the castle. As Col's eyes adjusted to the darkness, he could see that from here, he commanded the main gate and the greater part of the courtyard. The only places from which the citadel's archers could shoot down on them were the towers that stood at the junctures of the walls. Those towers had to be taken. The archers of the Southern Forest could then hold this position, guarded by ten pikemen at either end of the platform. There was no other way of approach.

With the archers crouched in a line behind the rear ledge and the pikemen in position at both of the stone staircases, Col and Ord moved out to secure the towers, each with a team of axemen and archers.

The habit of unchallenged mastery had made the guards fatally careless. One by one, the towers fell with brief struggle and so little noise that the others were not roused. In each tower were stationed two archers and an axeman, with orders to bar the doors and hold out to the death.

With the last tower taken, Col wiped his sword clean and reviewed the plan of battle. All had gone perfectly so far. By now the main force would be crossing the lake. On so dark a night they stood a good chance of reaching the walls before they were seen and the alarm was given. In those first frenzied seconds, when the defenders were running about half-awake and confused, the little band of archers inside the walls could decide the outcome of the battle. Col felt his hopes rise, and had to force himself to remember that they were still but a small force in the enemy's stronghold, outnumbered and outweaponed. Their only advantages were position and surprise. If the castle guardians should be roused too soon, before the full attacking force could arrive, the invaders would be in grave danger.

He studied, unnoticed, the four men with him, who were going intently about their tasks. A few days before, they had been strangers to one another; now they shared a bond as close, in its way, as brotherhood. They relied on one another for their lives. Wherever they went after this battle, whatever paths their lives followed, however long or short the future lay before them, they would remember this night and those who stood by their sides in battle. Tonight would change them all.

Col reflected on how greatly he himself had changed in such a short time. At first he had not really wanted to leave the Headland. The thought of being head of the family and master of Vannen's holding, wearing a magnificent blade at his side and hefting gold in his hand while the Headlanders who had once scoffed at him and his brothers now looked on enviously, had been a tempting one. If not for Ord's taunting and Staver's surprising firmness, he might well have stayed at home. Even in the

Fissure he had wavered and had been prepared to turn back.

Once across, though, all thought of the Headland had vanished from his mind, like so much dust blown from a smooth tabletop. Once they met the woodwards and heard the words of the Dark Prophet, his thoughts had turned to the kingdom that lay before him, not the life he had left behind.

And now, when he was preparing to seize his kingdom, all that really mattered to him was the welfare of his followers. He wanted to win this battle to prove himself to them and then go on to rule them wisely and benevolently. If he could learn to lead in war, he could also learn to lead them in peaceful ways and to help make a better life for those who had staked everything on their faith in him.

Col waited, silent, until he judged that sufficient time had passed for the main army to be on its way; then he rose, took up his sword, and beckoned to one of the three archers to follow him. The last and most dangerous step of their plan lay before them.

In the wall below was a sally port. It had to be taken and opened for the main force, and secured until their arrival. Since the inner gate opened on the courtyard near the troops' quarters, there was greater danger of discovery in this part of the mission than in any other—thus it was put off for as long as they dared. Now it could be postponed no longer.

Wrapped in cloaks taken from the fallen guards, cowls pulled well forward to hide their features, Col and the archer, a young man named Habeshaw, slipped from the tower, crossed the platform, and made their cautious way down the narrow steps to the courtyard. Silence lay all around them, and the darkness was broken only by a line of light under the door of a long, low barracks close to the wall and by the lantern glow from the tower windows and the inner door of the sally port, which stood open just a crack.

With his sword drawn, Col pushed open the door. Habeshaw stood behind him, an arrow nocked and ready. Light spilled forth, and Col eased forward and looked inside.

"Ellart? Is that you, Ellart?" said a gruff, irritable voice. "Come in, you idiot, before I drag you in."

Col dashed inside. Behind him, Habeshaw swung the door shut and slid the bolt into place. Before the guard could rise from his stool, Col's blade was at his throat.

"Don't kill me!" the guard said, his wide, terrified eyes on Col's, his hands flat on the table.

"Who's Ellart? When is he coming back?" Col said.

"He's the other guard."

Col urged the sword point so it depressed the flesh of the guard's throat but did not break it. "When is he returning?"

"Maybe not tonight. He took sick, went to the barracks. It was a while ago."

"Who else is here?"

"No one," the guard said.

Keeping his sword at the throat of the guard, who remained rigid as a wooden image on his stool, Col made a quick visual inspection of the little chamber. Walls and floor were bare stone. Opposite the door through which he had entered was another door, larger and more heavily built, bolted at top and bottom. This was the sally port. By the stone fireplace, in which a fire burned low, stood the table and two stools. Beside the fireplace was an archway that opened into blackness; in the opposite wall was a larger archway through which the firelight fell on stone steps.

"What's up there?" Col said, pointing to the steps.

"Inner passage to the archers' ports."

"There?" Col indicated the dark archway.

The guard hesitated a moment, then said, "Storeroom."

Col was about to give Habeshaw the order to bind the prisoner when he heard a faint scuffling sound from the storeroom. He turned, bringing his sword around. The guard acted at once, slamming his heavy fist into the pit of Col's stomach, doubling him up. As he raised his stool to smash Col's skull, Habeshaw loosed an arrow. The guard gave a low gurgling sound, like a cough, and clawed at the arrow that transfixed his throat.

Col pulled himself erect, gasping. The guard fell to his knees, blood spurting from his mouth. He looked up at Col with wild, white-ringed eyes, then pitched forward on the stone floor. Habeshaw came to Col's side and took his arm to steady him.

"I'm all right now. Thanks, Habeshaw."

"He took me by surprise," the bowman said.

"Me, too. Nearly had me. But you got him."

"Yes, I—"

Habeshaw sprang back, fitted an arrow to his bow, and let fly in a single smooth flow of motion. Col followed the arrow flight to the dark archway. He saw the missile strike the chest of a gray man and shatter as if it had hit the stone wall of the chamber.

This gray man carried the same long hook-bladed weapon as the others. It moved forward in a deliberate shuffle, like a sleepwalker. A second arrow splintered against its cheek, and it turned its blank gray eyes on Habeshaw.

Col stepped before it, sword held level, the burning pain in his stomach forgotten in the face of this new danger. The stony eyes fell upon him. The gray man raised its weapon and struck down hard.

Col caught the blow on his blade, turning it. The shock stung his hand and sent a jolt up his arm. Before he could strike a blow of his own, the gray man swung again. Col took a step back, and the gray man lurched in pursuit, bringing the long hooked blade around and down.

Col retreated another step and came up hard against the table. He jumped aside, and the gray man's blow splintered the heavy planking. The hooked blade lodged in the table momentarily.

Col snatched the lantern from the tabletop and flung it against the gray man's chest. Oil splattered over the creature, blazed up in ribbons of flame, and turned the gray man into a walking torch. It tugged the blade free, brushed the table aside, and shuffled forward as if Col had done no more than fling dust in its face.

Col gripped his sword with both hands. The gray man came on, and Col felt the heat of the flames on his face. The hooked blade descended, and Col brought his sword around and down, severing its sword arm above the elbow.

The creature stood rigid. Col could not understand how it still withstood the flames; and then he remembered that the other two had been beheaded before fire took effect on them.

The gray man dropped his blank gaze to the floor, where its severed arm still gripped the weapon. Habeshaw's third arrow rebounded from between the creature's shoulders. Ignoring the blow, it stooped, and as its flame-encased head lowered, Col moved in and struck it from the gray man's neck. The creature toppled forward, inert, and fell on its side, burning. Habeshaw took up another lantern and flung it on the fallen thing, sending up a bright burst of flame.

Habeshaw drew back from the heat. He turned and looked at Col in wonder. "You slew a gray man," he said.

"I did it noisily, I fear."

Habeshaw ran to the inner door to see if anyone had been roused by the sounds of the conflict. Col leaned against the wall, breathing deeply. He felt as if a giant hand inside him were clenched on his vitals. He pressed on his stomach and winced.

"I see nothing, my lord. They seem not to have heard," Habeshaw said, securing the peephole.

"If they can sleep through—"

Col was interrupted by a cry from a far part of the courtyard. More shouts broke out, then a bell began clanging. Col and Habeshaw flattened themselves against the wall beside the door. The shouting grew louder, and a group of men ran past the door with the heavy, clanking tread of armored warriors.

"It's not for us. It's the attack!"

Col dashed to the sally port. Beyond, in the vague murkiness of the water's edge, he could faintly distinguish figures moving. Loosening the bolts, he opened the door wide and beckoned them on.

In the opening moments of the battle, the defenders of the citadel seemed to be in a hopeless position. Roused by an alarm that had never rung before, they found an enemy within the walls of their stronghold. They ran, helpless and confused, from one peril to another. Doors were bolted against their passage; towers and parapets were manned by hostile bowmen secure behind a bristling shield of pikestaffs. Death was all around them.

A third of the defenders fell in those first turbulent minutes. Even breastplates and mailshirts were no protection against those arrows, longer than a man's arm, that hummed out of the darkness and struck down men on all sides. Death from nowhere, dealt wholesale by an enemy who could not be reached, threw them into disarray and threatened to demoralize them completely.

But the defenders held. They pulled back to where those deadly arrows could not reach them and took time to study the situation. The attackers hammering at the gates were a band of outlaw rabble with not one man in armor among them. Marksmen were within the walls, but there could be no more than twoscore or so all told; had there been a stronger force, the defenders would have been wiped out. The castellan heard his lieutenants and agreed: though the situation was bad, it need get no worse. A direct strike at the archers who held the north wall would be costly, but it was necessary. The danger within had to be rooted out, and then the mob at the gates could be cut down like ripe wheat.

Under a steady protective hail of arrows from their own archers, the men-at-arms moved along the walls, dodging from shadow to shadow. Five more fell on the way. At the foot of the steps they massed, and at a signal they rushed up both sides to slash at the wall of thrusting pikes. In the melee of struggling bodies, the invaders were forced to loose their shafts with caution, for fear of hitting their own pikemen, while the castle archers poured arrows on the parapet without hindrance.

The first rush brought the armored men nearly to the top, but a counterthrust by the pikemen drove them off. For a time both forces waited, regrouping, counting their losses.

The stone steps were cluttered with dead and dying. On the parapet half the forest bowmen had fallen to the arrows of the defenders. Five pikemen held one end of the platform, and four survived at the other.

In the first faint morning light the defenders saw the pitiful size of the force that stood against them and were roused to rage at their own earlier disarray and failure. They gathered for one final rush, vowing to sweep the enemy from the platform or die in the attempt—but never to be driven back by these forest vermin.

Then rose a great cry among the bowmen in the court-yard, as ragged figures poured into the castle through the sally ports and closed with them, slashing with axes and thrusting with pikestaffs at the bowmen who milled in panic, unable to use their weapons and unable to flee from the mob that flowed like a murderous tide around them.

The marksmen on the parapet were forgotten as the armored men charged into the wild struggle, slashing at every man not dressed in the livery of their master. Even here, the detestable pikemen were in the way, fending them off, driving them back out of sword's reach, while the axemen hacked a swath through their milling arch-ers. But pikes could be battered aside by a heavy sword; and once within reach, a pikeman was as easily spitted as a straw dummy.

The swordsmen, safe behind their armor from thrusting pikes, wrought great slaughter among the invaders. Even the axemen gave ground before them. And yet their ene-mies still swarmed about them. For each attacker a swordsman cut down, another appeared. And now the surviving handful of archers on the parapet began to pick away at the armored men, and others in the towers and among the invaders from the sally ports joined them. The range was now too great for all those long shafts to pierce armor, and most of the arrows glanced harmlessly aside. But some drove into flesh and bone: every joint in the armor was vulnerable; legs and forearms were un-protected; faces were exposed; and in the growing light, the aim of the bowmen was deadly.

At the height of the battle in the castle yard, the de-fenders of the main gate were overrun. The drawbridge crashed down, the portcullis was forced up, and a shout-ing band of foresters poured in to rally their bloodied comrades.

Now the fall of the citadel seemed assured, and the price of victory was clear: there would be no surrender, and the Cairnlord's followers would fight until the last man had struck his dying blow. The stronghold on the lake isle could be purchased only with lives.

Fewer than a hundred men-at-arms still lived, and about the same number of bowmen. They drew together into a solid mass and smashed their way to the keep to make a final stand. Fully a third of their number fell in the attempt. When they reached their goal, their track was littered with fallen men and bright with blood.

Col and Ord had been everywhere that day, it seemed —and always where the battle was most fierce. Now they were at the head of their men, on the heels of the retreating enemy. They wielded their swords as fiercely as ever, even as their stomachs revolted at the carnage.

Inside the keep two men-at-arms turned to confront Ord. He brought his blade down on the helmet of one, staggering him, then turned to block the slash that the other aimed at his knee. Disengaging, he swung in a downward arc, stepping into the blow, driving the swordsman back with blow after blow until a rush of his own men drove them apart and swarmed over his opponent. All around him, steel rang on steel like the hammering in a hellish forge.

Col fought his way to the steps where a knot of men-at-arms had rallied around the castellan. Waving his axmen back, he lowered his sword and addressed the enemy chief.

"Surrender and your lives will be spared. We have no wish to slay you," he said.

"Our lives belong to the Cairnlord," the castellan replied.

"Your master places little value on them, to let you die like this."

"We die a worse death if we surrender."

"You'd be spared. You have my word."

A hoarse bark of laughter burst from within the castellan's obscuring helmet. "You might spare us. The Cairnlord spares no one."

The castellan sprang forward, cutting at Col's neck, and Col heard the blade shear through the air as he ducked under the blow. He brought his own sword around in a level swing, with both hands, and felt it grate through armor and bone. He twisted the blade and jerked it free. The castellan dropped his sword, staggered, and as the blood poured from his side, he took two lurching steps, like a gray man, and then pitched forward.

Arrows zipped past Col, and his axemen charged into the men-at-arms. Another armored man stepped forward to take his fallen leader's place, and as Col engaged him, a second attacked from the side. Col felt a sharp blow on his arm—but no pain—and circled quickly to put his first attacker in the way of the second.

Around him all had grown quiet. As he slashed, parried, and beat at the two swordsmen, he realized that they were the last two enemies still erect and fighting.

Then Ord was at his side, drawing the second assailant away, and he was left with a single opponent. The swordsman retreated up the stone steps, slowly, until they were on the upper platform. Col felt a stab of pain in his arm, glanced down, and saw his hand dripping blood. The swordsman drove at his chest, dropping low and thrusting the sword upward. Col struck it aside and brought his own blade full across the man's helmet, cleaving it to the nosepiece. The battle for the citadel was over.

The fallen swordsman's blade clattered down the steps, and then all was still. Col turned to face the men below. He raised the bright blade, brandished it high, and shouted, "We've won! The Cairnlord's citadel is ours!"

For a moment Col's followers could not grasp what he had said. Battle weary, bloodied, some badly wounded, they could scarcely believe that their hope had come about. The years of resignation were now swept aside as fulfillment of the dream of generations was upon them. A cry went up, and grew, and soon echoed off the stone walls of the keep.

Col made his way slowly down the steps. The battle done, he felt suddenly weary and drained of strength. He was swept up by his exultant followers when he reached the bottom, but he was aware only of a mass of faces, milling figures, and reaching hands. He made his way outside. Men poured out of the keep to surround him, shouting his name.

Ord suddenly appeared. His face was bruised, and his

lips were bloody. He limped slightly but seemed otherwise uninjured and quite cheerful.

"Nice work, brother," Ord said. "I never saw you use a sword as you did this day."

"I never had as good a reason."

They looked at one another, panting, breathless, exhausted, and exchanged a broad grin. It was hard to put their feelings into words.

"That's a bad gash on your arm," Ord said.

"I'll have it looked after. What happened to your face?"

"Fellow butted me with his helmet. Had me dazed. Kinnaury took care of him before he could finish me."

"How is Kinnaury? How are the others?"

"Kinnaury's whole. Goodbowe took an arrow in the leg, but he'll be all right. They were lucky. We lost a lot of men, brother."

Col looked at the bloodied, battered crowd that stood before them, and at the bodies that covered the ground. He nodded. "The Cairnlord's men fight to the death. I can't understand such loyalty to one so evil."

"Maybe they're afraid to die like Goss."

Col had to think for a moment to recall the incident in Long Wood. It seemed like something that had happened years ago in his life, in another world. He remembered the agonized face of the strangling man and knew what Ord had meant.

"Do you think so, Ord? What a terrible way to win loyalty!"

"But very effective. I wonder what he promises them. Well, no matter—we've beaten him." Ord laid a hand on his brother's shoulder and smiled. "You're Master of the Southern Forest now. Colberane Whitblade has come into his kingdom."

Col smiled back and was about to speak. Before he said a word, an arrow streaked from the parapet above the gate and sank deep into his chest. Before the archer could loose a second shaft at Ord, a storm of arrows had been released from the crowd, and the figure that toppled from the parapet, bow still in hand, bristled with arrows as thick as thorns on a witchfinger bush.

Col raised his blood-covered hand to touch the arrow

and looked at Ord with a dazed expression. In a faint voice he said, "I've come to my kingdom . . . to die, Ord. All this . . . only to die. . . ."

Ord caught his brother as he collapsed and laid him gently on the ground. Numb with the shock of sudden grief, he pulled a cloak over Col's still form. He looked upon Col, thus struck down, and thought of Staver missing, and Vannen dead, and he remembered the words of the Dark Prophet. She had said that a time would come when they would curse her name and her words. She had spoken truly, for as Ord fell on his knees beside his brother, he cursed the Dark Prophet through his tears with all the bitterness his soul could brew.

15

The Solitary Sorcerer

Staver came awake shivering. He climbed stiffly to his feet, hugging himself for warmth, but the night chill clung to his damp garments and the thin morning sunlight that sifted through the trees was insufficient to drive it off.

His boots squished with water when he put his full weight on them, and he stooped at once to pull them off. As he leaned forward, his sword swung around and unbalanced him. He snatched at a tree trunk to steady himself and brought down a shower of drops that set him to shivering anew.

Forgetting the boots for a moment, he looked miserably around to see if he was alone. He remembered Jem Underhill clutching at him as their boat overturned, but after that he recalled nothing. A dart of pain in his forehead made him wince. He brought up his hand, touched a tender lump the size of a small egg, and let out a yelp.

"Staver! My lord Staver!" cried a voice nearby, and with a great rustling and cracking, Jem burst into sight, blinking sleepily.

"Jem! Are there any others?"

"I saw none. I fear we're alone."

"Where are we? What happened?"

"Steersman brought the boat around, and a great wave took us broadside. Clean overturned, we were."

"I remember that," Staver said. "What then?"

"I saw you go down. You must have hit your head when we went over. I got hold of you, grabbed an oar, and started to kick for shore. All turned round we were, though, and the waves took us, and now we're on the far side of the Fool's Head, up north."

"Are you sure?"

"Oh, yes. At first light, I climbed a tree to get bearings. On the east bank, we are, on the forehead of the Fool. The mountains are a day's march to the east of us," Jem said.

"Is there a faring-house near?"

"None on this side. Cairnlord's men smashed them all."

"Did you see a sheltered clearing, then? We have to dry our clothing, and we don't dare light a fire," Staver said through chattering teeth.

"To the south and east there's a clearing on a hillside. We'll have sun all day."

"Let's go."

No path led through these woods, but the ground around the high old trees was free of undergrowth, and the two boys made fair progress, trotting along as much for warmth as for speed. The only obstructions they encountered were branches blown down by the storm and now and then a felled tree. Once on the hillside, in the mid-morning sun, they stripped off their wet garments and spread them out. Staver drove four branches into the ground and hung up their boots to drain and dry, while Jem foraged for breakfast.

Fed, warmed by the sun, his clothing drying under the clear blue sky, Staver pondered their next move. Everything was up to him now. Jem would do whatever he was told, but he would initiate nothing. He would not even offer suggestions. He looked to Staver for wisdom.

Staver did not feel at all wise, but he tried to be logical. It seemed pointless to search for the others. The two of them could cover very little ground, and they would be even worse off if they were separated. They dared not shout or light signal fires; the Eye of the Fool was too near.

The best course seemed to be to press south. If the others had escaped the storm, they were sure to head in that direction. And if Staver and Jem were the only survivors—awful as the thought was, it had to be confronted—then Staver had no choice but to proceed south and take up their mission alone. He could only hope that the forces rallied by the Dark Prophet would accept him, a boy, as their leader; and that he would somehow become worthy of the role.

The thought of the others all being lost plunged him into bitter gloom. Together they had overcome gray men, crossed the Fissure, and thrown off the beclouding power of magic. To do such deeds and then to die uselessly in a sudden storm was to be the victims of some merciless joke. The outlying world was not like the Headland, Staver was learning. The Headland was a good place, a comforting place, and Staver missed it sorely. The world beyond the Fissure was no world for him. It was a tangle of pitfalls and treachery and indifferent deadliness, and he wanted nothing more to do with it, as king or commoner. Such wild storms as last night's did not swoop out of nowhere to trouble Headland waters. Only once, last summer . . .

"Jem, do such storms come often?" Staver asked.

"That was no common storm, Lord Staver. It was sorcery brought that storm upon us, and no doubt."

"Why do you say that?"

"I saw the blue light. It rose from the Eye and flew above the water, and as it—"

"A blue light—a globe of light that moved freely?"

"Just that."

So the storm was the work of the Cairnlord. And if Col and Ord and the rest of that band of brave men were dead, their death was on the Cairnlord's head. Staver felt despair enfold him. What could he hope to do against such an opponent except throw away the lives of more good men? Had he and his brothers any right to ask these men to lay down their lives so that three

Headland adventurers could seize a kingdom? Their mission was surely wrong. If he persisted, he would be as evil as the Cairnlord.

A cloud drifted over the sun, and Staver hugged his shoulders against the sudden chill. His fingers touched the buried amulet. At once his mood grew brighter. His despair came to seem cowardly and his doubts, foolish. Let the Cairnlord raise storms—it would do him no more good than the sending of his gray assassins. Staver and Jem lived, and now Staver was sure that the others had survived, too, and were moving south to continue the struggle. It became clear to him that whatever he might want, he could not turn aside or retreat, only advance to the confrontation that awaited. The Cairnlord could defeat him only if he gave in and lost the will to resist.

"We're going south, Jem," Staver announced. "As soon as our things are dry, we'll be on our way."

"Right, my lord Staver."

"And until we're among friends, you'd best remember to call me Staver."

By late afternoon their clothing was dry. The boots were still damp and chafing to their feet, so they removed them and made their way barefoot along the leaf-cushioned forest floor. They had no trail nor markers to follow, but they knew that the wood here was a narrow strip, with the Fool's Head on their right and the river on their left. Though they might zigzag a bit, it would be nearly impossible for them to lose their direction completely.

They ate as they walked. That night they slept comfortably on a bed of leaves, with a blanket of fallen branches over them. At dawn they started on their way again.

Thus they went on for days. Their progress was slow. This portion of the wood had been badly battered by the storm. They climbed over scores of toppled trees. The ground was thick with broken branches that snared their ankles, and others dangled limp from splintered trunks, the newly exposed wood at their bases gleaming pale as flesh. Staver was idly remarking the destruction when a hoarse voice came into his head as clearly as if the speaker had been at his side.

Over here, you great ninny! Over here, you bone-headed bumpkin, here, by the fallen oak! Achalla and Ylveret, make the simpleton turn his empty head!

Staver halted in his tracks. This was not the mindless mumbling of ground-dwellers or the chatter of birds—it was a human voice, yet it came to him as the voices of animals had come before.

That's it, that's the way. . . . Stop, you mooncalf! Stop and look around! Oh, you great swaggering tat-terdemalion, look this way! Wrothag freeze his ears if he doesn't turn!

Jem caught up to Staver and stopped beside him. Staver swept the forest floor carefully with his glance but saw nothing among the dirt-clotted roots of the downed tree.

Two of them now. Two—and not half a brain be-tween them! Thickwit! Dumbbell! Here at the base, here, you ninnyhammers! Walk over here and look! Achalla, Ylveret, Wrothag, lead them to me and I'll see that your praises are sung by a thousand unborn generations. Don't let them pass and leave me!

Staver came closer, moving cautiously, and saw a flutter of motion among the meshed roots at the base of the oak. "It's all right. I see you now," he said.

He spoke! Can it be that . . . that this raggedy lum-mox, with a sword at his back too big for a grown man, understands me?

"Yes. Quite clearly," Staver replied.

The voice was silent. Staver came closer, parted the entangled roots, and there, glaring out at him with angry orange eyes, was an eagle owl. It was a big bird, a bit over a quarter-mark in height, and woefully bedraggled. Its loose, soft plumage was dirt-encrusted, and the black-and-tawny-and-buff feathers were all uniform muddy brown. Even the long ear tufts that curled hornlike over its eyes were matted and dirty. The bird's head was lowered, and its wings spread, drooping, one much lower than the other. Its habitually fierce expression was even fiercer, as if intensified by sheer humiliation and discomfort. From all appearances this was a very angry owl. Staver reached out slowly, carefully, to touch the creature.

"Careful," Jem warned.

"I'll be careful."

See that you are, boy. My wing's hurt. Easy there. Easy, you lout!

"It doesn't look as though it's broken."

I didn't say broken, I said hurt. Broken or not, I can't fly. You'll have to take me home.

"Is it far?"

No distance at all. Right on your way. I'll be eternally grateful.

"All right. I'll have to carry you. Ready?"

Staver slipped his arm under the owl and lifted it gently, supporting the heavy body with his other hand. The uninjured wing flapped indignantly several times, then both wings folded close and the bird leaned against Staver's chest.

Careful, now. Steady. Gently, gently!

"You're digging your talons into my arm!" Staver cried.

I don't want to fall.

"If you don't stop digging into my arm, I'll drop you!"

All right, boy, all right. I'm just taking precautions. Is that better?

The talons hooked in Staver's forearm relaxed, and the dirty, disheveled bird huddled closer. Staver sighed with relief. He brought his other hand under for added support.

"I'll be stopping from time to time. You're heavy."

It's dangerous in these woods by day.

"I know. But you're heavy, all the same. Now, where's your home?"

Head for the river. You have to cross the river and then go just a little way into the mountains.

"That's not on our way. You said your home was right on our way. We're going to the Southern Forest."

Then you have to cross the river. You're heading for the mistlands, boy. You wouldn't last a day in the mistlands. One of those great flapping black monsters would burst from the water and drag you under for dinner. Both of you.

Staver recalled words of the Dark Prophet: the mistlands were deadly for a small band unequipped for the
crossing. That certainly described Jem and himself. She
had not mentioned monsters, but Staver was not surprised to learn that such things lay ahead. Yet the
Dark Prophet had also warned them against the river
and the mountain trail. Staver stood irresolute, unable
to choose between the dangers. The talons pricked his
arm in reminder.

Well? Let's be going.

"We don't dare go near the river. It's watched by the
Cairnlord's men."

*I know a crossing where we won't be seen. Remember,
boy, you gave your word.*

"Then give me yours. Promise you'll get us safely
across and back."

Jem, who had been hearing only one side of this
dialogue, burst out, "My Lord Staver, we must avoid
the river! Those was her orders—I heard them!"

"Then you heard what she said about the mistlands,
too, and you know we can't hope to cross them alone.
We'll do as I think best, Jem," Staver said irritably. In
the same tone, he addressed the bird. "Do I have your
word?"

*What makes you think an injured bird can promise
you safety?*

"You're no ordinary bird. You're a wizard, and if we
help you, you have to help us in return."

After a pause the voice in Staver's mind said, *Very
well. I'll see to it that you reach the Southern Forest in
safety.*

"Fair enough," Staver said. "Jem, we're heading for
the river. You lead the way."

The river was farther than either of the boys had
anticipated, and Staver had to stop twice to rest. The
first time there was no exchange between him and his
passenger. But the second time he stopped, with the
river in view, glittering through the trees, Staver heard
the voice once more.

How do you know I'm not just another owl?

"Birds don't talk the way you talk."

No, I suppose they don't. Never thought of that. But how would you know?

"I just know, that's all."

Why do you suppose a wizard might turn himself into an owl? Answer me that.

"He might want to travel unseen and unheard. Maybe he's trying to spy on someone or escape from someone— or maybe he's just trying out a spell. I don't know why wizards do the things they do."

Don't you?

"No. I'm no wizard."

There was no reply, but Staver felt the ghost of a soft, low, chuckling sound rustle within his mind. He said nothing more but took up the bird and started for the river.

They kept to the edge of the wood for a time until the owl directed them to a ford. Here they crossed the wide river easily, scarcely wetting their feet, and climbed up the stony slopes of the opposite bank with little difficulty. The owl was in complete charge now, directing Staver this way and that, behind a boulder, beneath a ledge, around a rockfall, until the broad road was in view before them. They did not cross at this point, but worked their way farther north.

Jem kept mumbling under his breath about risking their hides for a dirty old rat-catching mouse-gobbling owl, and the owl poured out a roster of insults regarding the forest boy's intelligence, and finally Staver, caught in the middle, told them both to be quiet and concentrate on the trail. In a short time they reached a place where a narrow cleft ran into the mountainside on the far margin of the road, and here they crossed, swiftly, running at a half-crouch, as if the eyes of a watching army were alert for their transit.

The cleft was very narrow, and Staver had great difficulty squeezing along with his excitable burden, but the owl assured him that the way would soon be easier. In a short time the cleft widened to a trail about a half-mark wide, winding between two smooth walls of stone. They traveled on until Staver became acutely aware of the fact that they had not eaten since early that morning. His stomach growled angrily.

"How much farther is it?" he asked the owl.

We're practically there.

"What does that mean? When will we get there?"

Very soon, very soon. It's no distance at all, now.

"You said before that it was right on our way, and we've come a long way north and deep into the mountains."

You ought to be grateful and not complain. If I hadn't come along to stop you, you'd both be in the belly of one of those bog creatures by now.

"At least we wouldn't be starving."

I'll feed you. Turn left here.

They entered a narrowed, darker crevice that wound and turned until they could no longer tell in what direction they were going, nor how far they had come. After a particularly intricate series of turnings, the track ran straight. Staver looked ahead and groaned.

"Look what you've done! We're lost!"

We are not.

"That's a blank wall of rock! There's no side trail, just a cliff!"

Don't carry on, boy. Just keep walking.

"I'll run into that stone face if I do."

It will hit me first, but I'm not worrying. Do as I say, and keep walking.

Staver did as the owl bade him. He had no choice. As he drew closer to the sheer rock face, it appeared ever more solid to him—no hidden doors or crevices or hinges —just solid rock. As it loomed before his face, he faltered. The talons pricked his forearm, and the voice inside said, *Walk on!* Staver closed his eyes and took a step forward, then another. He met no resistance. He walked on, and had the feeling of passing through a curtain of air, and when he opened his eyes he was in a brightly lit, roomy chamber.

No entrance could be seen. On three sides, the walls rose to a shadowed height. They were lined with books, and tucked in among the books were objects that Staver did not recognize. He had never seen their like. Some of them appeared to be alive.

The fourth wall held a low flight of steps that led to a

balcony. Beyond the balcony a starry sky sparkled with unfamiliar constellations.

"How did we get here? Where's Jem?"

Your friend is outside. It will do him good to fret for a while. Teach him some manners.

"Get Jem in here at once!" Staver demanded angrily.

Watch your manners, boy. Always be polite to a wizard, or he may make you very uncomfortable.

"You're not much of a wizard if you waste your time scaring little boys."

The talons dug in a bit, but Staver did not flinch. A moment later he heard Jem's voice shouting excitedly, "My lord Staver, you're safe! He didn't betray us!"

Satisfied, boy?

"Yes. Now will you feed us?"

There's work still to be done. I'm hungry myself, but this comes first. Here, through this doorway.

Staver ducked through a low doorway in one wall and emerged in a spacious chamber. It held only a massive round table. Around it stood six candlesticks in which blue candles guttered low. As he approached the table, Staver could distinguish a line of symbols drawn in a ring of colored dust that ran around the rim of the table.

That's close enough. You don't want to break the ring, or try to cross it. You'd go out like a pinched candle, and I'd be an owl for the rest of my days.

"What do the marks mean?"

You'll see. Just bring me a bit closer. A little higher, if you please. Good. That's fine. Better close your eyes now.

The owl rose awkwardly from Staver's forearm perch and fluttered down toward the center of the table. As the bird crossed the ring of symbols, a great burst of light drove Staver back, his hands over his eyes. When he looked again, he saw an old man sitting up on the table, cross-legged, rubbing his arm. The owl was gone.

"Good to be back. I won't try that one again soon," said the old man to no one in particular, like a man long accustomed to conversing with himself alone. Staver recognized the voice.

"You were the owl!"

"I was," said the old man, still rubbing his arm tenderly. He rolled up the sleeve of his robe to reveal a large purple bruise just above his elbow. He touched the spot gingerly with a fingertip, winced, and shook his head. "Next time, I'll turn myself into a dragon. A flying dragon, spitting flame and covered end-to-end with impenetrable scales. No more owls."

"Why did you become an owl in the first place?"

Without removing his attention from the bruise, the old man said, "You had it right, boy. I wanted to find things out, and I chose to travel silently in the dark. Owl's best for that kind of work. I'll be burned to cinders by the fires of Panathurn if I can figure out how they knew where I was, though."

"Who?"

The old man turned his gaze on Staver and looked on him coldly—as if he were deciding whether or not the boy could be trusted with the truth. Then he climbed down from the tabletop, rolled down his sleeve, flexed his fingers, and studied Staver again, more closely. At last he said, "The one who made the storm, that's who. Aoea, the Windwraith, and her master, whom you yourself fear."

"The Cairnlord? Is he your enemy, too?"

"One of many," said the old man with great bravado.

"Then you thought the storm was raised against you, not us."

"Of course it was! Do you think the Cairnlord wastes his power on boys? You've got a mighty poor knowledge of wizards, whoever you are. And just exactly who are you, if I may ask?"

"Just a swordsman, seeking my fortune," Staver said innocently. "And very hungry. We're both hungry, and you said you'd feed us. Would it be—"

"Don't change the subject."

"I'm not changing the subject. The subject is hunger."

"Your name is Staver, isn't it?"

"Yes, it is."

"Well, hear this, Staver. If you want to know the real reason why I became a bird, it's because I don't like people. And I live here alone because I don't like people. I don't like the company of other sorcerers, either. They can't be trusted any more than ordinary people. And I particularly don't fancy little boys with big swords and foolish explanations. Where'd you steal that sword, anyway? Out of a grave mound?"

"I didn't steal it!"

"Don't be so sensitive. A grave mound is the only place to get a decent sword these days. They don't make them the way they did in the days of the Old Kingdom."

"This sword is a legacy from my father."

"Ah. I see . . . I see. Well." The old man nodded his head. He said nothing for a moment, then he beckoned to Staver. "Come, eat. There's something in the other room."

They sat around a low table, the boys stuffing themselves with hard bread and strong cheese, the old man gobbling bits of crust and crumbs of cheese and sipping cold water, all the time seeming very preoccupied and almost oblivious to the boys' presence. Staver took the opportunity to study him in the brighter light of the book-lined room.

The wizard was a stumpy man, stooped in posture, no taller than Staver. He had a patchy white beard and a crooked nose, and his skull was as smooth and tan and round as a pecan. His voice was raspy, and no matter what he said, he made it sound angry. That was understandable, considering his long ordeal, Staver conceded. And yet there was nothing frightening about him; in fact, he seemed almost comical. When he thought of him as a dirty, bedraggled owl, Staver found it hard to hold back a smile. He was glad that the old man was ignoring him. Then, without warning, the wizard spoke. His voice did not sound angry this time, but there was nothing comical about his words.

"Now it's time you told me everything, Staver."

"I've told you who I am."

"You have not. You've given me a name, nothing more, and that's not nearly enough. I'm a curious man. That's what led me to this life. And when a young fellow appears with a companion who calls him 'My lord Staver' and that young fellow carries a sword from the Old Kingdom, and understands the language of birds, and thinks it possible that the Cairnlord might have summoned up his windwraith to raise a storm against

him, . . . well, my curiosity just gets all out of hand.
And there's something about you—the nose . . . the
shape of your chin—reminds me of someone I once
knew."

Staver hesitated before speaking. He knew that he
and Jem were at the wizard's mercy—virtually his prisoners. If they should ever escape from this place, they
would be hopelessly lost in the mountains. Yet he felt
no fear and no sense of danger. This old man had put
his life in their hands; without their help he might now
be dead—or close to death. Staver decided to repay trust
with trust. He took a deep breath and began to tell his
whole story, from Vannen's sudden illness to the storm
on the Fool's Head. The wizard listened without inter-
rupting him, only nodding now and then.

". . . and I heard your voice, just as it sounds now,
only it was inside my mind. And then I found you, by
the hollow tree," Staver concluded.

"Yes. Good. Very interesting," the wizard said. "Very
interesting indeed. So, you're the ones Ambescand
foretold. I should have known. That nose . . . and the
chin."

"Did you know Ambescand?"

"Of course. I knew them all—all but the Cairnlord.
Who, or what he is, and where he comes from, no one
knows. But the others, the ones he commands—I know
them all. And now the struggle is upon them. I wonder
if they realize . . ." The wizard fell into a thoughtful
silence, which Staver was reluctant to intrude upon.

At last, unable to restrain himself, he said, "You're
not going to warn them, are you?"

"I? Warn them?" the wizard laughed loudly. "I'm
happy to see them kept hopping, and I hope you put up
a good long fight. While they're busy with you, they won't
have time to bother me. I'll be able to rest and store up
power for when they turn on me."

"Then you don't think we'll win," Staver said.

"Certainly not. But you'll fight bravely and win much
glory, and if anyone survives, they'll tell tales of your
bold deeds for generations to come. That's all you
swordsmen care about, isn't it?"

For the first time since entering the cave, Jem spoke.

"We want to be free. We don't care for praise. We want to be rid of the Cairnlord once and for all."

The wizard looked at him suspiciously and said, "I've heard that sort of talk before. The nobles wanted to be free of Ambescand, and then my fellow wizards wanted to be free of the nobles, and all the while, the people wanted to be free of nobles and wizards alike. And all that ever came of it was blood and suffering. That's all people care for, blood and suffering, and may Erendu and Gleede consume the lot of them."

"It's the Cairnlord and his followers who bring the blood and suffering now," Staver said.

"And I suppose you think you'll turn the world into one endless Snow Moon festival, if only you get rid of the Cairnlord. Well, things don't work that way. There's always a dark spirit somewhere, and there's always blood and suffering. You won't change that, not even with the powers of Ambescand himself."

"Are we to do nothing then?"

The wizard shrugged. "Do whatever you please. It's not my concern. I tried to warn my fellow sorcerers before they got involved, but they listened to the nobles. Stupid of them." He stared into the distance, then shook his head resignedly. "Never fails to amaze me how learned a person can be in some things and how ignorant in others. Korang was always something of a fool, and Ulowadjaa and Rombonole weren't much better, . . . but Cei Shalpan and Jashoone had the makings of really great wizards. Cei Shalpan might have been a shape-changer himself one day. And now the Cairnlord has them all. . . ."

"But they're all dead!" Staver protested. "The people put seven to death, and Ambescand executed four more. Even if he can bring them back to life, what good are dead sorcerers to the Cairnlord?"

"Wizards may die, but their power doesn't. The Cairnlord has learned how to recapture the power of the lost seven. He can summon them up and force them to do his bidding. And they do it willingly enough, out of hatred and the hunger for revenge on the descendants of Ambescand and his people. The Cairnlord gives them a bit of life, a space of freedom from that awful abyss where their spirits howl in darkness, and they would do anything he asks in return." The wizard gazed up into the darkness. "Oh yes, the Cairnlord is a powerful sorcerer—many times as powerful as Ambescand was." He fell silent for a time, staring upward, and when he spoke again his voice was distant with reminiscence. "They never suspected Ambescand's full power, and that undid them. He was a fearless man and a mighty warrior, that much they knew, but his mastery of the white art was unknown. On the day he entered the High City, home from the war in the dry lands, his power was at its height. I was gone from the city then, but I could feel it, even from far away. Their cause was lost. They tried to use their magic against his, but for too long they had wasted their strength. Ambescand had saved his magic for the confrontation, and his power swept over them like a tidal wave. At the first touch of his force, they forgot they were sorcerers. They became frightened men, fleeing for their lives, with a mob at their heels."

In an awed voice Staver said, "One wizard . . . more powerful than eleven!"

"Ambescand was ready. He had built up power, stored it for this battle. The eleven had weakened themselves needlessly, working petty enchantments in the service of the usurpers. Magic takes a heavy toll, boy. Overuse can leave you drained and weak. That's what puzzles me about the Cairnlord—he uses his power freely, and yet he seems to grow stronger, not weaker, as he should. He sustains those gray men of his and gives them their strength. He keeps the four broken sorcerers in human form, walking about. And he's summoned up the others from the depths of Shagghya four times since summer. That's powerful magic, and I can't understand where he draws it from. He has to have some source, but I've never been able to learn what it is."

"And are all those sorcerers your enemies?"

The wizard frowned and fixed a cold eye on Staver. "Do you think Aoea churned up the Fool's Head and blew down half Long Wood because she likes me?"

"She raised the storm to stop me and my brothers. You ought to help us, for your own sake."

"I've held them off for more generations than you can count, and I'll hold out for a few more before I start to worry. They'll burn up their power fighting you, and I'll be storing up mine, and growing, here in the mountains."

Staver looked at him scornfully. "So you'll let us fight while you hide here, and then reap all the benefits."

"Men love to fight, Staver. That's why they're always doing it."

Staver glared at the old man sitting comfortably across from him. He could think of no arguments to use against him and wanted only to be quit of this place and on his way south, where brave followers awaited him. He rose and said, "Let us go. Show us the trail, and we'll be on our way and trouble you no longer."

"I promised to get you to the Southern Forest in safety, and I will. But first I must offer you a reward for saving my life. I'm obliged to," the wizard said. His words appeared to make him uncomfortable.

Jem's eyes grew wide, but Staver said, "I don't want a reward. I want to find my friends."

"I owe you a reward. A spell. Any spell you like. Love, power, great wealth—"

"I don't want any spell. I might misuse it."

"—strength in battle, long life . . . Pick one, Staver."

"To be truthful, wizard, I fear magic."

"A very sensible view, but irrelevant at the moment. Go on, choose."

"I'd rather not."

The edge of anger reappeared in the wizard's voice, and he said a bit more loudly, "You must. I won't owe you a debt. Choose your magic."

"I really don't want to, if it's all right with you."

"It is not all right with me!" the wizard cried, springing to his feet with an agility that surprised the boys. "If I let you leave without rewarding you, I'll be—" He choked off his cry, took a series of deep breaths, and in a gentle, wheedling voice said, "Wouldn't you like to be big enough and strong enough to use that sword properly, Staver? Or would you prefer—yes, this is an excellent magic—something to slow the passage of time, or speed it up, whenever you like? That's very handy."

"Just get us to the Southern Forest, wizard."

"If you leave like this . . ."

"What of it?"

"I'll owe you a rescue, that's what of it!" the wizard cried, all patience gone. "You saved my life, and unless you accept some sort of payment, I'll be obliged to save yours. Whenever you call on me, wherever you are, whatever I'm doing at the time, I'll have to go. I'll have to burn up my magic by the bucketful, go into the Cairnlord's kingdom, all because you're afraid of a little spell."

"I won't ask your help. You owe me nothing, if you'll only get us to our friends," Staver said.

"You can't release me from the obligation."

"Oh, all right then—if it will make things easier—"

"It's too late now. The obligation is marked," the wizard said petulantly. "When you need me, call my name: 'Zandinell, come to me,' will do. And I'll be there. Once, and once only, so don't be hasty."

"You needn't worry. I won't use it."

"Yes, you will," the wizard said with obvious disgust. "Now, about getting to your friends . . . Just let me check the proper wording. . . ." He went to one wall and began to inspect his books, finally pulling out a great dust-covered volume upon which rested something flat and pale—about the size of a child's cap—with large eyes. It squeaked and scuttled behind the other volumes when the wizard plucked it out of its resting place. Ignoring it, Zandinell leafed through the pages of the book until he found what he was after.

"Go and stand before the doorway," he told the boys.

"But that doorway only leads to the other room," Staver objected.

Zandinell looked up from the volume with an expression on his face that discouraged further discussion of the matter. "That doorway leads wherever I tell it to lead," he said slowly, pronouncing each word distinctly. "Now, stand there. And when I tell you to walk, walk!"

He lowered his head and began to read aloud. The words—and even the sounds he made with his breath—were utterly unfamiliar, as if he were reading things not meant to be spoken by a human throat. His voice rose and fell. Jem glanced uneasily at Staver and moved as close to his side as he could.

"Take hold of my belt, Jem," Staver whispered. "We don't want to be separated this time."

"Walk!" the wizard commanded.

They stepped forward. The opening was dark, and a pitchy mist swirled around them, engulfing them in its humid touch as they entered. Staver walked on into the blackness. He could feel the desperate clutch of Jem's grip tugging at his belt.

Then, suddenly, their eyes were dazzled by sunlight.

16

A Meeting on the Lake Isle

Before them the sun drooped low over a long expanse of grassy hills. They turned to put the blinding light at their backs and looked for the portal through which they had come. There was none.

Staver ran to the top of the nearest rise to get his bearings. Jem was close behind him. Their view was long and unobstructed, and most reassuring. To the south, the hills leveled to a plain extending to the edge of a forest that covered the horizon. To the north they saw the faint outline of a distant range of mountains; and off to the west, a low obscuring sea of mist.

"We're past mistlands! Wizard kept his word!" Jem cried.

"I thought he would. But I'm still glad to be out of that place."

"Bad place it was. Bad food, too."

"Yes. I'm still hungry."

"Be food out in grasslands, likely."

"We'll gather what we can on the way. We can make it to the forest by dark if we hurry," Staver said and started down the hill with Jem at his side.

Still chary of lighting a fire, they dined that night on

roots and berries, which they found in abundance as they passed along the plain. Once again their blanket was leaves and boughs, and they slept in the windless shelter of a hillock.

Birdsong awoke them, and they started south at once, foraging as they went. The trail they followed was a narrow one and old, but as they proceeded, it widened and showed traces of recent use.

"Score of men, or more, passed this way in great hurry. Not more than a day ago," Jem said, kneeling and studying the trail.

"Which way?"

"South, same as us."

When the path forked, they took the branch that showed most recent use. By late afternoon they had made fair progress south but had seen or heard no one.

Late the next day, they came upon a hamlet in a clearing. It was no more than a rough semicircle of small huts built around a spring, but they welcomed the sight of human habitation. They approached it cautiously. No challenge came, nor any greeting—only silence. All the doors were shut. No smoke rose from the chimneys.

Closer they came, and closer still, until they were well within the clearing—still they heard no sound. Jem looked nervously at Staver. Staver drew his sword and started for the nearest hut. Snatching up a length of firewood, Jem followed at his heels.

With Jem close behind him, makeshift club held high, Staver went from hut to hut until he had inspected each one. Behind one hut a man's shirt and a child's dress were spread out to dry. In two others, dried-up food stood in bowls on the table. Spare cloaks and hoods hung by the door of one hut, and gardening tools were neatly stacked beside three more. Not a living soul was to be found.

"I can't understand it. It looks as though everybody decided to leave—all at once," Staver said, sheathing his blade.

"Might have been a raid. Cairnlord's men."

Staver shook his head. "No trace of a struggle. Nothing broken or overturned. No blood anywhere."

Something about this scene impressed Staver as the setting of a hurried but orderly removal. Surely in a settlement of eight huts there would be children and a few old men and women who could not travel as easily as others—yet no one had been abandoned. Another fact kept nagging at Staver's mind, just out of conscious reach, until his eye fell again upon the hoe and spade stacked beside one hut. Then it came clear.

"Jem, they didn't run away—they went somewhere, but they're coming back. That's why the doors are all closed, and the tools are stacked, and things are left behind," he said.

"It might be so. But where did they go?"

"I don't know, and it's getting too dark to follow a trail. I think we ought to stay here tonight. There's food and real beds to sleep on. We can start on their trail early in the morning."

Jem was quick to agree. Secure within the largest of the windowless huts, they dared to build a small fire. Jem turned up a bit of meat that was still mostly edible, and some porridge, and cheese, and half a loaf of bread, and they ate slowly and with great relish. The beds were no more than sacks of straw, but they were far more comfortable than the ground, and the two boys slept long and soundly.

They left as soon as it was light enough to follow a trail and found that this particular trail might almost have been followed on a moonless night. The villagers had made no attempt to conceal their tracks. Jem estimated a band of about thirty, including several small children who were carried part of the way.

At midmorning they came to a place where the trail fanned out into three, and here they were faced with a dilemma. The tracks divided. A part of the band had followed each of the three branches.

They studied each new trail closely and determined that a small group—four or possibly five—had gone west, and an equal number northwest. The others, including all the children, had taken the southwest path. Staver sat on a stone by the wayside and tried to decipher the facts.

"Up to now it looked as though they were all going to

somewhere definite," he said, as much thinking aloud as addressing Jem. "But now they seem to be going to three destinations."

"Maybe going for help."

"That makes sense. They sent the children to safety, then went to get help . . . reinforcements, . . . so they ought to be coming back this way—unless they're assembling for a battle off to the west or north. . . ." Staver halted, uncertain.

He rose and began to pace up and down the trail, muttering to himself, trying desperately to work out this problem. If men were assembling for battle, then it almost certainly involved his brothers. The Dark Prophet had spoken of a struggle, of going into battle, and rousing their followers; the villagers whose track he pursued might well be among those followers, hurrying to join Col and Ord.

Or they might be the enemy—and in that case, following them would be marching to his death and Jem's. At that thought he was plunged once again into indecision. Should he send Jem to safety and follow the trail alone? Where was safety? And which trail should he follow?

Staver tried to determine how much time had passed since the storm on the Fool's Head and realized that he could not be certain. He knew how many days they had wandered in Long Wood and here in the Southern Forest, but he could not tell how much time—if any—had passed in the wizard's stronghold. Zandinell had offered a time-spell to Staver, and Staver had no doubt that such a spell existed. A wizard who could change form and annihilate distance could manipulate time as easily. And, uncertain of the day, Staver could not easily judge whether these foresters might be on their way to join his brothers or in pursuit of them.

He closed his eyes and tried to remember the Dark Prophet's words on that day at the bridge, a day that now seemed part of a remote, half-imaginary past. She had spoken of mistlands . . . they were to cross mistlands . . . , and fresh the memory returned of the sight of the mistlands lying to the west.

If their followers were rallying here in the Southern Forest, then some of them were sure to be at the border of the mistlands to receive their promised leader and escort him safely to the main force. Though all else was confusion and uncertainty, that made sense.

"The northwest trail, Jem," Staver said. "That has to be the right way."

They set out at a fast pace. Staver was haunted by visions of a wood teeming with armed men—friends and enemies, his followers and his pursuers—crossing and recrossing the maze of trails, all within shouting distance of one another but never within view, always concealed by the mute obscuring curtain of green on all sides and arching overhead. Col and Ord and an army of foresters might be waiting just ahead or marching toward them, or to the south, and he had no way of knowing of their presence, nor they of his. The frustrating possibility drove him to an exhausting pace. Jem fell farther and farther behind, and at last Staver, too, had to admit his fatigue and stopped to rest.

They spent a cold and uncomfortable night by the side of the path, starting awake at every fancied footfall. At last they sank into a deep sleep . . . and woke stiff and hungry in broad daylight.

At midday they came to the edge of the Southern Forest. Far off, beyond the plain, lay the eastern limits of the mistlands. Just at nightfall they crossed the track of a great army, heading south. This was what Staver had been seeking: if an army marched south, his brothers were sure to be at its head. They followed the army's tracks the next day and the day after, the trace of hundreds of feet leading them ever forward—and yet not a single human being to be seen or heard. . . .

Until dusk on the second day, when they were halted by a man who stepped from the roadside into the path about four marks ahead of them. He held a bow, an arrow nocked and ready.

"Identify yourselves," he called to them.

Staver had no wish to dissimulate or delay. Folding his arms and holding his head high, he declared himself. "I am Staver Ironbrand, and I seek my brothers, Colberane Whitblade and the Scarlet Ord. If you know them, take me to them at once."

The archer paused before saying suspiciously, "It was thought that you were lost in a storm."

"You can see for yourself that I was not. Where are my brothers?"

When the archer still hesitated, Jem cried, "Do as your leader tells you! Can't you see the blade at his side?"

Lowering his bow, the archer said, "They've left for the lake isle. Tonight at the full of dark, they lead the attack on the citadel."

"I have to be with them. Take me to them, quickly."

"My lord, I can't leave this trail unguarded."

"There may be gray men in the citadel. My sword will be needed."

"Our camp is a short way down this road, my lord. Some were left behind, and one of them may be able to lead you," said the archer.

Staver pushed past him and ran down the trail. Darkness was gathering when he came upon a camp large enough for thousands, where only an old woman and two small children could be seen.

"Where's the trail to the lake isle?" he demanded of the woman. "I must join them."

"Too late, laddie. They've all gone away," she replied in a soft and faraway voice.

"Where did they go? Show me the way!"

"All off to battle. All gone to be killing the wicked swordsmen who took my boys," the woman said. "They're all gone now, every one. We won't see them again."

"Who's that? Who speaks?" said a hard male voice from the darkness.

"I'm Staver Ironbrand. I want to join my brothers and fight at their side," Staver said.

A tall man came from the shadows and stood before him. He reached out a hand, touched Staver's chest, then lightly laid his fingers on Staver's brow and ran them over his face. The man's fingers were soft and gentle as feathers, and Staver did not flinch from the touch. He could now distinguish the cloth that bound the man's eyes.

"You are true brother to our king, Colberane Whitblade," the man said. "I can tell that from your features and your voice."

"I want to join my brothers, but there's no one to show me the way."

"Will you be led by a blind man, my lord Staver?"

The very suggestion seemed preposterous. Then it occurred to Staver that on a moonless night, in deep forest, unable to light a torch, all men were equally blind. He said, "I'll be glad to follow any man who can take me to my brothers."

"Then follow me," said the blind man. "I knew these trails well before the Cairnlord's men took my sight from me, and I've learned to see each step of the way without eyes since then. The others would not take me to fight, so I fight in my own way."

"Lead, then. I'm ready."

"You are not. Your voice is weary and your features tell me that you've traveled far and long. Refresh yourself as best you can. Take food and drink before we go, and wash away the dust. We have a long trail ahead and a hard battle at the end of it," the blind man said. "Who is the boy with you?"

"Jem Underhill. He's coming, too."

"He walks noisily."

Staver had heard nothing, but soon he could hear Jem coming closer. When the boy reached his side, Staver said, "We have a guide. We'll take something to eat and pour cold water over our heads, and then be off."

He saw Jem staring at the blindfolded man and gestured to him to remain silent. The blind man reached out, touched Jem's face, and felt his garment between his fingers.

"A forester's son. From Long Wood. One of the northern settlements, near the river," he said.

Jem drew back. "How did you know that?"

"Your clothing, your skin, the bones of your face, all tell me things. Why have you come south?"

"I serve Staver Ironbrand."

"Serve him, then. Bring food and water from the old woman. Hurry, boy!" When Jem had scurried off, the blind man said to Staver, "They left at midday. All the fighting men and women, all those who could help the

fallen and bear messages among the commanders—
everyone but this mindless woman, and a score of crippled old men, and the infants . . . and me."

"Can we reach them before the battle?"

"They will set out for the lake isle tonight, when the
skies cloud over. I doubt that we can reach them before
the battle begins, but we will surely arrive˙ before it
ends." The blind man turned his head, then said, "Your
servant comes. Call me when you wish to leave. My
name is Helmer."

He turned and disappeared into the shadows. Soon
after, Jem appeared, carrying a pitcher and an armful
of fruit. They ate, drank, and then washed their faces
in the cold water. Refreshed, Staver made ready to
leave.

Jem laid a hand on his arm, In a low, guarded voice
he said, "My lord, I don't trust the blind man. I fear
him."

"Why? Just because he's blind? In this darkness, in
an unknown country, we're the blind ones, Jem."

"Not right, blind man leading," Jem said stubbornly.

"We've been wandering through the Southern Forest
for days, Jem, and it's only luck that brought us to this
camp. We need a guide. I don't care who he is if he
gets me to my brothers."

Jem mumbled unhappily, then was silent. Staver
clapped him on the back for encouragement, then called
out for Helmer. The guide appeared almost at once and
handed Staver a rope.

"Hold fast to this rope and have your servant do the
same. The way will be dark, and we must not become
separated," he said.

Once they were out of the campsite and into the forest, Helmer set a surprisingly rapid pace. Moving at a
steady walk, Staver could hear the blind man's staff
tapping the ground before him, striking at trees that
stood near the road, cutting at low-hanging branches.
By the aid of these sounds, which served him as trail
markers might serve a sighted man, Helmer walked the
pitch-black trail as surely as a man strolling through his
own garden at high noon. He moved without hesitation,

sure-footed and silent, while Staver and Jem stumbled noisily behind him, hard pressed to keep up.

They went on without pause for a long time. Staver glanced up frequently, and often he saw a point of light through the foliage overhead and sometimes a cluster of stars when the trail went through a clearing. But after a time he saw no stars at all. The sky had clouded over, and the darkness was unrelieved.

Then Helmer signaled a halt. As Staver and Jem drew closer to him, he said in a low voice, "The camp is ahead. We must go carefully. There will be guards."

They went only a short distance before they were challenged. Staver at once gave his name and his mission, and was astonished to hear a familiar voice say joyously, "My lord Staver, you're alive! We thought you at the bottom of the Fool's Head, but you're alive!"

"Is that you, Forben?" Jem asked.

"Jem Underhill, too! Ah, here's a sure sign fortune is with us this night," Forben said.

"Where are my brothers? Has the attack started?" Staver asked.

"It has, my lord. They left as soon as the sky went black. You might catch up to the main party, though. They'd be happy to have a swordsman to lead them."

"But where are my brothers?"

"They took a special mission on themselves, my lord. I know no more than that." Forben sighed. "It was my luck to be left behind as a guard. I won't even get to strike a blow."

Staver jumped at a gruff voice close by, demanding, "How did you find us? Did we leave such a trail that strangers in our country can follow us in the dark?"

"I guided them," Helmer said. "I've led them this far, and I'll lead them the rest of the way."

"We did wrong to leave you behind, Helmer," said the gruff-voiced man, after a pause. "Do you know the path around the lake to the southern shore? Follow it to Barger's Point. The rafts are leaving from there."

"But the western end of the isle is protected!"

"Not tonight. The barricade has been breached, and the guards will not trouble us. On so dark a night our forces might make it to the walls before an alarm is given. I'd give all I have to be with them," the gruff-voiced man said with sudden feeling.

"Then go," Helmer said.

"I can't leave my post."

"I'll take your place." Before the other could object, Helmer said, "I know the footfall of a forester, the smell of his garments, the sound of his breathing. You know I can aim an arrow by sound better than most men can by sight. You say it's a dark night—then I can see as well as any man."

"You've earned your right to take part in the battle, Helmer."

"No. I would only hinder others. It was a foolish idea. I don't know the terrain of the lake isle, and I'd be in the way of the others. I can do my best here. Bring me a bow."

"I will. And thanks, Helmer. I will not forget this," said the gruff-voiced man.

"Our thanks, too," Staver said. He reached out to clasp the blind man's hand.

"Whetter will guide you well. He's a good bowman and brave. Strike a blow for me, my lord," Helmer said, taking Staver's hand in a firm grip.

"I hope we have the chance."

They were on their way at once. Whetter was able to move no faster than Helmer had, for the night was as dark as the bottom of a beggar's sack. Only when they reached the edge of the forest and saw the reflections of the distant lights in the citadel was there relief from the blackness.

Barger's Point was silent, but the trampled ground underfoot attested to the passing of a multitude. Gathering scattered scraps of wood, the three constructed a crude raft to float them to the isle.

Once ashore, they followed the northern path. All was strangely silent, and as the dawn broke, they could see the traces of a great army's passage. They hurried forward, and as they cut across a field, they heard the first faint sound of battle—a distant shouting and clattering as if noisy business were being conducted far off.

When they came within sight of the gate, they heard a great shout go up, and grow louder, and echo from the walls of the citadel, and they knew it was the foresters' cry of victory. As they passed under the gate, bloodied and battered men embraced them, and hailed them, and cheered and cried out and wept for sheer joy. The first stronghold of the old enemy had fallen and was theirs. After years of flight, and fear, and hiding, the foresters and mistlanders were tasting victory, and it was sweet and intoxicating.

Staver pushed his way through the crowd and was entering the castle yard when a second shout arose—no shout of triumph this time but a low moan of pain drawn from a thousand unbelieving throats. A great flight of arrows lofted from the bowmen in the yard, and Staver followed their flight to see a bristling body pitch headlong from the battlements.

An awful premonition gripped him, and he sensed what had come about even before the first shocked words reached his ears. Thrusting through the milling foresters, he came at last upon his brothers.

Ord was on his knees, his face buried in his hands. Before him, a man lay on the ground with a dusty cloak pulled clumsily over him. His face was visible, and Staver recognized Col. He lay pale and still, and an arrow jutted from his chest. With an agonized cry, Staver ran to his brothers.

They lifted Col carefully and carried him to an empty barracks, where they laid him on a pallet. Staver sat by his side, watching his pale brow film over with cold sweat, hearing the shallow, irregular breathing, and all the while close to bursting with the sense of his own helplessness. Here he sat at his brother's side, watching him die, unable to cure him or even to ease his pain. Whatever his destiny might be, whatever thrones and powers the future held, in this place and this situation he was no more help than a baby.

Ord paced the floor restlessly, angrily, unable in his agitation to remain still despite the injury that forced him to limp. His face was puffed and discolored, his lips swollen. A rag was knotted around his leg just above the knee. "It's all the fault of the Dark Prophet. Curse that witch and her schemes!" he said bitterly.

"She saved our lives at the bridge," Staver reminded him.

"For her sake, not ours. I hate to be a pawn in someone else's game, sprig, and that's how I feel now." He seated himself across from Staver and, leaning forward, said intensely, "I love gaming, because I always play my own hand. I'm not doing that now. None of us is. The Dark Prophet is using us, and our brother is dying because of her."

"Jem and Kinnaury are questioning everyone. There may be someone who can help."

Ord shook his head. "I doubt that there's a healer alive who could remove that arrow. Look at it, sprig! It must be touching his heart. One slip in removing it and Col will die. If we don't remove it, he'll die more slowly. We're helpless."

"I never thought it would end like this. The prophecies didn't mention—"

"Prophets are always very careful what they don't say."

They sat in mutual silence for a time, thinking their private thoughts. For all his concern Staver found himself nodding and dozing. A sharp rap at the door brought the two brothers wide awake. Kinnaury's big frame filled the entry.

"There's no one can help with the healing of my lord Colberane. We've asked all, and there's not one dares try," the forester said. "It needs more skill than anyone among us has."

"It's all right, Kinnaury," Ord said dully.

"My lord Ordred, you must have your own wounds tended. The folk be looking to you for leading them now."

"I'll see to it, Kinnaury. Leave us now." Ord looked down on his brother's still form and said, "He was learning to be a leader, sprig—the first of us to become a king. He would have been a good one." Ord rose and stood at the foot of the pallet. "We were closer in these last few days than we've ever been. No arguments between us, only trust. I saved his life in there, in the keep, in the very last minutes of battle. We were talking, just talking easily, like brothers, when that arrow came. . . ."

In the silence a light blazed through the doorway, and the booming of a great wind stirred the flimsy walls. The light faded, and the wind died, and the Dark Prophet stood in the room.

"Whose life do you seek now, witch?" Ord demanded.

"Colberane will live," the prophet said.

"Who's to heal him?"

The Dark Prophet pointed across Col's supine form. "What are you willing to do to save your brother's life, Staver Ironbrand?"

Staver looked up wide-eyed at the hooded figure and felt a clutch of fear at the thought of what sacrifice she might ask of him. He hesitated for only a- moment, then said, "I'll do whatever must be done."

"Careful, sprig," Ord said, moving to his side. "I don't want to lose both my brothers to a witch."

"I can't refuse, Ord."

"No. No, I suppose you can't."

"If Colberane recovers and Staver returns unharmed, will you trust me?" the Dark Prophet asked.

"Yes, I will."

"Then our work may yet be accomplished. Staver, come with me. There are skills you must learn and master."

Staver shook his head and raised his hands as if to fend her off. "There's no time! Col is dying!"

"There is time, for those who know its ways. Quickly, Staver—outside."

The words made no sense, but she had promised that Col would live. Even a lying promise offered more hope than Staver could rouse in himself. He stood and followed her out the door.

Ord remained within. He saw the Dark Prophet enfold Staver in her robe, and then a brilliant light erupted to blanch the mild morning sunshine, as if a thousand lightnings stitched the earth of the castle yard. The building swayed and creaked in the buffeting wind, and Ord had to grip the back of a chair to keep erect. Then all was still, and pale sunlight shone through the door. Staver entered alone. In his hands he bore a small wooden chest.

"It's all right, Ord. I can cure him now," he said.

"How? Magic? You've had no time—"

"I have, Ord. Believe me, I've had time. I must get to work at once. The Dark Prophet will explain everything," Staver said. He threw off his white cloak and set the chest down beside the pallet. Opening it, he removed a bottle of pale blue liquid, poured it on Col's chest around the jutting arrow, and began to rub it into the skin with a gentle motion.

Ord looked at him in bewilderment. Staver was changed. He was dressed in different garments now—he had worn no cloak when he walked out the door only moments ago—and he seemed a bit taller as well. His voice was deeper. He had carried no chest before, nor had the Dark Prophet. And yet they had been gone no time at all.

Staver drew a piece of white cloth from the chest and dried his hands. "It's all right, Ord. I can do it. Col will recover," he said.

There was a certainty in his voice and manner that Ord had never heard before, and the look of confidence was in his eyes. Ord nodded, turned, and left him to his work.

Three days later, the brothers talked for the first time since their boats had set out on the Fool's Head. Col was propped up on the pallet, a broad bandage wound around his chest. He was pale and spoke little, and then only in a weak, weary voice; but he was alive and recovering.

Ord sat on one side of him, Staver on the other. The bruises were almost faded from Ord's cheek and temple, and the swelling was gone from his lips. Staver alone was uninjured, but he had the look of great weariness upon him and age far beyond his years. Under his puffed eyes were dark crescents, his face was drawn, and he slumped in his chair like a man pushed beyond exhaustion and drained of all strength.

"Staver's done it all, brother. How, I don't know, but he's done it—all alone," Ord said.

"Saved me . . . I know . . . Col whispered.

"You—and twoscore others at the very least. He's

been cutting out arrows, and stitching up gashes, and setting bones since the battle ended, with no more than a few minutes' sleep at a time. He's too tired to stand," Ord said, and Staver seconded his words with a long, loud yawn, "but he keeps going."

"Not much longer. Most of the work is done now," Staver said.

"And wait until you hear how he learned. It's incredible, but I know it's true, Col. I saw the results, and I can't doubt. The Dark Prophet is amazing! I never suspected. . . . I'll believe anything she tells us from now on."

Col turned to Staver. "Tell me . . . how. . . ."

"I don't know exactly, Col. The Dark Prophet wrapped me in her cloak, and all at once I was in a white city. A beautiful place it was, though I saw little more of it than the first glimpse. I worked with an old man and a young woman. People were brought to us, terribly injured—the city was in the midst of a war—and we healed them. At first I only watched, then I helped, and then I began to work alone." Staver paused to yawn. He stretched and rubbed his eyes, then went on. "I don't know how long I was there, but it seemed like a long time—two winters passed, I know that—and yet when I came back, no time had passed here at all."

"And the ointments and drafts he brought back with him—unbelievable, Col! He rubbed something on my face, where that fellow had bashed me with his helmet, and the swelling was down in minutes. He put something else on my knee, and now it's healed. And Goodbowe—he took an arrow in the thigh, remember? Today I saw him walking in the castle yard with scarcely a trace of a limp!" Ord said with great enthusiasm.

Staver nodded, but his expression was somber. "They were wonderful medicines, but they're nearly gone now, and there's no way to replenish them here."

"You won't need any more. You've cured everyone."

"Not quite everyone, Ord. But there's enough left for Col and the ones with the worst injuries."

"Thanks, brother," Col said, smiling.

"You ought to rest now. I'll come back with something for you to eat."

Ord and Staver rose, and after Staver had instructed one of the older women to keep watch on his brother, they left the barracks. As they crossed the yard, every man and woman they passed greeted them warmly. The castle yard was neat and orderly now, with most traces of battle removed. The last of the Cairnlord's followers were being buried this day at the far end of the island. From the forge came the ring of hammers as the foresters set about repairing the weapons they had taken. Masons were at work on the main gate and two of the towers, and one of the barracks was being rebuilt.

"We can outfit a good force of armored swordsmen with what we captured here," Ord said. "It will take some work, though. The swords were poor stuff, and the armor wasn't much better."

"The Cairnlord has his weakness as an armorer."

"He does, brother. It's a strange thing—there's not a nick in my blade, or in Col's, but the ones we took are all hacked and battered. They look as though they'd been used for quarrying."

"There's something special about our blades, as the Dark Prophet said. I only wish I'd been here to help."

"You did more good with your healing. We'd have lost at least forty men and another hundred crippled or maimed if it hadn't been for you. And the Dark Prophet, of course."

Staver yawned and smiled wearily. "You've changed your mind about her, haven't you?"

"Col is recovering, you're safe—I believe she means us well. I don't doubt her power or her intentions now, not after seeing you come back and heal Col."

"She has some kind of power over time. The wizard in Long Wood spoke of such a spell."

"You've had an interesting time these past few days. I want to hear more about that shapechanger. But now I think you ought to rest," Ord said.

"I'll rest soon."

"Rest now, brother. Col is being watched, and the others are all doing well. Get some sleep. I'll see that you're awakened if anyone needs you."

The full weight of his fatigue seemed to bear down on

Staver as they spoke, and he realized that Ord's advice was sound. The most pressing work was done. For the sake of those who still needed his care, he had to consider his own state. Taking leave of his brother, he went to his chamber and slept soundly until the morning.

17

A Mission to the North

Col recovered slowly. Much of the governance of the citadel fell on Ord, who handled things capably in his brother's stead. He set Staver to teaching his healing skills to others and organized the foresters to complete the harvesting of the island's crops and to prepare a store of food against the oncoming winter. Much work still remained to be done on the citadel and the island's defenses, but food was the most immediate need.

On the twelfth night after the battle, as Ord and Staver sat discussing plans for the defense of the island, the Dark Prophet came to them. Before they could rise to greet her, she silenced them with a raised hand.

"Colberane Whitblade is Master of the Southern Forest once again. The first part of the prophecy is fulfilled. Now we must move quickly to bring the rest about," she said.

"We can't leave Col," Staver objected. "He won't be able to walk for another month."

"There's too much still to be done here," Ord added wearily.

She brushed their objections aside. "What must be done here can be done by others. The people are well organized, and Goodbowe is reliable. I will remain here for a time to assist him. But you must go, both of you. The Cairnlord surely knows of his defeat by this time and is gathering his power. He will send a force to recapture the citadel—but not before spring. The interval is ours; if we act at once, we retain the initiative."

"We're not ready for another battle. We have barely enough men to hold the citadel now, and if we draw off men to fight elsewhere, we might lose everything," protested Ord.

"No one need leave the citadel but you—Ordred, to the city on the Plain, and Staver, to the freemen's settlements near the Fastness, in the mountains to the north."

"Just the two of us?"

"You will need a guide for each of you, but no more than that. Speed and secrecy are most important."

Ord nodded. "And I suppose we must leave at once."

"You may leave in the morning."

With a weary sigh, Ord said, "We'll do as you say, but this time you must tell us more. We came south not knowing where we were heading, nor why. This is a hard way, prophet. Tell us our destination and our purpose. Don't hold things back to protect us. We won't shrink from what must be, I promise you."

The hooded figure did not respond at once. Finally, she said, "Perhaps it is time that you know more. Listen, then. Centuries ago, the Cairnlord undertook to destroy the Old Kingdom. Until now, he has succeeded without a setback. Using the sorcerers he had restored to life, spirits summoned up from Shagghya, gray men created by his magic, and foolish humans lured to his cause, he has broken down all that was achieved by generations of our ancestors and brought to a peak by Ambescand.

"But Ambescand foresaw what was to come and took precautions. In the days of his greatness, he forged the three blades of liberation, hammering his blood and his knowledge of the white art into the hot steel. He stripped himself of all his magic but one final spell and poured it all into those blades, which he hid in a safe place, to be used by his descendants when the time was right. Then, stripped of his magic, powerless and unprotected, he fell under the Cairnlord's attack.

"The Cairnlord knew that some magic had been worked against him, but he was not then strong enough to seek it out. Restoring the four broken sorcerers to life had drawn deeply on his magic. When he was ready, he began the long struggle against Ambescand's descendants. He brought forth the four he had recalled to life. Bellenzor the Blightbringer he sent upon the High City, and as the people sickened and died, he sent Cei Shalpan the Weather-master to bring freezing rain and hail. He launched Korang the Warmaker against the Fastness. After it had fallen, he loosed Skelbanda, Destroyer of Hope, on the people of the lake isle. When all else was in his power, he sent an army of gray men and humans against the cape where rise the Crystal Hills, the last stronghold of the Old Kingdom. His forces could not conquer, but they smashed the bridges and sealed the cape off from the world.

"The Cairnlord held dominion over all the land and ruled long where once the children of the Old Kingdom held sway. But the magic swords still existed, hidden in secrecy, and they gathered power as the generations passed. Now the citadel has fallen and a descendant of Ambescand is Master of the Southern Forest once again. This is the beginning. Next, Ordred must be established as Keeper of the Fastness and the Plain, and then Staver will go to the Crystal Hills. By then the Cairnlord will know that the final confrontation is at hand."

The brothers sat silent, transfixed by her account. She raised a pale hand and pointed at them in turn. "Make no mistake—his power is great, far greater than yours, though yours increases as you grow ever more attuned to the force in the blades and as they attune themselves to you. If we move silently and secretly it will soon be some danger for him to strike at you."

"He's struck at us already. He's sent his windwraith and the Rouser of Envy—and two gray men," Ord pointed out. "And we've handled them all."

"He has treated you as a minor annoyance. Had he suspected who you are, and what you bear, he would have turned his full power on you, as he is certain to do in a short time. At present the longer you stay together, the greater the danger to you all. The time will come for you to rejoin forces and fight as one. Some day, you must face the power of the Stone Hand. I pray you will be ready."

"You make it sound as though there's little hope for us or our cause," Ord said.

"While you live, there is always hope. The Cairnlord is powerful—but not invincible. He had ruled unchallenged for long and is less wary than he once was. His mind has long been fixed on new conquests. Signs and prophecies

that might have warned him of your coming have gone
unheeded. If you can arouse the people enslaved in the
High City and unite the fugitives who live in the mountains around the Fastness, you can seize both and bring
about the second part of the prophecy," said the dark
figure.

"We two—Staver and I—will capture a city and a
fortress? You may overrate us a bit, prophet," Ord said
with a smile.

"Just as the foresters rallied, so will the people of the
city and the mountains." The Dark Prophet pointed to
Ord. "When you show them that their masters can be defeated, they will take heart and follow you."

"How will I defeat the masters of a city single-handed?"

"I said once before that when your moment comes,
your weakness will be your strength and your vice your
virtue. You thought I spoke in riddles, but I said the
truth."

Ord laughed and shook his head, bewildered by her
words. "Prophet, my only vice is gaming. Am I to win
the city in a toss of the sticks?"

"It will not be so easy. The masters of the city are
in thrall to a demonic game. It occupies all their waking
time and fills their minds. The gray men keep the slaves
in check, the players of the game rule the gray men, and
the Cairnlord dominates all. But you are a gamester,
Ord, and always have been. Defeat the players, and you
will shatter their will. Their hold will be broken, and their
master's power lessened. The city will rally to you, and
you will then march on the Fastness." Turning to Staver,
the Dark Prophet went on, "You will tell the free men
who live in hiding in the mountains that they must prepare for an assault on the Fastness. When Ord arrives,
your combined forces will strike together."

"You make it sound very simple," Ord said.

"It will be difficult and dangerous, and you may both
be lost. But it must be attempted. The first steps have been
taken, and the rest must follow. If the Cairnlord is not
made to divide his forces, he will turn all his strength
against this citadel in the spring and recapture it. But
with an unknown enemy in the High City and the Fastness and new life stirring in the Crystal Hills, he will

begin to doubt his powers, and will fear and become weakened. And then the final days will be upon him."

"It seems we can't avoid our destiny even if we want to," said Ord. "But you pick an odd champion, prophet. I'm a gambler, to be sure, but I know nothing of the game played in the city. How can I defeat such devoted players at a game I don't even know?"

"You must not seek to learn it."

"Not learn . . . ?" Ord looked at her in amazement, but there was only darkness to be seen under that hood.

"There is a prophecy in the city that a man with red hair, a stranger to the city and the game, will defeat the masters and end their rule."

"If that's true, they may not be too hospitable to me."

"They will greet you eagerly," the Dark Prophet said. "Their faith is all in themselves, and they thirst for a new challenge."

"That's some help, I suppose," Ord admitted grudgingly. "But I still don't see how a man can win at a game he doesn't even know."

"Custom allows you to choose three gamesters to assist you. Choose the one who speaks your mother's name and allow him to select the others."

"How would they know . . . ?" Ord checked his question and waved his hand helplessly. "Never mind. There's so much I don't know, I won't even bother to ask."

"Have faith in Ambescand and in yourselves. That will bring you through."

Ord shrugged, pushed back his chair, and rose. As Staver stood, Ord said to him, "You'd better have a look at Col before you go to sleep. He was restless when I saw him last."

"I'll go to him now."

When Staver had said his farewell and passed out of earshot, Ord asked the Dark Prophet, "Why must he go north—to a stronghold of the Cairnlord? Staver's not a warrior, he's a healer—a most effective one, thanks to you."

"The word must be brought to the freedmen of the mountains."

"Why can't you carry the word? You told the foresters

and mistlanders of our coming—why not the mountain people?"

"The people of the mountains have waited long and heard many prophecies. They want no prophet—they want a leader. You think of Staver as a boy and no warrior, but I tell you this—the Iron Angel at his side will strike the blow that destroys the Cairnlord."

"Staver . . . ?"

"Yes. I can not say how or when, but this is foretold." When Ord turned an incredulous eye on her, the Dark Prophet said in a voice more human than he had yet heard issue from that shadowed hood, "Are you surprised that I admit ignorance? There is much I do not yet know."

Ord seemed surprised by these words. "Goodbowe told us . . . he said you could see the future . . . visit the past. . . ."

"So I can. But time is long, and life is short. Even the life of a wizard is too short to seek into every corner of time for the secrets others have buried so carefully. And yet I must seek until I find them—for your sakes and for all the generations to come."

"Is our struggle really so important?"

The Dark Prophet clutched Ord's hand. Her grip was warm, and living, and as she turned to him, Ord glimpsed the outline of a pale face under the obscuring hood. "No more important struggle has ever taken place than that of the sons of Vannen against the Cairnlord. Remember this when you enter the High City, Ord. Remember it in all you do," she said intently.

They departed early the next morning, quietly and without ceremony. At first light Ord and Kinnaury, whom he had picked to go with him, went to the sally port in the southern wall. The Dark Prophet awaited them in the guardroom.

"Staver will be here shortly. He's taking a last look at one of the injured men," Ord explained.

Kinnaury, at the gate, said, "He be coming now, my lord."

"Who's with him?"

"Helmer."

Ord groaned. "Helmer? The blind man? Has my brother gone completely mad to choose a blind guide?"

"There's no man knows the mountains as well as Helmer, my lord. Blind he may be, but he can see with his ears and his hands better than most with two eyes," said Kinnaury.

"I've heard that, too, and I know Staver trusts him. But Staver is my brother, and I think he risks too much by this—"

"Staver is to be a king, like you," the Dark Prophet broke in, "and he must make his own decisions unhindered. Say nothing about his choice."

Ord took a deep breath, as if preparing to launch into a speech, but instead he was silent. He glowered at the Dark Prophet, then out the gate at his brother and Helmer approaching, then he threw up his hands. "Why bother complaining? A blind guide is no crazier than anything else that's happened to us these last few weeks."

The Dark Prophet said, "Staver must move through guarded lands, where the safest time to travel is by night. What better guide in the darkness than a blind man? He had made a wise choice—as wise, in his case, as your choice of a forester to guide you."

Ord was resigned. "I won't argue, prophet, but I'd feel better if he had a skilled man-at-arms to travel with him."

"Helmer's a fine bowman, my lord. If he can hear a thing, he be hitting it dead center," Kinnaury volunteered. "He be as good as any man I know with the quarterstaff, too."

Ord nodded and said no more. The others entered, and after a quick exchange of greetings, Kinnaury and Helmer left to load the waiting skiff.

"One final thing before you leave," said the prophet. "I must place a concealing spell on your swords, to make them appear like ordinary blades taken from a gravemound. Best that the Cairnlord's followers see nothing to arouse their suspicions."

"What of our followers? We want them to recognize the swords, don't we?" Ord asked.

"Very few know the prophecy Goodbowe knew. But

if you must reveal the true nature of the blades, you may lift the spell by an act of will."

The Dark Prophet took the swords in her hands, one by one, and spoke words in an unfamiliar language. Staver thought, at one point, that he recognized sounds similar to those used by Zandinell when he spoke the spell of the door, but he could not be sure. The language was guttural and unpleasant to the ear. Again, Staver had the thought of words not meant for a human throat.

The spell was quickly made. The Dark Prophet laid a hand on the shoulder of each of the brothers and guided them to the outer door. As they left, she touched first Staver, then Ord, on the shoulder blade where the amulet was implanted. At her touch they felt a sense of renewed confidence—strength seemed to flow through them. They looked back from the water's edge, but the outer door was closed, and the castle was silent and dark in the misty dawn.

They rowed to the northeast bank, and there they beached the skiff. With Kinnaury in the lead, they set out directly north. The forest was bright with autumn now, and the leaves lay thick underfoot in many places along the trail. Nights were chill, but they lit no fires except for a small smokeless cooking fire at midday.

They marched north along winding trails, passing on their way abandoned hamlets like the one Staver and Jem had found. But these had long stood empty. They investigated one and found evidence of disorderly flight. Nearby in the woods, they came upon four skeletons.

"Cairnlord's men killed them. A raid," Kinnaury said.

"Why? Do the Cairnlord's servants steal from these people? Is it to punish them?" Ord asked.

Kinnaury squatted down beside the bleached bones of a child. He laid his hand on the little skull and stared blankly into the dark wood beyond. "They did not raid our village to punish us, and we had nothing for them to steal. They killed for the joy that killing gave them—no other cause."

"Madness . . ." Ord whispered.

"Not madness—evil," said Helmer. "Thirty years ago they killed my parents and all the others in my village. I was in the woods alone, hunting for berries, else I would have died with the rest. Above the sound of the flames and the groans of the dying, I heard their laughter."

"It's as though they must be killing and killing without stop. You would think they be living on death," Kinnaury said.

They covered the skeletons and proceeded north. On the fifth day, they reached the edge of the forest. Grasslands stretched out before them, and far and faint in the distance the outline of mountains was sketched against the sky.

They crossed the grasslands by a trail Kinnaury knew and went on into the foothills. When they reached the mountains, Kinnaury fell back and allowed Helmer to guide them. No words passed between the two men, but the shift in leadership was clear. Ord, still doubtful, said nothing but observed closely.

Their plan was to travel directly north through the mountains, until they were well past the watchtower at Southmark. They were then to split up, Ord and Kinnaury turning eastward to the coast, while Staver and Helmer kept to a northern track. Under Helmer's lead, their time of travel changed. They went on into the dark hours and laid up in a guarded camp during the daytime. It seemed to Ord that they covered more ground each day, but still he doubted the wisdom of being led by a blind man.

Ord's skepticism came to an end on their fourth night in the mountains as they made their way in the shadow of a high cliff. The skies were cloudy and the moon was young, but Helmer strode along confidently, with no more than an occasional delicate, almost soundless tap of his staff on the path ahead to guide him. Suddenly he came to an abrupt halt and waved the others to cover.

Ord, crouched a few paces behind him, took a firm grip on his hilt. He did not wish to risk the noise of movement; he could only hope that if a patrol came upon them, the blind man would get safely out of the way before the fighting started. To his amazement Ord saw Helmer fit an arrow to his bow. As he watched, the blind man raised the bow, pointed it down the trail, and slowly drew it back.

A vague shape came into view around a curve in the trail ahead and vanished at once into the shadows. Helmer released his arrow. No sooner had Ord heard the soft thump of the arrow hitting flesh than Helmer was drawing his bow for a second shot. A startled cry came from up ahead, then the thud of a second arrow, and then a scream that faded as the wounded man plunged over the edge.

Helmer waited for a moment, then rose and walked ahead. He stopped by the body of a man wearing the conical helmet of the Cairnlord's mountain patrol. Quickly running his hands over the body and finding nothing, he tumbled him over the edge.

"Incredible shot, Helmer," Ord said.

"My second shot was hurried. I had to take the rearmost man first, so the other could not retreat."

"You did it perfectly."

"The second man should not have cried out. My aim was poor."

"It was better than any other man could have done."

"I thank you," said the blind man. In a low confidential voice he added, "Do you think now that Staver has a man-at-arms to protect him?"

Ord recalled his remark back at the guardroom and regretted it. "I think he made a wiser choice than I would have made," he said. "Now I know he'll be safe."

Two days later, they separated. Ord looked back from the trail to the seacoast and saw the two figures on the mountain ledge. Staver's hand was raised in farewell. Helmer stood motionless, hands clasped on his staff, eyes shrouded, facing them.

Ord turned and went on for a time. When he looked back again, they were not to be seen. He set his eyes to the east and walked toward the city, where the game and the gamesters awaited.

18

Challenge to the High City

Ord and Kinnaury walked eastward across the plain on
roads no human foot had trod for generations. All around
them was the wild tangle of rich land long neglected and
now overgrown, and often they came upon a young tree,
thick as a man's thigh, sprung up in the very pathway.
The evidence of abandonment, though it was disheartening, at least offered promise of safer passage. And, indeed, the two men journeyed unhindered to within sight
of the city of the game, once the High City of the Old
Kingdom.

Several times along their way, they heard the sound of
living creatures, and the sounds were of a kind not comforting to hear. Kinnaury walked with his axe at the
ready, and Ord's hand was on the hilt of his dark sword.
But they saw no one and believed themselves to be
unseen, their passage unknown.

Ord's first view of the city came at sunset, and he was
stunned by the sudden clutch of its beauty at his heart.
The sun was at their backs, on the rim of the mountains.
All the plain behind them and around them was in
shadow. They climbed a low rise, and the ground fell
gently away before them; and there in the distance, ablaze
with the golden glow of the declining sun, rose the city.

It stood on a hill between the sea and the plain. Its
walls were of pale stone the color of honey, and the cop-
per roofs of the turrets glinted like mirrors under the
leaning shafts of light. The domes and towers within the
city shone like jewels, as if all were part of some fabu-
lous diadem wrought in gold, flashing in motionless splendor under the deepening blue sky.

The Headland held no sight to compare with this. Ord
stood entranced until the topmost spire was sunk in
shadow. He turned, still dazzled by such magnificence,
and felt a sudden flare of anger at the thought of this city

defiled by the power of the Cairnlord and the presence of his minions. It was as if he had seen a fair woman helpless in the grip of some loathsome beast.

They camped that night on the lee side of a steep rise overlooking a stream. Despite the fact that they had as yet seen no one, they took turns keeping guard, for they had heard disquieting sounds in the thick growth on either side of them during the daylight hours and had no wish to be taken unaware, especially at night, by whatever creature made them. On his second watch Ord heard the rustle of movement below them and saw a ripple in the tall grass, approaching their camp. He felt a tingling in his shoulder and drew his sword. The moon flashed on the bright blade as it came forth. At once the noise ceased and was heard no more that night.

In the morning they washed in the stream, and as they dried under the early sun, they ate the last of the food they had brought with them. Once dried, and warmed, and fed, they buried their traveling clothes and packs in the soft soil of the bank. The time had come to don the outfits the Dark Prophet had given them on the morning of their departure.

They were to come to the city in the clothing of a people to the south and west, of a little-known kingdom beyond the forest and across a wide river. The garments were of fine stuff, expertly woven and sewn, and as Ord put on one after another, he felt his spirits improve. On the Headland he had won the reputation of being a dandy because of his conviction that one ought to dress in attire suitable to the occasion and the undertaking, and to his own particular temper. Actually he was not quite the coxcomb he was thought—and pretended—to be. He would have been quick to agree that a battlefield was not the place for finery; he had, in fact, felt comfortable until now in the patched, stained, much-worn garments and the borrowed cloak and boots that he had worn on his travels. But he was now on his way to topple the rulers of a great city—to strike a defiant blow against a powerful enemy and seize a kingdom with no more to aid him than his own wits and courage—and one loyal follower. The task at hand seemed to call for a certain magnificence, and he was pleased to find, as he opened the pouch tucked in among the garments, that the Dark Prophet had provided magnificence even beyond his imagining. The pouch contained four heavy rings, the smallest stone in them the size of his little fingernail, and a medallion on a heavy chain.

Ord inspected himself in a still pool beside the stream, turned to his companion, and said, "Come, take a look at yourself, Kinnaury. It will warm your heart. We're as splendid a pair of princes as ever walked through the gate of the High City."

And so they were. Kinnaury was in gray, while Ord was in black from head to foot. Each of them wore a close-fitting black hood that concealed all but his eyes, nose, and mouth. The hood covered neck and shoulders, and came to a point on the chest and back. Around his neck Kinnaury wore a heavy silver medallion. Ord's medallion was of gold, with a large lenticular diamond set into it.

"It is finely clad we are, indeed, my lord," said Kinnaury.

"Yes. Perhaps the masters of the city will be so overwhelmed by us that they'll turn the place over to us on the spot," Ord said, grinning at his reflection. "That would save everyone a bit of trouble. I must say, Kinnaury, I'd prefer that to playing a game of which I know nothing. However . . ." His smile faded, and he was silent for a moment. Then, rising and throwing back his cloak, he turned to Kinnaury and said, "Let's be on our way."

The road soon began to show unmistakable signs of use, and the roadside fields, of cultivation. Still they encountered no one until they came to a crossroads quite near the city, where they passed a small boy and an old woman. The pair scurried out of their path and stood by the wayside with heads bowed. Ord went on about a dozen paces and then stopped and shook his head.

"Stay here, Kinnaury," he said. "I'm going back to talk to them."

The old woman and the boy stood frozen as he approached. He smiled to reassure them, but they showed no sign of ease.

"Good day to you," he said. When they made no reply, he reached out to pat the child on the head. The boy

made a strange, unintelligible noise and recoiled as if
from a blow.

"We did no wrong, master. We did nothing, nor said
nothing. Boy can't speak, and I'm old and sick. Let us
be, please," the old woman whined.

"I'm not your master, and I'm not going to hurt you."

"Not about to hurt us?"

"No. Why should I?"

"It be the way of folk in the city to do as they please
to us."

"I'm not from the city."

The old woman seemed no less suspicious. "You wear
sword . . . like the guardsmen of the city do."

"Men wear swords in the country I come from."

"You come from otherwhere? And travel to the city?"

"I do."

Now she studied him more closely. With a dirty finger
she pointed to his hood. "You cover your head. Why do
you cover your head so no one sees the color of your
hair?"

"It's the custom of my country."

"And is it that your hair is bright red?"

"Would it mean something if it were? Are red-haired
men unwelcome in the High City?"

"A far country you come from, truly. Since my own
father's father was a small boy—smaller than this fellow
here—no one has spoken of the city by that name."

"Perhaps it's time to speak of the High City again. And
of the Old Kingdom," Ord said. He took the medallion
from around his neck and slipped it into his pouch, then
reached up to pull off his hood. "I've come to the city to
play the game they play, though I know nothing of it.
And I mean to win."

The old woman gaped at him for a moment, then let
out a cackle of joyous laughter and cried, "He's here! The
red-haired man has come!" Hugging the boy, she said,
"The Dark Prophet told my father, and he believed and
told me, and now I've seen it come about, boy! They
don't want to believe me, and they don't listen anymore,
but it's happened, just as was foretold!"

"What was foretold?" Ord asked her.

"All! The day of your coming, and the clothing you'd wear, and the ones you'd meet on the way . . ."

Ord asked, "Do the masters of the city know of this prophecy?"

"They know nothing but the game. It consumes them, as it did their fathers and those before them."

Ord nodded thoughtfully. "Then go to the people who refused to believe you before. Tell them I'm here and that they are to be ready."

"Ready?"

"Ready to rise up and overthrow their masters."

Her eyes widened. "There be gray men in city! No one can fight gray men!"

"You've forgotten your own prophecy. The gray men will fall beneath my sword."

The old woman took the child by the shoulders. "You'll be witness, boy—the red-haired man has come! I'll tell the people!"

She shuffled back down the side road, the boy at her side. Ord watched them go, returning the old woman's wave when she turned, and then he slipped the hood over his head once again. Kinnuary watched with a grave expression. Ord sensed the forester's disapproval.

"You think that was a rash thing to do," he said.

"She could be spy," Kinnaury said uneasily.

"True, she could." Ord was silent for a time, then he burst out, "But what am I to do? I come here without instructions, knowing nothing and no one. How are the people to know I'm here?"

Kinnaury said as uneasily as before, "Dark Prophet gave us hoods to wear."

"She said to wear them when we enter the city, and we will. But I have to trust someone to alert the people. That old woman can spread a message quickly."

Kinnaury frowned and said nothing. Clearly he was unhappy with Ord's action. Ord himself wondered if he had been too impetuous and perhaps forewarned his enemies. Still, he needed support and he knew of no way to seek it without confiding in someone and risking betrayal. He might be able to beat these mysterious gamesters at their unknown game, but he knew that he and Kinnaury alone could not hope to defeat the guardsmen and their gray allies as well. He could only hope that the old woman was trustworthy and that her word would be believed. The more he thought of this, the flimsier his hope seemed, and he did his best to force his misgivings to the back of his mind. What was done was done, and there was nothing more to do but to go on.

A cool breeze from the sea tempered the warmth of the autumn sun, and they moved along the road briskly. They passed others more frequently now, and they too cringed and stood aside as had the old woman and the boy. Ord and Kinnaury went on unchecked until they reached the great west gate of the city.

It was past midday. Having walked since morning and eaten only a few scraps of food on starting out, they were hungry. When they came to the gate and found it shut—and a sullen crowd of ragged men and women standing listlessly before it—Ord's small stock of patience ran out.

"Why is the gate shut?" he asked one man.

"Guards don't choose to open it. Been waiting here since early day, but guards won't open gate," the man said dully.

"Why not?"

The man turned a bemused glance on him, and others who had overheard the exchange looked on with wary interest. When Ord repeated his question, the man waved a hand in aimless gesture and said, "Guards do as they please is why not. You must know that. Us, all we can do is wait until guards feel like letting us in. No good to ask why or why not."

Ord looked at the gate and the heavy walls all around. His eye was caught by a large bell, tarnished to a dark brown, that hung above the gate to its left.

"What's that bell? Is it an alarm?" he asked.

"It's for challenge," a second man volunteered. "When men used to come to play masters at the game, they rang bell to announce themselves. Bell doesn't be rung for a long time now."

"There be men full grown has never heard it ring," added another. "It is that long without a challenge."

"This should prove a memorable day then," Ord said. Turning to Kinnaury, extending a gloved hand in invitation, he raised his voice and said for all the crowd to hear,

"Announce us, Kinnaury—and be sure the bell is heard all through the city."

Kinnaury slung his axe behind him, threw back his cloak, and rubbed his palms. Stepping up to the bell rope he took a firm grip and pulled. A deep note sounded over the crowd. He pulled harder, and the note came again, louder. Again and again came the deep, penetrating sound, and as Kinnaury tugged harder at the rope, little showers of mortar spilled from the bell brackets. The bell lurched forward a bit and hung for a moment at a precarious angle. Then Kinnaury tugged at the rope again, and just as the gate swung wide and the officer of the guard stalked forth with sword drawn, his face red, and four guards at his back, the big bell ripped loose from the wall and crashed to the ground scarcely an arm's length from his side. The red of his face changed quickly to a ghastly white.

Kinnaury looked down on the guardsmen, the futile rope hanging limp from his hands. "It was loose," he said.

The officer glared at him, and the guards moved out to encircle him. Ord stepped forward between Kinnaury and the officer and raising his open hands, said, "I've come to play the game of the city masters."

The officer waved the guards to a halt. "Who are you?" he demanded.

"I come from a kingdom far to the south. Take me to the masters. I wish to present my challenge."

"There are no kingdoms to the south."

"None you know of, apparently. Well, come along, bring us to the masters," Ord said impatiently.

The officer of the guard looked at this newcomer uncertainly, then turned his eyes from Ord's unblinking gaze. No challenger had arrived in the city in his lifetime, and he had no instructions for dealing with such a man.

"You've broken the challenge bell," he said, his voice somewhere between accusation and sulking.

"That bell hasn't been rung since you were a baby. Now stop this foolish talk and take me in," Ord said.

The officer sheathed his sword and said decisively, as though he had just thought of it, "I'll take you to the masters. You can give your challenge to them." Turning to the guards, he barked, "Back to your posts, all of you.

See that this bell is taken inside, and have it back in place by morning. Round up a dozen of these beggars to do the work."

"Don't bother. You'll have no more need for the challenge bell once I've finished with the masters," Ord said.

"No one beats the masters. No one ever has, no one ever will."

"I will," Ord said.

For the second time that day he reached up and pulled off the black hood. At the sight of his red hair, the ragged crowd at the gate stopped in their tracks and gaped at him. The officer looked at them, then at him, and seemed to sense something amiss but could not tell quite what it was.

"A warm day, captain. A hood is most uncomfortable on such a day," Ord said pleasantly.

"Why are they staring?"

"Perhaps they've never seen a red-haired man before. Would you lead on, captain?"

The captain of the guard glared back and forth between Ord, the crowd, and his men, but could think of nothing to say and of no course of action but to lead on. They passed over the flagstones under the dark echoing archway of the gate and emerged onto a sunlit avenue. Before them in the center of the avenue, a fountain hurled a rainbow spray five marks into the air. Beyond the fountain stood a building made of the same honey-colored stone as the walls.

Ord did his best not to show it, but he was deeply impressed by the sheer magnitude of the High City. He had hoped, on his way, to observe and gauge sizes, distances, numbers, and any other information that might be of help in a battle waged within these walls. Now he saw that it would be futile to try. The city was immense. There was nothing like it on the Headland, and even the citadel on the lake isle was small in comparison. Nevertheless, he observed what he could.

The avenue on which they walked was broad and smoothly paved. On either side lay an expanse of grass. A ribbon of shimmering water, debouched from a fountain on either side of the gate, flowed through the grass on each side. Beyond the grass stood a row of buildings, some tall enough to obscure the city walls behind them. The smallest building appeared to be at least four marks high, and the largest, perhaps eight marks from the ground to its topmost tower. The buildings were broad, flat-fronted, with narrow streets and alleys running between them. The distance from the façade of one building, across the grassy strips and the avenue to the one facing it, Ord estimated at about seventy marks.

He glanced over his shoulder at the gate and saw that it formed the third side of a formidable trap. Anyone entering was surrounded on three sides, completely in the open, with no shelter from missiles raining from rooftops and towers. He could not see them clearly from this angle, but Ord was certain that those canals in the green strips were too wide to be vaulted. The city was secure against frontal attack. Its water supply appeared plentiful. If food had been stored—and he was sure it had—this city would be self-sufficient behind its high, thick walls, able to withstand any besieging army.

The central fountain loomed larger and larger as they approached. Ord had never seen such a thing before and was filled with wonder. He understood what it was but could not imagine how it worked. The men who had built this city were clearly no ordinary breed. Looking at the ragged, scrawny, hangdog lot that shuffled on the avenue, shrinking from the path of the guard captain, he wondered if these people could be the descendants of the builders. It seemed impossible to him that a race that could build such a city should ever fall to this wretched state.

But as he walked on and observed more closely, he saw things to qualify his first impression. The city people were gaunt, but their leanness was not weakness; there was muscle and toughness in it. He watched a pair of men maneuvering a heavy paving block into place at the edge of the avenue and others digging in the grass under the lazy eye of an overfed guard. He caught the sidelong glance of one of the diggers at the guard, the burning eye that looked hungrily on the sword, and he knew that the spirit of resistance still smoldered in these people.

Far down the avenue by the fountain that now towered over them, they came upon another group of workers replacing paving stones. Ord stopped the guard captain. Raising his voice over the sound of falling water, he said, "Wait here a moment. I want to observe these men at work."

"Why stop for this rabble?"

"There's much stonework in my kingdom. Their method is unfamiliar, and I'm interested in seeing how they work."

"You'll not be going back to your kingdom. No one has ever left the tower of the game victorious except the masters."

Ord smiled and nodded, as if he were humoring a child, and walked to where the party of nine men were working. The guard started toward him but fell back at a gesture from the captain. The workers at first ignored him; then, one by one, they noticed his red hair and his sword, then looked at him more closely with awakening interest.

Close to the fountain as they were, their voices could not be heard by the guard or the captain. Pointing to one of the paving blocks, Ord said, "I'm supposed to be asking you about your work. Don't stare at me, act as though you're explaining it."

A young man hunkered down beside the block and gestured for Ord to join him. Ord crouched, and the young man said, "Are you come to challenge the masters?"

"I am."

"And do you know the way of the game?"

"I know nothing of it."

"There's an old tale . . . something about a man with red hair."

"I know the prophecy. I've come to fulfill it. Stop staring, will you? Point at the stone."

The young man did as Ord bade him. "What do you want of us?" he asked.

"You must be ready. When I defeat the gamesmasters, they'll be demoralized and confused. That's your opportunity. You must rise up and strike at your guards. You outnumber them about twenty to one, near as I can judge."

"They're armed."

Ord took up a sledge and hefted it. He handed it to the young man and said, "So are you."

A second young man squatted on Ord's other side. "Gray men be in the city. We have no weapons against them. No one dares stand up to a gray man."

"You take the guards and leave the gray men to me. How many of them?"

"Hard to tell. Gray men all look alike," the newcomer said. "I'd say ten. Might be twenty."

"I'll handle them. Are you with me?"

"Yes," said both men.

Peering closely at the stone, as if studying its dimensions intently, Ord said, "Be ready then. You'll have to hit fast and hard as soon as you get the signal. If I can't get to you. Kinnaury will." With a sidelong glance he indicated the tall forester.

Rising, brushing his gloved hands together, he rejoined the guard captain and Kinnaury. They walked on, around the fountain, to an open parklike area where Ord could see trees and a body of water in the distance. The area was dominated by the building of honey-colored stone. All around it stood small tents and pavilions. Many were occupied, and the people within sat before tables, motionless and silent, totally absorbed in some occupation Ord could not fathom. Behind the building and the gaudy tents, surrounded by green, stood an octagonal windowless tower of squat design and dark stone. The guard captain pointed to it.

"The tower of the game," he said.

19

The Game of God and Demon

Ord had assumed that the manners of the masters would reflect their elaborate surroundings and anticipated considerable ceremony and ritual before getting down to the work at hand. In this he was wrong. Scarcely had the guard captain taken him into the building of honey-colored stone and announced his challenge than he was surrounded by pallid men and women in robes of various

colors, all exhorting him to commence play at once. He
was taken aback for a moment by their sudden appearance and their feverish eagerness to play, but he
quickly recovered his composure, shook off their hands,
and waved them back.

"I've come a long way, and I'm hungry and thirsty.
There'll be no play until my companion and I have eaten
and drunk and shaken off the dust of the road," he said
firmly.

He and Kinnaury were ushered at once to a hall where
a table awaited. Food and drink were set before them.
The meal was excellent, but Ord's pleasure in it was
diminished by the hovering anxious presence of a crowd
of robed gamesters. People entered the room, observed
him, and left again in deep conversation with one another,
and newcomers took their places. Only as he listened to
their chatter did Ord come to understand the reason for
their eager excitement. For much of their lives—in the
case of the younger ones, for their entire lives—these
gamesters had played only against one another, constantly
practicing and preparing themselves for the coming of an
outsider, a true challenger, one with whom the game
might be played to an ending, with full rewards and
penalties. The last few outsiders to challenge them had
been desperate adventurers, half-trained, trusting to luck
and bluff. Surely, the masters repeated to one another,
surely this stranger in black with hair of a color never
seen in the city, surely he would prove to be a worthy
opponent and lead them through a regenerating sequence of moves and countermoves, feints and stratagems,
until at last they triumphed.

For they would win in the end; they had no doubt of
that. The game was their life and more than their life—
it was their reason for being, their entire universe. Even
to think that an outsider might overcome was a heresy
bordering on madness. Outsiders chose to think otherwise, and that was good. It brought challengers, and
stimulation, and life to the masters. But the game existed
for the masters, giving them sustenance; and they in
turn lived only for the sake of the game. In the nature of
things victory belonged to them.

Ord listened to their talk and said nothing. He and

Kinnaury finished eating and, at his insistence, were taken to a private chamber to rest and clean themselves.

When they were alone, Ord said, "If anything happens to me, Kinnaury, it will all be up to you. Take my sword, cut your way out, and rouse the people."

"What can happen to you, my lord?"

"I don't know. I feel uneasy, that's all. Playing a game I know nothing about . . . why should I play? The gamesters are weak and their guards are flabby and careless. We could take this city in a day."

"Dark Prophet said you must play."

"I know she did and I'll play—but I'd almost rather fight gray men. Though, I imagine I'll soon have my fill of that, too. There may be twenty of them in the city." Ord smiled ruefully and shook his head. "I hope the Dark Prophet knows what she's about."

"Dark Prophet said your brother would rule on the lake isle, and he rules there."

"True—but he nearly died in the process."

Neither man felt like talking after that. Ord flung his cloak and hood on a bench, stripped off his rings, and removed his gloves. The rings he placed in the pouch with his medallion. He splashed cold water on his face and neck, dried himself, and brushed the dust from his clothing. Turning to Kinnaury, he held out his hand. "Wish me luck," he said.

"All the luck in the world, my lord," Kinnaury said fervently.

"Now let's get to work."

They were surrounded by robed men and women as soon as they emerged into sight. Ord, the challenger, was now to choose his assistants. Once this was done, play could begin.

He was led from the building to the open area separating it from the tower. Here, brightly colored tents and pavilions stood all about. In them, at practice and at study, were the gamesters from whose number he was to select three to assist him. At his arrival most of them rose and hurried to present themselves before him, reciting their names and an unintelligible litany that he took to be their credentials. It all meant nothing to him. He listened for a single word.

A gray-haired man pushed his way to Ord's side. In a low voice he said, "I urge you to choose me, and my daughter Ciantha."

Ord studied the man. There was nothing special about his appearance that Ord could see. Like all the others, he was thin and pale. He wore a robe of blue so deep it was almost black. Around his neck hung a medallion of gold set with blue stones. Ord had noticed similar medallions on several others since his arrival.

"Why you?" he asked. "And who is to be my third?"

"I am a first-level master," said the man, laying a hand lightly on the gold medallion. "There is no finer gamester in the city. My daughter is the best of the third-level players, and the third I will pick is a former first-level master, now disgraced."

"Disgraced?"

"He lost to a challenger. Now he is mine. His skill is still great, I assure you."

Ord tried to gather his thoughts. It was difficult to concentrate, with the crowd pressing all around him, calling out names and victories, plucking at his arms, forcing themselves upon him. He was still uneasy about his role in this affair, still unwilling to trust his fortunes to strangers on the strength of the Dark Prophet's word, more ready to trust all to his own skill and swordsmanship than to place himself in the hands of others.

"If your skill is so great . . . ," he began.

The gamester responded before Ord could finish. "In order to exercise our skill to the full, we require your strength and vitality—your newness. And you, in order to have any chance at all, require our skill."

Ord knew he had no choice. "Come, then, and assist me," he said.

"You honor me, challenger. My name is Maridon, and I will serve you to the last play," said the man.

The crowd nearest them was still for a moment; then a low murmur ran through the assembly as one turned to another to remark Ord's choice. The words that he could distinguish were encouraging: apparently Maridon was the expert he claimed to be and the crowd saw the exciting prospect of a long and complex game, one to be reviewed and replayed and studied for generations to come—when the challenger was long dead and forgotten, and the names of Maridon and Ciantha were sunk in defeat and disgrace. For he would surely lose, the gamesters said knowingly to one anther. The game was the masters', and no challenger could hope to overcome. And to align oneself with a challenger was to choose certain defeat.

The others quickly left them, hurrying to the dark tower, and at Maridon's signal a girl and a very old man joined them. The girl was dark-haired and quite beautiful, but her solemnity of manner, and the intensity of her expression, discouraged the interest her beauty aroused. The old man was silent, bowed, his head low and his gaze fixed on the ground at his feet. Ord would have guessed from the man's posture that he was in disgrace even if Maridon had said nothing of it.

All the others were gone now, and the four stood alone. The tents and pavilions stood empty, their flaps and pennants lifting and falling in the gentle breeze, looking like a field of bright flowers under the late sun. In the stillness a bird called and another answered it. In that moment the world was a good and desirable place to be and Ord was loath to turn his back on it and enter the windowless tower of the game.

He turned to Maridon and asked, "Do you expect me to win?"

"In all the history of the game, no one has ever defeated the masters."

Pointing to the old man, Ord asked, "What about him? You said he was defeated."

"He was. But his challengers played on, and I defeated them, and they and all they had became mine."

"So that's how you do it. Just wear the challenger down. A challenger can win a battle, but he can't hope to win the war."

Maridon pondered those words for a moment, then said, "That is a reasonable image."

"Then tell me this, Maridon, and tell the truth: if you don't expect me to win, why do you risk your disgrace, and your daughter's, and this poor old man's, by assisting me? That makes no sense that I can see."

Maridon nodded as if he had expected this question, but his reply was slow in coming and was halting and uncertain. "Words came to me, challenger. . . . A dream or a vision, I am uncertain, but you were part of it. . . . Your appearance, your manner of coming. . . . Tell me, what do you know of the game?"

"Nothing."

Maridon and Ciantha exchanged a glance of recognition in which there was a trace of fear. "Even that was foretold," Ciantha said.

"I still don't see why this would make you align yourselves with me," Ord said.

"In my dream or vision—my revelation, I must call it —your coming was a portent of great change and upheaval. I sensed that the game might never be played again and I knew then that I had to play. Not as one of many masters contending against a hapless challenger, but as the chief antagonist against all. Can you understand?"

"I confess I can't, Maridon. The game is everything to you, and yet you'd be the one to help end it forever."

"The game is our heritage and our way of life. Without the game, there is nothing. If it must end, what greater meaning could I bring to my life, and my daughter's, than to be the last and greatest player? Could I allow such a deed to be done by another?"

Ord looked from father to daughter and saw the fixed expressions of the possessed. Even the old man had lifted his head at Maridon's words, and an eager light shone in his ancient eyes.

"No, of course you couldn't," Ord said. "So lead the way, Maridon, and may you have the victory you crave."

As the three gamesters walked before him, Ord said to Kinnaury in a voice too low for the others to overhear, "Stay close. No telling what goes on in that tower. I think we've come to a city of madmen."

Kinnaury's earlier confidence was no longer evident. "No madder than we are to be here," he said glumly, then quickly added, "if I may say so, my lord."

Ord looked at him with quick severity, then burst into laughter. "You may, Kinnaury. Well you may. Do you know, it never occurred to me to ask what the stakes are? I don't even know what we stand to win or lose."

"Perhaps it were best not to know."

"That's a thought," Ord said, as they followed the trio

of gamesters into the shadow of the dark tower. "We'll learn soon enough."

Within the tower high torches cast restless light on a narrow flight of steps that rose between dark stone walls. As they ascended the curving steps, Ord heard heavy doors shut behind them, and the torches fluttered, sending shadows weaving underfoot and all around them. He went on, around in what he judged to be a full circle, and as he rose, the light grew brighter. They emerged on a platform illuminated by a soft glow that came from the center of the tower.

Then Ord saw the crystal, and he stared in wonder.

The interior of the tower was about six marks from wall to wall. The platform, which ran all around the inside, was just over a mark in width. Here by the steps it was flat and open, but opposite the staircase were three ranks of benches that curved a third of the way around the tower. At its inner edge, running unbroken around the platform, was a railed fence of lacy metalwork, sloping inward as if it were meant to support people gazing downward into the interior of the tower. There, in the well of the tower, its nearest surface an arm's length below the level of the platform, a curving dome of crystal shone with a pale inner light.

Ord turned to Maridon with a question, but the master was preoccupied, speaking closely with Ciantha while his slave dragged high-backed wooden chairs into place near the rail. Ord then noticed that the other masters had ranged themselves on the opposite side of the platform, where they were seated on the stone benches, their eyes intent on the crystal dome.

Maridon touched him lightly on the arm and said, "Come to the railing. We must be ready."

"What shall I do?"

"Watch. Learn. The game may unfold itself to you. Do not interfere."

They stepped to the railing and stood side by side. Ciantha came and stood next to Ord. Across from them three men and a woman rose and came to the opposite railing. All four wore the gold medallion. The sight recalled to Ord the gift of the Dark Prophet, which he still carried in his pouch. He drew out her gold medallion and

placed it around his neck. One of the opposing gamesters
saw him and quickly spoke to his companions. Maridon
turned to Ord, noticed the medallion, and said, "You
have power, challenger. You were clever to hide it until
now."

"I hope it's power enough."

"No more. It begins."

The crystal dimmed and grew dark. In the darkness,
far and faint, tiny points of light appeared and swiftly
grew brighter and more numerous. Soon they had swelled
to blurred discs of light, and they grew still more into
slowly spiraling pinwheels of glowing pale dust. Ord felt
the platform solid under his feet; yet at the same time he
felt himself inside the crystal, hurtling through an infinite
cold emptiness, while ages passed between the beats of
his heart.

The wheels of light grew, and one by one receded as
they grew, until only three remained, huge against a
backdrop of white-speckled blackness. Ord felt himself
pulled toward one of the spirals; then a force tugged him
away toward another, and it was into this wheel of light
that he plunged. Brighter and brighter it grew; then the
surrounding light shattered, and once again points of light
burst around him, and he soared like an arrow in ever-
swifter flight among them. Huge glowing spheres these
became—of gold and blue and ember red, and other
colors for which he had no name—and their beauty tore
at him like pain. They swung round on the track of a
mighty circuit; some of them circled each other in pairs
and triplets, and one group of five whirled around and
around like jewels tossed by a juggler; and behind them
all, sweeping across his vision, was a veil of pure white
trailing streamers and tatters of light behind it.

Again he felt the tugging, and his will was buffeted.
He was pulled toward a blue light, then he veered away
toward a deep red, and then to a pale yellow. As he came
closer to the yellow ball, the others all grew faint with
distance, and their color faded. Soon they were only tiny
points of brilliance, then these too vanished in the growing
yellow light.

Ord saw then that four beadlike objects spun around
this yellow sphere, like toys at the end of a string that a

child whirls around his head. His path began to curve so as to intersect with the track of one of the smaller spheres, and soon, to his surprise, he was skimming over the surface of a world unlike any he had ever imagined. And all the while, his hands were tight around the railing and his feet firm on the platform.

This was a world of smoke and flame. As Ord dipped lower, dusky clouds shut out the light from above, and the light below him rose up red and gold as it burst from mountaintops and ran like fiery honey down their flanks, slow and bright.

Ages whirled by in instants. Rains came, and the world below was swept by turbulent seas. Then the clouds dissipated, and the skies cleared; the waters receded, and the surface of the world was covered with greenery, and living things appeared. Huge some of them were, and grotesque, and some were hideous monsters. They multiplied, and flourished, and then were gone, and a new creature walked where once their tread had shaken the ground.

This new being was small and agile. It had blue skin and a mane of silvery white on its head and over its shoulders. It walked erect on two legs and carried weapons in its hands.

The blue creatures grew in number and spread across the face of the plain on which they first appeared. Soon they had built settlements and had begun to clothe themselves in differing ways and separate into different bands. A plague came among them, and the blue creatures fell, and writhed in pain, and turned white, and died in great numbers until only a scattered handful were left. Those who lived began to rebuild.

Ord realized that he was watching men like himself, though he did not understand how he could see these things, or where they were taking place, or whether they were real or imagined. The people were strangely colored and oddly shaped; their garments were peculiar, and their buildings outlandish; but they struggled and suffered and fought to stay alive and save those around them, as men do.

Plague struck the blue people again and again, and flood and famine devastated their land, but always the survivors gathered their strength and rebuilt a better life

from the wreckage of the old one. Their settlements grew
into towns, then into cities. They learned to master the
plague, and control the floods, and plan for times of
drought and hunger. They learned to navigate the waters
of their world and built vessels that took them far out to
sea, where they found new lands and new races. One of
these races, a hairless violet-skinned people with high
crests of flesh on their heads and webbed hands, greeted
the blue voyagers with friendliness, welcomed them
ashore, and then cruelly slew every one.

In time other blue people came. These were more wary,
and when the crested race attacked, there was battle.
The blue people retreated. But eventually they returned
in great strength, and a long war began that ended with
the defeat and subjection of the crested race.

Age followed age as Ord stood fascinated on the platform in the tower, with the game unfolding before him
and around him. The crested race won equality with their
conquerors, and at last the two races became one, pale
blue and hairless, with a crest on its skull.

Ord watched generations come and go, and the shape
of land and waters change, cities and whole civilizations
rise and fall, and slow inexorable time pass with the
speed of a lightning bolt—and yet not too swiftly to be
perceived and understood as if he were a participant.
He began to grasp the sense of the game, and feel the
exhilaration it brought to those who gave it their life. As
the lives and the destinies of these little people unfolded
before him, he came to feel like a god—their god; they
were his people, in his power, subject to his will, vulnerable beneath his hand.

A twinge in his shoulder, like the prick of a dagger
point, brought Ord out of his reverie. He was clutching
the rail, both hands white-knuckled, and his garments
were drenched in sweat. He glanced at Maridon and
Çiantha; they stared fixedly down at the crystal, as did
the masters opposite.

When Ord looked again, the blue race had spread over
their entire world. Their cities dwarfed the High City and
were filled with buildings of odd form and unimaginable function. Small shining objects traveled at great
speed over the land and sea, and through the very air.

War came upon them again—the blue people of one continent against those of the other two—and this war was utterly devastating. When it ended, the world was smoldering under a black blanket, with glowing pits that burst and bubbled through the ash. The blue people were nowhere to be seen. Ord glanced up at the rail where his opponents stood and saw them lean forward and turn to one another with pleased expressions.

Then a tiny band of blue people appeared, and the old struggle began anew. Death was all around them now. It blew in the winds and rode on the rain and burrowed in the soil. Monstrous things rose from the glowing pits to stalk the sick and weakened survivors. Their number shrank to a handful; they fought on, increased, and shrank again under the deadly onslaught.

Now, on all this world only a score of the blue people remained alive, and they were making their way across the deadly surface to a place of refuge. Far to the west a shimmering cloud of poison gathered and rolled forth to intercept them. The things from the glowing pits crawled toward them from all sides. One of the blue people fell, then another, and then two more. The rest staggered slowly on.

Ord could not bear to watch their final extinction. He lifted his eyes and saw, across the crystal dome, the masters looking down on the little tragedy with expressions of triumph on their flushed, glistening faces. In an instant of revelation, the nature of the game burst upon Ord: the blue people had to be saved, or he and his cause were lost. He did not understand how such a thing could be or how he could know of it, yet he knew beyond a doubt that it was so.

Maridon, and Ciantha, and the old slave were clinging desperately to the rail, leaning forward, taut as bowstrings, their faces contorted with the strain of concentration, their breathing loud and labored. Below them the deadly cloud drifted nearer, and the monstrous pit creatures closed in for the attack. Ciantha swayed, and a trickle of blood ran from the corner of her mouth.

Instinctively Ord reached out and laid his hands on theirs in a firm grip. As his fingers closed, he felt a surge of strength inside him. The medallion around his neck grew so heavy it seemed to pull him down, and it burned against his chest. Something poured into him from the medallion and passed through him and into the masters, and with the power of the medallion, something of his own substance was being drained away, for he felt a weakness coming over his. His legs grew weary and all became dim before his eyes. His grasp on Ciantha's hand and on Maridon's loosened and slipped.

As he was ready to let go, a warm pulse beat faintly in his shoulder. Ord knew then that he was not alone. The pulse strengthened and spread through his body. His grip held firm; his legs were steady; his vision cleared. He looked at the masters opposite and saw that they no longer appeared so certain of their victory; some were shaken and dismayed by his recovery. Beside him Ciantha, Maridon, and the old man breathed evenly once more, and the strain was gone from their faces.

In the world of the crystal, the blue people had reached sanctuary. They were rebuilding once again. Green had appeared here and there on the plains and hills, and the creatures of the glowing pits were no more to be seen. Ord focused his attention on the game.

This time the blue people rebuilt their civilization in a different way. No cities grew, no tall buildings rose, no strange casings were forged to carry them from place to place. Their development was not outward but inward—to the depths of their own natures and beyond, to the secrets underlying all things. They had entered an age of magic.

Ord felt the medallion stir on his chest. His shoulder tingled as the amulet under the skin sensed occult presences. New forces shaped the game; mists and shadows moved over the world of the blue people, bringing good and evil in their wake. They contended long and fiercely, and after an extended conflict, the evil force was put to flight.

The good reigned in triumph. The forces of evil withdrew to a dark and distant valley, where they abided long in secrecy and grew strong; and when the blue people had all but forgotten the struggle, they began to seep forth and engulf all things in their path. In time the shadow of evil lay over all the world but one small mountain village where a single wizard stemmed the encroaching darkness. As the dark powers gathered around this little patch of light, the wizard steeled himself for the final confrontation with the enemy. Ord, too, felt the end of the struggle approaching.

The blue people fled from the dark tide to take refuge in the wizard's tower. Behind bolted doors they fed their courage with light and song, while their protector climbed to the parapet to face the demon lord. Age had paled the wizard's blue skin to near-white, and his crest was high and translucent with the passing of time and the unrelenting struggle. Yet his step did not falter, and despite his knowledge of the ordeal that lay before him, his will was unshaken. Ord knew this, because when the blue wizard set foot on the parapet of his tower and looked out at the surrounding sea of evil, he and Ord were one.

A dark cloud rose and thickened and whirled around him; foul things brushed his face, plucked at his skin, pawed him; the air was filled with whines and shrill cries and soft mewling laughter. The wizard Ord spoke a phrase and light enveloped him, driving the minions of darkness back. The tower shook under him, and with a single gesture he split the mountain and ringed his stronghold with a moat of glowing molten rock—the tower was steady once more.

Then the blue wizard Ord attacked. Raising his hands, he called forth lightnings to rend and shatter the retreating darkness. The black sea clotted and congealed into titanic shapes that lurched toward the tower, and Ord gave form to the lightnings, turning them into great winged dragons of light that fell on the dark forms with tearing claws and withering breath of fire. The darkness fell back still further and thinned to a murky gloom. Ord flung up his hands, and called on the winds to scatter the lowering clouds.

For a moment the skies brightened; then a cloud of impenetrable black loomed in the north and sped for the tower. Ord, weary and aching in every bone and sinew, braced himself for the meeting. He had broken and driven off the minions of the dark power, and now the demon lord himself came forth to battle.

Ord armored himself in light. A pounding hail of black-

ness drilled into his shield from all sides, forcing it in
upon him. The dark tide rolled forward and lapped at
the base of the tower. Ord summoned fire and light from
the heart of the mountain; the demon lord smothered the
fire and brought forth a rain of ash. Ord's armor shrank
still further. Bolts of violent hatred hammered him back
until he was pinned against the door of the tower. Before
him the eye of the demon lord rose like a sickly sun over
the parapet, and words crawled in his struggling mind.
*Lost . . . Forever lost . . . Eternal agony . . . in the deep-
est pit . . . Torment . . . despair, defeat . . . All lost . . .
Hopeless to defy . . . to presume against the dark power
. . . Hopeless . . .*

The huge yellow eye hung before him, and the darkness closed on him, crushing and choking him. Ord's mind
whirled; his hands trembled; he groped for the medallion
around his neck, and with his last strength he tore it free,
raised it high and hurled it into the eye of the demon
lord.

And then he was Ord again—only Ordred Vannenson
and no blue wizard—in the tower of the game in the High
City, standing at the rail weak and dizzy. The medallion
was gone from around his neck. The crystal dome lay
shattered at the bottom of the tower. Its light was fading.
The echo of its destruction troubled the tower for a few
moments; it died, and all was utterly silent.

Then a wail went up from the masters opposite, a high
keening cry of desolation. Gamesters stumbled aimlessly
to and fro on the platform, tearing at their robes and
lamenting. One after another they hurled themselves over
the railing onto the jagged shards of crystal below. Those
who were not killed outright, or stunned by the fall,
groped among the shards with bloody hands for a fragment with which to saw at their wrists or throats, or to
drive into their hearts.

Ord turned away, sickened, and saw Maridon slumped
beside him. One arm was hooked over the rail, and the
chain of his medallion was caught on a point of ironwork.
He hung limp, a smile frozen on his face, and Ord felt
for a pulse and found that Maridon was dead. The old
man lay dead beside him in a pool of blood. Ord turned
to Ciantha, who was on her knees clutching at the rail-

ing. She was alive but dazed and helpless. As he knelt beside her, a hand fell on his shoulder.

"Best we leave this place, my lord," Kinnaury said.

"Yes. Yes, it is," Ord said, rising stiffly. His damp clothing clung to him. He staggered and gripped the rail to steady himself.

"Are you well? It looked for a time as if you were in a bad dream."

"I was. Was it I who shattered the crystal, Kinnaury?"

"You did," the forester said. "Flung your medallion right down on it. Smashed it to bits."

"So the game is over. And now the fight for the city begins." He took a deep, weary breath, straightened his shoulders, and said, "Let's be to our proper work then. We'll take Ciantha with us and put her somewhere safe."

"She was one of the masters," Kinnaury said dubiously.

"She was on our side. Can't just leave her here. They might decide to take out the defeat on her."

"I'll take her then," Kinnaury said. He lifted the girl as if she were a child and slung her over his shoulder.

They emerged from the tower into deep night. Ord had no idea of how long they had been inside; the game might have gone on for hours—or for ages. Crossing the open space where all the pavilions now stood empty, they reached the palace. Here, too, all was dark and still. Lamps and torches were burned down. Doors stood half open, and rooms were in disarray.

Kinnaury placed Ciantha on a couch in an upper room, while Ord searched for food and drink. He came upon the chamber where they had dined and found the table still spread with cold meats, fruit, and wine. He and Kinnaury ate ravenously, and when they were satisfied, Ord poured himself a goblet of wine, spilling a good deal of it in the gloom, and went to the window.

The High City was dark from end to end—and silent. He wondered for a moment if he had indeed been in that tower, caught in some timeless web of sorcery while an age passed outside and the city was abandoned. He knew that this could not be so—the food was evidence enough of that—but the thought was suggestive.

He drank deeply and looked out the window once again, and this time he saw a little point of light far away, by the gate. Another appeared, and then many more, and they moved and grew brighter. Ord gulped the wine, tossed the goblet aside, and ran to the door, Kinnaury at his back.

A low roar burst upon him as he stepped from the building. Now he could clearly see that the lights were torches. The roar was the cry of a people risen from their chains and turned on their former masters. Ord lifted the obscuring spell from his blade and went forth.

All through the night and into the early daylight hours, battle raged in the streets and passages of the city. When the sun cleared the eastern wall, its slanting rays fell on a gory prospect. Like the defenders of the citadel, the city guardsmen had fought to the last man. Only two had attempted to surrender, and both had been throttled by a ghostly hand at the moment they threw down their weapons. The rest had fought on furiously, and none fell who did not take an attacker with him.

A pyre blazed in the center of the city, reducing six-teen headless gray men to ashes. Ord knelt on one knee before it, leaning on his sword, nearly faiting from exhaustion. His arms and legs were leaden; his head throbbed; and when the people of the city raised him to their shoulders, he could scarcely feel the men supporting him.

They carried him to the palace of honey-colored stone. He picked a score of men—those who had shown good judgment as well as courage in the night's fighting—and put them in charge of caring for the wounded and burying the dead. If they had questions, they were to bring them to Kinnaury.

With their jubilant cries rising all around him, Ord waved, turned, and stumbled inside to collapse on the nearest couch, where he slept until late afternoon. He awoke with a start. His muscles were stiff and he ached in every joint, but he could sleep no longer. He was Keeper of the Plain now; half the promised kingdom was his, but more work lay ahead, and Staver was awaiting him. He climbed stiffly to his feet, sent Kinnaury to rest, took up his black sword, and set about bringing order to the High City.

On the second day he went to Ciantha. She had lain

in a fever since the shattering of the crystal, and only now was she recovered and strong enough to speak. He had feared for her, but when he thought of telling her that she alone survived of all the gamesters, he feared for himself—fighting gray men and wizardry was easier than bearing such news.

Ciantha now looked far different from the dour, obsessed servant of the game that Ord had known. She was pale and seemed weak, but nevertheless she spoke with an animation that had been missing from her earlier manner. She was like one freed from a spell; she seemed to feel liberation as fully as the oppressed people of the city, even though she herself had been one of the oppressors. When Ord entered her chamber, and she smiled in recognition and reached out her hand to him, he forgot everything but her beauty.

"You've won. The city is yours now, and all in it," she said.

"It wasn't as simple as you make it sound. We had to do some fighting."

"My father is dead, isn't he?"

Ord sat beside her and took her hand. "He died in the tower. He won the game for me, Ciantha. That's what he wanted, and he accomplished it."

She pulled her hand free, lowered her eyes, and shook her head slowly. Ord watched the shimmer of her dark hair and scarcely heard her say, "It's you who won. At the end you were that blue wizard. My father was dying then . . . all the life had been drained from him. He would have lost, but you entered, actually became a part of the game, and seized the victory. Maridon would never have dared such a move. No master has ever done such a thing."

"No one will ever do it again. The game is ended."

"What of the others? Were they slain?"

"They threw themselves on the shards of broken crystal."

"Had you lost, they would have slain you and enslaved us. They feared the same treatment from you."

"I didn't come to kill or enslave anyone. I came to free them."

She took his hand in both of hers and looked into his

eyes. "We had no desire to be free of the game. Now that it's over, I feel as though a blindfold has been torn from my eyes and chains struck from my limbs. But while the game existed, I wanted nothing more than to give my life to it. It seemed to offer everything."

"I know. I felt it myself. It was like being a god, infinite and all-powerful—but it was all illusion."

"I understand that now."

"How did it happen, Ciantha? How did you all become slaves to the game? Where did it come from, anyway? There was no such game in the Old Kingdom," Ord said.

"I know very little. Only tales from childhood."

"Tell me," Ord prompted her.

"It happened long ago, many cycles of play before I was born. A plague had come upon the High City and taken a great toll. So many died that the living were too few to bury the dead. Corpses lay rotting in the streets. The water became corrupted and deadly, and a blight fell over the fields all around, destroying the crops. There seemed to be no hope."

"Not even flight?" Ord asked.

"The only survivors were members of the noble families. Some were blood descendants of the Scarlet Ordred, last Keeper of the Fastness and the Plain. But they lacked the strength and hardiness of Ambescand and his sons and were further weakened by hunger. They could not hope to survive a long journey, so they remained in the city and waited for death.

"Fewer than two score were still alive when the first gray man came through the open gate. Others soon joined the first. They were fearsome creatures to look upon, like giant men made of stone, but they delivered the survivors from certain death. They carried the corpses from the streets and from the houses where they lay and buried them far away. They drained the ponds, and cleaned the wells and waterways, and brought food.

"Soon afterward a force of guardsmen came, in unfamiliar armor, and placed themselves at the nobles' service. With the help of the gray men, they scoured the Plain and brought all those they found to the city, to do the needed work and tend the fields beyond the walls. The city began to thrive once again."

"Did the nobles never wonder where the gray men and the guards came from?" Ord asked.

Ciantha gave him a puzzled look. "They were nobles. They were accustomed to being served. It did not occur to them to question."

"Too bad. But go on with your story, Ciantha."

She closed her eyes for a moment, collecting vague memories, then went on. "One day the gray men began to gather huge blocks of stone outside the city wall, stone from no one knows where. Soon they built a tower—a squat tower, windowless, for an unknown purpose. When the tower was complete, the gray men went to the parapets of the east wall, where they stood like statues, facing out to sea.

"A boat came—a small boat, no longer than this chamber and narrower than a man's outstretched arms. It came from the east, with no oarsman and no sail, moving swiftly against wind and tide. A man was in it, dressed in a plain robe of coarse cloth, and he came into the city like a father rejoining his children. His white hair shone like a sunrise, and he was fair to look upon.

"He went to the tower, where he stayed long. When he emerged, he gave the nobles a book, *The Book of the Game,* and returned to the tower. The nobles studied the book and were fascinated by what it contained, and when the man emerged again from the tower, they surrounded him and besought him to tell them more of this game that held the promise of all things. He led them into the tower, which was as you saw it. Since that day, the nobles of the city have been the people of the game, and this has been the City of the Game—until you came to end it all."

"The man from the sea was the Cairnlord," Ord said.

Ciantha shook her head. "I never heard his name. He was the bringer of the game and was always spoken of with reverence."

"I hope you revere him no longer."

"No. When I think of all the generations, all the lives . . . Some cycles of the game cost scores of lives. And all those people, driven by the gray men and the guards, working to feed us and keep the city running while we gave our lives to the game. It was a great evil."

"It was. But it's over now, and you're free."

"We'll never be completely free of the game. I was a mere third-level master, and you played only once, but the game has touched us both. I can understand why you live on, but why was I spared?"

"There's a reason," Ord said. "I've learned that there's a reason for everything, though it may not be apparent."

"There can be no reason for me to be spared," Ciantha insisted. "I'm the last of an ancient line. A new age is here, and all things will be different. There is no place for me in the city."

Ord was silent for a time, deliberating within himself, and then he spoke decisively. "I think you were spared to be my wife." When she looked at him in astonishment, he said, "The blood of Ambescand is in you, as it is in me. My name is Ordred, and I'm called the Scarlet Ord. I was destined to rule here, and a greater ruler than Ambescand will come from my descendants. I think we must marry. We have no choice, Ciantha."

They looked at one another for a moment; then Ord reached out to Ciantha, and she came to his embrace. He forgot the dangers and hardships that lay behind and before him and rejoiced in the fate that had brought him to this woman.

20

The Fastness

Staver watched until Ord and Kinnaury were two motes on the emptiness of the plain; then he turned to Helmer and said, "Let's be on our way."

"It will be safe to travel in the daylight for a time. Would you prefer that?" Helmer asked.

"I would."

"Then we will do so," Helmer said and led off at once with his long sure strides.

Since it was safe to travel by day, Staver assumed that it was also safe to break the cautious silence they had observed in the mountains. He was full of questions for his guide.

The blind man was at first reticent, answering in a word or a phrase. But Staver persisted, and Helmer began to speak more freely. He told of his own youth, and his family, and of the settlements he had visited in the lands under the Cairnlord's dominion. He recited old legends, scraps of history, tales of the scattered peoples, and told Staver stories of bold but futile blows struck against the Cairnlord's forces by brave, doomed men. He himself had been a solitary fighter in the days after his family and his village were destroyed.

"How did they come to blind you?" Staver asked. "Don't speak of it if it will pain you, but if you're willing to speak, I'd like to hear."

"I was young and reckless, and I grew overconfident. I set a trap for the Cairnlord's men and fell into one they had set for me. They debated for a time whether to cripple me, cut off my hands, or blind me. They tossed the throwing sticks to decide."

"Why didn't they kill you?"

"I've never understood that myself. Perhaps they thought it would be too easy on me. Or perhaps they had their fill of killing. They'd butchered an entire village two days before."

"Why?"

"I think it was for pleasure."

Staver was silent for a time; then he said, "Helmer, I don't understand how there's anyone left. Between his human followers and his gray men, the Cairnlord has enough strength to wipe out everyone he can't use as a slave. Yet thousands of free men and women live and resist him. We raised an army in the mistlands and the Southern Forest, and I'm told there are settlements on the Plain and here in the mountains. How have they survived all these years if the Cairnlord's followers are such butchers?"

"It's a mystery, my lord Staver. Perhaps we're too spread out and too well hidden. Perhaps they don't think it worth their while to hunt us down."

"But if they kill simply for love of killing, they'd have wiped out everyone long ago. That's what troubles me, Helmer. I think there's another reason for all the bloodshed, but I can't imagine what it could be."

Helmer nodded and fell into a thoughtful silence. Staver did not disturb him. They walked on until they reached a pool by a waterfall, and here they stopped to eat and wash and rest for a time. As they reclined in the shade of a thicket, Helmer returned to Staver's question.

"Long ago, my lord, in the days when I was learning to live in darkness, I listened much to others," he said. "I spent many hours thinking of what I had seen in my own wanderings and comparing it to what others told me, and it seemed to me that despite all the Cairnlord's casual butchery, the same number of people died each year and the same remained alive."

"That hardly seems possible, Helmer."

"I thought so, too, and soon lost interest in what seemed a foolish speculation. But your words recalled it to me."

"Do you mean that the Cairnlord's followers kill the same number of people, year after year?"

"No. The same number die, but not all by the hand of the Cairnlord. In a year when plague, or famine, or hard weather claimed many victims, the Cairnlord's men took fewer. And when no natural disasters befell the people, the Cairnlord's men struck more frequently and fiercely. It seemed to me, my lord—from what I heard—that this was so, year after year."

"I wonder. . . . Perhaps a certain number must remain alive, for some reason, to maintain the Cairnlord's power. Why else would such a creature let his enemies live when he has it in his power to destroy them?"

"I cannot understand the reasoning of wizards, my lord."

"No more can I," Staver said despondently. "But we know so little about the Cairnlord that anything we learn might help us fight him."

"Your brother may learn something in the city. Perhaps the mountain people know things we do not."

"I hope so. Are we near their settlements, Helmer?"

"In four days we will be near the place where their

settlements were when I last came to the mountains. By now they must have moved, but I can find them."

Staver had no doubt of the blind man's tracking ability. He had seen Helmer do too many things that would have taxed the powers of a sighted man. In the end, though, Helmer's skill was not required. The mountain people found the travelers.

It happened at night. Farther north, deeper into the mountains where patrols from the Fastness were likely to be encountered, Staver and Helmer had again taken to traveling in the safety of darkness. As they followed a narrow trail, Helmer dropped back and in a low voice informed Staver that they were now being followed by two men.

"Should we stand and fight?" Staver asked.

"They are not Cairnlord's men."

"Then we must let them know who we are."

"I think it best to let them make the first move. They'll observe us and decide whether or not to reveal themselves."

Staver considered the reply and said, "We'll do as you say, Helmer."

They went on for a time, and Helmer informed Staver that they were now followed by three men, and another was on a trail above them, keeping parallel to their track. Soon after this, he told of two more men, armed, waiting directly ahead. Staver, who had heard nothing and could barely make out the way under his feet, marveled at Helmer's senses. He did not doubt the information.

The mountain men were waiting at a bend in the trail. When they stepped into view, Staver could see how their outfits of gray-brown blended with the rock and stone all around them, making them almost invisible. Helmer halted, raised his staff overhead, parallel to the ground, gripping it with both hands spread apart, and said, "We come in peace. We are two and no more."

For the first time, Staver heard footsteps behind him. He turned and saw a bowman poised about three marks away. An arrow was nocked, the bow half-drawn. Staver looked up at the ridge opposite and caught a glimpse of motion.

"Who are you, and where from?" called a man from ahead.

"We come from the lake isle," Helmer replied.

The man on the trail ahead said something to his companion in a voice too low for Staver to hear—then, aloud, he said, "The lake isle is a long and dangerous way from here. Are you fugitives?"

Before Helmer could answer the question, Staver stepped forward and said, "We come as messengers, not fugitives. The only fugitives from the lake isle now are the followers of the Cairnlord, and few of them remain alive."

There was no immediate reaction to Staver's words; then exclamations came from before and behind him, and the man who had been questioning them stepped forth to approach Staver. As he passed by Helmer and saw the cloth covering his eyes, the man paused and stared. When he stopped before Staver, there was a look of perplexity and expectation on his plain, blunt features.

"Tell us your message," he said.

"The citadel has fallen to an army of woodwards from the north, of mistlanders, and of foresters. Colberane Whitblade is Master of the Southern Forest once again. The Scarlet Ordred is on his way to free the High City, and when he has, he'll come here to reclaim the Fastness. You must be ready to receive him and to fight under his banner," Staver said.

The mountain man glanced once again at Helmer, then peered hard into Staver's face, as if studying his features. "And you who bring this message—who are you?" he asked in a hushed voice.

"Staver Ironbrand, Mage of the Crystal Hills. The sword at my side is the Iron Angel," Staver said, willing that the cloud lift from his blade, and it be revealed to these men.

The mountain man looked hard at him, turned once more to study Helmer, then glanced down on Staver's blade. His expression changed to one of awe. He stepped back unsteadily, then fell to one knee. Staver looked around and saw that the others had done the same. He held out a hand to the man before him and bade him rise.

"It's as the Dark Prophet said: a youth—come by night —led by one who walks in darkness as others walk in the sun," the mountain man said, still overwhelmed. "Ironbrand his name and a gray-winged blade at his side."

"How long have you waited?"

"The Dark Prophet came to us at the end of summer and said that the time was near. But the prophecy was old when my father was a child."

"And now it's come true," said a second man.

"There's much planning to do. We must have an army awaiting Ord when he comes and be ready to move quickly against the Fastness. Are the mountain people willing?" Staver asked.

"They are eager but few in number."

"Fewer than the defenders of the Fastness?"

"Slightly fewer, we think. And it will take a great army to capture the Fastness."

Staver smiled reassuringly. "The defenders of the citadel thought the same, and the citadel fell in a few hours. But we ought not discuss our plans in the open. Will you take us to a place of safety?"

They proceeded north, with the mountain man, whose name was Wenman, now leading, and before dawn they entered a cave. The way led deep into the mountain, downward for a long distance. It twisted and turned like the path of a butterfly before it rose sharply. In time Staver could see a pinpoint of light ahead of them that grew steadily until they emerged into early morning, in a shallow valley ringed by sheer cliffs. From the thinness of the air, Staver judged that they were at a considerable height. A cluster of stone huts stood veiled in chill mists in the center of the valley. While the others led Staver and Helmer to a hut where they were given food and water, Wenman at once went to the largest of the huts.

He soon returned, bringing three older men with him. At sight of the travelers, these three bent their knees before Staver as the others had done. Staver set his bowl aside, rose, and urged them to their feet.

The oldest of the mountain men, a gaunt white-haired man weighted down with years, clasped Staver's hand and clung to it. "That it should come about in my lifetime . . . That I should live to see the rising!" he said in a voice that cracked with feeling.

"It's close at hand. There's much work to be done before we march against the Fastness, though."

"We've sent for the leaders of the nearby bands. Will you rest until they come?" their guide asked.

Staver and Helmer needed no further invitation. They finished their meal and rolled up their cloaks for a sound sleep. The others arrived late in the afternoon, and they all assembled in the large hut just as the sun touched the peaks.

Each of the newcomers offered Staver the same obeisance. Their actions showed no doubt in their minds that deliverance from the yoke of the Cairnlord was at hand, that the generations-old prophecy was on the brink of fulfillment, and that Staver would lead them to freedom. But their information was disheartening. As one leader after another numbered his men and his weaponry, Staver realized that the army awaiting Ord would be small and poorly armed.

He asked about the Fastness, and that news was equally discouraging. The Fastness, he learned, was a huge, walled fortress-city—larger than the citadel, larger even than the High City, and old beyond memory and legend. Why and how it had been built in this remote desolation of stone, and what forgotten race had built it, were unknown. When the High City was founded and the calendar begun, the Fastness was already ancient. Before the age of magic, before the Old Kingdom, before the coming of men to the plain and the forests, the Fastness had stood impregnable in the mountains.

Despite its age, it was no crumbling pile. Over the centuries the walls had been thickened and extended until four concentric rings of stone, the thickest and outermost of which was four marks at its narrowest point, now encircled the central tower. The walls were scrupulously patrolled and maintained; there was no chance of scaling them unseen. Indeed, even if the walls were to stand unguarded for days on end, the thicket of downcurved spikes near the top, and the rounded edges that afforded no purchase for a grapnel, would have made ascent impossible.

Staver saw no way to breach that fortress. Yet his coming had brought the promise of victory to the mountain men, and they encircled him, full of quiet confidence as he studied the objective. He knew he could not let them be disappointed; they would have to have hope of victory if they were to pledge their lives to Ord. But assault on that brooding man-made mountain seemed like an act of futility close to madness.

As Staver studied by the feeble light of smoky rush lamps, the diagrams and drawings provided by the leaders of the mountain men, he grew even more frustrated. Finally he swept the material aside and said, "Is there no entry but through the gates? No tunnels, no drains? Where does the water come from, and go to?"

"There's an underground river, my lord," one man explained. "It feeds a lake, which serves as cistern for the central halls. The current of the overflow is used to carry off slops and filth. But no man has ever found the source of the river—or its end."

"Has it been sought?" Staver asked impatiently.

"For generations, my lord."

"What of escape tunnels?"

"We know of fourteen. All are sealed off."

"How long would it take to dig through?"

"The enemy did not seal them off. Our people did."

Staver looked at the speaker curiously, and another man said, "There is a thing that roams the tunnels. It must not be allowed to escape among us. It is monstrous beyond imagining."

"When the Cairnlord's men besieged the Fastness, they discovered the escape tunnels. To guard against our return through the tunnels and to make certain that none of their captives escape, they loosed a creature in the great central cave from which the tunnels open," the first speaker said.

The other added, "We think this thing is too big to come through the tunnels, but our fathers would not risk its escape. They labored long and hard in constant danger to seal it in."

"I'll trust to your fathers' judgment. I'd not care to come upon a monster in a dark tunnel," Staver said. He shuffled the diagrams and sketches that lay all before him, and finally threw up his hands in despair. "The walls are unscalable, that's certain. There's no way in or out by water, and we don't dare try the escape tunnels."

"The Fastness has no weaknesses we know of, my lord. It held out against the Cairnlord's army for nine years and fell only because it was betrayed from within."

"No weaknesses you know of, and none I can find. But it must be taken. Tell me, are there others who might know more about it?"

The mountain men looked at each other uneasily. One older man said, "We know of settlements to the northeast and to the west beyond the Fastness. In one of them there is a collection of ancient writings in which much is told of the Fastness. I know of no one who has seen these writings, but I once heard that they spoke of ways of secret entry."

"Will anyone lead me to those who hold the writings?"

A fearful look crossed the older man's face, and he stepped back into the group. Again there was an uncomfortable silence. Someone said, "It would be very dangerous traveling, my lord."

"It must be done. Who will guide me?" Staver asked again.

Wenman stepped forward. "I will."

"We'll leave when you're ready. Just the two of us," Staver said.

"Dawn is the best time, my lord," Wenman said.

Helmer laid a hand on Staver's arm. "My lord, I should go with you."

"You're needed here, Helmer. The mountain men must be told of all that's happened, and your memory is far better than mine."

"As you wish, my lord."

Staver perceived the disappointment in Helmer's voice. He gripped the blind man's hand firmly and said, "When the time comes to fight, you'll not be left out, Helmer. I promise you."

In the first gray light Wenman and Staver stepped from the cave on a peak far from where they had entered. Staver had placed the obscuring spell on the Iron Angel once again. He and Wenman now appeared to be two ordinary travelers. With the sun low at their right hands, they set off to the north.

They exchanged few words. All their attention was on keeping a wary eye, an alert ear, and a steady pace along the narrow trail. Twice that first day they dove for cover at sight of a moving figure on the ridge, and both times they crept out, relieved and grinning, at the sight of a rock goat bounding up the heights.

On the third morning, as they sat in a patch of weak sunlight and ate the dried fruit and hard bread from their packs, Wenman warned that this day would begin the most dangerous part of their passage. The Fastness lay only a few greatmarks due west of the trail. They would have to skirt outposts and avoid patrols all this day and for several days following.

"Why are the men of the Fastness so cautious?" Staver asked. "I can see no cause for them to fear."

"They fear nothing. They're watching for fugitives. This is one of the old routes between Long Wood and the High City, and many still use it, despite the danger."

"Is there still much traffic to Long Wood?"

"Yes. The power of the Cairnlord is not quite so strong there as it is in the eastern lands. Or so some people believe. Myself, I feel better in the mountains. They're safer than woods any time."

Again Staver thought of the perplexing mystery of life and death under the Cairnlord's rule. A merciless lord, brutal followers who killed at whim without mercy or remorse—and yet people survived and escaped to resist. It might be that the power of the Cairnlord was limited— though the storm on the Fool's Head and the attack of the gray men on the Headland made that difficult to believe. It might be that the Cairnlord was holding back his power, hoarding it for the proper moment. There seemed to be no way of learning the true situation.

The morning passed without the sight of another human being. Wenman and Staver reached a low point in the trail, where it ran between narrow walls and then turned and began to rise, twisting in a series of switchbacks up the side of a sheer cliff. It was a bad spot, with no cover and only one way of retreat; but once past this, the worst danger was behind them.

Staver was the younger, but Wenman, despite his years and greater weight, was accustomed to the heights. He drew ahead as Staver lagged, panting in the thin air. They were halfway up the steep switchback trail when Staver saw his guide stagger and fall forward as he rounded a turn. He ran to his companion, turned him over, and found the broken shaft of an arrow jutting from his chest.

The scrape of a boot sounded on the trail ahead. Looking up, Staver saw a bowman aiming at him. He wore the conical helmet of the Cairnlord's guard.

"Move, and you'll get an arrow in your guts," said a voice from behind Staver.

Staver remained very still. Footsteps came closer, stopping directly at his back. His hands were jerked behind him and tied tightly and painfully. A noose was slipped over his head and tightened until it fit like a collar.

"Back the way you came, now. We're taking you to the Fastness, boy," said the voice.

"He's got a sword. We ought to take his sword," the bowman pointed out.

"Let him carry it. He'll have no chance to use it."

The bowman laughed in a way that Staver found unpleasant. "Right enough. Not now, nor ever. Not when he goes down to meet the Lool."

21

In the Tunnels of the Lool

Four massive gates swung open one by one before Staver and his guards and rumbled shut behind them. Each ring of the wall rose higher than the one before, and the way grew darker, even in midday, as they walked in their deepening shadow ever nearer to the tower that stood at the center of the Fastness.

Within the tower Staver was relieved of his sword and dagger. His guard tossed the dagger into a corner, but he held the sword up to the torchlight and inspected it closely.

"What gravemound did you steal this from, boy?" he demanded.

"No grave mound. I got it from a dying man."

"Cut his throat for it, did you?"

"No. He was sick. He couldn't use the sword any longer, and he gave it to me," Staver said.

"It's a poor fit for you. Tell me, can you lift it with both hands?" the guard asked, and he and his companion laughed.

"I've never had to use it on a man."

"Lucky for you," said the guard. He hung Staver's sword over his shoulder, then rubbed his hands together briskly. "All right, boy, I want some answers now. Speak up, and you'll save us both some trouble. Where are you from, and where headed?"

"I come from the Southern Forest. I wanted to reach Long Wood."

"Why? One wood's the same as another."

"My brother heard people say that Long Wood was safe."

"Your brother's the one we killed, is he?"

Staver shook his head. "That man was a guide. My brother and I were separated in the mountains. I was lost. The man found me, and offered to take me to Long Wood. He said he was going there himself and didn't want to travel alone."

"You trusted a stranger?"

"I had to. I needed a guide."

The guard looked suspiciously at Staver for a time, then said, "Why'd you take the mountains if you didn't know the way? You're lying, aren't you?" He cuffed Staver, hard, with the back of his hand, then jerked the rope around his neck. "I want the truth, boy, and you'd better tell it. Why'd you come this way?"

"We thought it was safer. There are monsters in mistlands."

"You can skirt mistlands. There's a road to the west."

"A traveler told us it was unsafe."

The guard hit Staver again, harder. "Truth, boy. What are you doing here?"

Staver blinked. He was dazed from the blow, and his

mouth was bloody. "We wanted to get to Long Wood, that's all. This was the best way."

"Why'd you head right into the mountains? Why didn't you work north on the Plain, and then strike due west?" The guard jerked the rope until Staver choked, then demanded, "Why not?"

"There are things on the Plain. We were afraid."

"There are things in the mountains, too. Right here in the Fastness. You'll find that out soon enough."

The interrogation went on for a time, and Staver endured more blows and near-strangulation, but in the end the guards accepted his story. They freed his hands and slackened the noose around his neck, and pushed him to a bucket of water.

"Clean yourself. You're going to be taken to our master now," the first guard said.

Staver winced at the sting of water on his cut and swollen cheek and lips. Two of his teeth wobbled slightly, but they bled hardly at all now. Nothing seemed to be broken, though his treatment had left him sore and bruised from head to foot. As he rubbed the water from his eyes, the guard said, "It's our master's wish to see all prisoners. What he'd want with a cheap thief, I don't know, but you'll be taken to him same as all the rest."

"Then it's down to the Lool, eh?" the other guard said.

"That's usually the way. Come along, boy."

They left the guardroom, traversed a long hall lined with guards, and climbed a wide stone stair, also guarded. Staver walked with hands unbound, but the guards' grip on the noose around his neck was firm. At the top of the stair, they passed through high iron doors and entered a throneroom.

Before them on a canopied throne of glistening black wood sat the most splendid man Staver had ever seen. As they approached the throne, Staver felt wonderment rising in him, driving out all other sensations. Even his fear was forgotten in this sudden overwhelming flood of awe. When the guard pushed him to his knees, Staver bowed willingly, and looked up with timid amazement. This was a being worthy of homage.

The man on the throne was tall and sturdy of frame;

even Kinnaury would have seemed small beside him. His broad chest was encased in a glittering golden breastplate, and a thin circlet of gold ringed his forehead. His hair was deep gold in color; his face, fair; his large eyes, a deep blue with a look of cool majesty in them. When he rose and folded his bare arms, his every motion was full of easy grace. He moved like a gymnast, smooth and supple, despite the fact that he was the biggest man Staver had ever seen. His voice, when he spoke, was clear and deep, and as mellow as the note of a distant hunter's horn. Staver felt that he was in the presence of a demigod.

"I am Korang the Warmaker, who rules the Fastness and all the mountains and the Plain. You've trespassed in my domain, and you must be punished for it. Where were you traveling, boy?" the golden man said.

Staver gaped in confusion, unable to respond, and a warning thrust of warmth came alive in his shoulder. His thoughts settled. He remembered his story to the guards and said, "I was fleeing . . . to Long Wood."

"And why did you take such a dangerous course? What did you fear, and what did you hope to find in Long Wood? Speak, boy."

"I sought . . . safety."

Korang's laughter was like the tolling of great bronze bells. He put his hands on his hips, threw back his head, and laughed like a god amused by the follies of men. Pointing disdainfully at Staver, he repeated, "Safety? There is no safety for you. No refuge, no sanctuary anywhere in the world, boy. Don't you know that yet? Run until you drop, and you won't reach the limits of my power. And beyond me, guiding me and giving me strength, is another more powerful than I or any who live. You were foolish, and now you'll suffer for your folly."

He strode across the room with graceful silent tread and gestured for the others to follow him. Staver, led by the guard, came after. Korang stopped at the brink of a well in the floor of the throneroom. At his nod the second guard took a torch from a wall bracket and held it over the opening.

"A creature dwells below," said Korang. "It was placed

there long ago to guard us against secret attack through the ancient tunnels. There's been little work for it in recent times, and it grows restless. So we deliver our guests to it when we're done with them. And we're done with you now, boy."

"You have your choice," the first guard said. "Climb down willingly or be thrown down."

"Think on it, boy. If you're flung down, you might break your neck instantly, and then you'd know nothing, feel nothing. I should think this is the easiest way," said Korang, and his voice was filled with what sounded like genuine concern.

The second guard said, "Then, on the other hand, if you climb down you might be able to run and hide and stay alive for a day or two. Might even find an open tunnel and escape!"

"Which will it be, boy?" said the first guard, coming closer.

The amulet burned in Staver's shoulder, and he understood what he must do. "I'll climb down. Give me my sword," he said.

The guard stared at him, amazed, then gave a loud guffaw. The others joined in his laughter. For a moment the three shared a camaraderie of mockery at their prisoner. Then Staver repeated his demand, and they fell silent. The first guard glanced at Korang. Staver turned and saw a smile on those perfect features, even white teeth gleaming and a light in the dark eyes. Korang nodded. The guard slipped the sword belt free and tossed the weapon to Staver, grinning as he did so. Staver flung off the noose and slung the sword belt over his shoulder.

"You think to fight the Lool, do you?" Korang said. "I do."

"Fight it, then. Be a brave little thief. And if you slay it, you'll have a reward: I'll make you Captain of the Nether Guard and throw you prisoners to dine on."

Staver lowered himself over the edge of the opening. It was round, a bit more than half a mark in diameter, with handholds cut in the rock down one side. The last sight he saw as he descended into the darkness was the smiling face of Korang.

When he touched ground at the bottom of the shaft,

a shout reverberated down after him. He looked up to
see the torch hurtling toward him. He stepped back, his
foot crunching down on something that snapped beneath
his weight, then he snatched up the torch gratefully. He
knew that it had not been given him as a kindness;
most likely, the flame was a signal to draw the Lool to
him more quickly so those above would not have long
to wait for the sounds of his struggle. But light, however
hazardous, was a comfort.

Under his foot, the brittle fragments of a rib cage
crackled like dry crusts. As he raised the torch, its light
glinted off shards of white that lay scattered all around.
Apparently the Lool had dined often on this spot.

That was reason enough to move. Unnerving shadows
swooped around Staver with every step he took, and he
walked warily. The roof of the cave was high overhead,
and the ground fell away all around the shaft in irregular undulations. It was spongy beneath his feet. He climbed
to the top of the highest mound he could see, raised the
torch, and looked in all directions. Nothing moved, and
there was no sign of a tunnel, no breath of air moving.

Staver decided to keep going, away from the shaft, in
search of one of the escape tunnels. Fourteen were
known. If he could locate one, he might be able to dig
himself out before the Lool reached him. With luck, he
might even find an unblocked tunnel, unknown to defenders or mountain men. Should the Lool come upon
him, it would be easier to hold the creature off in a narrow tunnel than in this dark arena where a hunter had
room to stalk and pounce.

As Staver stood on the mound, deciding his course,
fatigue came over him, and a great desire to sleep. He
was weary, and his senses were dulled; a rest would be
good for him. Surely the Lool was nowhere near. If he
lay down in some concealed spot, he would be fit and
rested for the struggle when it came. His eyes grew heavy.

At once he knew that this was madness and he fought
against it. His mind seemed cleft in two. He felt an awful
sensation, as if something had crawled over his conscious-
ness and left behind it the slimy track of a slug.
He turned quickly and caught a glimpse of motion. One
of the mounds had moved.

Though he had never seen the Lool and never had it described to him, Staver knew that the shape out there could be nothing else. Again the feeling of a groping slimy thing in his mind made him shudder and this time he had a revolting moment of communion with the creature.

The Lool was a single-minded hunger; a great crawling mass of appetite abiding in the darkness to await the moments of satiety that followed when little scurrying creatures with fire in their hands came trembling from the shaft to be his food. Staver felt hunger, anticipation, hideous joy pouring like a foul current into his own thoughts, and the contact left him shaken. It was not like the innocent speech of animals and birds. There was animal in the Lool, but there was something else, as well, and it was different from everything Staver had ever known.

He jammed the torch into the soft ground until it stood upright, casting its light in all directions, and then he drew his sword. Flight would be useless; he could not run on this yielding, clutching ground. Better to face the thing than have it close in and fall on his back in the darkness. He would make his stand here.

He drove the Lool's intruding thoughts from his mind and focused all his attention on watching and listening. A quiver of motion to his right caused him to turn, but he saw nothing. From behind him came a faint liquid sound, as of some viscous substance being slowly rolled over the ground in a huge barrel. He spun around, but nothing was there.

Then light and shadows swooped crazily as the torch was plucked loose from its socket and flung through the air. It fell in a bright spray of sparks and smoldered dully. In the dying glow Staver saw the hand that had held it melt back into the mass that lay on three sides of the mound, rising and falling slowly in regular pulsations.

With a gurgling sound the mass of the Lool surged up to enclose its victim. Staver struck with the Iron Angel, slashing at shoulder level into a yielding substance that clung to his blade as if he had tried to cleave a vat of cold honey. The thing moaned and fell back. It rolled in upon him again, and he drove it back a second time, and then a third.

It waited. He opened his mind cautiously to its thoughts and found that it was not seriously injured. Blades could pierce the Lool, but it quickly healed itself. Even the power of the Iron Angel could do barely more than irritate it. The resistance shown by this victim puzzled the Lool and roused a certain curiosity in its mind. But hunger surged above all, and the thing pulsed with its desire to consume the little stinging creature that stood so tauntingly within its grip.

It moved silently in the darkness, and Staver felt its substance clutch at his legs to pull him down. He fought it back, slashing and thrusting wildly into the flowing mucid heap. Once more it fell away from him.

At the top of the mound, Staver sank wearily to one knee. He was sore from mistreatment, weary from long travel, and his arms felt heavy as lead. His empty belly growled its hunger. Before long his strength would give out, and the Lool would have him. Even now, he could sense the thing's assurance. The struggle was serving only to whet its appetite and add zest to the inevitable banquet.

Flight was impossible. Staver looked at the distant speck of light that marked the shaft opening. He could never hope to outrun the Lool across this uneven ground in the dark. And if by a miracle he made it to the shaft, he would find no sanctuary there, only men waiting to fling him back down to death. He must fight where he stood.

He thought of Col and Ord, and wondered what they were doing at this moment, when he was so close to death. Together they could defeat this creature, but they were far apart. He remembered Helmer, and Jem Underhill, Goodbowe. . . . His mind went back to the camp in the forest, the inn, the long sleep he had enjoyed at the citadel. . . . Sleep. It was time to sleep now, too . . . time to rest and rebuild his strength . . .

His head jerked upward and he scrambled to his feet, shocked by the realization that he had drifted off to near-sleep. He had to fight off the lulling power of the Lool and stay awake. To sleep was to die. And if the amulet in his shoulder should pass into the body of the Lool, what effect might that have on his brothers? Staver rubbed his eyes hard, breathed deeply, and flexed his aching muscles. If only his brothers could be here—or the Dark Prophet. She would know a way to defeat the Lool. But he was alone, utterly alone, buried beneath the Fastness without a friend to call on.

Then he remembered.

It was as if new life had been poured into him. He threw back his head and shouted, "Zandinell, come to me! Help me, Zandinell!" The cry echoed and re-echoed through the emptiness. At the base of the mound the Lool moved with a syrupy burble. Staver shouted again and took up his stance with renewed courage. Help was on the way.

The Lool attacked, and he fought it off once more. But the struggle was fierce, and Staver felt that he could not endure another like it. He stood panting, aching from head to foot. The Iron Angel weighed like the world in his hands. He braced himself for the next attack.

A rush of wind pressed at his back. He heard the flap of leathery wings, and there came a burst of fire that turned the caverns into a midday world. As a stream of flame poured around the mound, driving the Lool back, Staver saw a dragon settle lightly to the ground a few marks away. It lowered its head and fixed bright red eyes on the Lool.

"Zandinell? Is that you, Zandinell?" Staver cried.

You didn't expect me to come as an owl, did you?

"I didn't really know. . . ."

I told you I'd never again become anything smaller than a dragon. I meant that, boy. I enjoy being a dragon.

"Be careful. The Lool is dangerous . . . subtle."

I know the Lool. Just keep out of this, the dragon said, a harsh voice deep in Staver's mind.

In the bright light of the dragonfire, Staver saw the Lool clearly. It was poised, still, at the foot of the mound, a hemisphere of shimmering jelly two marks high. It had no arms, no eyes, no face or features—but he could sense its vigilance and its sudden uncertainty.

The dragon belched forth a ribbon of flame. The Lool divided, and as the fire passed harmlessly between its halves, they flowed out to either side of the dragon and flung out thick tendrils to clutch at him. The Lool moved with a speed that astonished Staver, but the dragon was ready. He countered with bursts of flame. The Lool re-divided and encircled its enemy. As the tendrils closed in, the dragon rose, and the Lool flowed together to thrust forth a single long tentacle to wind around this attacker, but as it did so, the dragon spewed out a great ring of flame that encircled the thing. The Lool drew together, flowing in on itself, and the dragon poured forth more fire, closing the ring.

Staver was hypnotized by the eerie spectacle. Into his unprotected mind came a message that burned with shrill desperation. *Kill the firething! Strike at it and kill it! Lool will spare you . . . share food. . . . Kill the fire-thing for Lool!*

Staver staggered drunkenly and fell. He turned all his strength to driving the Lool's voice out of him. His head throbbed. It became a battlefield, and he writhed as the Lool's cries grew wild—until Zandinell's voice cut in to urge strength on him.

In time all was silent. A foul burnt stench was sharp in Staver's nostrils. He sat up and saw the dragon, seated on its haunches, licking a forepaw with an audible rasp of its tongue. The Lool was a puddle of blue flame under a canopy of coiling black smoke.

The dragon unfolded its wings with the sound of a cloak being shaken. It flapped them slowly until the thick smoke was blown off.

"Thank you, Zandinell. I could never have fought it off alone," Staver said.

Pretty stupid of you to get mixed up with the Lool in the first place, I'd say.

"I didn't have a choice."

Well, now I've paid my debt. We're even.

"Stay, Zandinell. There's a battle to be fought. We need your help."

I want nothing to do with men and their battles.

"But we're fighting the same enemy! The man who put me down here to be eaten by the Lool are followers of the Cairnlord. Korang is their leader—you spoke of him, Zandinell."

I know Korang. Stupidest wizard I ever met.

"We've started to fight back, and with your help we can—"

Don't look for my help. I've used up a lot of magic to come here.

"We need you, Zandinell."

Men always confuse what they need with what they want. That's only one of the reasons they're not to be trusted.

"I saved your life. You trusted me then."

And I saved yours in return, Staver, and owe you nothing. Men slaughtered my brother wizards, and I'll never forget it. They were cruel wizards, I admit, and they misused their knowledge. But the men fell upon them with a bestiality I found abhorrent. I trust no one, Staver. Even the good and just Ambescand, a wizard himself, punished my erring brothers most severely.

"But those other wizards are trying to destroy you!"

True, they are. And I'll defend myself against them. But I won't join you or our common enemy. I live alone and will stay alone and apart while the rest of you betray and kill each other. The dragon flexed its foreclaws and gave a flirt of its wings. In the ruddy fading glow of the Lool's dissolution, its outline began to blur. *There's a tunnel open to the outside, Staver. Relight your torch and seek it. And be careful in future. I won't rescue you next time.*

The dragon's outline had faded, and its voice had risen to a higher tone as it spoke. Before Staver's eyes it shrank and darkened and became a great bat that rose, circled the pool of dying flame, and shot off into the darkness.

Staver sat atop the mound for a time, dazed. Weariness, hunger, and pain wound like chains around his body, dragging him down, and he longed to give himself over to a long sleep. But he forced himself up, sought out the torch where the Lool had flung it, and brought it back to where the last flames glided on the oily surface of a dark stain that had once been the guardian of the tunnels. Here he rekindled the torch.

For an indeterminable time he wandered through the gloom and murk of the caverns under the Fastness.

Without food or water, he felt his strength failing steadily. His head grew light and his feet, heavy and clumsy. He stumbled frequently and several times fell heavily on the rank and spongy ground. At last he sank to his knees, too weak to go on. He fixed the torch in the ground and stretched out, dropping at once into a dream-filled sleep.

Staver awoke to a reality worse than his nightmares. He was hungrier than he had ever been in his life. His mouth was sore and dry, and his head ached from hunger and fatigue and the struggle against the Lool's insinuating voice. One side of his face was stiff and swollen, and his arms and shoulders were sore from wielding the weight of the Iron Angel. The torch, jammed upright in the clammy ground beside him, burned low, nearly gone.

He fell back, eyes closed, sinking into a paralysis of despair. After a time he felt a breath of air. The breath rapidly became a breeze, then a wind, then a roaring gale. Staver opened his eyes to a blaze of cool blue light that faded to a soft glow in the upraised hand of the Dark Prophet.

"Up, Staver, quickly! You must be ready for the Lool's attack!" she urged him.

He tried to reply, but only a wordless rasp came from his dry throat. The Dark Prophet drew a small flask from her robe and approaching, held it to his lips. She allowed only a few sips, then withdrew the flask. The substance worked instantly, miraculously. Staver's thirst and hunger vanished. His head was clear, and strength flowed through him, and he rose to his feet with no difficulty. He flexed his arms and rubbed his shoulders and his back. There was no pain or stiffness.

"It will last until we leave this place," the prophet told him. "But you must ready yourself to face the Lool."

"The Lool is dead."

"Dead? How did you slay it?"

"I didn't. I fought it, and it was overcoming me. But a wizard came in the shape of a dragon and slew the Lool with fire. Zandinell is his name."

"Zandinell does not come to the aid of men."

"Do you know him?" Staver asked.

"Zandinell was the only one of the company of sorcerers who would not join the revolt against Ambescand.

For that, his fellow wizards turned on him, and afterwards, men condemned him along with the others. He has not been seen since the revolt."

"I met him in the forest after the storm on the Fool's Head. I saved his life then, and he saved mine in return."

The Dark Prophet was silent for a moment, deep in thought, then she said, "All this is a surprise. I knew you would be here, but I knew nothing of your friendship with Zandinell. So . . . the Lool is dead."

"Yes. And according to Zandinell, there's a tunnel open to the outside. We must find it and let the mountain men know of it. When Ord comes, they'll have a way to attack this place."

"I know of the tunnel, Staver, and have told the mountain men."

"Then they're on the way!"

"Not yet. But they will come. And the battle will be hard. The Cairnlord's followers do not surrender."

"I know. I'll help as much as I can. But sometimes I wonder. . . ." He lowered his gaze; then, looking up in appeal, he said, "I'm not as big as Col and not nearly so good a swordsman as Ord. The Iron Angel is a fine sword, but it's too heavy for me. What good am I in this struggle?"

"You may be the most important one of all."

"What can I do that's so important? I keep getting lost, and being saved, and led around—what's important about that?"

"Your time is coming, Staver. You must face Korang in single combat."

Staver looked aghast at the Dark Prophet. "Me? Challenge Korang?" he asked weakly.

"You must."

"But Korang is twice my size, Prophet! His armor alone weighs more than I do—and I don't even have any armor."

"Your protection is within you. No armor ever forged can withstand the sword of the Warmaker, but the strength of Ambescand can turn aside any blow."

"Korang's not just a swordsman, he's a wizard as well—though I've never heard of a wizard who looked so magnificent. I thought all wizards were wrinkled old men like Zandinell, but Korang . . . he looks like a god!"

"Korang appears strong and noble, but this is all an illusion to conceal the hideous broken thing that he really is. The dark power finds strength in illusion, in deceiving simple people into thinking that evil is good."

Staver, greatly `relieved, said, "Then that big strong warrior isn't really Korang?"

"The warrior is real and will strike hard blows. He is real, he is Korang—but he is also an illusion, created and sustained by magic. It will cost Korang dearly to withstand an equal. It will drain all his magic and draw on the magic of his master. This is why he must be challenged to single combat."

"But not by me, Prophet. I'm not his equal."

"You can become his equal, and his better, if you are willing to sacrifice a portion of your life. I speak of magic, Staver, and magic is a costly art. It gives much, but it demands much in return. The Cairnlord has paid an awful price for his great power and the power of his servants. You must expect to pay dearly for the strength to withstand them."

"Is there no one else?"

"There is only you, Staver."

Staver sighed. "I'll do what I must, whatever the price. But tell me, Prophet, what would have happened if I had fallen crossing the Fissure or drowned in the Fool's Head? What if the Lool had eaten me before Zandinell arrived? Would there be no one to fight Korang?"

"I have no answer to that, Staver. I know only that you and your brothers are the last males of the line of Ambescand. Perhaps from one of your descendants, a leader would come forth, but I think not. Even so, that would come only after a time, and very soon all hope would be lost, for the Cairnlord's power grows with the passing of time. He has been husbanding his power since the fall of the Old Kingdom, letting his human servants do the work of empire while he amassed his magic. By striking at his strongholds, you and your brothers are forcing him to expend magic—to waste it, since he is unprepared for the strength of your attacks. Every new drain on his magic forces him to delay. This is why you were called forth now to do the things you have done. No, Staver, there would be no other," the Dark Prophet said decisively. "Only you can challenge Korang, and then go on to confront his master."

"Confront the Cairnlord?" Staver's voice was small with astonishment.

"I think one day you must. It is not yet clear."

"But not for a long time. A very long time."

"It will come when the time is right. Until then, you and your brothers must attack his servants and force him to delay."

Puzzled, Staver asked, "What's the good of making him delay if his power grows with time?"

"Your attacks will make the delay costly to him. Meanwhile, I use the time thus gained to search out his plans."

It was all getting much too complicated for Staver, who could see nothing but contradictions in what the Dark Prophet said. "Don't you know yet what he wants to do?"

"Much is still concealed. I know only that he planned to move westward, into Long Wood, and then north to seize the Headland. You yourself have seen his gray men on the Headland."

"But why does he want the Headland?" Staver pressed her.

"To secure his borders. He would then spread east and south, and across the sea, to bring the world under his dominion."

The sheer immensity of such ambition left Staver speechless. He knew that the world was a large place, big enough to contain the Headland, and the forests, and mistlands and mountains, and surrounding seas, and perhaps a great deal more besides, though the nature of that other reality was vague in his imagination. To think of one man seeking to dominate all was staggering. Even the great Ambescand had not had such ambitions.

"It will take the Cairnlord long to achieve this," the Dark Prophet went on. "It may take ages. To him, that means nothing. The Cairnlord long ago passed beyond all human reckoning of time. He is patient. One day he hopes to be master of all the Earth. And I think that this is only the first step in his plan."

Staver was dumbfounded. He tried to conceive of such magnitude, so long a view of time and such a thirst for power, and his mind rebelled. He could only cry out, "How am I to stop such an enemy?"

"Only when the time is right, Staver. Only when you are ready. First you must face Korang." She opened her arms. "Come with me—into the corridors of time. As you once learned the ways of healing, now you must learn the ways of war."

Staver stepped closer. She folded one slender arm about his shoulders. The blue light dimmed and died, and he felt her other arm enclose him, clasping him tightly. The Fastness fell away into a blacker emptiness, and a great wind rushed by on all sides while they stood calm and untouched at the center. Staver felt no fear. He had come this way before.

22

Bane of the Blightbringer

By the time the first snow fell on the lake isle, Col was fully recovered. He immersed himself, for a time, in the repair and strengthening of the defenses of the citadel and the reorganization of his fighting force. There was not a great deal of work awaiting him; Goodbowe and Mullerin had seen to the provisioning and housing of the fighting force and of the newcomers who ventured in small groups from the forest as word of the victory spread; Bolter had kept the able men on a regular training schedule. All was in good order at the citadel.

Throughout the winter the foresters worked steadily to refit the citadel into a stronghold all but impregnable. They did not doubt that the Cairnlord would strike back, and they hoped to be prepared for whatever mortal force he might send against them. To protect them from his magic, they trusted in their king.

The underwater defenses were increased and made stronger, and a regular patrol was maintained around the isle and on the lake. The outer walls were filled and patched and coated with smooth mortar. The old sally ports were blocked, and new ones built. The ground before the citadel was graded, and the towers refashioned to give the archers long clear fields of fire. Captured weapons and armor were reforged and fitted to the defenders, and everyone able to bear weapons was set to regular drill.

Col took a strenuous part in the training, eager to get his body back into fighting condition after his long idleness. He made frequent visits to the outer parts of the island and the surrounding forest, picking sites for outposts and building a defense perimeter against the inevitable counterattack by the Cairnlord's forces. Nights he spent in planning and consulting with his chiefs.

As the short gloomy days wore on, Col became increasingly restless. He found the duties of kingship manifold and complex, and thorny with frustrations. He seemed never to have time to deal satisfactorily with one problem before another, more urgent problem arose to trouble him, and all too often he had to admit to himself that he had not the wisdom or the experience his role required.

Winning a battle, taking a fortress, proclaiming oneself king—these were straightforward acts, deeds to be planned and carried out and seen to completion. Once done, they were done forever. Kingship was different. It involved uncertainties and alternatives. One seemed always to deal with things that changed even as one dealt with them. What appeared sound and workable at the outset often turned out to be unsound and impossible when one was halfway through. Agreement turned to disagreement overnight; decisions wavered; results never seemed to be what had been planned but something different that had insinuated itself along the way. Nothing was properly manageable.

When the sickness first came upon his people, Col thought it was simply one more pointless, annoying complication in his plans. But the sickness remained and spread among them. The work parties in the forest and on the island began to fall behind. Soon noticeably fewer people were to be seen working in and around the citadel.

An air of neglect began to settle over everything as those who remained well were forced to take more and more work upon themselves. Each day, a few more people took to their beds. No one seemed to recover from the mysterious illness. At a conference with his chiefs, Col asked about the situation.

"It's been twelve days since the first victims complained, my lord," Goodbowe told him. "Now we have a hundred and thirty-one people ailing."

"I've heard of no deaths."

"No. They don't die. But they don't get well, either. It be always the same," Bolter said. "Three days they sweat and shake; two days they have an awful thirst and hunger; then the sweats and the shivering return, and it goes on and on, first one and then the other."

"Where did this sickness come from? I've never heard of anything like it. Could the Cairnlord's men have poisoned the water or left some kind of poison here to destroy us after they're gone?"

"We all be drinking the same water, my lord, but not all has the sickness."

"Might be that the newcomers from the west, or up in Long Wood, brought it with them," one man suggested.

"Not likely. It be touching old and new equally," said another.

"Have the healers found any cure?" Col asked.

Goodbowe shook his head. "They've bled some, and roasted some, and cooled some, and purged some, and the rest they've left alone, and they're all the same. The medicines are nearly gone, and it's too early to gather new, and nobody believes it makes a difference, anyway, whatever they do."

Col looked up, frowning. "The people are losing heart."

"They are, my lord. I've heard them saying that before spring is here we'll all be sprawled about the citadel, weak as water, and if we don't die of the sweats and the shivers we'll be cut to pieces when the Cairnlord's armies come to storm the walls."

"I've heard more than one say that he might slip off and take his chances in the forest," Bolter added.

"Those who do are helping to fulfill their own prophecy. If no one's left but the sick, we'll have no hope of defending ourselves. How are the defenses progressing?" Col asked.

"Slowly, my lord," Goodbowe replied. "I took men from the island defenses to help complete the forest outposts. If I don't lose any more men, we'll be ready by summer."

"The Cairnlord could have an army here before that. Has there been any word?"

"None, my lord," Bolter said.

Col went around the table, asking each of the chiefs in turn how he was coping with the situation, and he grew more concerned with each reply. Important work was going undone; supplies were dwindling; morale was low; and fear was on the increase. The bond that had been forged in attack and victory was beginning to crack under the slow attrition of sickness and uncertainty.

"Where's Mullerin?" Col asked when the last chief had reported.

"He came down with the sickness this morning, my lord," another mistlander replied.

Col sighed and shook his head wearily. "The rest of you—all of us—must care for ourselves as best we can. We have to find a cure for this sickness. In the meantime take whatever precautions you think wise. If you find anything that seems to be working, come to me at once."

"Will my lord Staver be returning soon? He was a fine healer of battle wounds. He might know of sicknesses, too," one of the chiefs said.

"Staver's gone to the Fastness. I don't know when he'll return."

"Might you send after him?"

"We can't spare men to search the mountains. Staver was sent north by the Dark Prophet. If he's needed here, she'll see to it that he returns," Col said with a show of confidence that he did not truly feel.

The next day, only three people came down with the fever, and two more on the day after that. Col felt his spirits lifting; clearly the worst was now behind them. But on the following day, twenty new victims were reported. And on that same evening, a messenger arrived from the east with dreaded news: an army of humans, reinforced by gray men, was gathering in the eastern forest beyond Broad River.

"How many?" Col asked.

"About six hundred humans and a score of gray men when I saw them, my lord."

"That's a small force to besiege this place. Were more expected?"

"A larger force was to come from the City of the Game, but none arrived. This has troubled the men somewhat, but they expect to conquer nonetheless, with the aid of sorcery."

"How are the Cairnlord's men armed?"

"One in three is a swordsman. The rest are archers. Some of the gray men are different, my lord—bigger than any I've ever seen."

"And who leads them?"

"I could not learn. He remains in a tent at the center of his forces. The tent is always guarded by gray men."

Col thanked the messenger and dismissed him. He sat late that night by his window, in the quiet light of a full moon, thinking. Somewhere to the east, the Cairnlord's minions were making ready. They might number twice his present strength before they struck camp and moved against him, and while their army could only grow, his was dwindling.

Col stretched out on his bed, fully clothed, his body weary but his mind too troubled to permit him to sleep. He could only hope that when the attack came, he could meet the Cairnlord's forces on his feet, sword in hand. He did not want to be butchered in his bed, enfeebled and quaking with sickness, oblivious even to the blade descending. He longed for the wisdom of the Dark Prophet.

She came as if at his wish. First the glimmer in the darkness, swelling to a dazzling oval of light; then the roar and press of wind; then the shimmering dark band that grew to a hooded figure, and she stood before him in the moonlight. Col sprang to his feet.

"The Cairnlord's army is assembling, and a sickness weakens my people. You must help us," he said.

"I can help somewhat. The struggle is yours."

"I'm doing all I can. How can I fight sickness?"

"Face the one who calls the sickness down on you. He

is Bellenzor, the Blightbringer, Waster of Life. It was he who sapped the strength of those in the High City and left it defenseless. He hopes to do the same to the citadel."

Col was silent for a moment, then he asked, "Am I strong enough to face such a wizard?"

The Dark Prophet spoke confidently. "The blood of Ambescand is in your body and in the blade you carry. His power is with you. The amulet in your shoulder is very powerful. Your magic is fresh, untapped. . . . You bring innocence to the confrontation. Yes, I think you have the strength to face Bellenzor."

"But I know nothing of magic, and he's a wizard."

"The magic is in you, and around you. It will work through you when the time is right."

Col was still dubious. "Bellenzor is one of the Stone Hand. He's lived twenty years for every one of mine—perhaps longer than that. He's learned things I can't even begin to imagine."

"Learned—and forgotten," said the Dark Prophet. "His days of mastery were few, and he wasted his gifts. Since the crushing of the rebellion, Bellenzor has been in thrall to one more powerful. He has given himself to evil, and now only evil sustains him. He is still a man, Colberane, and can be overcome. The fall of Bellenzor will be a great blow to the Cairnlord."

"I have no choice, do I?"

"None. Ordred has freed the High City, so no help will come to the Cairnlord from that quarter. But the Blightbringer is strong. If he is not stopped, the citadel will fall to the Cairnlord's army, and then they will turn all their strength against the High City. Darkness will descend again on this corner of the world, and none will rise to drive it back. You must confront him now."

Col nodded and took up his sword. "I only wish Ord and Staver were here. The three of us together might have a better chance."

"Just as a hand has five fingers, the Stone Hand has five wizards. Ord must confront one and Staver another."

"Can they hope to win?"

"Place your trust in Ambescand, in his blood and his power, and you will all overcome the enemy."

"I will, prophet. I'll trust him—and you." Col smiled

and added, "I already owe you my life. I'd be foolish to doubt you."

When the hooded figure spoke, the affection was unconcealed in her voice. "Three brothers, and yet how different. Staver is trusting. I need only tell him what must be done, and he is willing. Ord does not even require that; his own impetuous nature drives him to his destiny. And you, Col, must ever be convinced and persuaded before you act. Yet you all do what you must, each in his own way."

"Isn't Staver a bit young for such a contest? I trust and respect him, Prophet—indeed, I love him dearly—but he's scarcely more than a boy."

"You were a boy not long ago. Now you are a king. Boys grow to be men, and sometimes they must grow quickly."

Col threw his cloak over his shoulders and said, "Lead me to Bellenzor, Prophet."

The Dark Prophet stepped closer to him. She spread her cloak, raising her arms high, and a blackness enfolded Col, shutting out the moonlight. He felt himself suspended, as if the earth and skies had dropped away and he stood alone among the stars; he felt no wind, nor any sense of physical movement in himself. It was as if the world moved around him while he remained apart.

In a moment the darkness eased. Points of light appeared above and ahead of him, and then the full moon broke through, and he could distinguish an encampment in a clearing surrounded by trees. It was deep night. The ground was firm beneath his feet. He stood at the perimeter of a cleared circle, with rows of small tents at his back and all around. At the center of the circle was a single huge tent, where gray men stood on guard. Col became aware of muted sounds of a sleeping camp; the smells of food and of fire burning low; the regular tread of a guard on his rounds. He looked around quickly; he was alone and unseen. He moved into the shadows and studied the large tent in the circle.

The tent was oval in shape. Giant gray men stood at intervals around it, positioned so that no one could pass through the circle of guards unseen. Col recalled the mes-

senger's words and knew that this must be the tent of
Bellenzor.

He acted at once; his plan was direct and simple. He
plucked an armful of fresh grass and threw it on the nearest fire. As the smoke thickened, he slipped off and took
up a position in striking distance from the nearest gray
watcher.

In the tents nearest the fire, men began to cough and
to swear loudly at the smoke. The gray man, ever vigi-
lant, turned toward the noise and as it did, Col ran silently behind it, sword drawn, and beheaded the creature
with a single stroke. Placing his hand against the thing's
knobby back, he thrust it toward the row of tents. The
headless gray man lurched forward, hooked blade slashing. Col ducked into the shadow of the tent and waited
for his chance to strike at the next guard.

When the third headless giant had been sent stumbling
toward the tents, Col heard a great outcry go up—the
first of the gray men was among the sleeping army, slashing blindly as it strode inexorably on. The din increased
as the second gray man burst upon the sleepers. Shouts,
screams of pain and terror, the clatter of arms hastily
seized or thrown down in panic, all rose around the great
tent. In the confusion Col eluded the three remaining
guards and entered the tent.

As the flap dropped behind him, Col gave a start. He
was in no tent but in a corridor of glistening black stone
that extended before and behind him to limitless darkness.
Torches flared high overhead. No entrance was in sight.

Col blinked, and stared, and found that the walls were
not featureless, as they had first appeared to be. He could
distinguish the outlines of doors set into the walls at irregular intervals. As his eyes grew accustomed to the
wavering light, he could see that the doors were of different shapes and sizes. Some were as high and broad
as castle gates; others were narrow as cupboards or
low and squat as ovens; and some were like no doors
he had ever seen.

He felt a great desire to fling wide these doors and enter all the rooms that lay beyond, one after the other, to
find what awaited him—treasure, beauty, adventure,
glory, a joy beyond description or imagining. The thought

danced in his mind, enticing him, drawing him, and he reached out for a broad, rounded door that radiated a rainbow of fluid color. The handle rose to meet his grasp, but before he could touch the door, a jolt of pain in his shoulder made him draw back his hand with a start. The door at once faded and vanished, as did all the others.

Col saw that he was at an intersection. Unbroken corridors of gleaming black, torch-lit, silent and empty, led off to his left and right, curving and branching in a labyrinthine web of stone. He could not tell which way he had come, nor which way he had meant to go. All ways were the same. As he stood indecisive, he heard a faint scraping sound from far down one of the corridors, as of something moving. He turned, and the sound shifted so that it now came from his left. When he turned to his left, the sound was behind him, louder, and drawing closer.

He turned, and turned again, but always the sound was elsewhere. He saw that the corridors were shrinking. Overhead, the lights had begun to fade. The sound was nearer; close at hand; just behind him; always out of reach. To the scraping was added the snuffling of a great beast's breath. Col felt panic rising in him at the gathering darkness, and the encroaching walls, and the sound, all of them closing in on him, tightening like a net. Sword in hand, he stood numbly waiting.

The jolt of warning came again from the amulet in his shoulder, and with it came awareness. Col closed his eyes and slashed out with the white blade, straight for the black walls that now nearly touched him on all sides. His blade struck no stone, but he heard the crash of shattered glass. He struck again, and there was a tearing of cloth, and he knew that he had overcome the wizard's first defense.

When Col opened his eyes, he was in a tent. A man stood before him in a blood-red robe, holding a black staff tipped with a red stone. His face was pale and sunken, and his large dark eyes were ringed in red, like those of a man in the grip of fever. Col avoided those eyes and leveled his sword at the wizard's breast.

"It was all illusion, Bellenzor. That's all you are," Col said.

"The world is full of illusion," the wizard said. His

voice was hoarse and low and rasped like the croak of a man on his deathbed.

"Is the sickness of my followers illusion? Will it vanish when you die?"

"You will never know."

"I will. I've come to finish the work of Ambescand. The Cairnlord won't bring you back this time."

Shouts and cries and the sound of running came from beyond the walls of the tent. There was a commotion outside the entry flap, and a guard burst in, sword in hand.

"The gray men, master! They've gone mad! They—" At sight of Col, he sprang forward on the attack.

Col's return slash cleft his helmet, and the guard fell just as two more entered. As Col engaged them, Bellenzor sidled toward the entry. Col struck furiously, driving the guards aside so he could block Bellenzor's escape. One guard went down, then the other, and Col turned to the wizard.

He felt a sudden blow, and his leg gave way beneath him. The first guard had rallied for one dying stroke and driven his sword deep into Col's thigh.

Col fell to his knees. Supporting himself with one hand, he thrust up at Bellenzor. Their eyes met. The wizard darted back and threw his staff to the ground before Col.

It sprang to life, a slim black serpent with a single eye of blazing red. It twined itself around Col's arm like a whiplash, A pain burned Col's sword arm, as if he had plunged it shoulder-deep in hot coals.

"Let the blade fall, swordsman. Let it fall, and the pain will end," the wizard said.

Col struggled to his feet, dizzy with the agony that seared bone and muscle. He steadied his grip on the white sword with both hands and stepped clumsily forward. The red eyes blazed before him, weaving, taunting him. He fought to avoid them. Bellenzor gave way, and Col came on, eyes fixed on the point of his blade. The wizard came up against a table, tried to turn, and fell. Col threw himself on the struggling form, driving his sword through Bellenzor's chest and into the ground.

The pain faded from his arm and his head cleared. He leaned on the blade to steady himself. He looked down, and his gorge rose at sight of the putrescent blot that lay before him. Tugging the blade free, he drew back, a groan of horror and loathing breaking from his throat.

He raised his sword and saw that the tip of the blade where it had pierced Bellenzor, was dulled and darkened as if he had plunged it into some corrosive. The tent was silent. Bellenzor and one guard lay dead, the other two guards wounded. Col turned to leave, and a stab of pain in his leg made him stagger and reach out for support. His lowered eyes fell on the wizard's staff; it lay where Bellenzor had flung it, a black stick with a cracked red stone at its tip.

The camp was in uproar now, and Col felt as if he were at the eye of a storm. Bellenzor was dead, and his evil influence was ended. The people of the citadel might be rising from their sickbeds at this very moment. But there would be no invading army for them to face. The Cairnlord had been beaten back once more.

But each victory was harder won than the last.

Col thought of his brothers and wished them strength, and then the glow of the Dark Prophet's coming filled the tent.

23

Death of the Stormlord

Ord was busy all through the cold, wet winter. As word of the last game and the battle spread, little groups of exiles from the far corners of the Plain came cautiously to the gate and were welcomed by the freedmen.

The tower was demolished. Its stones were dragged from the city and tumbled into the sea. With the weapons of the beaten guards, the freedmen built their own force to defend the city. The long, hooked weapons of the gray men lay untouched in the armory. No man could wield them.

Late one gloomy night when rain was sweeping in from the sea, the Dark Prophet came to Ord and told him to make ready to march on the Fastness. He was to take only a small force and to follow the trail she mapped out for him. She brushed aside his worried questions about Col and Staver, assuring him that they were safe, and was gone before he could ask further about his mission. Only a map remained on the table.

Ord left with a force of thirty men on the fifth succeeding day. Kinnaury remained behind; he and a tough, dedicated young freedman named Parrill were to oversee the city in Ord's absence. Kinnaury was especially charged with Ciantha's safety. She and Ord were to be wed upon his return.

They took their farewells at the palace, and again at the fountain, and still again at the western gate. As he marched before his men, Ord looked back and saw Ciantha waving to him from atop the gate tower. He waved in return until he could see her no more.

Less than two greatmarks' distance down the road, Ord and his men passed an old woman and a boy, and Ord called a halt. He recognized the two, and from the smile that lit the woman's lined face and brightened her eyes, he knew she recognized him, too. This time the boy did not flinch from his hand.

"You saw me entering, and now you see me leave. And much has happened in between," Ord said to the woman.

"You're not as red-haired as you were. I see that."

Ord reached up to brush back the white streak that ran from his temple. "I've not been since I played the game, but you're the only one honest enough—and unpleasant enough—to tell me so."

She laughed happily. "Oh, I knew you had hard task before you. I knew that. I knew you'd win, too, and send all crashing down, and make the city as it once were. All foretold, it were."

"Well, what else is foretold? Do you have another prophecy to tell me about?" Ord asked.

"I do, I do. This one is for all of you—but especially for the young one. He's the one will do the great deed. Colberane battles the Blightbringer. Scarlet Ord strikes at the Stormlord. But Staver's Iron Angel will blend with three ages and strike at the Cairnlord's heart."

"It sounds good. I don't understand it all, though," Ord said.

"It be prophecy. Prophecy don't be rightly understood until it come true, then all see it plain as sunshine."

Ord looked at her narrowly. The bright black eyes in that webbed face told him nothing, and he could not decide whether she was taunting him or speaking with simple sincerity. Her expression was as innocent as the child's.

Ord took his leave from them and proceeded westward until they reached the first crossing, then turned north. They followed this road for five days, the sea always on their right, the far mountains on their left. Under the spring sun, snow-mantled mountains and spangled sea glittered alike.

They reached a point where the foothills jutted forth onto the Plain. Here Ord stopped and sent out scouts. One party came upon a long unused trail westward, and they followed this trail into the mountains, ascending a shallow grade that grew steadily steeper until they were no longer walking but climbing. After a day of this, the track leveled. They were high in the mountains now. The air was chill, and snow lay in all the sheltered places. Nothing was to be seen but the walls of higher mountains.

On their second day in the heights, Ord became aware of a tingling in the amulet in his shoulder. Danger was near. He moved to the front of the line and remained there, alert, but saw nothing. Twice he heard loud booming noises echo from far away, but nothing and no one came into view.

Next morning, as they started on their way, the earth swayed beneath their feet. The tremor passed in a moment, but that single touch of sickening motion where no motion should be was enough to unnerve every man. They thought of the narrow ledges they had worked their careful way along, and of the slopes of scree and broken stone they had climbed, and imagined what would have befallen them had the tremor struck at those places. They were quiet after that, and Ord sensed their tension as they walked behind him.

No more tremors came, and their confidence gradually returned. By the next day they were marching along as

boldly as ever. Then the sky began to darken. The wind
rose, and dusky clouds rolled swiftly from the west. A
cold rain spat at them with coin-sized drops that soon
changed into a steady downpour. In the night, as they
huddled miserable and fireless in crevices that left them
half-exposed, the rain became sleet, then heavy snow,
and changed at last to icy rain. When they looked around
in the pale morning light, the world was armored in ice.
They had only a glimpse of it before fresh thick snow began to fall.

Ord was taken completely by surprise at this turn in
the weather. He had little knowledge of the mountains,
and the men of the city knew no more than he. It had
been long since any but guardsmen had ventured beyond
the Plain and come back to tell of the journey. Ord and
the others had known that the weather would be cold and
had worn heavy cloaks and high boots to protect against
it, but they had not conceived of such extremes.

Since their food supply was adequate, Ord decided to
have them stay in this place until the storm abated. The
snow continued falling all that day and night. The next
morning dawned clear and still on a world so white it
pained their eyes to look upon it.

Ord weighed the thought of backtracking. This was the
trail the Dark Prophet had marked, but he was certain she
had not meant for him to risk his men's lives in such
weather. There was sure to be another route to the Fastness.

The scouts returned with their reports. The way ahead
was snowy, slick in places, but passable with caution. The
trail behind them had vanished, drifted over a mark deep
in heavy, clinging snow. Ord listened to the scouts and
remembered the crossing of the Fissure. When something
wants you to go forward, he reflected, it makes certain
that you can't turn back. He gave the order to move on
and took his place at the head of his men.

The footing was treacherous, and their progress slow.
Men slipped and slid on the glassy surface; each rise
and dip in the trail was a major obstacle. By nightfall
they had gone only eight greatmarks.

Next day they climbed higher and came to a saddle
between two peaks. Ord led the way across the crusted

snow, walking gingerly, his boots sinking in a hand's breadth before they held firm. Two of the freedmen, Denrick and Flawn, were close behind him.

Once again the earth stirred beneath their feet, like a restless giant stretching in his sleep. Ord heard a sound like a colossal sigh at his back. He looked back in time to see the snow crumble and fold in upon itself, to fall with a great roar and an upflung blossom of white that curled and hung in the windless air. Three men were gone.

"It's a crevasse. The snow covers them, makes a bridge, but it can't hold a man," Denrick said.

Flawn looked into the deep gap that now separated them from the others and said, "We were lucky. It could have gone when we were on it."

"How do we know we'll stay lucky?" Ord asked.

"We do not," Denrick replied. "In snow like this there's no way to test."

Flawn raised his eyes from the crevasse and looked at the others fearfully. "What shall we do?"

Ord thought again of the unknown power that drove him remorselessly forward, forbidding all return. "We go on," he said. "We can't turn back, and if we stay here we'll freeze to death. The wind is rising. We go on, and hope our luck holds."

"I can't see anything beyond the peak. Maybe we've reached the crest, and we'll start moving down to where it's warmer," Denrick said.

They signaled to the others to circle around and join them at the peak. Then Ord turned to lead his two companions on, and as he looked ahead, he saw three figures at the peak, motionless, looking down on them. His shoulder gave a twinge of warning.

"Who are they, my lord?" Flawn asked.

"No friends, I'm sure. Two of them appear to be gray men," Ord said, stepping forward.

Wind hit them like a blow, staggering them. A whirl of blown snow enclosed them on all sides, obscuring everything behind a barrier of featureless whiteness. Ord strained forward, walking with caution yet trying to get to the peak and close to his enemy before his men were scattered and lost in this savage, ever-rising wind.

Each step was harder than the one before. Ord felt like a man trying to force his way through a congealing wall. The wind tore the breath from his lungs, blinded his eyes with tears, drew the life and warmth from his body, and cloaked him in ice. He covered his face with his gloved hands and forced himself on, step by agonizing step, until the wind grew so strong that he could barely stay erect.

In a rage he unsheathed his sword. At once he felt new strength. The naked blade seemed to draw him on, stronger than the wind that howled and shrieked about him and tried to force him back. As the wind diminished and died, his step became firm and sure. He reached the peak just as the light began to fade.

The gray men started to life at the sight of him, but he was quicker than they. He cut the legs out from under the nearest and turned to draw a blow from the other. Dodging aside, he struck off the creature's sword arm at the elbow and charged full force into the gray man, sending it over the edge to vanish down the side in a plume of snow.

The third figure did not move. It stood motionless at the very peak, its white cloak enfolding it, one hand and its face only exposed. In the hand was a long staff, higher than its head. The face was that of a man, lined and weathered, with eyes as pale as ice. The hair was white, lifting over a high forehead.

"It's you who brought the snow and rain, and the ice, and the wind," Ord said, words tumbling out of him without knowledge of what put them in his mind. "You shook the earth beneath our feet. You thought you'd destroy us."

"I will."

"You tried on the Fool's Head, and you failed."

The white figure blinked once, disdainfully, and gave a soft humorless breath of laughter. "You think you face Aoea? That is a mere windwraith, a minor spirit subject to my bidding. I am Cei Shalpan. I rule the world and the weather and shake the mountains."

"You don't rule me or my brothers. Soon you'll rule nothing."

"Contemptible little thing of flesh and bone," Cei Shalpan said, lowering his staff.

Ord started for the white figure. As the staff came level with his chest, he automatically brought up his sword. A bolt of shimmering colored light shot from the staff; he parried it, and as the light touched the blade, he felt a power tear through him, like a flood through a narrow channel. It was not painful or even unpleasant in any way; neither was it pleasurable. It was a sensation utterly unlike any he had ever felt before, and when it drained from his body, he felt different—as though something new and unfamiliar had become a part of him.

"This little thing of flesh and bone still stands," he said.

"Not for long, swordsman. Nothing human can withstand the power of the Stone Hand."

"So you say. Your power is unimpressive."

"I can bake and freeze these mountains until they crumble into dust. I can turn the Plain into a desert, the forest into a wasteland of ice, and make the land heave and roll like the sea."

"But I'm not a mountain or a forest. I'm Ordred Vannenson, and I bear a sword forged by Ambescand."

Cei Shalpan lowered his staff quickly, but Ord's guard was up. The light splattered against the silver blade and lit the darkening sky with a shower of dying flares of deep violet, and red, and pale green. Again and again the blast poured forth, and each time Ord caught it on his blade and flung it aside to illuminate the sky with streaks and ribbons of blazing light.

Ord's two companions huddled below, paralyzed with fear at the sight of their king in combat with this uncanny figure. The rest of their party, farther down the mountain where the peak was obscured from their view, saw only the light wildly dancing in the sky and trembled at the thought of what might have caused it.

Alone at the mountaintop, Ord battled a protean enemy. The wizard before him was a man no longer; he flowed from shape to inhuman shape. He became a huge form that towered over Ord with an upraised blade of dark fire. Ord set himself to fend off a mighty blow; but when it fell, and he turned it aside with his blade, the blow of the giant figure was no stronger than that of a man. Again Cei Shalpan changed, now to a squat hulk of brute muscle, swinging at Ord's head a mace that could shatter an oak. Ord ducked beneath the blow, thrust, and felt his blade sink home. The hulking form shrank to something more nearly human—but still long-limbed, huge of frame, gaunt-featured, wielding a broad-axe in one hand, clutching a dagger in the other. Ord dodged the axe, and as the expected dagger thrust came, he cut at the hand. The dagger fell, and Ord slashed again and again at the axe hand.

Then the wizard turned into something more hideous than Ord could face—a great formless mound of gray-green sponginess, lurching toward him on stumpy legs, flailing with boneless, whiplike, leprous arms that caught at flesh and clothing to draw him toward a clacking white beak. Ord fell back a step and groaned in horror. The thing closed in on him; it grew larger; its grip was firmer, hooking into him and pulling him to the gaping beak.

Ord closed his eyes, raised his sword in both hands, and struck at the clutching arms. The grip of the thing loosened. Ord took heart and struck again. He opened his eyes and saw the thing shrunken and falling back under the blows of the sword. He understood then the nature of their struggle and the weapons involved. Cei Shalpan fought with terror, and the fear he raised in his opponents became his strength. Ord gave vent to a peal of triumphant laughter. He strode forward, slashing at the formless thing that writhed under his attack, cringing and shrinking before him until it became at last the white-robed wizard.

Cei Shalpan glared at him. Fear mingled with the hatred in those icy eyes. Ord continued forward on the attack. The wizard parried his blows with the staff, but now no fire burst forth against him. Cei Shalpan retreated, and the fear grew in his eyes, and Ord saw despair there as he drove the wizard back and battered him to his knees.

The staff fell from Cei Shalpan's hands, and the white cloak fell away. Ord saw the wizard's body, twisted and misshapen, as if it had been crushed in a giant grip and then clumsily reworked into human form. He stayed his hand for an instant touched by pity for the pain this creature had undergone. Cei Shalpan scuttled forward, groping for his staff. Before his fingers could close on it, Ord brought his sword down.

The wizard shuddered and lay still. His white cloak crumpled inward. Where the body of Cei Shalpan lay, a mist arose. One wisp of it drifted to Ord, and he fell back, gagging. The mist rose, and the wind drove it off, dissipating it to nothing. The cloak fluttered and flapped, blew along the crest, and floated down the mountainside. Nothing remained but a dark stain on the bare rock, and even that faded and disappeared before Ord's eyes.

Ord turned and made his way down from the mountaintop. The crippled gray man lay motionless as a statue, its upraised slashing hand arrested in midstroke. He stepped over it and stumbled to where Denrick and Flawn rushed to greet him.

"It was a wizard! You overcame a wizard!" Flawn cried.

"Cei Shalpan. One of the Stone Hand," Ord mumbled.

"You fought him and beat him!"

Ord turned dazed eyes on them. "You saw? You saw those things he raised against me?"

"We saw only you and the gray men and the wizard," said Denrick.

Ord nodded and said nothing. He felt drained of all strength. He sat down, drew up his knees, and lay his forearm and head on them, breathing slowly in great sighing breaths. His sword was still firm in his hand, lying across his ankles.

Denrick and Flawn looked at their leader and exchanged a fearful glance. In the midst of the blade, where it had struck the fallen wizard, the bright sword was darkened as if etched with acid. And Ord's hair was as white as the snow that blew around them.

24

Scourge of the Warmaker

Korang was armed for battle. He settled the plumed gold-
en helmet on his head and reached out to take up his
sword. A rasp and a dull clang sounded behind him, and
he whirled, blade at the ready. He saw at the door to
his throneroom, his hand on the massive bolt he had just
slammed into its sockets, a man nearly his own size with
a plain iron breastplate and helmet, and a great winged
sword at his side.

"Where did you come from?" Korang demanded.

"From the place of the Lool."

"You lie! Nothing escapes the Lool."

"Your creature is dead, Korang. The tunnels are open,
and the mountaineers are entering. While your men guard
the outer walls, your enemy will enter the heart of the
Fastness."

"Another lie. The mountain rabble are gathering outside to storm the walls. I've seen their fires, night after
night."

The intruder laughed. "A few men can make a great
many fires, Korang. For one who deals in deception,
you're easily deceived."

"Let them pour through the tunnels by the thousand.
The only way up from the tunnels is through this room,
and no man will climb from that well and live."

Korang took a step toward the well in the throneroom
floor. The intruder moved quickly to block his way. The
Warmaker stopped, lowered his sword, and looked the
iron warrior over. He was a good size and quick for one
so big. His plain armor told nothing, but the broad face
and green eyes struck Korang as familiar. His gaze fell
on the dark-winged blade, and that, too, plucked at his
memory.

"I've seen you before. Who are you?" Korang demanded.

"When you take on human form, you take on human frailty. A wizard has a better memory than a swordsman."

"Answer me."

"I'm your enemy, Korang."

"Unfortunate for you. My enemies don't live long."

Korang gripped his sword with both hands and took up fighting stance. Staver drew the Iron Angel and held it before him. They circled, taking one another's measure. The throneroom grew still, with no sound save slow breathing and the soft padding of wary footsteps.

Korang struck first. His blow was turned aside. Staver moved back, circling to his left. When Korang lunged at him again, Staver countered with a series of hard strokes that pressed the Warmaker to a steady retreat. Staver broke off the attack and lowered his blade, and only then did Korang see that another backward step would have sent him over the edge of the well.

"You're a fair swordsman. But you cannot hope to defeat me," Korang said.

Staver made no reply. He came to guard, waiting for Korang to move on him. The Warmaker advanced, feinted to one side, then the other, and then swung in an overhead arc straight for the neck. His attack was turned aside, more easily this time than before, it seemed to him, and Staver's counterstrokes fell harder.

They circled and struck—lunge and feint and slash coming in ever more intricate sequence. Blow and counterblow rang in the stillness. The shock of steel on steel had hands and forearms smarting, palms sore and bruised. Always the footsteps fell lightly, but now the sound of breathing was louder and more labored.

After a furious passage of arms that carried the swordsmen the length of the throneroom and brought Korang, in full retreat, hard up against the stone wall, they broke off. For a moment they faced one another, panting, the sweat on their exposed skin gleaming under torchlight. Korang, with a wild cry, sprang forward and cut at Staver's midsection. The blow was blocked, and Staver's counterblow, a high flat slash, sent the crimson plume spinning from Korang's helmet and jarred the Warmaker's clenched teeth with the impact.

Korang staggered back, came up against the wall,

and quickly slid to one side where he had room to maneuver. He raised his sword to block the expected blow, but his opponent made no move to follow up his advantage. Korang blinked and shook his head and studied the iron warrior more closely. Something about his appearance was maddeningly familiar.

"You've been here before. I've seen you," Korang said.

"You have."

"Who are you?"

"I've told you, Korang. I'm your enemy."

Roused by the intruder's coolness, Korang attacked again. Staver met his blows without flinching or yielding a step; he brushed them aside with an ease that was close to contempt and then took the offensive. Korang was scarcely able to block the blows that fell so hard and so swiftly on all sides. Once again he was driven back in full retreat. In rage and desperation he sprang to the side, feinted high, and cut at his opponent's legs. His blow went wide, and the flat of Staver's sword landed full on the temple of his helmet, stunning him momentarily. He struck out in panic, flailing wildly at empty air, until his head cleared and he saw the iron swordsman standing motionless, a mark away, with lowered sword.

"You think you can overcome me," Korang said. "No one defeats Korang."

"No one, until now."

"I'm Korang the Warmaker. My power is great, and I serve a master many times more powerful than I."

"All that power seems to do you little good."

"Who are you to invade my throneroom and defy me? Tell me your name!"

"My name is Staver Ironbrand, brother to Colberane Whitblade and the Scarlet Ord."

"Again, you lie. Those three are long dead."

Staver raised the Iron Angel. "Do you think you've been fighting a dead man?" he asked, advancing on the Warmaker. He struck methodically, while Korang wielded his blade with increasing desperation. They moved nearer the well, and when Korang caught sight of it, he broke off the struggle and vaulted to the far side, placing the opening between Staver and himself.

"Where will you run next, Korang?" Staver taunted him.

"I'll defeat you. You're an imposter. Staver Ironbrand and his brothers died in the days of the Old Kingdom."

"Are you so certain?"

"My brother wizards slew them. Dead men do not return."

Staver laughed and made a contemptuous flourish of his hand toward Korang. "And what of yourself? You were a heap of shattered bones and torn flesh when the Cairnlord brought you back to life."

"I am no ordinary man. I am Korang, a wizard, and servant of a far greater wizard."

"But you're vain and foolish, for all your dark knowledge. You had to appear a man, and greater man than all around you—and that was your undoing. You mistrust your magic, Korang, and I think you even doubt your master's power."

"No!"

"You could not believe that true strength does not depend on stature and sheer physical force. You had to create the thing that you are, and now it's failed you," Staver said.

He moved to his left. Korang circled in like manner, keeping the well opening between them. When he came to the inner edge of the well, the side that opened on the throneroom, he broke for the throne, but Staver caught up and forced him to turn and engage. When they separated, Staver stood by the throne. He caught Korang's hungry glance past him.

"Is this what you were after?" he asked, pointing with his blade to the tall staff that rose from a crystal socket at the right hand of the throne. With a backhanded stroke he slashed the staff in two. The upper portion fell to the floor, and the pale blue stone in the top was shattered.

Korang paled and seemed to shrink. He stepped back. His face was contorted with sudden fear. Staver raised his sword.

"This is the Iron Angel, Korang. It was forged by Ambescand himself, and his blood and his magic are in the blade," he said.

The battered helmet fell from Korang's head. Golden hair and fine features corrupted before Staver's eyes, and he looked upon a skull covered in skin as dry as ancient parchment. The sword fell from Korang's skinny fingers, and his twisted legs sagged under the weight of armor. He sank to his knees, wailing in despair, and crashed forward, imprisoned in his golden breastplate. Staver's single thrust was an act of mercy.

The battle for the Fastness went on for a night and a day. Caught between two forces, the followers of the Cairnlord had no chance of turning back the attack of the mountain men, but they fought to the last defender all the same. A handful, here as at the High City, offered to surrender and then died horribly, strangled by an unseen hand. The others chose to die by the sword.

At sundown, on the day of battle, Ord and Staver were shocked to meet each other on the outer wall. Their first sight of each other stunned them both, and the shock was doubled by their mutual recognition at precisely the same moment.

"Staver, what's happened to you?" Ord said in a voice gentled by bewilderment. "It's you, I know it's you, but you're twice the size you were when I saw you last, and more than twice the age."

"You've changed, too, Ord."

Ord laughed and ran a hand through his tangled white hair. "Yes, I have. When they call me 'Scarlet Ord' in the future, they'll have to be talking about my red cloak."

"How did it happen?"

"It started at the tower of the Game. Then I fought Cei Shalpan. I defeated him, but it was an awful struggle. The price of victory is high."

"It cost me twenty years to overcome Korang."

"But how, brother?"

"The Dark Prophet can move through past and future at will. I don't understand how, but she's done it twice with me. She took me back in time—to the High City, I think—to learn healing so I could save Col's life. And then she took me to the Old Kingdom, in the early days when there was much battle, and there I stayed and learned to be a warrior the match of Korang."

Ord shook his head. "All those years . . . and yet we parted only at summer's end."

"In your eyes, we did. But I've not seen you or Col for half a lifetime."

"That's a harder price to pay than a few white hairs."

"It had to be paid. Korang had to be beaten into submission by a better swordsman to end his magic forever. The Iron Angel was the proper weapon, but I had to learn to use it. It took a long time."

Ord smiled ruefully. "The adventurous life is something more than we expected, isn't it, brother? Doing fine bold deeds and slaying evil sorcerers . . . I think often of the Headland. I've begun to miss it."

"I can scarcely remember it now."

"Will we ever see it again?"

"I think not, Ord. We still have much to do."

"I hope we'll have a time to rest. To tell the truth, brother, I'm weary."

Staver looked out thoughtfully to the peaks that rose in the north, where the way led to the Crystal Hills. "I think there'll be a time of peace. The old pattern has been broken by our arrival in the south, and we must wait for a new pattern to emerge."

"Will the Cairnlord wait?"

"I think he must. Three of the sorcerers of the Stone Hand are gone, and their magic is gone with them. Three of his strongholds have fallen. It's possible that he is still unaware of us, and who we are, and why we've come. The Cairnlord has to learn the situation, and rebuild his power, and lay new plans. The longer he waits, the more powerful he becomes."

Ord grunted. "Perhaps we'd be wise to move against him now. What do you think?"

"We're not strong enough," Staver said flatly.

"Are you so sure? Everyone seems terrified by the Cairnlord and his magic, but we've defeated him three times. We've overcome his gray men, escaped his spirits, taken his strongholds, defeated his sorcerers. It was hard, and we paid dearly for our victories, but we won. Maybe the Cairnlord just seems formidable because nobody ever dared to stand up to him before—like the Quarrier brothers, back on the Headland. Do you remember them?"

Staver laughed. "I do. They never expected us to take on the five of them. But the Cairnlord is no barnyard bully, Ord. We've won only because he left us to his servants. I doubt he'll make that mistake again."

"What will he do?"

"He'll wait. Build his magic." Staver frowned, gestured helplessly, and went on. "We still don't know what he wants or why he's done the things he has. It's clear that time means nothing to him. Perhaps the loss of fortresses, and armies, and even fellow sorcerers means nothing and he considers us unworthy of his power. I don't know, Ord. These are the things the Dark Prophet is trying to learn."

"I wish her success," Ord said fervently.

Darkness was coming on, and they walked toward the gate to descend to the courtyard. Neither of them spoke until they reached the stairwell; then Staver said, "I'm learning how little and weak we all are. We seem to have a bit of power, but it's all lent to us from somewhere beyond, and the price of that power is high—even for those who never sought it and had it thrust upon them. We've both seen that, and I'm sure Col has, too. When I think of the Cairnlord's power and his hunger for more, I shudder to think of the price that will be demanded of him."

"Perhaps he thinks that if he gathers enough power, there'll be none who dare to demand the price."

"Perhaps. I hope we can learn."

They crossed the courtyard, where the dead lay stacked like bloody cordwood, and entered the barracks that served as hospital. Here they parted. Ord had the work of cleaning up and organizing before him, and Staver now put to use his knowledge of healing. Both brothers worked steadily, with little food and less rest, through the following days. When they met again, it was to say their farewells.

"We can use your help here as long as you're willing to stay," Ord assured his brother. "You've saved scores of lives. The men are grateful to you."

"There's little more I can do here. Your healers have all the skill that's needed now."

"Only because you taught them, Staver."

"They learned quickly. It's time for me to go north."

"Must you go alone?"

"I'll have your messengers for company all the way to the coast. I would have asked Helmer to come with me, if he had lived. Perhaps it's best this way, though."

"Helmer led us through the tunnels. He was one of the first out and the first to fall. He was a good man," Ord said.

"He was." Staver reflected for a moment and smiled at a long-ago memory. "I found Helmer frightening that first night at the camp. So did Jem. Remember me to Jem when you see him again, will you?"

"I will, brother."

"And to Col. It may be long before we meet again."

"I hope not. We work well together. The three of us can unite this land and hold it against anyone."

The brothers embraced, and in a few moments Staver and the two messengers to the High City were through the gate and headed down the eastward trail to the coast road. Ord watched his brother's towering form grow small and then vanish around a bend, and he felt a sudden tug of sadness at his heart, a longing for the times they could never recapture and the people and places they might never see again.

Ord was Keeper of the Fastness and the Plain now, and his rule was undisputed. He had good reason to be happy and to look forward to a long reign. At the High City a woman waited to become his queen and help build a dynasty from which, one day, a great leader would spring. She was fair, the young Ciantha, and separation had only made him love her the more. The High City was a fine city to rule, and the Fastness was strong. But as Ord looked down the road, he thought not of what he had won but of what he had lost forever. He looked at the dark and barren walls that rose all around him, at the silent gray rock and the blank blue sky. With a sigh he turned to take up his duties.

Staver and the messengers took a clear, easy trail through the mountains and reached the western edge of

the Plain in a few days. Before them the green stretched
unbroken to the horizon. The air was rich with the scent
of new life and sweet with birdsong, and they strode in
good spirits along the old trail to the sea.

At the coast road they parted. They were near the
northern limit of the Plain. Staver could see the great
tower at Northmark, guardian of the passage to the Crystal Hills, looming in the distance. It rose twenty marks
from base to parapet and stood atop a hill twice as high
as itself. Even in ruin it was majestic.

It took him two days of steady walking to reach the
tower, and he arrived in the late afternoon of a gloomy
day, with sea mist hanging low in the sky, close around
the upper portion of the tower, obscuring all. He spent
the night at Northmark and remained there, resting,
through the rainy, misty day that followed. During the
night the wind shifted and the skies cleared. Staver awoke
at dawn to have his first sight of the Crystal Hills.

In the long rays of early light, the peaks were a tumble
of diamonds on a mound of ermine, glistening with a
brightness that pained the eyes even as its beauty forced
one to look. A long neck of land extended out to sea,
disappearing in the mist that still lay upon the water,
concealing the base of the mountains and the way to
them. Staver knew that the old bridges had been smashed
and that no easy access lay before him. But he did not
trouble himself with this. Out there lay his kingdom. He
was destined to reach it, and he would. The power that
had brought him safely across the Fissure, and the Fool's
Head, and through time and battle, would take him to the
Crystal Hills.

He stood long on the parapet, watching the shadows
sink and the peaks grow ever brighter under the climbing sun, and he thought of his lost home, and his brothers, and his solitude. Ord had spoken of a woman who
was to be his queen, and Staver had no doubt that Col,
too, would soon marry. But Staver's own middle years
were close upon him, and in his future he saw no love, no
tenderness—his future held the Cairnlord.

He had once had a friend in Jem Underhill, but the
Staver who was friend of Jem was gone now—lost in

the involutions of time, a sacrifice to the cause that dominated them all. Something of that young Staver still lived in the seasoned swordsman who now bore his name, but it was no more than a memory of years long past. This Staver was a man, with a man's duties on his shoulders.

The swordsman Staver might have found a friend in Helmer if that brave blind man had not fallen. So many had fallen—friends and strangers—that mourning one particular death seemed futile and almost self-indulgent. Woodwards, mistlanders, foresters, mountain men— all had given their lives to bring Staver here and prepare him for what lay ahead. The best memorial was acceptance of his duty.

He shouldered his pack, climbed down the long, winding staircase of the tower, and started north to his kingdom.

25

The White Haven

The sea mist furled around Staver, enshrouding him in milky white as he descended to the stony strand. At first he saw only the mist and heard no sound but the rhythmic crunch of his tread on the shingle; then he became aware of the lapping of the waves ahead of him and the rattle of sea-tumbled pebbles. And then, abruptly, as if come from nowhere, he saw the water lying like a dark smooth floor under slowly billowing swags of mist.

Here the sea was calm as a sheltered pond, but he knew that farther out from shore were churning currents, rips and overfalls that no human craft could navigate. Yet he went on, unperturbed. His destiny lay in the Crystal Hills, and while the way might seem impassable, the Fissure, too, had been thought impassable. The will that had shaken the earth to bring him safely across the Fissure would take him safely over the island chain to the Crystal Hills, if that was where he was meant to be. He need only be ready.

All day he followed the strand. Toward evening he heard the roar of distant waters. The sound grew louder as he walked on, and at length he came to the end of the neck of land. Inland, the ground rose, steeply now, to a rutted road that broke off in a sheer drop of three marks or more. The current rushed by below, curling, white-crested, loud with the force and speed of its passage. Out here at water level, with the empty sky overhead, the noise of the tideway lacked the brutal intensity of the voice of the Fissure. Nevertheless, it swallowed all other sound, and no human voice could have been heard above it.

Staver climbed to the high road and stepped to the brink, shielding his eyes, peering eastward to where the next island lay, two greatmarks distant and faint in the gathering dark. Between them raced the current, foaming over and around rocks that rose like the stumps of giant teeth. He stood for a time, studying the wild waters; then he seated himself at the edge of the road, took food from his pack, and ate. As darkness fell, he rolled himself in his cloak and slept in the lee of a tilted granite block.

He awoke chilled. Moisture was beaded on his cloak and hung heavy in the air. The mist was thick with morning. The first thing he noticed was the silence. He climbed stiffly to his feet, stamping to warm them, rubbing his cold hands together. He shook the droplets from his cloak, wrapped it close around him, and clapped his hands hard against his upper arms. The mist absorbed all sound, and he felt as if he had been swallowed by a cloud. Then he heard a voice.

Come, Ironbrand. You must go to the Crystal Hills.

"Where are you?" Staver called aloud.

On the southern strand. Come.

From where he stood Staver could barely distinguish the far edge of the road. Taking up his pack, he made his way cautiously down the steep bank. Once on the strand, he looked in both directions, but saw nothing. And then, as if the mist had taken form, a white shape moved toward him. The tip of its nose was black, and its eyes were a pale gray-blue, but all else was white. A great white wolf padded noiselessly out of the whiteness and stopped less than a half-mark away.

Come. The boat awaits you.

"Are you to be my boatman?"

You need no boatman. She will bring you safe to shore. I am your guide to where she waits.

The wolf turned and trotted into the mist. Staver followed. At the water's edge he stopped and peered out. A boat lay just off shore. It was not beached, nor was it tied, but it was as immobile as the land. Only then did Staver notice that the stillness around them was absolute. There was no lapping of water, no stir of the shingle. Nothing moved. Even when the wolf splashed into the water to spring aboard the boat, his passage made no sound and raised no wave.

The boat was narrow. It had no oars nor oarlocks, no sail nor sailing thwart, yet the moment Staver had taken his place amidships, the little craft set off smoothly into the mist. The wolf settled at his feet. In the eerie silence Staver could hear the great beast's regular breathing.

Soon they were skimming the still waters at a speed that caught at Staver's breath and sent his cloak flaring and snapping behind him. On each side the water swept back in a long white curl, and still no sound came to his ears. At last, when his eyes were weary from squinting against the buffeting wind, he felt the boat slowing. Out of the mist loomed a gray shape, and the boat drew up to a narrow beach of white sand that ran along the foot of a cliff.

The wolf sprang to the beach in a single smooth bound. Staver stepped ashore behind him. He was about to draw the boat up on the sand when the wolf turned.

Come.

"I'll beach the boat first."

The boat obeys her. Come.

Staver rolled up his cloak and swung the pack to his shoulder. He glanced back for one last look. The boat was gone.

Follow, urged the wolf, and Staver obeyed.

They went a short way over the white sand, then, when the gray cliffs gave way to a gentle slope, they turned inland. Soon they were above the mist, ascending in bright morning sunlight to a broad plain. At the crest Staver called for a halt. This was his first clear sight of his promised kingdom, and he found it of a grandeur that dazzled him. He wished to savor the moment.

The island rose out of the mist like a vessel riding a calm sea of milk. The air was warm and sweet with life. Splashes of color caught his eye everywhere on the Plain. The ground sloped gently, rising inland, and beyond everything towered white-capped mountains that glimmered under the cloudless sky. All was serene and still, calm in the majesty of its own special being, as if the peaks themselves were aware of their magnificence.

"This is my promised kingdom, wolf. I am Mage of the Crystal Hills. And a beautiful kingdom it is, too," Staver said.

She awaits, came the imperturbable reply.

"Who is she who awaits me?" Staver asked, without stirring.

She who sees what was and what will be. She who travels the paths of time and knows before and after as one.

"Is she called the Dark Prophet here?"

She is the Mother of Days. Come.

The answer was not revealing. Still, Staver felt certain that he was to see the Dark Prophet once more, though for what reason he could not imagine. He had come to his kingdom; his destiny was fulfilled. Yet the beast's description of a woman who knew past and future could only refer to the Dark Prophet, whatever name the creature might give her.

As they moved inland over the Plain, Staver's thoughts wandered from the approaching meeting. He felt unseen life all around him. It was not the life of the growing things, or the insects that hummed and clicked about their business, or the birds that circled lazily high overhead—these were all manifest to his senses. Another inner perception whispered to him of the presence of human life. And yet it was not human life of a kind he knew—this life had a chill in it, a remoteness, as if it were reaching out to him from across a gulf. The sensation was sttange but in no way frightening. And as he walked and wondered, Staver's mind went back to that morning half a lifetime ago—and yet not a year past by the world's reckoning—when he, a boy, first heard the voices of the creatures of the earth and understood. Now he experienced a similar feeling of revelation, as if a sense unsuspected and long dormant had stirred to life.

"Who dwells in this place, wolf?" he asked.

The Mother of Days. My pack, and the gathering of Hlir, and many smaller ones.

"No others like me? No people?"

Only the Mother of Days.

Staver was puzzled. There was life here, and it was human life. Though of an unfamiliar kind, it was as human as he was. The white wolf could not be speaking truly, yet he sensed no deception in the beast. He said nothing more, but he wondered.

The ground leveled. Far ahead at the foot of the mountains, Staver saw buildings—unmistakably the work of human hands.

"Hurry, wolf! I'll not fall behind," he cried eagerly.

The wolf broke into a loping run, and Staver ran at its side, keeping pace. The distance was less than a greatmark, and as they closed, Staver saw a slender figure, clad all in white, rise from a bench and stand before the largest of the buildings. It was a woman, and she waved a welcome to him as he drew near; then she folded her hands demurely before her and waited.

Her long hair was very fair. As he came near, he saw that it was white. Her face was lined and worn, but her beauty had not faded. She was plainly dressed, in a long dark gown of linen cinched at the waist with a golden cord. A golden fillet around her forehead bound her hair, which fell to her waist.

Staver stopped before her, and the white wolf, his tongue lolling, settled on his haunches at her side. Breathing heavily, Staver dropped his pack and his rolled-up cloak to the ground and looked down on the woman. She returned his gaze with queenly dignity, her clear green eyes unblinking.

"Welcome to the Crystal Hills, Staver Ironbrand," she said. Her voice was low and sweet, and familiar to his ears.

"Thank you, lady," he replied, bowing. "So, you're the Dark Prophet."

"I am known to some by that name." She laid her hand on the wolf's head, and said affectionately, "My companions here call me the Mother of Days. And in other places, I have other names."

"What shall I call you, lady?"

"Call me by that name you would have used if this task had not been placed upon us and we had lived as others live."

"And what is that?"

She looked up at him, her green eyes shining, and held out her slender arms. "I am Ciantha, wife of Vannen, and your mother, Staver."

For a moment he was too stunned to react. Then he flung out his arms to embrace her.

"Mother! All these years we believed you dead! You were sick . . . and an old man came . . . took you away. . . . We never heard anything more," Staver said, exultant now, but no less confused and wondering.

"Only Vannen knew the truth, and he could never tell."

"But why?" Staver put his big hands gently on her fragile shoulders and looked hard into her eyes. "It was so soon after my birth. . . . Did I make it necessary for you to go away?"

She reached up a hand and laid it on his. "At your birth things converged. An old age ended, and a new one began. We were all in great danger in those early days, and in order to keep you safe, I had to leave."

"Vannen said—just before he died—that you had protected us all those years. You gave him the amulet, and you left the black potion to revive him."

She lowered her eyes and nodded slowly. Her expression showed that the memory of those times was still fresh and still painful. "Vannen was very brave," she said, her voice subdued. "He knew he'd be found one day. Not all my magic could have saved him from the Stone Hand. But he watched over you until the time was right."

"Your sons have weakened the Stone Hand a bit, I think. Only two wizards remain."

"They are the two most dangerous, Staver. Skelbanda

shrivels hope and turns men against themselves. And the Cairnlord . . . The power of the Cairnlord is a hundred times greater than the power of all the others combined."

"Even now—with three of his chief followers dead?" Staver asked, incredulous.

"Even now. But you've taken a bit of his power from him and you've forced him to change his plans, and that will give you time to prepare for the confrontation. His strength will grow in these years of waiting, but yours will grow faster."

Staver sighed and shook his head. "I can't believe that I'll ever be a match for the Cairnlord."

"He's been turned back before by mortal men like you."

"Yes, but he always returns. Always. Humans can delay him, force him back, but in time he rebuilds his power and returns to threaten a new generation. Isn't this what has always happened? I'll face him, Mother. I'll give my life, if I must. But can't he be defeated once and for all time?"

Her expression became thoughtful. Taking Staver's hand, she led him to the bench where she had been seated when he first caught sight of her and bade him sit at her side. Her voice, when she spoke, was taut and intense. "If I can learn one thing, Staver, perhaps the Cairnlord can be stopped forever. Somehow—and I do not yet know how—I must find the locus of his power. When we know that, we may be able to cut him off from the source of all his magic."

"I don't understand."

"Have you never wondered why wizards are so reluctant to tell their true names, Staver?"

He thought on her words for a moment, then shook his head helplessly. "In truth, Mother, I've never noticed that they were. Zandinell told me his name freely. And everyone seems to know the names of the Stone Hand wizards."

She smiled and patted his hand, as if to chide him gently. "Not their true names, Staver. They're known by the names of long-dead figures. They've concealed their own. And the Cairnlord himself is so ancient that he may never have been given a name. He was in the world before things had names."

"What of Zandinell? Is he like the others?"

"Zandinell uses his true name. He learned that much before he broke with the company of sorcerers: just as one has a strongbox or some other hiding place for material treasures, so anyone who traffics in magic needs a safe focal point of power, where it remains hidden, secure from all others. Many wizards make their true name the locus of their power. Whoever learns it gains access to their power and can destroy it, so they guard their names very carefully. But some locate their power elsewhere—in a beast, or an object, or a conjunction of events at some particular time and place—and then it can be difficult indeed to discover. Zandinell has done this. So has the Cairnlord."

"Can we ever find it?"

"I've sought it in the past and the future. So far, I've learned only that the locus of the Cairnlord's power is an object—not a person, or a beast, or anything living, because living things are too ephemeral. But it might be almost anything, anywhere: a single stone on the beach, or one coin in a treasure at the bottom of the sea, or a mountain, or a symbol carved deep in a cave—anything."

"Have you any hope at all of finding it?"

"I must find it," she said simply. They sat in silence for a time; then she rose, held out her hand to Staver, and said cheerfully, "We both have hard work ahead of us. I must continue my search, and you must learn much before you can truly be Mage of the Crystal Hills. But tonight, we will have a feast to welcome you home."

He took her hand and rose, smiling at her words. "A feast—for just the two of us?"

"All your subjects will attend."

She said no more, and her manner made Staver reluctant to press for more information. He knew he would learn this day what he wanted to know, and that satisfied him.

His mother led him through the large building before which they had met. It was plainly furnished, with large and well-lit rooms, most of them containing shelves of great books in ancient, cracked bindings, draped in thick

dust. He was reminded of the hidden home of Zandinell.
In the largest room he pulled down an armful of the
books and laid them on the big round table that stood in
the center. The first two were in a familiar script, and he
recognized the words, although their meaning was not
clear. The third book was written in a curving, coiling
script that made no sense to him at all. As he studied it,
frowning, his mother stepped to his side and began to
read aloud. Staver listened until she was done.

"I've heard that language before. You used it to place
the spell on our swords, and Zandinell spoke it when he
transported Jem and me from the mountains."

"The ancient writing contains all the magic ever
learned. Read that writing, and the secret is unlocked.
Learn to speak it, and the magic can be yours."

He turned to her, perplexed. "Is that all one must do
to be a wizard—learn to read and speak an ancient
tongue? If it is, then it's strange to me that the world is
not full of wizards."

His mother smiled, then laughed affectionately, and
laid her hand on his. "The words are only the beginning,
Staver. The way is long and the discipline hard. It is easy
to destroy oneself in a terrible way. Most men and women
have no taste for it."

"I don't much want it, myself," Staver confessed. "But
I must learn, mustn't I?"

"You must, Staver," she said. "There is no other
choice."

That evening, in the great hall of the chief building,
Staver and his mother took their places in high-backed
chairs, elaborately carved, that stood at opposite ends of
a long banquet table. They were dressed in simple garments of white, all unadorned. The Iron Angel hung at
Staver's side. The table was covered by a plain white
cloth that reached almost to the floor. On it stood three
golden candelabra. There was no other source of light in
the hall. The corners and the high beamed ceiling were
deep in shadow.

Staver unfastened the Iron Angel and laid sword, scabbard, and belt on the table beside the golden bowl and
goblet that were set before him. When he had done so,

a man and woman dressed in white appeared on either
side of him. The woman gave him meat and bread, and
the man poured wine. Staver wondered at this, for he had
seen no servants that day, and in his wandering during
the afternoon had found no trace of livestock, no crops,
and no vineyards. He, his mother, the wolf Harzai, and a
few birds flying high overhead appeared to be the only
living creatures on the island.

He noticed then that the man and woman who stood
by his seat were not as substantial as he had first assumed.
Their outlines were vague, and their flesh translucent. He
felt again the sensation of life near at hand; and all
around him now, the room began to brighten. Points of
light appeared, flickered, grew strong, and took the forms
of men and women. More and more of them appeared,
and soon the room was filled with ranks of luminous,
white-clad figures. Staver could feel more of them gathering outside, and above, and behind him, hovering everywhere, and from all of them emanated the same aura of
love and devotion. He heard a soft brushing sound beside
him—and overhead, the flutter of wings; he looked and
saw the white wolf and a companion stretched out sphinx-
like on either side of his chair, and a trio of white falcons
perched on the high back, one over each shoulder and the
third, Hlir, above his head.

The chamber was now as bright as midday. Light
flooded every corner, and a sweet sound—neither song,
nor speech, nor the voice of any instrument, but a pure
inward resonance of surpassing beauty—swept over
Staver like a healing rain. The white figures were everywhere, and every glittering bright eye was on him.

He took the goblet in one hand and rose. Drawing the
Iron Angel from its scabbard, he raised it aloft, and
raised high the golden goblet, and said, "I pledge my life
and my strength and my faith to all who dwell in the
Crystal Hills. With your help, I will be what I must be
and do what I must do. I pledge this on the blood of
Ambescand."

As he emptied the goblet, the light grew steadily
brighter and furled around him like a cloak of radiance;
the sound swelled to a long drawn-out chord of a sub-
limity that caught at Staver's heart and brought tears to

his eyes; then sound and light receded, and the room held only Staver and his mother, the wolves, the falcons, and a pale misty light slowly fading, returning the corners and niches and beamsides to shadow.

Later that night, before the fire in her chamber, Staver questioned his mother about the visitation. "Are they all spirits?" he asked. "Do you live here among the dead, and I am to rule over a kingdom of dead souls?"

"They are not dead, Staver. They live on a different plane from ours, and the crossing is difficult and dangerous. They visit rarely."

"How so? They were once like us, were they not?"

His mother did not respond at once. At length, fixing her gaze on the fire, she said, "They were men and women who had suffered in the turmoil after the death of Ambescand and made their way here, through great dangers, to what they believed was the last refuge. All else had fallen to the minions of some unknown evil power. When that army of murderers poured over the causeway, they knew they must drive them off—or perish to the last soul. And they drove them off, at a terrible cost. Reduced in numbers, believing that their enemies ruled all else, they decided to leave this world to the evil beings that hungered for it. They besought their mage to deliver them, and he did. But they found that they are human, and this is their world, and they miss it sorely." After a time she turned to Staver and said, "Tonight is the first time they all returned together—in order that they might see you. Now you are Mage of the Crystal Hills, and they will be loyal to you."

"I felt it. They spoke to me—all of them at once, and yet I heard each one distinctly. Not in words. In a kind of music, but something more than music. They were within me, part of me, like blood and breath."

"Some of them will come to teach you. Some will be your army."

He scratched his chin thoughtfully. "An army of spirits. Whom will they fight, mother?"

"Perhaps an army of gray men. Mortals cannot withstand gray men, but the folk of the Crystal Hills can."

Staver turned to her, his lined and weathered face looking weary. "It's a hard life I have before me, Mother—

learning the ancient tongue, mastering the wizard's art, leading an army of spirits against the gray men, and one day coming face to face with Skelbanda and the Cairnlord." He sighed and rubbed his eyes. "I hope you can discover the locus of his power. If we can stop him forever, it will all be worthwhile."

"Even if I cannot find the locus, you must face him when the appointed day comes."

"I know that," Staver said. "I only wish we could be sure of final victory."

"Victory is never certain, Staver. There is a power beyond ours, beyond even the Cairnlord's, and it rules all. With all our effort, all our sacrifice, all our faith, we can never be sure of overcoming. Nor is the Cairnlord, for all his planning and patience and knowledge, sure of victory. A few generations ago, he seemed to have won everything —and now he has suffered defeat, and his enemy grows stronger. Yet he is still very powerful and might yet destroy us."

"So we can only try."

Her voice was steady and confident when she replied, "We will do what we must do when the time comes and hope that if the Cairnlord must be fought again, someone will rise to face him. Perhaps all we do, all we have done, is meant only to survive in some half-remembered legend that in some distant future will inspire the one destined to defeat the Cairnlord forever. It is possible, Staver."

"And what do you think will become of us?"

After a long pause she said simply, "I think we will defeat him."

Staver awoke to sunlight and gave a start when he saw Harzai seated beside his bed, pale eyes fixed on his face. He threw back the covers, sat up, stretched, and reached out to scratch Harzai's forehead. He felt well-rested and fully at ease in this big, book-filled room. It was already his home.

She awaits. Today you begin.

Staver yawned, then nodded and said, "I'm coming, Harzai. You can tell my mother so."

The white wolf padded from the room. Staver splashed his face and hands, dressed quickly, and had just turned to the door when his mother and Harzai entered. She carried a tray bearing bread and honey and a pitcher of milk.

"We'll work here, Staver, so there's no point in wasting time going up and down stairs," she said, setting the tray on the table. "Come, we'll break our fast together."

The bread was crisp, still warm from the oven, and the milk was foaming fresh. Staver could not imagine where his breakfast had come from, but once having tasted it he did not care. If this was indeed food from some other plane, it tasted better than anything he had eaten on this one in a score of years.

As if she had read his thoughts. his mother said, "Food from the Headland, Staver. I knew you'd like it."

"The Headland? How did you . . . ?"

She turned away, and he detected a touch of embarrassment as she said, "It's a simple spell. We can't have servants here, Staver, and this is the only way we eat. You'll learn how to do it soon enough."

He nodded, said nothing, and took another bit of bread. Such a piece of homely magic—on a sunny morning with the mountains glittering beyond his window and the tang of the sea on the air—swept away the last trace of his misgivings. He was eager now to begin learning.

And learn he did, in the years that followed, though not without effort and pain and some moments of extreme danger. He persisted, and soon had learned all his mother could teach. His next master was a shimmering white wizard, the ancient Mage, who spoke in a voice like wind in a dry forest and unlocked doors of long-forgotten knowledge in the years he swirled and glowed at Staver's hand. When he and those he summoned up had taught Staver all they could, he returned to that other plane where Staver's followers dwelt and brought with him the love of their leader.

In all the time of study, Staver made it a point to spend some time each day out of doors, seeing his realm with his own eyes, smelling the sea breeze and the dark forest, scaling the peaks, and gazing far out over the turbulent waters, feeling the hard rock and the yielding forest floor beneath his feet, while Hlir and his companions swooped and called overhead and Harzai trotted silent at his side.

He kept in practice with the Iron Angel, and when one of the creatures of his kingdom was injured, he healed it. He was healer, swordsman, and wizard all in one, and he valued all his skills.

A time came when he could learn no more in isolation, and so he spoke words of concealment and went among the men and women of the mainland, where he sought out missing fragments of the ancient knowledge. While he traveled in this world, his mother, wrapped in the mantle of the Dark Prophet, searched the hidden ways of time for the Cairnlord's secret.

Staver encountered some old acquaintances in his wandering—but never a soul who recognized him. He revealed himself to only one of them, and that was at the end of his travels.

They met at an inn in a wood far to the south and west of the three kingdoms. Staver had found—as he had often found before—that the people of this unknown distant land were little different from the people of the familiar places. They all respected an aging healer who walked their roads at a slow and halting gait, with only a great white beast for company; they listened respectfully to his tales and spoke openly and freely before him. The healer, whom they came to know as Crookstaff, from the twisted stick he leant upon, bestowed his gift of healing freely and never asked for recompense, accepting only food and drink and a night's shelter for his help. He seemed content to hear the old tales and legends and to have the places of mystery pointed out to him. They could not understand this, but they accepted it as a fact that the gifted are entitled to their own odd ways and treated Crookstaff as he wished.

One day, when the healer had saved a woman in childbirth, her husband took him to the inn to celebrate her miraculous deliverance. Staver sensed the presence of another wizard as soon as they turned down the lane to the inn. He laid a hand on Harzai's head to reassure him and halted.

"Go on ahead, friend, and order a mug of beer for me and a bowl of water for my companion. We'll join you soon," he said to the husband. Then he knelt, as if to examine Harzai's paw.

When the husband was out of earshot, he said, "You feel it, too, don't you?"

Another with power, close by. Yes.

"At the inn, I think." Staver drew a plain silver band from his finger. Holding it before his eye, he sighted down the lane. "Only one. A man, I think, but it's hard to tell. There's a strong barrier."

I feel no evil. There is caution—and some fear.

"I can sense no ill-will, either. And we haven't been attacked." Staver climbed stiffly to his feet, brushed the dust from his knees, and said, "Let's have a look at this wizard."

They knew as soon as they passed over the threshold. In a corner seat, deep in shadow, where one could see all within and yet remain unseen by all but those who sought most carefully, sat a bent figure in a worn, dusty, travel-stained cloak. This much any eye could see. But when Staver tried to see deeper, he was repulsed by a wall of magic that armored the figure against sorcery. He at once spelled a barrier of his own and then turned to greet the husband, who beckoned him to a bench where he sat with two others.

"Over here, Crookstaff," the man called, half-rising, and the others lifted their mugs and smiled in greeting.

Staver joined them and listened to the husband recount his feat of healing. It was not two hours old and already the exaggerations had crept in. He knew that before long the people hereabouts would be telling tales of Crookstaff, the healer who raised women from the dead and turned spindly little early-borns into robust babies. But he said nothing, and let the man go on. After a time he turned their talk to local events and asked for news of strange happenings and mysterious travelers. They could tell him nothing.

This in itself was informative. Whatever the wizard in the corner feared and fled from, it had not occurred near-by. And the wizard's presence was unknown—that be-spoke a powerful magic.

Staver kept up a show of attention while his mind turned over the problem. He did not want to reveal himself

to Skelbanda or the Cairnlord, if the wizard was indeed
one of them. To clash with either of them here might
mean the death of all the unsuspecting people at the inn
—and perhaps his own as well. Yet his enemies had no
scruples about mass slaughter, he knew; and so this hidden wizard had to be another.

He probed at the barricade and found it impenetrable.
He could not pierce it without bringing into play powers
that might cause havoc for greatmarks around. After a
long time he decided to deal openly with the stranger and
take his chances.

He brought a sleep on all those at the inn. When the
last farmer nodded off, Staver swung round to face the
hooded figure in the corner and said, "I think we are in
the same trade, you and I."

For a time there was no response. Staver felt the prick-
ling as the other probed at his barrier, and then the wizard turned toward him. Still concealed by the cowl of his
cloak, the wizard said in a raspy voice, "No, we're not.
I'm not a healer, and I don't play tricks for farmers to get
myself a mug of beer. Now clear off, or I'll turn you into
a flea on your own familiar."

Staver knew that voice at once. It had lost some of its
strength but none of its crustiness. He leaned back, placed
his elbows lazily on the table, and gave vent to a deep,
slow laugh of pure relief.

"Think it's funny, do you? I'll make you a louse! A
nit!" the other cried, enraged.

"There was a time when you could breathe flame. Now
you make threats about fleas and lice—quite a comedown
for a shapechanger, Zandinell."

"You're free with names. What's yours?"

"Lately, I'm known as Crookstaff the healer. When you
knew me, I was a boy, with a sword too big for my
strength."

"In the wood—after the storm!"

"And beneath the Fastness, where you saved my life.
It's Staver, old friend. And my companion is Harzai, of
the Crystal Hills."

The other's hood was flung back, and Staver saw the
familiar smooth pate and crooked nose. The wizard's
beard was whiter now, and longer, and there was a dark-

ness around his eyes. His face was pale and noticeably thinner.

"You're much changed, Staver. And far from home," he said.

"I was thinking the same of you."

"Are you fleeing?"

"No. I've come in search of knowledge that will help me withstand our old enemy. And you?"

Zandinell paused and looked about, checking carefully to be certain that the rest were asleep and no one else would hear his words. He beckoned to Staver to join him. When Staver was seated facing him and Harzai stretched out beside them, Zandinell leaned forward and in a subdued, reluctant voice said, "I'm running, Staver. Trying to hide. They attacked my refuge, destroyed the entire mountain. I lost all my books, all my . . . special equipment . . . everything. Nearly lost my life as well."

"Who attacked you, Zandinell?"

"The Cairnlord and another. Skelbanda, I think, because I felt such an emptiness and desolation when they approached that it was difficult to make myself resist. Though it was little difference my resistance made."

"Had you no warning?"

"Ample warning, I thought. They came upon me openly, and I foresaw their coming well in advance and made ready to repel it. But the power, Staver! I never knew such power—never imagined it. It was awesome," Zandinell said. His voice rose, and he spoke more rapidly and excitedly. "When I sensed them near, I obscured all around me and sent forth shapes to lead them astray. But they came unerringly to the very spot where I stood. The stone began to grow hot, and in mere moments it was glowing and beginning to melt. I could only try to escape, but as soon as I emerged, a flock of black gryphons descended on me—ghastly things, clawing and raking at me. My fire had no effect on them."

"You fought them as a dragon, then?"

"Yes. A mistake, too. Air is the thing to use against gryphons. But I doubt that even a tempest would have driven these monsters off. The smallest was almost my size. And as I tried to evade them, the mountain burst apart. Fragments the size of this inn, glowing white, were hurtling through the air. Black smoke everywhere . . . jets of flame. . . ." Zandinell broke off, settling his face in his hands.

"But you managed to escape."

"I escaped. I turned into a fly. A fly, Staver!"

"You escaped. That's what counts."

"So I tell myself. But I fled, and I'm still fleeing. I thought I could stand up to the Cairnlord, Staver, and he crushed me as if I were a novice—sent me running for my life."

"But why did he attack? There must have been a reason for his turning such power against you."

Zandinell shrugged. "Sheer malice is reason enough for him. He bided his time, let me get confident, then he struck like a hurricane. Things had been so quiet and peaceful, I began to think he might have gone away."

"Is it really so peaceful in the kingdoms, Zandinell? It seemed so to me, too, and I wondered."

"There have been no raids by the Cairnlord's men for years. Your brothers have done their work well. There's peace and safe travel. It's all changed."

"Then why didn't he attack them? Why you?"

"The Cairnlord doesn't attack mortals. He sends his own mortal followers against them or one of his subject spirits." Zandinell groped thoughtfully in his beard. "In fact he seldom confronts anybody himself, not even another wizard. He must have been terribly angry at me."

They were both silent for a time; then Staver announced, "I must return. If he strikes at the Crystal Hills, I must be there."

Zandinell looked at him dubiously. "If the Cairnlord attacks, you're safest far away."

"I don't think he will. Not for a time, anyway, and the interval is ours. His power is linked with death somehow, and there's been less death in the three kingdoms of late —if all we've seen and heard is true. His attack on you must have taken a lot of power. He'll have to build it up before he turns to his next enemy." Rising, Staver said, "No, we need fear no attack for a time. When it comes, we'll be ready."

"I was ready, Staver. And you see me now."

Staver held out his hand. "Come with me, Zandinell."

"To a place the Cairnlord might attack? No thank you, my friend."

"Are you safer wandering alone among strangers? You'll use up all your magic in concealment," Staver said. When Zandinell's expression became thoughtful, Staver pressed his offer. "The two of us together are stronger than either one alone. Between us we might spell a barrier that can stop even the Cairnlord."

"I hardly think so," Zandinell said. "Though I must admit, that was a fine barrier you put up. Very nice work. Quick, too."

"There's much magic in the Crystal Hills. And books —more books than I can count. I've mastered a few of them, but there are many that are beyond my grasp. You might be able to find the magic we need."

"Books? A lot of books in the old language?"

"Most of them."

Zandinell gave a little grunt suggesting interest and approval. Half to himself, he said, "I miss those books of mine. It would be nice. . . ." Looking hard at Staver, he said, "The Crystal Hills are far from here."

"Not so far. Come with me, friend. I need your help."

Zandinell frowned, then nodded once sharply and rose from his place. "I guess you do. It's not easy to follow the old language. Yes, I'd better come—just for a short stay . . . to clear up your problems, you understand. Rest a while and get my strength back. Then I'll be off to a safe place."

"That's all I ask," Staver said.

Zandinell's acceptance left him much relieved. He could sense the momentum of events building all around him, the destined crossing of his future and the Cairnlord's coming ever nearer. Zandinell would be a valuable ally. He felt equally a sense of obligation: beyond doubt, the attack on Zandinell was related in some way to the struggle between the sword-bearers and the Cairnlord. Twice now, hardship and danger had been brought down on the old wizard by that struggle, and Staver believed that he owed him sanctuary.

Zandinell left the inn and waited at the end of the lane. After rousing the patrons Staver stayed for a safe interval, then took his own departure. The two wizards met at the appointed rendezvous. Arm in arm, with Harzai trotting at Staver's side, they turned their footsteps north. By hidden ways they passed over land and water to the Crystal Hills, where with the aid of the Dark Prophet they made ready for the final confrontation.

26

A Gathering of Kings

> The white blade and the black were forged to
>   break the men of stone
> And hew a bloody pathway for a king to mount his
>   throne;
> But not the Iron Angel—
> Upon that hallowed brand
> No blood would ever run, for it was forged by
>   Ambescand
> To war with wraiths and shadows, and strike the
>   single blow
> That ends the age of darkness and destroys the an-
>   cient foe.
>
> —From *The Last Deed of Ambescand*

For the span of a generation, Colberane Whitblade ruled in the Southern Forest while Ordred governed the Fastness and the Plain. In all this time they heard no news of Staver.

They thought often of their younger brother and asked all travelers from the north for word of him. Word never came, for no man now traveled to the Crystal Hills, and it was believed that no man, not even Staver Ironbrand, the vanquisher of Korang, could cross the waters beyond Northmark. All the bridges lay in ruin, and a cold sea thundered over the rubble and the jagged outcroppings of the northern archipelago with a fury that devoured every craft to dare the passage. But Col and Ord knew their brother. Despite the long silence they never ceased to hope for his return.

The brothers did not remain sequestered, Col in his citadel and Ord in the High City, listening only to the advice of favorites. Their rule was active. They traveled among their people, asking questions and listening patiently to grievances. Their laws and policies grew out of their subject's needs, not their advisers' whims.

Ord's travels were mainly between the High City and the Fastness, with occasional tours of the frontiers. It was Col who became the far voyager. He went beyond the limits of the Southern Forest to study the ways of lands to the south and west and east. Often, with no companions but his chamberlain, Goodbowe of Long Wood, and a small band of archers, he set off without warning on a long trip to some unannounced destination.

It was on such a journey, to a land of green hills and vineyards and placid river valleys, that Col was nobly received by a family descended from fugitives from the High City in the last days of its freedom. They had a daughter, Davasha, just turned twenty, and when Col saw her he knew he had found the woman he was to marry.

At winter's end Davasha returned north with Col as her betrothed. The wedding on the lake isle was the grandest festival since the similar event held two years earlier in the High City, when Ord and Ciantha were wed.

As the years passed, the two brothers grew closer in spirit, despite the distance and the duties that forced long separations. Col, who had been cautious in his youth, became curious in his maturity and ranged ever further in search of new knowledge. Ord, the reckless brother, learned to deliberate, and reflect, and carefully seek out and weigh all the facts before making a judgment. Between them they established a rule of law and impartial justice, tempered by compassion, that was undreamed of even in the days of Ambescand.

The people of the two realms enjoyed a peace they had never known before. Just as they had fashioned a system of laws, Col and Ord built a fighting force to defend their subjects from the scattered vestiges of the Cairnlord's armies, who still struck at remote settlements. Marauders were hunted down. The attacks became less frequent. In the twelfth year of the reign of the two brothers, no raid

occurred anywhere from Northmark to the southernmost
limit of the forest. Gray men attacked in the two succeeding years, but they were pursued and cut down by the
brothers themselves, and for long after that, there was
peace. The people thrived and prospered, and life was
good.

Then, in the twenty-fourth year after the fall of the
Fastness, a village at the foot of the mountains was attacked and burned, and all its inhabitants slain. While
Ord's forces were making ready to move against the
raiders, another small settlement, this one in the Southern
Forest, on the west bank of Broad River, was attacked
and devastated in similar manner.

A relentless pursuit began, lasting from the first days of
planting to the time of snows. Two bands of the Cairnlord's followers were hunted down. But the raids continued through the next year, and the next, ever bloodier
and more brutal, and the people began to live in fear as
they once had. It seemed to them that the horrors of the
past were returning, and no force of man could hold them
off.

The first green was on the trees in the twenty-seventh
spring since the fall of the Fastness when the Cairnlord's
challenge came. It arrived in the night, and no man knew
who had brought it—or how. It came at the same hour to
Col in the citadel on the lake isle and to Ord in his palace in the High City. The message to both was the same:
"At full moon in the month of Yellowleaf, my strength
will assemble on the Plain. Confront me if you dare."

It was written on human skin.

Messengers were dispatched at once, and within a few
days the brothers were met in council at the tower of
Southmark. There was no question that they would engage the Cairnlord's forces. Their people were eager for
a final confrontation with the ancient enemy, whose
threatening power they hoped to smash forever. Armories
clattered and forges rang as the old tools of war were
brought forth and made ready. Men and women spent
their days in the fields and then devoted the evening
hours to drill and practice with weapons that had long
stood idle in corners or gathered dust upon the chimney
piece.

Summer passed, and the ripening of the crops, and the harvest and gleaning. As the first day of Yellowleaf drew near, the forces of the two rulers began to assemble. Sixty score of axemen from Long Wood crossed the mountains, joined with a force of armored mountaineers bearing long swords, and marched to the rendezvous. Pikemen from the new settlements in the mistlands circled the foothills and joined a great army of archers from the Southern Forest to march north to the Plain. A force of picked men, in refashioned armor and bearing reforged blades, came from the High City with Ord at their head. Up from the south and west, led by Col, came warriors from lands where the Cairnlord's touch had not yet been felt but was feared. They wore garments and carried weapons unlike anything known to the people of the two kingdoms, and their language fell strangely upon northern ears, but they came from their unknown lands to lend their strength to the freedmen's cause, and they were welcomed as comrades.

The full moon of Yellowleaf shone on a great crescent of campfires that lay between the foothills and the open Plain, enclosing the armies of the Cairnlord like an arching wall. This portion of the Plain bulged out to sea. The armies of the two rulers extended, at the horns of the crescent, almost to the water's edge; the central portion curved westward toward the mountains. Seacoast and campfire line thus formed a rough ring around the arena where the armies were to meet. In the center of that ring stood a tight formation of dark tents.

Ord looked down from the rise near the shore where his own tent stood. All was ready for the final battle, and he had nothing to do now but wait for morning. The eastern sky was already beginning to brighten, and both camps were astir. He turned to Col, who stood by his side, gazing at the cluster of tents.

"Doesn't look like much of an army, does it?" he said.

"It isn't half the size of ours."

"There's a trick in this somewhere."

"I'm sure there is," Col said. "A challenge like that, coming out of nowhere . . . People had actually begun to doubt that Cairnlord ever really existed. I've spoken to children who'd never heard of him. And now we face him at last."

"But what can his trick be?" Ord turned to the tall red-haired youth at his side and asked, "Have all the scouts reported?"

"They have, Father. They've found no trace of the enemy anywhere but on the plain before us."

Ord tugged at his grizzled beard and shook his head dubiously. "It makes no sense. Can the Cairnlord have grown so desperate in so short a time?"

"He'll have his gray men," Col reminded him.

"None have been seen. And even if they come, we know how to fight them now."

They fell silent again, watching, tense with expectancy, and the gnawing sense of uneasiness that they could not quell. The skies brightened, and in the center of the dark tents was sudden activity. The distant cry of trumpets summoning men to battle floated on the misty morning air. All along the crescent of the free army, light glinted on naked weapons.

The Cairnlord's men struck their tents and moved into an arrowhead formation. Here they held. The crescent began to close on them.

"They're not even attacking!" Col cried, amazed. "They're going to stand their ground and be slaughtered!"

"Impossible. It's suicide," Ord whispered.

The crescent tightened on the wedge. For a moment the two forces paused, as if to gather strength; then a shower of arrows arched from both formations at the same instant, and the free army surged forward with a roar that reached the mound where the brothers stood. The two forces met with a clash, and the air was filled with the din of mortal combat, muted but not disguised by distance.

Ord and Col remained on the hill, alert to join the battle at the first sight of a gray man, but none appeared. Below them on the Plain, the crescent and the arrowhead merged. The northern arm of the arrowhead flowed out and turned on the wings of the free men's army; then both formations dissolved into a milling, hacking mob.

Col and Ord looked on, speechless with wonder and bewilderment. The armies of the Cairnlord fought hard and with undeniable bravery, but they had no hope of winning. Outnumbered, facing an enemy forewarned and fully prepared, fighting from a defensive stance in a position with no retreat, they had been doomed from the beginning.

Absorbed in the bizarre battle, Col and Ord were unaware of the strange sight that attracted the attention of Ord's son, Geerdran. The red-haired youth pointed to the east and cried, "Look, Father—someone comes from the sea!"

The brothers turned and saw a shimmering mist that lay over the waters a few marks from the land. Out of it, heading for the shore at the foot of the rise, came a small boat. Without sail or oar, breasting the strong current, it floated smoothly on. In it stood a tall white-haired man. He was dressed in simple robes, and a sword hung at his side. With him in the boat was a huge white wolf, and no other creature.

The boat came gently to rest on the sand, and man and beast climbed out. Guards converged on them at once, but Ord's loud shout turned them back.

"It's Staver! He's returned, at last!" he cried, waving a joyous welcome. "He's come to stand with us! Let him pass!"

The newcomer brushed past the guards and started up the rise with the step of a strong young man, the wolf trotting beside him. Halfway to the crest he caught sight of the melee; his face fell, and he shouted to Col and Ord, "Break off the fighting at once. No more must fall!"

"But we're smashing the Cairnlord's army," Col objected.

"Every man who falls gives strength to our enemy. Signal retreat, quickly!"

Ord was confused; he felt uneasy, and had a sense of danger near; but the sight of the Iron Angel at the white-haired man's side moved him to trust. He turned to his bannermen and gave the command to signal retreat. To his son, he said, "Go to the leaders. Tell them no man is to strike another blow until I give the order."

Col, who had also seen the Iron Angel at the tall man's side, said, "Speak in my name, too."

Geerdran hurried off, and the bannermen took up their flags. The white wolf yawned once, then settled on his haunches at Staver's side, looking impassively on the battle that still raged on the Plain. Staver, too, observed the fighting and said, "I hope I've not come too late. I thought I'd be in time to prevent this."

"I don't understand. We're destroying the Cairnlord's army, and you tell us to stop," Col said. "I trust you—but why should we spare them?"

"Those pitiful dupes are not the Cairnlord's true army. They're a sacrifice. Out of their deaths, and the deaths of your warriors, will come the power to raise the Cairnlord's real army. The more who fall here, the stronger that army will be." Staver turned to them and said in a weary voice, "He is more powerful than we ever imagined. We looked upon our lives and deeds as if they were important. To the Cairnlord, they're as the wink of an eye. He remembers ages past, and he plans for eternity. And he must be stopped here, now, this very day, for in a short time his power will be too great to resist."

Col shook his head in utter bewilderment. "How can he still be so strong? We defeated his armies; we captured his strongholds."

"Fortresses mean nothing to him. His power comes from the spilling of life. The battles at the citadel, and the High City, and the Fastness, fed his strength with slaughter. But since you two came to power, you've prevented his servants from killing—that weakened him, so he forced this battle." Staver pointed to the Plain where the armies of the two kings had begun to disengage and were now pulling back, though small pockets of furious fighting remained. "Those men are a reservoir of life and power for the Cairnlord's magic. As long as they take lives, he allows them to live on. If they fail, then he takes theirs. It does not matter to him whether the life he feeds on is that of follower or enemy."

"What manner of creature is the Cairnlord?" Ord asked.

"I've spent a lifetime—more than a lifetime—trying to learn that," Staver said. "I learned much while I lived in the Crystal Hills, but still some things remain hidden. He is not human, I know. He was in the world before men, even then prolonging his life and growing ever stronger on the lives of other beings. He was already a powerful sorcerer long before the rise of the Old Kingdom, but some greater force overthrew him and nearly destroyed him. He lay dormant for ages, until the time of Ambescand, when he saw a chance to regain strength and magic at once. It was he who roused the nobles to rebel against Ambescand, he who persuaded the company of sorcerers to join them—all but one. He knew their cause was futile. I believe he even foresaw the manner of their defeat and their punishment. But out of the bloodshed would come power for him. That was all he cared for.

"When the broken sorcerers were buried on the Stone Hand, he restored them to life to serve him. He was not yet strong enough to restore the others, but he learned to summon them up from Shagghya to do his bidding. When Ambescand died, the Cairnlord began to move openly in the world once more, as in ancient days."

"But why, Staver? What does he seek?" Ord asked.

"Yes, what? He seems to take no pleasure in the spoils of power," said Col.

On the battlefield the Cairnlord's forces re-formed into a circle as the crescent of the free army withdrew. The circle was pitifully small, and the crescent was ragged, with gaps in its line. Staver looked with apprehension on the bodies that lay strewn on the bloody ground.

"So many have fallen. This will give him great strength," he said. Turning to his brothers, he went on. "What the Cairnlord seeks is beyond our power to imagine. If he is not stopped, first he will overrun all the lands we know. Then, slowly, he will spread over all the earth. Everywhere he will cause battle and bloodshed, because from them come his strength and power. When he has slaughtered all the life of this world and taken it to himself, he will only be beginning. He will move onward and outward, beyond the moon and the sun and all the stars, until on all the worlds in all the heavens, for all time, there is only the Cairnlord. He will be all, and possess all, and all will be the Cairnlord, for eternity. He would make himself God."

His brothers looked at him and at each other, stunned to silence. Truly, such an ambition surpassed their understanding. It could be spoken and heard, but such magnitude of evil greed was beyond human imagining.

Finally Col said in a subdued voice, "And what are we to do, brother?"

"I must confront him. You must hold back your men and see that no more blood is shed."

"But if his army comes . . ." Col said.

Staver gestured to the shining mist that lay unmoving on the water and said. "I've brought my own army to face them. This battle must not be fought by mortal men."

"Our men will stay back," Ord promised. "Geerdran has brought the command to all the leaders."

"Geerdran . . . your son, Ord?"

"He is. A fine young man, too."

"And you, Col—you have a son?" Staver asked.

"Yes, and a daughter. The boy is with Kinnaury now, at the head of the axemen."

"Good. The two of you must keep the line of Ambescand alive." Staver glanced at the beards adorning his brothers' faces and touched his own smooth-shaven chin; they had all observed the old Headland custom. "I never married. I had other work to do."

"You look old, Staver—far older than your years."

"Magic takes a heavy toll. I still have my strength, but I've given much of my lifespan to learn the things I must know."

"Have you always been alone?"

"Not alone, though I had few human companions, Col." Staver laid his hand on the skull of the great white wolf. The beast turned its sky-colored eyes on him and rubbed its jaw fondly against the man's ribs. "I've had the company of beasts and birds and spirits. The Dark Prophet has taken me to far times and places, and taught me all she knows. We've searched the hidden corners of the past to find the Cairnlord's buried secrets."

"And have you succeeded?"

"One thing remains unknown. She seeks it still, but I had to abandon the search in order to be here. Even so, I arrived too late . . . and I wonder if this, too, is part of the plan. . . ." He fell into a brooding silence for a time. When he spoke again, he said, "The Cairnlord is powerful and devious. Often, what seems to be the strongest blow against him—like the slaying of his followers—only adds to his strength. I've learned that he caused

Vannen's death so that we would come south and raise an army against him and bring about battles that would renew his power. We ourselves were his dupes, brothers."

Col and Ord exchanged an uneasy glance. The more they learned about this enemy, the more forbidding he became. Staver saw the doubt on their faces and went on to encourage them. "Even the Cairnlord cannot foresee everything. He knew nothing of the swords of Ambescand or the amulet of Ciantha. I believe he knows nothing of them still, thanks to the last spell of Ambescand. The death of his servant wizards troubled the Cairnlord greatly—dying as they did, their magic was lost to him. And when you drove his raiders out of your kingdoms, his source of strength was cut off. Thus was he forced to this battle."

"So . . . even the Cairnlord can make mistakes," Ord said.

"But can he be overcome?" asked Col.

Staver drew his sword and held it before him. "Unsheathe your blades, brothers, and lay them on mine. Let Ambescand's blood and magic be rejoined."

White blade and curving silver crossed on the Iron Angel, and at the linking of the three, the brothers felt strength and confidence surge through their hands and arms into their bodies and their spirits. But as they lowered their blades, the foreboding came again upon Ord; it was as though an old forgotten sense was stirring to life within him, trying to rouse his attention. He drove it from his mind with an effort.

They sheathed their swords once more, and Staver embraced his brothers in farewell. As he turned to leave the hill, the white wolf whined; its fur rose; it lowered its head and bared its fangs.

A rumble arose from the battlefield, and a great cry came to the ears of the three brothers. In the center of the circle where the Cairnlord's men were gathered, the ground began to churn and heave. A head appeared, and shoulders, and arms, as a gray man twice mortal size clawed its way from the earth. Another broke the surface, and another.

"That's why the scouts saw no other army," Ord murmured, as he looked astonished on the sight. "I should have realized."

"The gray men are creatures of stone. The Cairnlord breathes life into them, and no mortal force can take it away," Staver said.

"This battle is ours," Col said, gripping his sword hilt. Staver laid a hand on Col's arm, restraining him, and said, "Not yet."

Staver reached out his hands to the sea and spoke aloud in a language unknown to his brothers. The shining mist began to stir and to sparkle with points of light. It rolled slowly toward the shore, growing ever denser and more opaque as it moved, spreading in a line that curved to enclose the seaward limits of the Cairnlord's force. Shapes appeared in the mist—and suddenly it was gone, and Col and Ord looked upon a legion of white swordsmen forming where the gray men climbed from the womb of earth. The two bands flung themselves at one another with the ferocity of ancient enmity. The remnants of the Cairnlord's mortal army struck at the white warriors, but their blows had no effect. One by one, the humans fell back to look helplessly on the struggle of forces beyond their understanding.

As the weird battle raged on the Plain, a dark cloud appeared on the horizon far out to sea. It grew rapidly, rolling landward, and soon the brothers could distinguish winged figures high in the moiling darkness. At sight of them, Staver flung his hands high and spoke again. A wind rose at his back, blowing out to sea. It grew in force until the grass of the Plain lay flat, and trees were bent and broken, and the human warriors were knocked from their feet; and as it blew out to sea and met the dark cloud, the winged creatures were tossed and tumbled, and the cloud was driven off.

Now, on the Plain, the gray men outnumbered the white, and still they issued from the churning earth, oblivious to the leveling wind and the dust that whirled past them. White warriors moved like points of light, striking and slashing at the towering creatures of stone. Gray men toppled and fell, and did not stir, but here and there a blow landed on a white warrior and the glow of his presence faded and vanished. As the gray men grew ever

more numerous, some of them turned to attack the freedmen's forces. At the sight of the gray giants lumbering
toward his followers, Ord drew his dark blade. Again
Staver restrained his brother.

"We're the only ones who can drive them back now,"
Ord said.

"I have an ally," Staver assured him. He covered his
face with his hands, bowed his head, and murmured
words Ord and Col could not distinguish.

"They need help now, Staver," Ord said.

On the Plain, a score of gray men had left the battle
and were striding with ponderous steps toward the crescent line of freedmen. The humans milled about in
confusion. Some fell back—others held their ground—as
the giant gray men came ever closer.

Staver pointed to the mountains. "Help has come."

A dot appeared in the sky, moving rapidly toward the
battlefield. It grew larger, and the brothers could distinguish wings and a long neck and could see the morning
light glint off its scaly sides.

"A dragon!" Col cried.

"An old friend," Staver said.

The dragon circled overhead. Staver raised a hand to
salute it, and the great red-gold creature fell like a falcon
on the gray men just as they came within reach of the
freed forces.

Staver took his astonished brothers by the hand. "My
battle must be fought elsewhere. I'll take my leave from
you now."

"Let us go with you," Ord said.

"You can't leave your men leaderless. This is my fight.
I've prepared for it, and I must face it alone."

"Good luck, brother," said Ord, embracing him.

Col embraced Staver in turn and said, "Be victorious,
brother. Come back, and we'll rule these lands together. We need your wisdom."

"You've ruled wisely and well without me. You need
no help to be great kings, but I'll gladly share all I know
with you when this is over."

Staver turned and started down the hill. The wolf
padded silently at his side and sprang lightly into the boat
after him. The narrow craft at once moved smoothly from

the shore and headed out to sea toward the island called the Stone Hand. Staver stood erect in the bow, eyes fixed on his destination. Watching him, Ord recalled a tale told by Ciantha, of the coming of the Game to the High City. Words of a prophecy spoken long ago came back to him.

"Staver's much changed, but he's still his old self in some ways. I think I'd have known him even without the sword," said Col.

"He's changed in ways we'll never understand."

"I hope he's gained strength. He's gone to confront a powerful wizard."

Ord was silent for a time; then he said, "I think we saw only a very small bit of Staver, brother. I have a feeling he's a mighty powerful wizard himself."

27

The Day the Magic Died

> Stone Hand,
> Bleak land;
> Dark sky,
> Cold eye;
> Sea still;
> Air chill;
> Men fear
> Death near.

—Sea-charm of the people of the Plain

The waters surrounding the Stone Hand were still and cold. No waves beat against that waste of lifeless stone. Nothing lived in the waters or on the land, and no living thing flew overhead in the gloomy sky.

Staver and his companion crossed the glassy surface and came to shore in the cove formed by two narrow peninsulas, the thumb and forefinger of the Stone Hand. They stepped ashore, and the boat drew up securely behind them. Harzai sniffed the air and looked about suspiciously.

No life. But something here. A power.

"Where?" Staver asked.

Center. In a high place. Stone at its back.

"I'll go to it, Harzai. You stay here."

You and I go.

"It will be dangerous."

You need help. Not alone. Strong power waiting.

Staver put his arms around the white wolf's neck. "You're a good friend, Harzai. I'm glad for your help."

They walked inland, across the dead bare surface, under a silent sky. The ground slowly rose. No sign of life could be seen, but Staver felt the amulet pulse in his shoulder. About forty marks from the shore, at the palm of the Stone Hand, the grade rose sharply and then leveled. At the center of the level space was a mound of gray stones the height of a man. Two figures stood before it.

Harzai's voice came into Staver's mind. *Them. They are the power.*

Staver took a deep breath and started forward over the smooth ground. His hand was on the hilt of the Iron Angel. Harzai trotted at his side. As he approached the two figures, Staver studied them. To the left of the mound stood a woman, dark-haired, white-faced, dressed in robes of black. She looked coldly upon Staver with dark and narrow eyes, and as his eyes met hers, he felt a chill brush his heart. She was Skelbanda, Destroyer of Hope, the last survivor of the band of sorcerers. Alone, by her soul-killing power, she had shriveled the lives of the dwellers on the lake isle in the days of the sons of Ambescand. Beside her stood the Cairnlord, and the first sight of him was a great surprise to Staver.

The Cairnlord was a small man, bright-eyed and apple-cheeked, with a cloud of fine white hair haloed around his head. He was simply dressed, in a robe of coarse cloth. He stood before the pile of stone, his pudgy arms folded, the sleeves of his robe pushed up, looking for all the world like a tapster, or a baker, or some honest crofter, and he greeted Staver and Harzai with a cheerful smile.

"Who can these visitors be? Speak up, old fellow, and tell us who you are and why you come to the Stone Hand," he said, and his manner was pleasant.

"You know who I am, and why I've come."

"I know a great many things. But I want to hear my answer from you."

Something slithered into Staver's mind to draw the words from him. With an effort he drove the intruding power out and remained silent.

Unperturbed, the Cairnlord said, "So, you choose to be mysterious. You wish me to guess. An old man and a beast come to this isolated island . . . What could be their purpose? Perhaps they're not an old man and a beast, though. Perhaps . . . perhaps the old man is a mighty wizard and the white beast is his familiar . . . Or perhaps it's the other way around. Now that would be clever—far more clever than all the other mighty wizards who have challenged my power." He looked at Staver with amusement in his eyes.

Staver looked into those bright and merry eyes, and his shoulder gave a sudden throb that jarred him to alertness. While the Cairnlord talked, his gray legions rose ever more numerous from the Plain. If they reached the human armies, blood would be shed, and the Cairnlord's power would grow. The Cairnlord would always delay; he had to be fought by deeds, not words and patience, not anymore. The time for patience was past. Staver drew the Iron Angel and stepped forward.

"Staver Ironbrand!" said a high cold voice. Staver turned, and his eyes met Skelbanda's. For a moment he could not tear his gaze free. The chill returned, enfolding his heart, and a sudden weakness came over him. The hopelessness and folly of his venture burst upon him like a revelation. For all his hard-earned knowledge, for all the power he had stored up within him, he could not hope to best the Cairnlord, the most powerful of sorcerers, ruler of all. The Iron Angel grew heavy in his hands.

But something else, some other force within him, drove him on. His shoulder burned, and he felt courage returning. Skelbanda raised her hands and took a step toward him. Cold and chill flowed sickeningly within Staver, and he faltered once again.

Then Harzai launched himself at Skelbanda, and his jaws locked on her upflung forearm. White fur and black robe rolled in a tangle on the bare stone, amid a demon din of snarls and shrieks. The spell snapped. Staver and the Cairnlord both moved at once. The Cairnlord waved his pudgy hand in a casual-seeming gesture, as if to brush away a fly, and Harzai yelped in pain and tumbled free from the sorceress. Before she could rise, Staver's sword came down.

It struck an empty robe and rang on the stone. Staver turned to the Cairnlord and saw a different smile on the round face—a smile of confidence in victory.

"Not this time," the Cairnlord said. "Skelbanda's power will not be lost to me."

"So you destroy your own follower."

"I take back what I gave."

"Yes, you need her power now. You're draining all your magic to pour out that army of gray men," Staver said. He raised the Iron Angel.

"I have more than enough magic left to annihilate you," said the Cairnlord.

On the mound overlooking the Plain, Col and Ord looked on as white legion and dragon battled the growing army of gray men in eerie silence. White blades swung in arcs of light among the towering gray figures. The red-golden dragon tore and slashed and spewed out streams of fire on the gray swarm. The Cairnlord's forces went down by the score.

But it seemed that for every gray giant that fell, two more clawed their way from the earth to shamble into the struggle, long hooked blades slashing remorselessly before them. The white swordsmen were engulfed by the gray wave. The dragon was surrounded on all sides by slow, lurching figures that hacked at his scaly armor even as flames poured over them. Three times the dragon rose from the melee, shaking loose from clutching gray hands and hooked weapons. The fourth time, he fell back to earth heavily with a torn wing, and his enemies closed in.

"He needs help," Ord said.

Col drew his gleaming blade. "We're the only ones who can give it."

"Let's go," Ord said, bringing his dark blade forth.

They ran down the slope and charged full tilt into the gray mass besetting their allies. The gray men, taken by surprise, went down like stalks of wheat. Slow and clumsy, unable to maneuver because of their own numbers, they reeled helplessly before this new enemy. The brothers cut their way to the dragon's side, slashing methodically at every gray figure that rose before them until nothing stood between them and the scaly red-gold mound of dragonhide.

Ord laid a hand on the cool metallic skin and shouted, "We're Staver's brothers. We've come to help you."

The dragon, in response, belched forth a ribbon of flame that sent the gray men reeling back to where the flashing cometfire of the white warriors' blades waited. Ord breathed deep and rubbed the muscles of his swordarm.

"Been a long time . . . since I used a blade . . . so strenuously," he panted.

"You'll use it more this day. They're regrouping."

"Let's hit them . . . before they can get set."

They dashed through the smoke and into the front ranks of gray men, hacking high and low, rhythmic as reapers, dodging the brute slash of hooked blades that hummed overhead and on all sides. Eight of the creatures went down before the attack, and the others hesitated, as if some touch of human fear had entered them.

With their backs once more to the dragon's side, the brothers drew in deep, heaving breaths. The years that seemed to fall away in the press of battle weighed heavily on their muscles when they paused, and their swords were heavy in their hands. As they rested, gathering strength, a distant roar came to their ears.

"What's that noise?" Col asked.

"I don't know. Wind?"

"No. Getting louder."

"Col, it's a battle cry—our forces are attacking!"

The brothers exchanged a glance of despair. Then they raised their swords and charged into the gray mass, and the dragon lumbered forth beside them.

Staver held the Iron Angel before him like a talisman. He could feel the icy brush of despair, like cold wings fluttering at his heart, but he was better able to resist it now.

"You can't annihilate me. If you could, I wouldn't be here now," he said.

"I can destroy you when I will. By cold," said the Cairnlord, and a shock of utter frigidity ran through Staver's body. "By darkness," he said, and a smothering blanket of moist, clinging dark closed around Staver. "By terror," and a harrowing apparition of slithering eyes and venomous jaws and engulfing, consuming loathsomeness rose up before Staver like a ravening mountain. But all were gone in an instant, repelled by the force of Staver's resisting will.

"And yet I live. It will take more than conjurer's tricks to destroy me," Staver said.

A whimper came from Harzai, and Staver glanced to where the wolf lay. The enchanter's bolt had struck him savagely and flung him some marks distant, where he had lain bloody and unmoving. Now he climbed clumsily to his feet. He crumpled and fell, whining with pain, but at last he stood erect. Staver turned to the Cairnlord.

"Your power can't destroy man or beast," he said.

The Cairnlord was silent. Harzai limped to his friend's side, tongue lolling, one broken forepaw raised. He trod the black rag that was all that remained of Skelbanda, and when he was half a mark away, he leapt for Staver's throat.

Staver saw the motion out of the corner of his eye. He swung the Iron Angel, severing the great white head, and as his sword struck home he saw the emptiness of death in Harzai's pale eyes. They were as stonelike and vacant as the eyes of the gray men.

The carcass hurtled on and crashed into Staver. Staggered by the weight of the great white wolf, he fell backward. As he lay sprawled on the stone, a shadow loomed over him, and he looked up at a towering hulk of horror.

"Now see me as I am!" the Cairnlord cried from a hundred mouths in a hundred inhuman voices. A writhing thicket of misshapen limbs spread wide to pluck with dark talons at the fallen man's flesh.

Staver struggled to his feet and took up fighting stance, with the Iron Angel poised. All around and inside him were the sounds of the Cairnlord's many mouths, softly laughing, mewing, mocking, slobbering in anticipation.

The Cairnlord had assumed all of Skelbanda's power to impose despair, and added to it the unmanning vision of his own appearance. Staver fought back and held the thing at bay, but he felt the struggle exhausting him.

Then there came a rushing wind and a glow that grew to a blaze of white light, and in the light appeared the flickering presence of the Dark Prophet. At once the monstrous vision of the Cairnlord vanished, and only the pudgy white-haired man remained. The light died, and the Dark Prophet stood between the adversaries.

"Staver, I have found—" she began, but a gesture from the Cairnlord struck her down where she stood, and she lay still.

The Cairnlord opened his arms, as if in friendly appeal, and turned to face Staver. "Why do you resist me?" he asked, and his voice was almost kindly. "Your friends are slain one by one—or turned against you. Your brothers will die, and their friends and followers."

"But we'll stop you. We'll destroy you forever." The brave words hid his fear. The last words of the Dark Prophet meant she had found the hiding place of the Cairnlord's power. But she had been struck down before she could reveal it.

The Cairnlord chuckled and shook his head. "No, you will not. I've been stopped before, and I've always come back stronger and wiser. And I'll never be destroyed— not by a pitiful mortal thing like yourself."

"Your wizards have all been slain. Your gray army is being cut to pieces," Staver said.

"They will die if they must. My humans are loyal to me."

"Loyal? What kind of loyalty is that? They know you'll strangle them if they hesitate."

"Ah, yes, you've witnessed my touch. But that's only my assurance. I seldom need to employ it. My humans follow me willingly. I promise them life, and I give it."

"What kind of life?"

"No one before you has ever inquired about the quality. They ask only about the duration. A long life satisfies most men, and they do my bidding gladly to obtain it."

"The men on the Plain will have no long life after this day," Staver said. He forced himself to keep his eyes off the huddled form of the Dark Prophet, to shield his mind from all thoughts of her and of Harzai, and to focus his powers on the confrontation with the Cairnlord. Now it was his turn to delay.

"They're all unimportant," said the Cairnlord. "Handy, I admit—but quite unimportant. My gray men will overcome the human forces aligned against them—and will then go forth to reap a great harvest in the northern lands. And then I will move freely in the world."

"No."

"Oh, yes. Do you really think, Staver, that this earth exists for the like of humankind? Your race is fodder for its superiors, nothing more."

"You're not our superior. You know nothing but slaughter."

The Cairnlord again chuckled softly, almost good-naturedly, as if he were conversing with an amusing but perverse child. "I deal in slaughter because it is the simplest way with beings such as your race. Do you truly believe that if you were to destroy me, men would cease to slaughter one another?"

"In time they might."

The Cairnlord laid his hands on his belly and laughed aloud. "Oh, Staver, for a wise old wizard you're very innocent indeed."

"At least they wouldn't kill one another merely to feed your ambition."

"No, they would slaughter one another for no purpose. Death would have no meaning at all. Is this what you would bring upon your race, wise Mage?"

"It's better than being slaves to a thing like you," Staver said. He spoke slowly, holding his mind to each word, blocking out all else but the exchange at hand. It was his only hope now of learning the Dark Prophet's message. If she lived, and could speak once more, the Cairnlord might yet be overcome. But if he were to learn what Staver had in his mind, he would turn all his destructive power on her. He had to be kept occupied.

Staver raised the Iron Angel and attacked.

Ord and Col were weary from hacking at the ever-growing army that swarmed around them. Their dragon

ally was panting and moved with lurching slow steps. The
battle cry of the freedmen's army grew louder as the vanguard closed on the field.

"They're coming . . . to save us," Col panted.

"They'll lose . . . everything," Ord replied.

"How . . . how stop them?"

Ord blinked the sweat from his eyes. He could think of
only one way, and it would put him and his brother
in the gravest danger. But the Cairnlord could not be
given new strength, not while Staver was confronting him
—perhaps even now locked in the death struggle. Ord
knew the risk had to be taken.

He stood by the dragon's head. That scaly fire-
breathing triangle drooped now, and the slitted eyes were
glazed with pain and exhaustion. But at Col's terse message the eyes brightened and narrowed; the long neck
drew back and arched the red-gold head high; the wings,
cut and wounded, stretched out and grew taut; and the
great creature slowly rose. It was unsteady for an instant, then it arrowed to the west, to the narrowing strip
of empty land between the gray men and the onrushing
human host. There it laid down an impassable barrier of
flame, stopping human and gray man alike. Newly ringed
in, the gray men turned all their strength against the two
brothers who stood back to back at the center of the
circle. The shimmering forms of the white legion drew in
to gird the brothers with a wall of light, but the gray
forces were an irresistible swarm. One by one the glow of
the phantom swordsmen winked out, and the gray ring
tightened.

Staver's arms ached from clashes with a dozen different adversaries summoned up by the Cairnlord. He had
vanquished all, and now the Cairnlord again stood before
him, pudgy, smiling, with that look of fatherly amusement
still on his round face.

But the wide pale brow now shone with sweat, and the
veins in the temples throbbed. Staver saw this and took
courage from it. The Cairnlord raised one hand in a
pacific gesture.

"You fight well, Staver. I had not expected to face
such an adversary," he confessed.

"I'll do better."

"But why, Staver? Why should two like us squander magic merely to injure one another? Surely we can think of another solution to our differences," the Cairnlord said mildly.

"The only solution is your destruction. You see it coming now, and you want to trick your way out."

"If I should . . . suffer a setback, be sure you would suffer worse. Are you so eager to thwart me that you would willingly give your life?"

"I was born to destroy you. I'm willing to die to accomplish that."

"How much better to achieve your goal and live to enjoy the victory! Continue the struggle and you will die, Staver. Regardless of what happens to me, you will die. We both know that. But there is a way for you to enjoy victory and glory, to reign long and much-beloved by all the people of the northern lands."

"Do you think I'd surrender to you?"

"No surrender. A sensible truce. You wish to save the race of man from me. Very well. I give you the human race. I will promise to withdraw and never to trouble them again."

"Am I to trust in your word?"

The Cairnlord frowned disapprovingly. "A mage such as you knows that there are unbreakable oaths, Staver. Cease your attack, and I will leave this world to the human race for as long as they exist. Only when they have passed will I enter the world again."

"By then you'd be so powerful that none could withstand you."

"Does that matter? Do you care what becomes of creatures who will walk this earth when a million snows have fallen? I offer you life, and honor, and security, Staver. Consider it my tribute to your steadfastness and courage. Accept it as your just reward. Reject it, and I promise you death."

Three voices spoke within the mind of the white-haired man who stood leaning on his sword. Young Staver the innocent, the healer; Ironbrand the swordsman, vanquisher of the Warmaker; the Mage of the Crystal Hills, vessel of a magic beyond his understanding; and all three voices, as one, cried "No!" and the cry burst from the mage's throat. No compromise was possible. Safety could not be bargained for with unborn lives as counters. The Cairnlord had to be fought to the end, defeated and destroyed—whatever the price of victory.

"Then fight on and die," the Cairnlord said.

"It's you who face death. The Iron Angel was forged by Ambescand to destroy you."

"That sword?" The Cairnlord pointed to the gray blade and gave a scoffing laugh. "You think to overcome me with that?"

"This blade, and others forged by the same hand, have slain your servant wizards and gray men. Ambescand poured all his magic into these blades, and now it's all flowed into mine."

The Cairnlord set his hands on his hips and smiled. "Ambescand is a fraud. He was an ignorant, dirty, ragged country lout who served me as a convenient figurehead. Those swords were forged at my command."

"No use to lie. I know the truth."

"Do you? Then use your mighty blade on me. Come, try it. I'll stand my ground. Come, Staver Ironbrand—destroy me!" the Cairnlord taunted him.

Staver knew that there had to be a trick in this. The Cairnlord was all tricks and lies and deceptions, the reality buried deep under layers of illusion, so deep that even now it might still be far from perception. But it had to be attempted. He sprang forward, across the mark's space that separated them, and brought the Iron Angel down to shear the Cairnlord to the breastbone. The sword passed through, and the pudgy figure stood smiling at him. Staver recovered and brought the blade around to behead the wizard. Again the Cairnlord stood to accept the blow unscathed.

Staver took a step back, confused and shaken. This had to be one more illusion, but he had been duped before, woven into the Cairnlord's plans, unknowing. It might be real. If the Iron Angel was a deception, then all was lost and this was the day of the Cairnlord's victory. In his moment of doubt, Staver felt the despairing power drawn from Skelbanda break over him like a wave. The Cairnlord swelled before him, growing more terrible than ever, and blasted him with a deadly bolt from his uplifted hand. Only the instinctive raising of the Iron Angel saved Staver. The sword still protected him—but it could not slay the Cairnlord.

Another blast followed and another even more powerful, and Staver warded them off. He was confused, and despair was all around him, battering to enter and erode him from within. But the despair could not breach his soul. Within him grew the certainty that a greater power than the Cairnlord was watching and guiding him. As he parried the shriveling death that poured from the Cairnlord's hands, Staver remembered the night of Vannen's death, when he noticed the darkness in their house and saved them from the gray man's ambush; the miraculous crossing of the Fissure; the warning from the birds and the Dark Prophet's arrival; the escape on the Fool's Head; the finding of Zandinell; the escape from the Lool. These and all the other events that had led to this moment were not accidents. He was not alone. His struggle was not unseen.

The despair began to fall away. The Cairnlord struck harder, but Staver turned aside every blast. Then the darkness overhead thickened and coagulated, and the winged forms he had driven from the battlefield circled and called high above him. One by one, they plunged.

As Staver set himself for this new attack, the ground humped and burst, and searching hands slid forth to grope at him. The air was filled with strange voices and haunting cries—laughter, and sobbing, and the groans of unimaginable creatures. The power of the Cairnlord was being turned full against Staver.

A human voice penetrated the horrid din. "Strike the cairn! His power resides in the cairn! Strike now!" it commanded.

All the menacing presences vanished on the instant. The Dark Prophet lay where she had fallen, but one pale hand pointed to the cairn. The Cairnlord turned to hurl a devastating bolt of destruction on her, and in that same instant Staver dashed forward and drove the Iron Angel deep into the pile of stone. Even as the sword grated home, the Cairnlord flung himself at Staver with a wild despairing shriek.

The ground trembled and split, and Staver went staggering backward. With a sound like the tearing of a cloak, it gaped wide, and cairn and Cairnlord plunged into a dark gulf that thundered shut after them. Staver rose and stood panting as the island heaved and buckled beneath his feet. He started for the Dark Prophet's side, but a tremor flung him to the ground.

The crash of a rising sea beat in his ears. He looked up to the brightening sky and saw the great dark wall of water rushing toward the island. He struggled forward over the churning ground, and as he fell, he clutched the hand of the Dark Prophet.

The waters closed over the Stone Hand with a spuming roar. When they receded, and the sea was still once more, the island was gone—and never again was the Stone Hand seen by mortal eyes.

On the mainland, Ord knelt over Col's body. All around him gray men lay in mounds of shattered stone. The white legion dissolved and flew from the battlefield in a shimmering cloud to hover over the churning waters that boiled and rolled where once the Stone Hand had lain upon the sea.

A figure seated himself on a fallen gray man, facing Ord—an old man with a patchy white beard, a crooked nose, and a shiny bald skull. His clothing was torn and dirty, and he had one blood-drenched arm tucked into his belt.

"It's over," the old man said.

"Col is dead."

"But it's over. The Cairnlord is defeated. Maybe forever."

"And Staver. He must be dead now, too," Ord said.

"They did what they had to do. We all did."

Ord raised his eyes and looked closely at the old man. "You were the dragon," he said.

"I was. Won't do it again, though. Nobody will, ever. Today I used up all the magic in this world. I'm just an old man now. Tired."

"We couldn't have won without you."

"No . . . you couldn't. But if you and your brother

hadn't come to help, those gray men would have brought me down."

"And now Col's dead."

The old man rose stiffly, grunting with pain, and laid a hand on Ord's shoulder. "Fire's dying out. Your men will be here soon. Greet them like a king."

At the old man's touch Ord was aware of an odd sensation in his shoulder. The amulet lay like a cold, dead, chunk of metal under his skin. It had never felt this way before. Truly, the magic was gone.

Ord started to rise, but his left leg buckled and he fell. The old man held out his good hand. Once on his feet, Ord put an arm around the old man's shoulder to support himself.

"What's your name, wizard?" he asked.

"Zandinell. And I'm a former wizard."

"Staver said you were an old friend of his."

"Met him a long time ago. He did me a favor, and I returned it. We've met a few times since then."

"I have hard work ahead of me, Zandinell. I'll need someone to advise me—someone I can trust as I did my brothers. Will you stay with me until I can get the kingdoms in order?"

"I'll stay with you as long as we can stand each other. We ought to get along. We're the last of our kind, you and I."

Ord looked down at Col's body, then off to the luminous mist that still hung over the turbulent sea. The sky was bright now, with the clear light of morning, and the mist grew ever fainter as he watched. Soon it was gone, the crescent of flame had burned out, and the free army was surrounding the two survivors and the fallen king.

Epilogue

The Promise of the Iron Angel

After the War of the Stone Hand, as the scribes and story-tellers named that day's battle, a new age began in the three kingdoms.

Davasha, widow of Colberane, ruled long as Mistress of the Southern Forest. She had been loved and praised for her beauty. After Colberane's fall she was honored and long remembered for her wisdom and statecraft. Through treaty and alliance she expanded the boundaries of her kingdom fourfold. Her oldest son, Vannen, succeeded to a realm that extended from the mistlands to the Red Mountains, and from the Western Ocean to the dry lands.

To the north, Ordred and Ciantha built the High City into a place of more splendor than in the days of Ambescand and turned the Fastness into a great caravanserai for travelers and traders crossing the mountains. In time it became the center of a mountain city. Roads were cleared and passes widened—traffic between Long Wood and the High City became commonplace. Ordred and Ciantha, and Geerdran after them, worked to unite all the lands to the north. By the end of Geerdran's reign, bridges once again linked the Crystal Hills to the cape at Northmark, and in the reign of his daughter Jemmesne, who succeeded him, a bridge spanned the Fissure, joining the Headland and Long Wood.

In the third generation of the new dynasty, when Jemmesne ruled the Fastness and the Plain and Colberane the Second was Master of the Southern Forest, it was possible for anyone to travel swiftly and safely anywhere from the southernmost tributaries of the River Issalt to the northernmost tip of the Cape of Mists. To all those who thought about such things, it was clear that the sons of Vannen and Ciantha had not merely restored the Old Kingdom, they had founded a new and greater one, and their descendants were raising it to ever more stirring heights.

Wise men, scribes, and scholars had written careful accounts of the great battle on the Plain, and their accounts agreed on all the significant details. But Zandinell, the counselor of Ordred, and Geerdran in the early years of his reign, paid scant heed to these records, saying that legend was better suited to that battle than cold history. And whether it was the doing of Zandinell or not no one knows, but before very long, legends were heard among the people of the north concerning the events of that day, and the deeds and sacrifices of the brothers.

Some of the legends gave rise to local superstitions. Among the people of Long Wood, it was firmly believed that lighting a fire on the Eye of the Fool after dark would cause a storm on the Fool's Head within three days. Those who crossed mistlands always avoided a place called Deepwater, where all the bog creatures were said to be lurking, waiting the return of the mistlanders who had gone to the south. Dwellers on the Plain attributed great virtue to a certain kind of brittle gray stone; wrapped in brown cloth and worn next to the body, it was said to make the wearer invulnerable to any blade. On the Headland a shielded candle was placed in the window of a home where a death had occurred; should it go out before dawn that was a sign of grave danger to the surviving family.

Such superstitions came and went, and were scoffed at by many. But there was a single legend known to all, and everywhere it was the same. From the terraced gardens of the steep southern bank of the Issalt to the stone-and-hide huts of the fisherfolk who live on the shore of the Sea of Storms, and from End-of-All in the west to the dunes of the dry lands, the tale of Staver Ironbrand was unchanging.

It was said that he never died, as common men die, but was taken by the Dark Prophet to a place of sanctuary, where he abides in peace, watching his people. His home is in the heavens, somewhere beyond human vision or understanding. But on a clear autumn night, between the constellations of the Callicrast and the Policorn, on a line drawn through the Great and Lesser Crowns, a cluster of stars points the way to his abode. These twelve stars, four of them bright and the rest very faint, visible only to the sharpest eye, form the Iron Angel. Here it hangs, eternally glittering, forever unrusted, ready to the hand of its master. And no one doubts that should the need arise, Staver Ironbrand will take up the Iron Angel, and rouse his white legion, and lead his people to victory.

In time evil moved in the world once more. An age of fire and anguish came, and a darkening of the hearts and minds of men. Many brave deeds were done, and there was much of horror, too. Eyes were lifted to the gleam of the Iron Angel, and the name of Staver Ironbrand was spoken hopefully.

But that is a story to be told elsewhere. This one is done.

Stories
→ of ←
Swords and Sorcery